What people are saying about …

Wishing on Buttercups

"A family tragedy, a woman scarred for life, a chance meeting, and a charming ensemble cast blend together to make Miralee Ferrell's *Wishing on Buttercups* a story that runs the gamut of emotions, from enthralling and heart-wrenching, to the enjoyable, satisfying end."

Vickie McDonough, award-winning
author of the Pioneer Promise series

"In *Wishing on Buttercups*, Miralee Ferrell invites us to enjoy the charm of the Oregon wilderness and a boardinghouse filled with fascinating characters. This romance will speak to many as a beautiful young artist struggles with mystery, pain, and shame from her past, and fears to step into a future filled with promise. Will she find the will to overcome her reluctance to trust again? *Wishing on Buttercups* is filled with enough questions, twists, and turns to satisfy the most demanding of readers."

Hannah Alexander, award-winning
author and author of *Keeping Faith*

"I loved *Blowing on Dandelions* for its wonderful characters, the variety and depth of the conflicts, and a storytelling style that kept me reading chapter after chapter. I've been eagerly anticipating this next book in the series, hoping it would be just as good. And it

is! Ferrell is a master at writing complex, fascinating characters and at building suspense and mystery in her books in a way that keeps me turning the pages until I finally hit 'The End'!"

Roxanne Rustand, award-winning author
of *When He Came Home, Harlequin*
Heartwarming, and *Summer at Briar Lake*

Praise for…

Blowing on Dandelions

"*Blowing on Dandelions* is a fun read with a beautiful setting in 1880s Baker City, Oregon. Ferrell has created characters you'll root for, and the attitudes feel appropriate for the time in this tender romance. The relationships of mothers and daughters in this story speak deeply of the need for acceptance, love, and respect from one's parents."

Susan Page Davis, award-winning author of
the Prairie Dreams and Texas Trails series

"As soft and gentle as the wisps of snowy seeds for which it is named, *Blowing on Dandelions* is an achingly tender love story that will lift your spirits—and your heart—high on a gentle breeze through the Oregon mountain valleys."

Julie Lessman, award-winning author of The
Daughters of Boston and Winds of Change series

"Miralee Ferrell's writing style is always a delight, even as her stories are captivating. *Blowing on Dandelions* is no exception. From the opening scene the reader is drawn into Katherine Galloway's life, and we care about her from that moment on. This is more than a heart-tugging romance—though it is that; it is also a mind-challenging read that will leave us in a different place from when we began."

Kathi Macias, multi-award-winning author of
forty books, including the Golden Scrolls 2011
Novel of the Year and Carol Award finalist *Red Ink*

"In Katherine Galloway, Miralee Ferrell has created a woman who models grace. As the story unfolds, readers see Katherine's faith lived out in a way that is authentic, challenging, and encouraging. A book you won't want to put down … and a story you won't want to end."

Stephanie Grace Whitson, author
of The Quilt Chronicles series

"In *Blowing on Dandelions*, Miralee Ferrell gives us an engaging story with strong characters who have hidden depths. The theme of the story is universal and will touch hearts and help heal longtime hurts. As with all of her books, Miralee weaves a satisfying romance through these pages. What else could a reader ask for?"

Lena Nelson Dooley, speaker and author
of the 2012 Selah Award winner *Maggie's
Journey, Mary's Blessing*, and the 2011 Will
Rogers Medallion Award winner, *Love
Finds You in Golden, New Mexico*

"Miralee Ferrell's *Blowing on Dandelions* is a deeply inspiring story about family conflict and the transforming power of rekindled love. A richly written story chock full of nuggets of divine wisdom, this book was, for me, a genuinely satisfying read."

Walt Larimore, bestselling author
of *Hazel Creek* and *Sugar Fork*

"Miralee Ferrell delves deeply into the issues of bitterness and family discord and shines a bright light on God's path to reconciliation for every hurting heart. You won't be able to read this book without shedding a tear as you identify with one or more of these true-to-life characters."

Louise M. Gouge, award-winning author

"The relationship between a mom and her daughter can be complicated. In *Blowing on Dandelions*, Miralee Ferrell writes a compelling novel about a single mother trying to raise two girls even as she works to mend the relationship with her own mother. Miralee's story takes place more than a hundred years ago, but the poignant themes of friendship, healing, and forgiveness will inspire readers today."

Melanie Dobson, award-winning author of *Love Finds You in Liberty, Indiana* and *The Silent Order*

"An interesting combination of the classic Western and prairie romances. No cowboys but a hero who loves his son and a heroine who loves her daughters. Mix in a boardinghouse, a mysterious boarder, and two matriarchs marking their territory. Katherine

Galloway is a heroine to root for! And Miralee Ferrell is an author to watch!"

"With characters who will both delight and dismay, Miralee Ferrell's compelling style has created a story that explores relationships and the deeper emotions behind the conflicts of ordinary people in extraordinary circumstances."

Wishing on Buttercups

Love Blossoms in Oregon Series

Blowing on Dandelions

Wishing on Buttercups

Dreaming on Daisies

MIRALEE FERRELL

A NOVEL

Wishing on Buttercups

Love Blossoms in Oregon

David C Cook®

transforming lives together

WISHING ON BUTTERCUPS
Published by David C Cook
4050 Lee Vance View
Colorado Springs, CO 80918 U.S.A.

David C Cook Distribution Canada
55 Woodslee Avenue, Paris, Ontario, Canada N3L 3E5

David C Cook U.K., Kingsway Communications
Eastbourne, East Sussex BN23 6NT, England

The graphic circle C logo is a registered trademark of David C Cook.

The website addresses recommended throughout this book are offered as a
resource to you. These websites are not intended in any way to be or imply an
endorsement on the part of David C Cook, nor do we vouch for their content.

This story is a work of fiction. Characters and events are the product of the author's
imagination. Any resemblance to any person, living or dead, is coincidental.

Scripture quotations are taken from the New King James Version®. Copyright
© 1982 by Thomas Nelson, Inc. Used by permission. All rights reserved.

LCCN 2013946239
ISBN 978-0-7814-0809-7
eISBN 978-1-4347-0748-2

© 2013 Miralee Ferrell
Publishing in association with Tamela Hancock Murray of The Steve
Laube Agency, 5025 N. Central Ave., #635, Pheonix, AZ 85012.

The Team: Don Pape, Ramona Cramer Tucker, Amy Konyndyk,
Nick Lee, Tonya Osterhouse, Karen Athen
Cover Design: DogEared Design, Kirk DouPonce
Cover Photo: iStockphoto and 123RF

Printed in the United States of America
First Edition 2013

1 2 3 4 5 6 7 8 9 10

112613

When you pass through the
waters, I will be with you;
And through the rivers, they
shall not overflow you.
When you walk through the fire,
you shall not be burned,
Nor shall the flame scorch you.

—Isaiah 43:2

For I know the thoughts that I think
toward you, says the LORD,
thoughts of peace and not of evil, to
give you a future and a hope.
Then you will call upon Me
and go and pray to Me,
and I will listen to you.

—Jeremiah 29:11–12

Acknowledgments

So many people worked to make this book a success. First, all glory goes to: God, my Father; Jesus, my best Friend; and the Holy Spirit, my Guide and Comforter. Without the three-in-one Godhead, I'd be unable to accomplish anything worthwhile. God gives me the strength to get through each day and the creativity to put the words on paper. I write for Him first. If He's satisfied, I know the rest will fall in place.

My biggest thanks goes to my family—most especially my husband, Allen—for being patient as I work toward my deadlines, while being supportive of all it takes to bring a new book into the world. My children, Marnee and Brian, and Steven and Hannah, and my mother, Sylvia, who is one of my closest friends, and my husband's parents, Chuck and Dolores, as well as Allen's daughter, Tricia, and our three wonderful grandkids, Mikayla, Dionte, and Damion, all offer encouragement and support. Also a special thanks to my church family, who pray as I write each new story and eagerly await the publication of every novel. You are special to me.

The writing of a book is never completely about the author; it takes a team working behind the scenes to bring it to life. First are my critique partners, Kimberly Johnson, Vickie McDonough, and

Margaret Daley, who also offer valuable brainstorming help. Sherri Sand also read and critiqued my manuscript when it was finished. Wilburta Arrowood, Ginny Aiken, Sherri Sand, Judy Vandiver, and Kimberly Johnson spent time on the phone brainstorming parts of the story line, and a number of friends gave me title suggestions. I love all these wonderful ladies who are an integral part of my team.

My publishing team starts with my agent, Tamela Hancock Murray, who champions my work and helps find it the best possible home. Tamela, a friend as well as a business associate, works diligently to make my career succeed.

This is my second book with David C Cook. They graciously accepted my request to assign an exceptional editor, Ramona Tucker, for this entire series. I'm so blessed to partner with Ramona and value her professional expertise and editing, as well as her friendship. The Cook team welcomed me from the start, and I've loved working with Don Pape, Ingrid Beck, Karen Stoller, Caitlyn Carlson, Tonya Osterhouse, Amy Konyndyk, Michelle Webb, Michael Covington, and Jeane Wynn, as well as the sales and marketing team. I look forward to interacting with more of these quality people.

And, last, to my readers—I value every email I receive, as well as the posts on Facebook, Twitter, Goodreads, and Pinterest, and I'd love to have you drop by. Thank you for your faithful support!

- My Facebook Fan Page: https://www.facebook.com/miraleeferrell
- Twitter: https://twitter.com/#!/MiraleeFerrell
- My personal website: www.miraleeferrell.com. View pictures of my book research and travels, family photos, upcoming speaking event updates

(via my blog link), and find announcements about future books.

- You can also drop me a note at miraleef@gmail .com.

Chapter One

Baker City, Oregon
Late August, 1880

Beth Roberts willed her hands to stop shaking as they gripped the cream-colored envelope. She hadn't heard from her magazine editor in months and had about given up.

Stepping toward a corner, Beth licked her dry lips. Dare she open it here? No one lingered in the lobby of the small post office tucked into the corner of Harvey's Mercantile, and the clerk was working on the far side of the alcove stuffing mail into the slots. Glancing out the window at the bustling street of the small city that became her home a few months ago, she scrubbed at the fabric covering her arm and wished her scars hadn't chosen this moment to itch. Only a handful of people knew her, so she shouldn't fear discovery.

Beth sucked in a quick breath and slid her finger under the flap. A folded page fluttered to the floor, opening as it landed. Her heart rate increased as a second piece of paper, long and slender, drifted several feet across the hardwood. They'd sent her another check.

Seconds passed while she stood frozen, unable to take in the renewal of her dream. She stepped forward, then crouched low to pick up her treasure.

Masculine fingers gripped the end of the check before she could snatch it up. Beth found herself staring into the twinkling brown eyes of Jeffery Tucker, a fellow boarder at Mrs. Jacobs's home. She bit back a gasp, fumbled for the nearby letter, and plucked it off the floor, praying he wouldn't ask questions.

She extended her hand. "Thank you, Mr. Tucker. How careless of me." Her stomach did a flip-flop as his gaze lingered on the paper, then lifted.

"Not at all, Miss Roberts. I apologize if I startled you." He offered the check, keeping those mesmerizing eyes riveted on hers.

Beth tucked the payment and letter into the envelope, then pressed it against her chest.

His brows drew down, erasing the warm smile as his gaze dropped to her hands. "Is everything all right?"

Panic gripped her, and she covered the scar on her wrist. Her loose sleeve had left her exposed, and she was sure he'd noticed. All she could think of was escape. "I'm fine. I must get home. Good day." She backed up two steps and bumped into someone behind her.

"*Umph.*" Firm hands gripped her arms and kept her from falling.

Beth gasped and scrambled forward out of the man's grasp. "Mr. Jacobs. I'm sorry; I didn't hear you come in."

"Forgive me, Miss Roberts." Micah Jacobs removed his hat and bobbed his head. "If I'd known you planned on getting your mail today, I'd have offered you a ride. Zachary and I would have enjoyed your company."

"No need." Beth sidled toward the door and avoided his stare. If only the sun weren't streaming in the front window and illuminating everything in its path. "It's lovely now that fall has almost arrived. I enjoyed the walk." She smiled, then turned and dashed across the lobby. When she'd entered, the place had been empty; now it seemed almost every person she knew had been drawn to the post office.

Thank the good Lord Aunt Wilma hadn't appeared. At least these men were too polite to ask questions. Not so with her aunt. That dear woman would dig and pry until she obtained every last shred of information possible. Not that she wouldn't tell Auntie her news, but first she wanted to savor whatever the letter contained.

Beth bolted outside, keeping a tight grip on the envelope. She had no intention of revealing her secret to anybody, except to Aunt Wilma, of course, who'd been like a mother. Beth had made it this far without anyone else knowing, and she intended to keep it that way.

A shudder shook her at the memory of Jeffery Tucker's quizzical look after he'd glimpsed the check. Had he taken in the dollar amount and the signature of the sender? Would he recognize the magazine from back East? Probably. Although from what she knew of the mysterious Mr. Tucker, she surmised he had secrets of his own to guard. She could only pray he'd be charitable and keep his own counsel.

Jeffery worked to keep his expression carefully neutral. No need to encourage questions from Micah Jacobs or his son, Zachary. Something certainly had Miss Roberts flustered. She'd appeared self-conscious and worried at the same time. Did the check contribute to her distress, or had he somehow disconcerted the young woman?

Another thought struck him. Why in the world would the timid Miss Roberts have a check made out to someone else? He assumed it was a payment, and a large one at that. She may have been picking up the mail for her aunt, but he'd swear the check was made out to someone named Corwin, not Roberts.

Not that he had a right to pry—time to quit attempting to solve mysteries that weren't his concern. He'd come to town for another reason entirely.

He stepped up to the window. "Mr. Beal, any mail today?"

A tall, gangly man pivoted quickly, his Adam's apple bobbing. "Mr. Tucker. Yes, sir, there is indeed." He pushed his rimless spectacles up his nose and grinned. "An envelope from a publishing house back East and a letter from your family. Your father or uncle, perhaps? Hope they're both good news."

Jeffery bit back a groan. Too bad the timid Miss Dooley wasn't working today. She never snooped in patrons' business. Not so with Mr. Beal. He knew the comings and goings of everyone in town, all by inspecting the outside of their mail. "Thanks." He tucked the missives under his arm and tipped his hat.

"Not so fast there, young man." The clerk leaned close, his warm breath fanning Tucker's cheek. "You mailed a package to that same publishing house some weeks back. Does this letter mean they've made it into a book or they're turning it down? If we're gonna have a famous author in town, I want to be the first to congratulate you."

He stuck his hand across the divider. Jeffery took the man's hand and shook it briefly, then backed away. "Sorry. I don't know what it might be, and I'm not famous for anything. Please excuse me." He strolled from the post office without looking back, then halted a half block from the building. Micah and Zachary were still standing in the post office lobby, a perfect target for prying questions from that obnoxious man. He'd better return and encourage them to leave or rumors would be flying through town faster than a rabbit fleeing from a prairie hawk. Of course, he'd never personally seen that type of chase, but he'd read about such things in his favorite dime novels.

He glanced at the envelope from his father and scowled. No telling what he might want, but based on his recent correspondence, it probably wasn't good. Jeffery's thoughts flitted back to Miss Roberts, and he grunted. Speculation about her behavior no longer seemed proper. He couldn't speak for anyone else, but his letter was only one of the things he'd prefer to keep private.

Beth slipped into the boardinghouse, hoping she could get to her room without being seen. Not that she disliked any of the other residents, but the letter from her editor begged to be read. She hadn't dared to stop along the way after her encounter with Mr. Tucker.

She'd made it to the foot of the stairs when the skin on the back of her neck tingled. Gripping the banister, she turned and peered over. "Aunt Wilma." She released the breath she'd been holding. "I didn't hear you come in."

Wilma Roberts crossed her arms over her ample bosom. "Why are you tiptoeing?"

Beth tried not to roll her eyes. Aunt Wilma never had a problem with subtlety. Maybe a change of topic would deter the dear woman from further prying. "Did you have a good visit with Mrs. Cooper? I hope she's not feeling poorly again."

"Frances is as strong as a horse. As long as her gout doesn't kick up, that is." Aunt Wilma narrowed her eyes. "You didn't answer my question."

"I'm going to my room to rest, Auntie. It's been a long day."

"What are you hiding?" The older woman took a step closer, and her eyes shifted to the handbag clutched against Beth's chest. "Did you get a letter?"

Beth glanced down. The corner of the envelope peeked out of her reticule. "It's nothing to worry about." She stepped onto the bottom stair.

Aunt Wilma raised her chin and glared. "Did that good-for-nothing rapscallion from Topeka have the gall to contact you after I told him to stay out of your life?"

"What?" Beth's thoughts spun, trying to keep up with the sudden shift in direction. "Brent Wentworth?"

"I'd prefer not to have his name spoken, but yes, that's the scoundrel I meant."

Fresh pain knifed Beth's heart. She'd worked so hard to forget the man who'd won her love a year ago. "I haven't heard from him since we left Topeka." She waved a dismissive hand at her bag. "It's nothing to worry you, truly. Now I want to go upstairs, if you don't mind." She touched the small locket hanging on a chain around her neck, finding comfort in the contact.

It wasn't often Beth spoke to anyone in that tone, but she didn't care to linger. She trooped up the steps, thankful beyond measure that Aunt Wilma had secured two rooms when they'd arrived in Baker City earlier this summer. As much as she loved the woman who'd taken her in as a toddler, she could be quite overbearing at times.

Sinking onto the brocade-covered chair near the window, Beth pulled out the envelope. What if they no longer wanted her work? This might be the last check she'd ever receive. But even if it was, did the money they paid her really matter?

No. She had not spent a dollar of it since the first one arrived. Getting that initial contract for her illustrations had boosted her confidence, but only in a minuscule way. After all, every drawing was published under the name of Elizabeth Corwin rather than Beth Roberts.

The skin on her arm prickled again. How timely. The scars on her neck, arms, and legs were a constant reminder of the shadows that had dogged her from the age of three. What made her think an important magazine would see her worth if they knew her real identity? So far they appreciated her drawings, but let them catch a whiff of the mystery surrounding her childhood, and that would end. She'd decided early on that hiding her identity would serve her purposes the best.

Time to quit ignoring the inevitable. If her editor decided he no longer needed her work, she wanted to know. With trembling fingers she withdrew the letter and spread it on her lap, not yet daring to look closely at the check.

Dear Miss Corwin,

Please accept this draft as compensation for the recent illustration you presented, along with an advance payment against your future contract. Our periodical has experienced an expanding readership demanding more depictions of the Oregon Trail as well as life in the West. We're contracting you to produce a series of four illustrations of your choice capturing the westward movement and living in a town out West. Possibly something with a boardinghouse or cabin theme would be appropriate.

Our readers are quite taken with your art, and we trust you to provide us with more exceptional work. Please sign and return the agreement, and submit your first drawing no more than thirty days hence.

Yours most respectfully,

Byron Stearns, editor, The Women's Eastern Magazine

Beth slumped against the chair, shock and excitement coursing through her body. Four illustrations of her choice, with a portion advanced. She'd assumed the check to be for the most recent drawing she'd submitted and hadn't noticed the amount. Her insides quivered so hard she almost felt sick. This couldn't be real.

Snatching up the letter, she read it again, savoring each word. They trusted her and liked her work. Their readers wanted more. Shivers of delight danced up her spine, chasing away the unease.

She grasped the check and held it to the light. One hundred dollars. "Oh my!" She placed her fingers over her lips to keep from shouting. This would keep her and Aunt Wilma in comfort for a couple of months. Then, as she scanned the document again, her heart plummeted, leaving her cold and shaken. Elizabeth Corwin. The check was made out to Elizabeth Corwin. How had she forgotten that detail?

It hadn't been a problem picking up her mail, as it came in care of Aunt Wilma. And there'd been no difficulty cashing the three smaller amounts when she'd lived in Topeka, with a childhood friend and confidant as her bank teller. If he still worked there, she'd simply sign and send it to him. Opening an account here in Baker City without proof of her identity—or, rather, confirmation of her alias—could prove difficult. Aunt Wilma could vouch for her, but would anyone really believe her to be an upcoming illustrator for one of the largest magazines in the East? People in this town knew her as Beth Roberts, the quiet, shy young woman who lived with her aunt on the edge of town, and she'd prefer it remained that way.

She leaned back in her chair and a sigh escaped. If she didn't cash the check, would the magazine editor think she didn't want the contract? Surely not. She'd sign the agreement and get it in tomorrow's mail before they changed their minds. It would be legally binding whether or not she spent the money. After all, Auntie had plenty of money of her own and certainly didn't need her help. She'd tuck it away for now and quit worrying.

And while payment was nice, it wasn't the reason she sketched. When her pencil flew over the paper, creating new worlds and half-forgotten scenes, she knew what it was to truly be alive. Something inside cried to be released and nothing satisfied so completely as her work.

No one could understand the depths of insecurity she'd lived with all her life—the bottomless pit of fear and anguish that struck her every time the shadowy memories surfaced. The scars on her limbs ... she had only vague recollections of where they'd come from, but a definite knowledge of what they represented. But all of that disappeared when she escaped into her chosen field.

Art. It drew her, calmed her, healed her, in a manner little else had ever done.

Somewhere along the way, a voice had started to whisper in the early-morning hours while she lay in bed. Often she thought it must be her own mind playing tricks, hoping to convince her the past didn't matter. She'd pushed it away at first, but it had persisted, pulling her into the warmth of its embrace. Trying to persuade her to accept—something.

Rising to her feet with new resolve, she neatly tucked the letter and check into the envelope. Tomorrow she'd sign the contract and place it in the outgoing mail. Right now she must make her way downstairs to supper and put on an unassuming face. How would she avoid Aunt Wilma's badgering questions? It didn't bother her to tell Auntie about the contract offer, but the world, including Aunt Wilma, must never see her uncertainty.

She touched a spot on her arm where the scars were prominent. Not knowing what exactly had happened in the past—or more precisely, why—had caused her so much pain.

And her early childhood was only a portion of what she'd had to endure. Beth's thoughts flashed to Brent Wentworth, the reason she and Aunt Wilma had left Topeka, Kansas. After years of guarding her heart, Beth had finally chosen to open herself to love. She'd been so certain she'd found a man who would love and accept her without condition. She lifted her chin. Never would she make that mistake again.

Chapter Two

Jeffery paced the narrow confines of his room looking for something to kick ... even if that action wouldn't solve his dilemma. The last thing he wanted was to return home, or worse, have his father come storming westward to "knock some sense" into him, as the recent letter from his parents had threatened. He didn't know how to respond, or whether to simply ignore the demand and hope they'd leave him alone.

Not that he didn't love his parents and younger siblings, but Mother and Father didn't understand his hopes and dreams. Sure, he knew they'd always hoped he'd marry the girl they'd picked out for him and settle near them. It made sense that as the oldest he'd want to travel that route, but his heart had never been inclined to live off his family's wealth or follow in his father's footsteps. Writing was life's sustenance for him. Even as a boy he'd penned wild stories rather than doing his schoolwork. One teacher had seen his promise and encouraged him, much to his parents' dismay. They'd grudgingly allowed his foray into the newspaper world, but their patience had waned when he'd left his last job and moved west, looking for inspiration.

This newest bit of correspondence left no doubt to their misgivings or expectations: "Come home and take your rightful place in the family," they demanded, "or don't expect an inheritance in the future." Not that he cared about his parents' fortune, but he *had* hoped for their understanding, if not their approval of his chosen profession.

Then there was the letter from the publisher to whom he'd sent a sample of his manuscript. Another rejection. Unlike what Mr. Beal suggested, Jeffery wasn't a famous author, but rather a failure who, it appeared, couldn't write anything worth printing. He'd been sure this newest idea would find acceptance, if not outright delight, but three editors had turned it down and only one remained. He'd gotten to the point where his heart sank at the thought of picking up the mail.

Jeffery tossed the letter on the bureau and grabbed his hat. He needed some air to clear the dust from his brain. Yanking open the door, he strode into the hall and collided with a soft body clothed in sapphire blue. His arms encircled her briefly, and his heart jumped as his hands touched the curls cascading down her back.

"Oh!" Beth Roberts leaped out of his grasp and stumbled over the hem of her gown.

"Pardon me, Miss Roberts. My fault entirely."

She shook her head, setting the dark curls to dancing. Just as swiftly she placed her hand over her hair at the base of her neck and took a step back. "No. I was daydreaming and didn't hear your door open. I'm on my way to supper." A flush rose to her cheeks and her eyelids fell, masking the radiant blue of her eyes. "Is—is that where you were headed?"

"Supper? I'd forgotten the time." He blinked but couldn't tear his eyes away from her face. Why hadn't he noticed the depth of her eye color before? "Of course." He extended his arm. "Would you care to accompany me?"

She slipped her hand through his crooked elbow. "Thank you."

He'd not taken especial note of her before, but he couldn't deny his intense feeling of curiosity since their encounter at the post office earlier today.

Maybe she would merit a bit more investigation. He drew in a long, deep breath, trying to calm the erratic beat of his heart. Surely his interest in Miss Roberts was simply that of a curious writer. After all, he'd been a budding journalist before he'd branched off on his own, hoping to write a book that would gain attention in the literary world—both careers his family disparaged, but he didn't care. Jeffery hazarded another glance at the quiet young woman beside him. The light touch of her hand on his arm sent a wave of awareness through him—another thing his family wouldn't approve. His mother had made it clear she hoped he'd one day marry a socialite from one of her circles. He turned an encouraging smile on Miss Roberts. He'd prove to his family he could make wise choices and prosper on his own and hopefully win a new friend in the endeavor.

Beth hesitated, drawn by the offer to accompany this man she knew so little about, but apprehensive at the expression he'd cast her way. Had he noticed her hand creeping to her neck, or did his curiosity go deeper? She couldn't risk her heart again, no matter how appealing the man.

She gave him what she hoped passed for a pleasant smile. She had hardly any practice in speaking with men … other than Brent.

But this was certainly not the time or the place to think of him. "I appreciate your offering to accompany me, Mr. Tucker."

A gleam lit his eyes, and he grinned. "We've lived in the same house for a number of months now, and I'd wager a guess I'm not too many years your senior. Would you be averse to addressing me as Jeffery? I'm afraid I have few friends in this town, and it would be nice to hear my Christian name occasionally."

She raised her brows. "But I barely know you, Mr. Tucker."

"Quite so. But that could be remedied."

Her mind raced. "So you'd like to be friends?"

"If that's acceptable and you're willing to have a go at it."

She shot a glance at the man striding confidently beside her. She'd never really thought about their age difference but guessed him to be somewhere in his mid- to late-twenties, possibly six or seven years her senior. His sandy brown hair, flecked with gold, was combed to the side rather than slicked back in the current fashion. Deep brown eyes crinkled at the corners and glinted with a hint of humor while his firm chin gave rise to ideas of strength mingled with tenderness. He'd be a pleasure to sketch.

Beth dragged her gaze away, praying she wasn't blushing. Where in the world had those thoughts come from? Certainly, Mr. Tucker was a fine-looking man—tall, well built, and impeccably dressed—but she had no business allowing her mind to stray in that direction. "I'm not certain. People might talk if they hear us use our Christian names."

He halted and turned. "No one at this house would give a fig if we do. But if it concerns you, we can fall back on more formal address outside the boardinghouse or when company comes to call."

She nodded, certain she'd heard a note of yearning. Or did she imagine it due to her own loneliness? Either way it shouldn't matter. He'd proven himself a gentleman since their first meeting, and there was no reason to disregard his request. "All right. I'll agree, Mr. Tucker, if you think it appropriate."

A captivating smile revealed a cleft in his chin. "Jeffery, if you please, Beth."

Her heart fluttered, and she dropped her lashes. "Certainly. Jeffery."

"Now let's make our way to supper before they decide to start without us, shall we?" He patted the hand she'd slipped through the crook of his arm, then moved his away.

Something akin to disappointment tugged at her when his hand no longer touched hers. How foolish. She must steel herself against this man's charm. Beth had felt the same emotions a little over a year ago when Brent swept into her life, and she still had the broken heart to prove it. He had abandoned her without explanation. How many times must she remind herself no one would see her as a prize worthy of marriage? Her own family had cast her off years ago. It wouldn't do to allow Jeffery Tucker or anyone else inside the walls housing her closely guarded secrets. No. It wouldn't do at all.

Chapter Three

Jeffery seated Beth at the table and sank onto the chair across from her. What had possessed him to suggest they drop the accepted formality and use their Christian names? One glimpse of those compelling blue eyes, and his heart had melted … but only for a moment. He'd made sure of that.

He couldn't allow any woman, no matter how sweet and unassuming, to get in the way of his attaining his goals for the future. How many times had his father berated him for allowing a girl to distract him from his studies? Father had done his best to squelch those budding friendships and drilled into him the need to focus on a career.

"Mr. Tucker." Wilma Roberts tapped his left arm with a fan. "I have a question, if I might be so bold." She accepted the bowl of mashed potatoes he handed her.

Jeffery mustered a smile. "Certainly, Mrs. Roberts." The only person bolder than Mrs. Roberts in this house was Mrs. Cooper, the mother of the establishment's owner. Frances Cooper and Wilma Roberts had settled into a tentative friendship that still amazed him, considering the high degree of conflict they'd encountered shortly after Beth and her aunt Wilma had moved to the boardinghouse.

"What exactly are you writing? You have never been forthcoming about your work, but I seem to recollect earlier this summer you rejoicing over an idea that struck you. I meant to ask about it, but not long after, Mrs. Galloway … er, I mean Mrs. Jacobs …" She cast a flustered glance at her landlady. "I'm sorry. You and Mr. Jacobs have only been married a short time, and I'm still adjusting to your new name."

Micah Jacobs smiled. "There's no need to apologize, Mrs. Roberts. We're still adjusting, ourselves."

Katherine took a sip of her water, then nodded sweetly toward her husband. "We've only been back from our wedding trip for ten days, so it's understandable you'd forget." She turned her attention toward Jeffery. "And I'd be very interested in knowing the answer to your question as well, if Mr. Tucker doesn't mind sharing with us."

He did mind but didn't see much hope in escaping the direct questions. He'd lived in Baker City for a number of months now and had managed to evade talking about his work. It looked like the time had come to open up to some extent, at least with these people he lived with.

He took a bite of roast beef, chewed it slowly, and swallowed. "I suppose I can tell you a little, if you really care to hear about it."

Mrs. Roberts clasped her hands. "Yes, I'm sure we all do. Is it a romance, Mr. Tucker? I do hope so." She removed a slice of bread from the plate in front of her.

Frances Cooper snorted. "What nonsense. I do not understand how anyone can read that drivel. Please tell me you do not immerse yourself in those dreadful books, Wilma."

The woman dabbed her lips with her napkin, then laid it carefully beside her plate. "Romance is not drivel. Some of the finest books and plays ever written are romance. Look at *Romeo and Juliet*, for one. Shakespeare was a genius."

"Piffle." Mrs. Cooper waved her hand. "It is impossible to understand half of what that man wrote. Poetry is far better. Mr. Henry Longfellow is brilliant. Even Queen Victoria recognized the man when she invited him to her castle." She turned to Jeffery. "I do hope you are writing poetry, Mr. Tucker."

Jeffery coughed into his napkin, trying to contain the laughter threatening to erupt. One minute these women were cozied up like two bosom friends and the next they were sparring like two fighting hens. "I am afraid not, ma'am. I don't seem to have a talent for verse and rhyme."

She harrumphed and crossed her arms. "More's the pity. So it *is* romance then?" She glowered at Mrs. Roberts.

"No, I cannot say that's the case either."

The excitement died from Wilma Roberts's countenance. "What then? Not a textbook or medical journal, I hope?" Her lips twisted in distaste.

Frances perked up. "Now, that would be a worthwhile endeavor. I am so glad to hear you are not stooping to penning trash."

Katherine's chuckle cut across Mrs. Roberts's attempt at a reply. "Ladies, if we could all calm ourselves, Mr. Tucker might enlighten us as to his subject."

Her older daughter, Lucy, nodded. "I hope it's a story for girls."

Jeffery laughed outright and leaned back in his chair. "Sounds like you folks have plenty of ideas. If I ever run dry, I'll know who to ask." He looked around the table, suddenly aware that Beth hadn't offered a comment. He hadn't expected one from Micah's fifteen-year-old son, Zachary, or Mrs. Jacobs's younger daughter, Mandy, but wondered at Beth's silence. He'd thought she may make an observation after their talk on the way to supper. But on second thought, she'd never been one to chatter and often kept her own counsel. A glimpse at Beth showed her lips were turned up.

He relaxed and allowed a hint of a smile to touch his own lips. "Maybe I should make you all wait until the day it comes out in print." A memory of the letter in his room returned. "That is, if it ever does."

"Oh no. That's not fair." Cries of disapproval echoed around the table, overlapping one another.

He held up his hand, surprise and pleasure warming his heart. "I had no idea you were interested in my work. I confess this comes as a bit of a shock."

Micah Jacobs rested his forearms on the table. "I can't remember you being willing to discuss it, Mr. Tucker. None of us wanted to press you for details."

Jeffery's conscience pricked him, and he nodded. Micah was right. He had been more than a little secretive since moving to Baker City. Fear of failure had driven him at first, but once he'd slipped into keeping his own counsel, it seemed easier to maintain that state. He looked from one eager face to the next. On further reflection, it might be pleasant to discuss his work with others from time to time.

"All right. I'm not sure what genre it might fit into, but it is definitely a novel. It is fiction, but …" He wondered what the reaction would be to his next announcement. "It has its basis in a certain amount of fact. I'm writing about a boardinghouse in the West, set in a small mining town, and populated with a number of colorful, interesting characters."

Mrs. Roberts placed her hand over her heart. "What a wonderfully delicious idea."

"Delicious? Are you quite sane, Wilma?" Mrs. Cooper's eyes blazed.

Mandy, Katherine's seven-year-old daughter, squealed with delight. "Am I in your book, Mr. Tucker? How about Lucy and Zachary? Can we read it when you finish?"

"I will not have it." Mrs. Cooper pushed to her feet. "I cannot believe you are penning a book of gossip. It is dreadful, that's what. Simply dreadful."

Mrs. Roberts laughed and clapped her hands. "Not at all. Think of it, Frances. We might be famous one day. You mentioned Queen Victoria inviting Mr. Longfellow to her castle. Why, if Mr. Tucker's book is widely recognized, President Hayes might want to meet all of us! I'm delighted, and you should be as well."

Micah Jacobs cleared his throat. "Ladies, it might be a good idea to allow Mr. Tucker to explain before we all get in a lather." He swiveled toward Jeffery. "Go ahead. We'd enjoy hearing more about your idea, if you aren't scared off yet."

Jeffery shook his head. "Not at all, but I didn't expect such a reaction." He glanced at Mrs. Cooper, who sank into her chair, a frown still marring her face. "Please don't distress yourself. I haven't used any of your names, and I have no intention of being disrespectful or employing gossip. Quite the opposite, in fact."

Beth dug her heels into the carpet so as not to jump from the table as Mrs. Cooper had done. Why in the world would Mr. Tucker—she could no longer call him by his Christian name and would tell him so at her first opportunity—think it appropriate to write a story using them as fodder? She'd appreciated the man's offer of friendship but now saw it for what it was. A ruse to worm his way into her confidence and dig into her life. No better than Brent. Well, it wouldn't work. She would not allow herself to be manipulated or used again, no matter how handsome or charming the man.

"Please, will you excuse me? I find I'm quite tired and not feeling well." She scooted her chair away from the table and stood.

Katherine's brow creased. "Would you like someone to walk you to your room?"

Beth felt a movement and saw Jeffery turn her way. "No. Thank you. An early evening will put me to rights, and I'll be fine tomorrow." She avoided his gaze. "I'll say good night now."

A chorus of well wishes followed her into the hall. Beth forced herself to walk slowly. No sense in letting them suspect her desire to get out from under Mr. Tucker's probing stare. How dare he write a story about the people who lived here? She didn't care if it was fiction and he didn't use their names. It would be nearly impossible to pen a novel set in a place he lived and not incorporate traits of the people around him.

She gripped the banister on the way up the stairs, then slipped into her room, closing the door behind her and leaning against it. Jeffery had been observing their actions for months, she realized. He'd probably made notes of their conversations. How he must have laughed at the antics of Aunt Wilma and Mrs. Cooper as they quarreled like a couple of chattering squirrels. From now on she'd make herself scarce. It would not do to let that man get close.

A rap at the door, followed by the rattle of the knob, catapulted Beth forward onto her bed.

Aunt Wilma swept into the room and quite deliberately shut the door. She stepped close and placed her palm against Beth's forehead, then drew back, lips pursed. "You don't appear feverish, and your appetite was fine through supper. Are you truly ill, or did your desire to leave have something to do with Mr. Tucker revealing his unique plan for his story?""

Beth cringed. She knew Aunt Wilma loved her, but her brusque manner could be abrasive. She didn't want to lie but didn't care to be frank about her reasons either. At least not all of them. "I suppose I didn't care to listen. I felt Mr. Tucker had taken advantage of our proximity to attain information about our lives."

"Nonsense. I'm sure that is not the case. But when you chose to leave, I felt obligated to follow, so I didn't get to hear all the details. There is nothing distressful about a story set in a boardinghouse, and I see no reason why you or Frances should take offense." She walked to the high-backed chair in the corner and settled into it, as though that put an end to the subject. "It has been a long day and my feet hurt. So. You are feeling fine. Your decision to leave was based solely on not wanting to listen to Mr. Tucker?"

"Not entirely. I am tired, and my stomach is a little upset." At least it had been when he'd made his announcement. It had tightened to the point she thought everything she'd eaten might be pushed right back up.

"Then you'd best lie back and rest. No sense in taking chances." Aunt Wilma beckoned toward the bed. "I still don't understand why all the fuss. I think Mr. Tucker has a perfectly splendid idea."

Beth blew a light breath between her parted lips as she settled against the pillow. "I am not comfortable with him watching our every move so he can put it in his book. I don't see anything splendid about it. What if he keeps digging and …"

"You worry too much, my dear." Aunt Wilma rose from the chair with a sigh. "Get some rest, and I'll check on you before I go to bed." Her face broke into a smile. "I'm going to the parlor to chat with Mr. Tucker and ferret out what fascinating things he has decided to include." Leaning over the bed, she stroked the hair off Beth's forehead. "Physical marks and family connections mean nothing, my dear. God looks at the heart, not the outward appearance. Never forget that." She pressed a warm kiss on Beth's forehead and headed toward the door.

"Maybe not." Beth whispered the words, not wanting Aunt Wilma to return and take up the debate. Her aunt meant well, but she didn't understand. Beth burrowed deeper into her pillow. God might love her, but she didn't know a single man who could look at her scars without cringing.

Wilma Roberts plopped in a horsehair chair near Frances Cooper and dropped her voice. She'd been worrying over her niece's strange behavior for the past four days and would burst if she didn't talk with Frances about it. "I'm not sure this is the best place to talk. What if someone comes in? Beth would never forgive me if she returns from her walk and hears me discussing her with you."

Frances lifted her chin and glared. "Exactly what do you mean, 'with you'? Does she have something against me that I am not aware of? I do hope you have not turned the girl against me, Wilma."

Wilma waved her hand in the air. "I did *not* mean it that way. You are forever twisting my words. I meant it would distress her to discover me discussing her with *anyone*, as I'm sure you understood."

"Nonsense. I take what people say, not what they hint at. Be more concise so you do not hurt a person's feelings."

Wilma rolled her eyes. She didn't care a whit if Frances noticed. At times like this she couldn't remember why she had worked so hard to befriend this woman. "I wasn't aware you *had* feelings, Frances." She worried her lip a minute. "Oh dear. That was unkind, and I didn't mean it at all."

The rigid planes of Frances's face slowly relaxed. "You are forgiven. I suppose *I* should not have snapped at *you* either." She gave a wry chuckle. "It *is* a lot of work trying to be the right kind of person, don't you think?"

"Most assuredly." Wilma nodded. Gratitude filled her as she remembered the early days of her friendship with Frances. Back then, they had both stormed out of the room and refused to speak for days, but God had done a work in their hearts that continued to amaze her. Frances still had times when she rubbed people the wrong way and snipped at everyone around her, but they didn't occur as often or last as long. "Now, getting back to Beth …"

"Do you know exactly what the trouble is?" Frances set her teacup on the cherry wood end table.

"I'm not certain, but I *am* concerned it might have to do with a young man she believed herself to be in love with in Topeka."

"I believe you mentioned something about a lost love." Frances fiddled with the handkerchief in her lap. "It may have been when I was questioning you about Beth's prospects."

Wilma chortled, trying not to take too much pleasure in her friend's discomfort. "Ah, you mean the time you tried to convince me to move out and find accommodations at the Arlington Hotel?"

"I was hoping you might not remember that." Frances turned her face away.

Guilt pricked at Wilma. "Now I must apologize for my rude behavior. I was only jesting, Frances. I didn't mean to bring up an unpleasant memory."

"Let's forget about it, shall we?" Frances squared her shoulders and sniffed. "I think we have both apologized more than enough for one day. I, for one, am quite weary of it. Now, what were you saying about the young man and Beth?"

Wilma glanced over her shoulder. She hadn't heard footsteps on the stairs, but it would pay to be cautious. "Four days ago she received a letter. I saw her slipping upstairs with it sticking out of her handbag. I accosted her and asked if Brent had written to her."

Frances nodded approvingly. "You were correct to do so, in my opinion. Young people can so easily get in trouble if left to their own devices."

"Exactly." It felt good to have a friend who understood and agreed, especially one who had raised two girls and was involved in her granddaughters' lives as well. "She claimed it wasn't from that rapscallion, and I needn't worry about it. I want to trust her, but back in Topeka she sneaked out one time to meet him without my permission. Which makes me worry all the more."

Frances sat a little straighter. "Did you pursue the subject?"

"She refused to speak more of it and stalked up to her room."

"Well, I never!" Frances exclaimed. "That certainly does not sound like the placid young woman we have come to know."

"That concerned me too. I've been keeping an eye on her since, to no avail. When she left the supper table in a huff the other day, I followed her to her room. But I may as well have been talking to the wall for all she'd volunteer. At least not beyond stating she did not care to be the subject of Mr. Tucker's book."

A smug expression settled on Frances's face. "I stand up with Beth on that account. She is showing wisdom beyond her years in disapproving of that nonsense. I hope some of what I said to Mr. Tucker influenced her." She held up her hand and frowned. "Do not get all high and mighty with me, Wilma. I remember Beth excusing herself from the table, not leaving in a huff. I think you were miffed because she agreed with me, rather than you."

Wilma gritted her teeth and held in the words she'd like to say. She forced herself to relax, not wanting another argument to mar this time with Frances. Besides, if she were completely honest with herself ...

"All right. I'll admit I didn't understand why she was upset when I thought his plan quite splendid." She thought for a moment. "Or maybe I do."

Frances laced her fingers in her lap and leaned forward. "And?"

Wilma frowned, not realizing she had spoken the last few words out loud. "I *am* sorry, Frances. I have spoken out of turn. I was reminded of something that might be troubling Beth, but I'm unable to discuss it."

Frances snorted and stood. "I declare, Wilma Roberts, you do beat all. You invite me for a cup of tea and a cozy chat, then refuse to tell me a thing. My patience has been stretched to the limit and beyond. I am going to my room to rest."

Wilma raised her hands in the air. "Frances, wait. I didn't mean to be such a goose, but …" What was there to say? She couldn't reveal Beth's concerns over her past or her desire to keep her work a secret, no matter what she thought.

"But what?" Frances stared at her.

"Nothing." Wilma allowed her arms to drop to her sides. "Nothing at all. I hope you rest well."

"Humph. That is not at all likely." Frances limped from the room.

Wilma's heart sank. Her friend's gout must be acting up again. Frances's body was hurting, and now she'd added to that pain by making her feel she couldn't be trusted, but there was no help for it. Beth's secrets were her own to reveal, no matter how much Wilma longed to share the burden of the girl's past with someone else.

But one of these days her niece might want answers, and if anyone could aid Wilma's investigation, it would be Doctor Caleb Marshall. Besides her brother, Arthur, Caleb was the only person who knew the details of Beth's childhood. Wilma gave a quick nod, her mind made up. It was time to write a letter and see if Caleb would be willing to help her unearth some old secrets.

Chapter Four

"Beth, wait for me, if you please?" Jeffery lengthened his stride. He was certain she'd noticed him follow her down the front stairs, but she'd walked on as though he were invisible. Not that he had anything vital to discuss, and he would readily admit that strolling behind her was pleasant, but it had been almost a week since they'd agreed to a tentative friendship and from all appearances she'd avoided him ever since. He sucked in a breath. "Miss Roberts."

She came to an abrupt halt and pivoted with a flash of irritation that she quickly hid. "Yes, Mr. Tucker?"

He hurried forward. "It's a lovely day for a walk, and it's been some time since we chatted. Do you mind if I accompany you?"

"I suppose not." Her cool tone didn't quite match the tentative smile that followed.

"Were you headed to town or out for a morning constitutional?"

She looked toward the house a block or so behind them. "I have no particular destination and don't plan to stay out long."

"Ah, I see." He didn't, but maybe with a little gentle probing he might. "You have not been down to the parlor in the evening lately, and I recall you weren't feeling well when you left the table last week. Are you quite recovered now?"

She started forward. "Yes. Quite. Thank you."

He didn't want to appear dense or too inquisitive, but neither did he care to let a lengthy silence ensue. He kept step with her brisk pace. "You and your aunt have been in Baker City for a few months now. Are you planning to locate here permanently, or will you be returning to your home before winter?"

Beth halted and stared at him, brows raised. "Why do you ask?"

He hunched a shoulder. "I was simply making conversation, but please do not feel obligated to share your personal information. I did not intend to pry." He sensed her relief at his declaration and chastised himself for choosing yet another subject that made her uncomfortable.

"I appreciate that, thank you. Please forgive me, but it is not something I care to discuss." Her blue eyes locked with his for a moment before she resumed walking, her long green skirt swaying with the movement of her hips.

Jeffery surged forward, averting his gaze from her alluring figure to a passing wagon. Why did his heart gallop whenever this young woman was around? "Is your friend ill?"

She turned her head. "I'm sorry. I don't know who you mean."

His mind clouded in confusion. Was it possible he had made yet another mistake? Surely not. "Elizabeth Corwin."

Her eyes narrowed, and she increased her pace as though she'd suddenly remembered an important engagement.

He rubbed his jaw. Possibly she hadn't heard him, but unease niggled at him. Should he change the subject again or continue to pursue this one? He hurried forward and tried again. "You picked up her mail last week when I spoke to you at the post office. I assumed she might be indisposed, and you were collecting it."

This time she halted so abruptly he nearly stumbled into her. "Mr. Tucker, you said you were not trying to pry, but it certainly does not appear that way. Miss Corwin is someone I do not choose to discuss." She tugged at the sleeve of her dress, straightening the fabric. "I hope you will forgive me, but I don't care to be questioned about my personal business or friends so you can use the information for your novel. I must be going." She hastened toward the path leading to the bridge crossing the Powder River.

He hurried after her and touched her arm. "I won't bother you further, but I must know. Is that why you persist in addressing me as 'Mr. Tucker' when we decided on less formality?"

She gave a brief nod. "I suppose in part, though I must admit I'm not entirely comfortable using your Christian name. I *am* sorry for appearing brusque, but in all honesty I wish you'd find some other subject than our boardinghouse for your novel. I am not happy about you digging into our lives and asking questions, even if you do need material. Now, if you'll excuse me." She picked up the hem of her skirt and stepped onto the walkway alongside the bridge, moving away from him at a rapid pace.

He waited, hoping she would reconsider and turn back. If anything, she increased her speed. Jeffery stared at her retreating back, baffled by her response. What did his book have to do with anything? It had never occurred to him that a work of fiction could affect her life one way or the other.

Jeffery wanted to race after Beth—no, Miss Roberts, as she'd made clear she preferred—and convince her of his good intentions. His mind returned to his last pointed question concerning Elizabeth Corwin and Beth's pained response. Somehow he'd hurt her again, and he didn't have an inkling of how or why. When she'd stopped and looked into his face, her expression exuded confusion and fear. His heart twisted. Somehow he must find a way to win her confidence and trust.

Beth held her chin up as she continued to town. Her heels thudded on the wooden planks of the bridge, giving emphasis to the pounding of her heart. Her illusion that she might find a friend in Jeffery Tucker was simply that: an illusion. That had become apparent the moment he admitted to shaping a story after their lives. The knots in her stomach had yet to untangle since the day he'd escorted her to supper. If only she hadn't allowed herself to envision a relationship with him. But no matter how badly she might want to take the chance, she'd found out the hard way that men couldn't always be trusted.

And asking about Elizabeth Corwin. *Oh my.* Beth's hand went to her throat. Thankfully it appeared he didn't suspect anything was amiss. Her stomach coiled tighter. She wasn't sure how she would continue to avoid his questions. Would he persist in trying to discover who Elizabeth might be, and if so, how would she answer?

Would it be so bad letting the world know she was the magazine illustrator whose reputation was slowly garnering wider acclaim? People often wrote under pseudonyms, and no one seemed bothered by it, so it shouldn't shock anyone to discover the truth about her. Aunt Wilma knew, and although she didn't put much stock in a woman having a career, she was tolerant of what she'd labeled "Beth's little hobby." Of course, her solution to Beth's life was to marry her off and make her dependent on a man. "That should be enough," Aunt Wilma lectured, "to fulfill any woman." Truth be told, most people felt the same way.

But Beth longed to succeed at what she loved most—being creative. Most men wouldn't tolerate that in a wife. They'd want her cooking, cleaning, and raising babies full time, not staring off into another place, allowing her imagination to simmer until it finally boiled over and produced another glowing image on her tablet.

Not that having her own family didn't pull at her heart, but she couldn't imagine it happening for her. She wasn't certain a man existed who would love her for herself. A memory of Brent flashed, followed by a vision of Jeffery's warm, inquisitive eyes. She shivered. Would she even be a good wife or mother when the time came?

A sound pulled Beth out of her reverie, and she moved in time to avoid a collision.

A man heavily burdened with wooden crates bobbed his head and smiled. "Sorry, miss." He sidestepped around her, his boxes scraping against the hotel wall.

She picked up her pace, determined to watch where she trod, or she'd cause an accident for sure. Why fool herself dreaming about marriage and babies? That future would never be within her grasp. Besides, she wanted a career—as long as her past didn't get in the way and ruin it.

That's when she knew. Elizabeth Corwin must continue to be the growing-in-fame illustrator, not simple, scarred Beth Roberts. No one other than Aunt Wilma could ever know her true identity.

Chapter Five

Jeffery flung the most recent letter from an editor onto the desk in his cramped room and scowled. This wasn't a rejection, but it might as well be. He stuffed his hands in his pockets and prowled the room. They wanted to use his story as a magazine serial. Of all the hare-brained, ridiculous notions he'd ever heard, this beat all. He plucked the letter off his desk and reread the pertinent section.

We feel your manuscript has merit, and we'd like to extend an offer. However, we're not confident readers would purchase your book with your status as an unknown author. Our magazine would like to serialize your book, chapter by chapter, one week at a time. If it garners enough interest, we will accept a proposal for a follow-up book to release sometime in the future.

There is one condition. Our magazine articles and stories are ofttimes accompanied by illustrations.

Jeffery groaned and sank onto his bed. He almost wished he'd not gone to the post office, but after his encounter with Beth yesterday, he'd wanted to get away from the house. He couldn't believe the public would care about a bunch of drawings woven through his work.

Snatching up the page, Jeffery searched for a clue. A sentence he'd missed caught his attention, and he froze. They thought his manuscript needed dressing up—readers would find the story more interesting with fitting depictions? What in the world were *fitting depictions*? He had no idea.

The publisher must not be convinced of the merit of his novel, or he'd print it immediately instead of putting it in a magazine. And if his tale were serialized, would his parents see it? If so, his father would scoff at his son's name being bandied about as a two-bit writer of dime novels.

His mouth twisted. He couldn't imagine the publisher would pay much for a monthly series—not as much as he'd hoped to garner for a book. But there was no way he'd go back to accepting help from his family. A knot lodged in his throat. He'd ended that a couple of years ago, but without a successful contract, he might not have a choice. However, returning to the newspaper industry would be an option … certainly a better one than giving his father control over his future.

Jeffery's glance fell on the fat envelope tucked into a cubbyhole in his rolltop desk. Stuffed with rejections. He'd saved each one. It smarted to do so, but someday when he acquired a modicum of success he wanted a reminder of the road he'd traveled. Now he wished he'd destroyed them all. Maybe he should go back to his family. In truth, it wasn't exactly charity when at least a portion would be his inheritance someday. His parents didn't think he should be writing; they'd made that abundantly clear over the years.

But Jeffery wouldn't take their money in order to live. He hadn't worked for it, hadn't earned a penny of it with his own hands. If his father chose to leave all or part to him in the future that was one thing, but living on it now was not to be considered. Not if he were to retain even a remnant of pride.

Then where did that leave him? He suppressed a shudder. Nowhere, really. The choice was simple. Allow the editor to do as he wished with his book and pray the readers loved it.

La Grande, Oregon, August 30

Isabelle Mason hugged her son, Steven, again, hating to let him go but knowing she must. He'd stayed close to her side over the years since her husband had died, and she loved him all the more for his tender solicitude. "You take care on your trip, you hear?" She followed him onto the packed dirt in front of their humble cabin and shaded her eyes against the rising sun.

He ran a hand over dark, wavy hair and frowned. "I don't know why my boss chose to send me to Baker City now. He knows you haven't been well."

She shook her head and smiled. "I haven't been well for several years, so you can't fault his decision. Besides, I'm better, and I'll get along fine while you're gone. Ina promised to help if there's a need."

"Give me your word, Ma, that you'll let her lend a hand every day, or I'm not going." His jaw tightened even more, and his blue eyes darkened. "Do I have your promise?"

"Ina's a good neighbor and an even better friend. More than likely she'll be over here with a hankering to work even if I don't ask." She heaved a sigh. "I suppose if that's what it'll take for you to go peaceful-like, I'll allow her to help."

"It is."

"All right." A smile tipped the corners of her mouth. "How many hours will you be on the stage?"

"I should arrive at company headquarters in two days."

She nodded. "I'll be praying for you until you get home." Biting her lip, she worried another matter in her mind. "One more thing, Son."

His back stiffened. "Now, Ma. We've talked about this before."

"Please. It can't hurt to ask around."

"You've got to let it go. All this worry is what's made you sick. Doc says you'll never get better if you don't move on."

"It's not that easy. I don't know how many months or years I have left, and I can't die without knowing what happened." Tears sprang, unbidden, and she blotted them, hating for Steven to see her like this. He had been strong for her sake over the years, and she must do the same. It wouldn't be right, letting her older child leave for God-only-knew how long, with the memory of his mother's collapse fresh in his mind. "Forgive me. You're right. Go on with you, now. It won't look good to your new employer if you miss the stage."

Steven hesitated, searching her face, then leaned over and kissed her cheek. "I won't be gone any longer than I have to. And I'll keep my ears open, Ma. I promise."

Isabelle wrapped her arms around his waist and hugged him one last time. "Thank you, Son. I'll be praying. Maybe this time we'll get some answers. Maybe God will listen at last."

Chapter Six

Beth slipped out the front door, praying no one would follow. Jeffery Tucker had been a bit too inquisitive for her peace of mind lately, and she didn't need him following or noticing the sketch pad tucked under her arm. She'd spotted a towering shade tree on a small rise a mile or so from the house some time ago and had wanted to visit ever since. It might have a good view of the valley, and she could use some inspiration for her work right now.

She loved this time of year, when the trees were starting to turn all shades of orange, red, and gold. But homesickness nipped at her heels as she stepped off the main road and swung up a dirt path. It had been months since she and Aunt Wilma left Kansas, and sometimes she longed to return ... yet not as much as she had at first, come to think of it. In fact, it had been days—maybe weeks—since she'd thought about her old home at all. Brent, on the other hand, she thought about frequently. She gathered her skirt in one hand and stepped over a fallen log. The morning sun warmed her face, and she lifted a hand to block the light. Good. No sign of anyone under the boughs of the tree or anywhere on the hillside.

Why couldn't she forget about Brent? He'd walked away without a word. She'd always thought Aunt Wilma had driven him away somehow, and part of her hadn't been surprised he'd left. It *had* surprised her that he'd been attracted to her in the first place. She had never seen herself as pretty. Her body was marred, and her personality was little more than a flat surface with no ripples or peaks to stir a man's imagination.

She trudged up the hill, forcing herself to plant one foot in front of the other. The man she thought she'd loved had disappeared without explanation, and although she cared for Aunt Wilma as much as if she'd been a blood relative, she didn't have a clue to whom she belonged. She bit the inside of her cheek. That wasn't fair. Aunt Wilma loved her more than she deserved and was the only mother she'd known ... or at least remembered clearly. Lately, snippets of memory flickered. Images kept coming and going, making it hard to discern what was reality and what might be imagination.

Then there were the dreams, and the memories and emotions they'd begun to stir.

The lush grass and soft breeze blowing the russet-colored leaves drew her, and she settled onto the green carpet blanketing the ground. The valley spread out before her. The towering Wallowa Mountains loomed in the distance while the Elkhorn Mountains guarded the other side of the valley, and the sparkling Powder River wended its way through the center, right at the edge of town.

The peacefulness of the setting should have soothed her, but the memory of her dreams tightened her shoulders. She had awakened in the night several times this past month, drenched in a cold sweat and shaking. Getting out of bed and rinsing her face helped break the spell at times, but at others she sank back into the murky waters as soon as she lay back down.

Beth blew out a frustrated breath. Time to get to work. She'd finished one drawing for the magazine but hadn't been able to concentrate of late. Opening her bag, she drew out her pencils, thankful she'd sharpened them last night. She closed her eyes, trying to envision what she'd bring to life, then bent over the pad. Her fingers moved swiftly, and an image emerged of dust kicked up from horses' hooves as they trudged across the page, moving away....

Away? From what? She paused, struggling to put her finger on what niggled at her mind. She saw smoke rise from an abandoned cooking pit and her pencil flew, filling in the details. No sign of life appeared, no scattered litter from the campfire or utensils showing people had recently camped there.

Wait. There was something … a child. Huddled on the far side of the clearing. Crying and clutching herself, rocking back and forth. She sketched in the scene until she noticed the red welts on the girl's skin and smoke rising from her burned clothing. *What in the world?*

Beth dropped the pad and stared at it as though it might poison her if she touched it. Her body shook so hard she didn't dare try to stand, as much as she'd love to flee from this place.

She remembered now. They'd left her alone.

Her parents must not have cared.

The smoke rising from her clothing. The pain. The horrible, searing pain. She rubbed the length of her arm. That was all she could recall. The rest was blackness. Awful, scary blackness. Until *they* came and carried her away.

What in the dickens was Beth doing on that hill? Jeffery stood at the bottom and stared toward the tree towering above its neighbors. Why didn't she come down? He'd seen her wander up the slope two hours ago with a bag looped over her wrist and a book tucked under her arm. He'd wanted to follow but hesitated. The last time they'd spoken he'd offended her somehow, and he still wasn't sure why.

Had Beth experienced the same loneliness he had since arriving in this mining town? Jeffery had hoped she'd want to be friends as much as he did. He hadn't realized how much he'd looked forward to getting to know Beth until she'd turned her back and walked away. Something about her drew him that he couldn't quite explain. Beth had shown a surprising spunk when she'd refused to answer his questions. He wasn't concerned that she didn't care to share her past—neither did he. But he grieved the loss of the relationship that might have been, if she'd only given them a chance.

What was she doing up there, anyway? He wasn't certain it was safe for a young woman to ramble on a hillside alone, although he could sympathize with the desire for privacy. Maybe he should hike up, approach her, and offer an apology for whatever he'd done to upset her.

Those curls the color of dark chocolate and deep blue eyes held a definite appeal, and when she smiled—well, now. He moved forward, joy sprouting.

Then a thought gave him pause. He'd assumed Beth would want companionship based partly on the amount of time she spent alone—unattended by a man. But she might not have any callers because she was promised to someone. His heart sank. That should have occurred to him earlier. It was more than possible her trek up the hill was a tryst with a suitor.

Jeffery headed back toward the boardinghouse, discouragement dogging his steps. It might be best to wait and see if he could speak to Beth another time and not impose on her now. Another thought struck Jeffery, and his pace quickened. Maybe he'd linger on the trail near the house in case Beth came home soon and accompany her back home.

Beth scrambled down the hill, anxious to get away from the memories and back to her room. She hurried along the trail, unmindful of where her feet led. All that mattered was putting her sketch pad away and burying her head under the covers.

She faltered. No. That was foolish. She'd responded the same way when Brent stepped out of her life. She hadn't so much as protested when Aunt Wilma dragged her away from her home and out here to the wilderness. She gulped in a shaky but resolute breath. This nonsense was going to stop. She was a grown woman with a mind of her own, and it was high time she used it.

Why had her aunt insisted on coming so far west? Aunt Wilma had never wanted to discuss her reasons and avoided the subject whenever approached. Not that Beth had tried too hard at first. Brent's abandonment had struck a hard blow and, coupled with the other dark things that had happened in her past, she hadn't had the energy to care.

This new contract had sparked something to life. Things looked brighter, and hope had bloomed again … until today. She had to talk to Aunt Wilma.

Beth increased her pace. She rounded a bend in the trail and tripped on a tree root. Her pad went flying into the dense brush, and she sprawled onto the ground, striking her foot on a rock. "Ouch!" The word came out louder than she'd intended, but sharp, paralyzing pain shot up her leg. She rolled over, hugging herself and rocking.

Footsteps thudded on the path ahead, and Beth stiffened. She didn't care to be found flat on her backside with dirt staining her dress. She hitched over onto her side and tried to stand, but her knee wouldn't allow it.

"Beth?" Jeffery Tucker slid to a stop, apprehension widening his eyes. "Are you all right?"

"I think so." Consternation bit deep. Of all the people who had to appear, why Jeffery—Mr. Tucker? She would not call him Jeffery, even in her mind. "If you would be kind enough to help me up, I'll walk home."

He bent over and extended a hand. "If you are sure you can stand? I'll find a buggy if you're seriously injured."

She shook her head. "Truly, I'm fine. I caught my toe on a root. My knee was numb for a moment, but it's better now." Reaching out, she allowed him to take her hand, but he didn't stop there. He slipped his other arm around her waist and gently lifted her to her feet. Warmth rushed through her body. She found herself trembling, although she wasn't certain it was solely from her knee.

"Are you sure? Do you think you can walk?" He steadied her for a moment, then dropped his arm from her waist but kept her hand firmly in his grasp. "Try it while I steady you. I do not want to take a chance of you falling."

She could still feel the heat from where his arm had encircled her waist. Maybe it wouldn't hurt to allow herself to at least *think* of him as Jeffery. Beth took a step forward and then another, and a spasm of pain shot up her leg.

His brows rose in alarm. "You're limping. I insist on procuring a buggy."

"No. My knee is getting better, and it's not far to the house. It would be foolish to sit here and wait for a buggy when I can make it back home."

His jaw set with a stubborn firmness, and his grip tightened. "Beth, I really—"

"Please, Mr. Tucker. I do not want you to go to any trouble. If you care to walk with me, I'd appreciate that, but I truly don't need a ride."

His eyes were soft but determined. "Beth, please call me Jeffery."

Her heart jolted. "I, uh … all right, Jeffery. But right now I want to get home and sit."

Jeffery nodded. "Forgive me for being insensitive." He extended his arm. "Would you take my arm and lean on me?"

"Thank you." She slipped her fingers through the crook of his arm. "Whatever brought you this way, I am in your debt. I must admit I might have sat there for a while before attempting to hobble home."

He shot her a smile, revealing a dimple. Why had she never noticed that attractive feature before? "I suppose I could say I was only out for a walk, but that wouldn't be honest."

"Oh?" Her heartbeat raced, and she couldn't bring herself to look at him again.

"I saw you leave the house and followed, hoping to talk."

Beth stumbled, and he steadied her. Why would he follow? The stark truth washed over her. Was he hoping to interview her for more information for his book? "But it's midmorning. I left the house quite early."

"Two-and-a-half hours ago, to be exact." He grinned. "I saw you go up the hill but didn't want to impose on your time alone."

Her tablet! She pulled to a halt and planted her weight on her injured leg. "Oh my." It had flown out of her hands when she'd fallen and must have landed in the brush, but she'd been in too much pain to remember. If he retrieved it, he might ask questions. No. He certainly would ask questions. That could be dangerous. He might even ask to see her drawings. All of her finished ones were initialed E.C. She started to shake, unsure what to do.

Alarm crossed his face. "You're worse. I knew I shouldn't have allowed you to walk. We're almost to the house, but you're not going to take another step." He wrapped a gentle arm around her and, with a quick motion, scooped her off her feet, cradling her against his firm chest.

Beth gasped and planted her hand against his chest. "This isn't necessary."

Jeffery held her tighter. "I'm not taking no for an answer."

Jeffery watched the path, careful not to jar the injured young woman. He'd expected the balance of the walk home would be tiresome but was pleasantly surprised. It was almost like carrying a child wearing voluminous skirts. "Are you quite all right, Miss Roberts?" She hadn't said a word since he'd plucked her off the ground, and he feared she might have gone into shock.

She lay rigidly still in his arms but didn't appear to be in pain. At least she hadn't fainted.

"I assure you I am perfectly capable of walking." Her voice was a bit muffled against his shirt. "Please put me down, Mr. Tucker. What if someone sees us?"

"What if they do?" He gazed at her. How close those liquid blue eyes appeared. And those lips. His mouth went dry. "You were injured, and I am assisting you. There is nothing inappropriate about that." He nodded. "See? We're almost there."

Her small hand gripped his upper arm, and the pressure increased. "Please, Mr. Tucker. If you care for my feelings at all, set me down and allow me to walk the rest of the way."

The front door banged open. "What in heaven's name has happened?"

Beth groaned. "Mrs. Cooper."

Jeffery came to a halt. What to do now? They'd been noticed, so he didn't see any difference in carrying her the rest of the way. "It's too late, Beth. And you shouldn't attempt the steps." He strode forward up the path, ignoring her efforts to remove herself from his embrace.

"I can walk, Mr. Tucker." She spat the words. "I'm fine, Mrs. Cooper." Her voice rose on the last two words. "I wrenched my knee, and Mr. Tucker found me around the bend. He insisted on carrying me home."

Mrs. Cooper hurried down the steps and along the path, tsk-ing all the way. "My goodness. What is poor Wilma to think? It is certainly a good thing we have no close neighbors, or gossip would be flying about town in no time."

"Pardon me, ma'am." Jeffery brushed past the woman and stalked the rest of the way to the house. "There is nothing to gossip about, unless it's somehow noteworthy when a gentleman assists a lady in distress."

Mrs. Cooper trotted along behind them. "How badly are you injured, my dear?"

Beth squirmed in his arms, and he shifted her weight before attempting the steps. "I will put you down when we reach the top. Please hold still, or we'll both take a tumble."

She quieted immediately and turned her head. "I'm fine, Mrs. Cooper. Or at least, I think I will be once I've had a chance to lie down and rest my knee. I'm grateful Mr. Tucker found me when he did, or it could have been much worse."

Mrs. Cooper puffed up the steps and moved ahead of Jeffery. She poked her head in the front door. "Wilma, you need to come out here right now. Something frightful has happened to your niece."

Chapter Seven

Aunt Wilma didn't say a word, just looked from Mr. Tucker to Beth and back, then beckoned them to follow her upstairs to Beth's room.

Beth squirmed in Jeffery's arms, trying to ignore the prickles of awareness being cradled in his strong arms fostered. "Truly, Mr. Tucker, I am sure I can make it to my room with my aunt's assistance."

He gently set her on her feet. "I don't care to take the chance of bumping your knee against the wall. I won't carry you up, but I insist on helping." He slipped his arm around her waist again.

Beth resisted the impulse to snuggle against his side as he helped her up the stairs. *Safe* and *protected*—those were the only words that captured what she felt for those brief moments. Something she had never expected to feel in regard to a man again. And she'd certainly never expected Mr. Tucker to be so strong. Aunt Wilma swept ahead and swung open the door to her room.

He stopped at the doorway. "Will you be all right now, Miss Roberts?" Deep concern shone from his eyes as he continued to steady her.

"Yes." The word came out with a breathy sigh, and Beth felt an almost physical pain as his arm slipped from her waist … a pain that had nothing to do with her wrenched knee.

He waited until she entered the room, then headed toward the stairs.

Beth limped to her bed and stretched out. She darted a glance at her aunt and waited for the eruption.

Aunt Wilma settled onto the mattress beside her, and Beth hitched over, grimacing at the pain.

"Tell me what happened. Why was Mr. Tucker carrying you?" Aunt Wilma's firm tone softened. "Mrs. Cooper seemed to believe you were badly hurt."

Beth relaxed into the pillows. She didn't know why she'd feared her aunt would be upset—possibly a result of her own shame at being held in a man's arms for so long. She probed a little deeper, not sure that the word *shame* conveyed her feelings. *Chagrin* or *embarrassment* might come closer, although the warmth stealing over her disparaged that conclusion.

"I spent longer on the hill than I'd planned and decided to hurry home. I guess I wasn't watching my footing. I tripped over a root and went flying. I wrenched my knee and struck a rock."

"But what of Mr. Tucker?" Aunt Wilma's brows beetled together. "How did he happen to come upon you? What in heaven's name were you doing up on a hillside alone?" She drew back. "And how badly are you hurt?"

Beth held up her hand and chuckled. "One question at a time, Auntie. I'm fine. Or at least, nothing's broken, although my knee is quite tender and sore. As for Mr. Tucker, apparently he was taking a stroll and came across me." She bit her lip. It wasn't a lie, as he *had* been taking a walk, but she couldn't face all the forthcoming questions if she explained. "I'm quite grateful he did, although I could have made it home well enough by leaning on his arm."

A curious sparkle lit her aunt's eyes. "I see. It seems he didn't agree?"

Beth ducked her head. "Well ..."

"'Fess up and tell your aunt all about it. What exactly happened out there?"

"When I fell, I lost my sketch pad, and Mr. Tucker misinterpreted my response as pain. He scooped me into his arms, even though I assured him I could walk. No protest convinced him, and he insisted on carrying me to the house." There. She'd told Aunt Wilma everything. Well, almost. Beth saw no reason to share her reactions to Jeffery's arms cradling her against his chest or the loss she'd felt when he released her. No. Aunt Wilma had no need for those details at all.

Her aunt stroked a curl off Beth's forehead. "And why, pray tell, didn't you simply inform him you'd lost your tablet? I assume you didn't mention it. Is it still out there in the brush?"

Beth nodded, misery knotting her stomach. "You're the only one who knows I'm an illustrator. Except for my publisher, of course. But even they don't know the real Beth Roberts. I guess I didn't want Mr. Tucker asking questions or insisting on seeing my work."

Aunt Wilma sighed. "I still don't understand that decision. It's not like your drawings are more than an enjoyable hobby. I realize you make some money from them, but one of these days you'll marry and want to raise a family. You won't have time for sketching. Why do you insist on keeping it a secret? Mr. Tucker would probably appreciate what you've done."

"No, Aunt Wilma. I will never marry or have a family. No man would want me if he knew everything. It's no one's business, least of all Mr. Tucker's. And it is *not* just a hobby. It's part of who I am. It fulfills me, and that will never end. Nothing else makes me feel the same way—at peace … worthwhile." Her chin firmed with determination. "I know you don't understand, but it's true. Besides, Mr. Tucker is too nosy. He'll want to know why I have a tablet full of drawings and what I'm doing with them. He's always asking questions, and I'm convinced he's attempting to find more material for his book. I, for one, don't care to be included in his story, and I wish he'd go away and leave us alone." She averted her eyes, unwilling to reveal the conflicted emotions swirling inside.

Her aunt patted her shoulder. "But dear heart, your peace can't come solely from your drawings, nor can you find your entire worth there. That must come from God."

"I'm afraid not, Auntie. It's not that I don't care about God, but there is so much I don't understand, like why God allowed the things in my life, and why I'm so alone now." She met her aunt's gaze. "Other than you, of course. I'm sure I have Him to thank for you taking me in, but there are so many other unanswered questions. My peace doesn't come from God, at least not at this point in my life. It comes from my work."

Wilma smoothed another of Beth's curls. "Now, there. I don't agree, but I hate to see you upset. I won't speak to Mr. Tucker about your drawings, if you insist."

Beth plucked at the brightly colored quilt she lay on. "Thank you. But I *am* worried someone will find my tablet. Or that it will rain, and the pictures will be ruined before I can retrieve it." Sudden determination pushed her up onto her elbow. "I'll go get it right now. I can't take any chances."

Aunt Wilma gently pressed Beth back against her pillow. "You'll do no such thing. If it's going to worry you that much, I'll find it when we're finished talking. Tell me where you lost it. I can't imagine it will be too hard to locate."

The tension seeped out of Beth's muscles. "Are you sure? It's not terribly far from the house, but I hate to ask you to traipse down a dirt path."

Aunt Wilma fluttered her hand in the air. "Nonsense. I am not a child, nor am I in my dotage." She leaned over and kissed Beth's cheek.

Beth nodded but continued to fiddle with the tufts of yarn decorating the squares on the quilt. "But first I have something to discuss."

Isabelle Mason stared at the journal. It felt like such a waste. All these years, pouring out her heart in the hopes that someone would read them before it was too late. Remorse plagued her, tugging her deeper into the darkness than even the sickness that constantly beset her. Her shoulders slumped, and she laid the pen aside, suddenly too tired to continue.

What had she thought this would accomplish? Her time would be better spent in the garden, when she could muster the energy to pull the ever-encroaching weeds and pour water on the struggling plants. Steven always toted the buckets from the well when he was home, but the barrel standing beside the modest garden plot was nearly empty. She hated asking Ina or her friend Karen to fill it, even though both women were stronger than she.

Why must she always fight against this reoccurring sadness that drained the joy and strength from her body? The constant ravages of the disease that had struck so many years ago had done its share to draw her closer to her eternal reward in heaven.

More and more she longed to leave this life and travel to the next. Only two things pressed her forward and convinced her to fight: Steven and—

Pain knifed through Isabelle's heart. She couldn't go there, even in her thoughts. Plucking the pen from its stand and moving the journal into the lantern's light, she squinted at the next clean page. Time to stop all the foolish pity and do what needed to be done. A record must be kept, and she was the only one who could do it.

Chapter Eight

Wilma's heart pounded as she looked into her niece's agitated face. What had stirred her up? Surely the loss of her sketch pad wasn't enough to carve creases between her brows. "What's worrying you, Beth? Is it the illustrations you're supposed to do for the magazine?"

"No. I've finished one and sent it in to the magazine, and already have a rough idea for another. I'm still working out the details, but it'll come." Her fingers, stained with lead, continued to pluck at the quilt.

"You spend too much time in your room hunched over your desk; it's going to ruin your lovely posture. You need to be out in society, doing things other young women enjoy. Drawing is pleasant enough, but it's consuming far too much of your time, child. Finish your obligation for these illustrations and don't take any more. You need to make a life for yourself and stop wasting your time with foolishness."

Beth jerked as though slapped. "You think my work is foolish? All this time I assumed you believed in me. That you wanted me to succeed."

Wilma's stomach clenched. It had been years since she'd seen such a bereft expression on her dear girl's face. What had she done?

The child shrank as though Wilma had taken something precious away and was refusing to give it back. Could her drawings mean so much?

Wilma scrambled for the right words. "Of course I want you to succeed, but there are other kinds of success. I simply believe you'd be happier as a wife and mother. You can still enjoy your work after you marry. In fact, I'd like to have a picture with some trees or mountains in it, if you'd care to draw one for me someday." She peered at her niece.

Beth dropped her gaze to her fingers. "I'd be happy to, Auntie." No joy tinged the soft answer. "But I'm not giving up my work. It's important to me. People have never filled that hole. You were happily married to Uncle George, so I'm certain you can't understand. But that's not what I wanted to talk about."

"What then?" Wilma was unexpectedly nervous.

Stark pain blazed from Beth's eyes. "Memories." The single word came out in a whisper. "Or maybe they've been dreams. I'm not sure. Mostly at night, but they carry into the day … sometimes, anyway. And into my sketches. Like today." She shifted on the bed again. "I want to sit up. I can't lie here while I talk about this."

Alarm bells rang in Wilma's head. "All right, but you mustn't get up on that knee yet." She scooted off the bed and plucked a pillow from the chair in the corner of the room. "Lean forward, and I'll tuck this behind you."

Beth situated herself against the pillow. "That's better. Thank you."

Wilma pulled the chair close to the bed and sank into it. "Now, what's all this about? Dreams, memories, and such … and you've put some of it into your sketches?" Dread filled her. She'd worried this day might come. She'd only told Beth what she felt the girl needed to know. There was no sense in making her feel worse than she already did, believing her parents hadn't wanted her. All she could do was pray memories hadn't surfaced that would plunge her sweet darling into the past. Not that her niece wasn't a strong young woman. Sometimes Wilma wondered if she really knew how deep the girl's resolve extended. But this was not the way she cared to have it tested.

"I drew something today that I don't completely understand, but it left me shaken and feeling sick."

Wilma straightened in her chair. "Can you share it with me?"

"I think so. I wish I had my tablet so I could show you instead." She rubbed her temples. "It was something I saw in my mind. My fingers seemed to fly across the paper of their own volition. Dust, disappearing into the distance. In the foreground a little girl sitting by a bed of coals, her skin swollen and covered with red blisters, and her clothing burned."

Wilma winced, hating the picture forming. "Was that all?" As though it weren't enough, but she had to know. Too much had been left unsaid for too long. "So you believe what you drew was a memory of something that happened to you?" As soon as the words left her lips, she knew how foolish they sounded. What else would the images be?

"Yes. At least, I think so. You've never told me much about my past, and I guess I never wanted to know. I always thought my parents hated me because of my scars."

Wilma gripped the armrests so tightly her fingers hurt. "You are not ugly and never have been. Those scars barely show. And I don't believe for a moment your parents gave you away due to you being burned."

"What if I was careless and fell in the fire, and they didn't care to be bothered? They may have already decided they didn't want me, and my injuries settled it. Besides, I *am* ugly and the scars *do* show." Tears welled. Beth blinked rapidly, then swiped at an errant droplet. "A couple of years after I came to live with you, I was playing a game with the neighborhood children. We were rolling around on the ground, and my stockings fell down. The children screamed and said my legs were scary, and they didn't want to play with me anymore. I was so hurt and confused that I shrieked an Indian word. Not long after that, most of them quit coming to play." Her lips trembled. "Even the girl who'd promised to be my friend abandoned me...."

Hot rage saturated Wilma's body, and it was all she could do not to curse. She'd never done so in her life and didn't care to start now, but if there ever were a reason to do so, this would be it. However, it wouldn't do to allow her fury to bubble over and alarm her darling girl. Not that Beth hadn't seen her angry more than once in the past, but this was different. Very different. She sucked in a deep breath and released it slowly. "I'm so sorry that happened. Why didn't you tell me about it then? I would have sought out those children's parents and insisted they be disciplined."

Beth shook her head. "That's why. The last time two of the children came, they said their parents wouldn't allow them to return. They'd told them what I'd said, and their parents asked around. Apparently, someone knew about my past, and the children were told they couldn't play with a 'dirty redskin.' I was old enough to know if you spoke to the parents you would be as wounded as I. They wouldn't have been shy about speaking their mind to you."

Wilma clenched her teeth. "Who were they?"

"It doesn't matter. After a time I forgave them. There's no reason to resurrect it." Her eyes glistened with a hint of moisture, and she brushed it away. "At least, there wasn't a reason until today. What else do you know, Aunt Wilma? About my past, that is. What haven't you told me?"

Wilma sagged against the chair, and all her righteous anger oozed away. Her girl had been hurt much worse than she'd imagined. All these years, she'd carried not only the physical scars, but the damage to her heart and soul as well. Now she believed herself to be ugly and not worthy of love. No wonder she'd fallen prey to Brent Wentworth's charms when he'd slithered into her life. "Very little that you haven't already surmised. You were badly burned …" A shudder shook her frame, and she placed her hand to her cheek.

Beth leaned forward. "But where did they find me? What did they say? I've always known we aren't actually related by blood, but why did you call yourself my aunt when you took me in"—her voice broke—"instead of my mother?"

Beth gripped a fistful of quilt and waited. She'd always wanted to ask, ever since she could remember, but hadn't wanted to hurt her aunt. Her adopted aunt. No, that wasn't right either. To her knowledge no papers had been signed. Or did it go deeper than that? Maybe her real fear came from the possibility of yet more rejection. Her parents had abandoned her, and Wilma Roberts had taken care of her but didn't love her enough to make it legal. What did that say for Beth Roberts, or whatever her real name might be? Beth didn't even have that knowledge to hold on to.

She had no identity, no understanding of her past or who her people might be, and—from what she could discern—no way to find out. A couple of times Beth had introduced the subject to Aunt Wilma, but she hadn't seemed willing to offer more than the fact that Beth had been found and brought to Fort Laramie as a child.

Aunt Wilma opened her mouth, but Beth held up her hand. "Don't say anything more. I don't think I want to know the answer right now. Do you think I could rest for a bit?"

The older woman's mouth snapped shut. She pushed back from her chair and stepped close to the bed. "I love you, Beth Roberts. More than you can imagine. What I did was to protect you from further gossip, not because I didn't want to claim you as my own."

"Please. I think we've said enough, and I really do want to rest. My knee is aching." Truth was, her heart hurt worse than her knee, but she couldn't admit that to this woman who'd raised her. She owed Wilma Roberts too much.

Deep inside, Beth knew her aunt loved her. Knew it with every part of her being. But she didn't want to hear the excuses as to why she hadn't adopted her. It must have to do with the stigma of her past. Aunt Wilma wouldn't have wanted people to know her daughter had been held captive—no, that wasn't fair. There was still too much they didn't know.

Regardless, it would have reflected poorly on Aunt Wilma, and her standing in society had always been important. Beth couldn't blame her, not after the way those children had treated her. At least that family moved out of town not long after, but no doubt they'd spread tales before they'd departed.

It was possible Aunt Wilma had gotten the same treatment when a scarred child arrived in her home. People would have questioned where Beth had come from and who she belonged to. How much easier to claim she belonged to a deceased sibling and quell the rumors of a foundling child rescued by the Arapaho.

Wilma hesitated at the door, casting a longing glance at Beth, then shook her head and walked out of the room.

Chapter Nine

The following morning Beth gingerly removed her covers and swung her legs over the side of the bed. She'd forgotten to ask Aunt Wilma to bring her sketch pad to her room before she'd gone to sleep last night, but her throbbing knee would have kept her from concentrating on her work anyway.

She lifted the hem of her nightdress and rubbed her fingers over her knee. The swelling was down somewhat, but prodding the flesh around her kneecap caused her to wince. She might need to spend one more day close to home. She slipped back into bed. It wouldn't be long before Aunt Wilma came to check on her. After the nearly sleepless night, catching a few minutes more rest sounded like heaven.

Sometime later a soft knock woke Beth from a doze. "Come in, I'm awake." She scooted up against her pillow. A dull pain throbbed in her head, and she felt far from refreshed.

Aunt Wilma stepped inside and closed the door behind her. "You didn't come down for breakfast. Is your knee any better?"

Beth smiled. Trust her aunt to go straight to the issue at hand. "A little. I suppose I should have gotten up." She struggled out from under the covers again and brushed her hair from her face. "I should get dressed and go downstairs."

"No need." Her aunt opened the door. "You can bring it in, child."

Lucy Galloway, the landlady's older daughter, walked in, balancing a tray in her hands. "Where would you like it, ma'am?" Her blond head swiveled as she scanned the room. "I can set it down and pull a chair over to the bed if you'd like."

Mortification pulsed through Beth. She was no sick invalid to be waited on. "I'm so sorry, Lucy. I'll eat downstairs with everyone else."

"There's no need. Besides, we've all finished, and Ma's cleaning the kitchen. She told me to bring this up and see if you felt like eating." Lucy set it on the bureau and grinned. "Mandy's helping with the dishes, so I'm not eager to return. It's time my little sister did more chores, even if she is seven years old. I've been doing my share for years now."

Beth worked to keep from laughing. The girl was thirteen, so it hadn't been too many years since Lucy was her sister's age, and no doubt had been as carefree at seven. "I thank you kindly for bringing it up, but Aunt Wilma could have brought it."

Wilma nodded. "I told her, but she insisted." She shot the girl a playful look, her lips twitching. "Now I understand why."

Lucy dipped her head. "Oh, I'll help plenty when I get back downstairs. Ma will see to that, and if she doesn't, Grandma will." She heaved a sigh. "Ever since Grandma came, she's made sure we do our share. Not that I mind too much, but I do enjoy fishing with Zachary whenever I can slip away."

Beth quirked a brow. "I imagine your mother appreciates the fresh fish you and Mr. Jacobs's son catch. It adds to the larder and certainly makes for some tasty meals."

"Yes, ma'am. Well, I'd best get back to the kitchen before Ma sends Mandy looking for me. I do hope your knee will be better soon." She turned toward the door, then stopped. "I forgot. Ma sent this up." She tugged at the deep pocket of her apron and extracted a glass bottle. "It's liniment for your knee. Grandma says it helps her gout, and it's good for what ails you, sore knees and all."

Beth waited until the girl shut the door carefully behind her, then stood and limped to the bureau.

"What are you doing?" Aunt Wilma demanded. "Trying to make your injury worse? That's why we brought breakfast up, so you could rest."

"I'm getting stiff and need to move for a bit. Besides, it's not as bad today, and I'm sure the liniment will help. Since I overslept, I'm not staying in this bed a minute longer than I must, even if I can't go outside for a walk." She took the tray to the wingback chair in the corner and settled into it. "Smells wonderful. Bacon and eggs and hot tea. My favorite."

The next few minutes passed in silence as Aunt Wilma allowed Beth to eat without attempting to engage in conversation. Beth took the final bite of scrambled eggs and wiped her mouth with a napkin. "I realized last night that I'd forgotten to ask you to bring my sketchbook directly to my room. I wonder if you'd mind dropping it by so I can get some work done. If I have to be cooped up resting my knee, I can at least be productive."

"Oh my." Aunt Wilma placed her hand over her heart and plopped on the edge of the bed.

A cold wave of dread washed over Beth as the color drained from her aunt's face. "What?" She set the tray aside and pushed to her feet. "Are you ill?"

Wilma gazed up at her. "No. But I'm afraid you might be after I tell you."

Beth gripped her aunt's shoulders and squeezed. "What is wrong, Auntie?"

"I'm so sorry, Beth. I know it meant a lot to you, and I can't believe I got busy and forgot. Please forgive me." Her words dropped to a whisper.

Beth sank onto the mattress next to her aunt. "You didn't look for my sketch pad? Auntie, how could you!"

Aunt Wilma didn't speak.

"Are you sure you forgot?" Beth jumped to her feet, pushing aside the knifing pain in her knee. She did her best to keep her voice level and calm, but it shook with the effort. "Yesterday you said my work is foolish, and you think I should stop. Well, I won't. And if I can't find my sketch pad myself, I'll go to town and buy another one. I can't replace what I lost, but I will not give up my work."

Wilma pressed her fingers over her lips. "Let me, please. I'm so sorry." She rushed from the room, her heels thumping as she headed toward the stairs.

Beth slumped onto her bed. Despair snaked its tendrils around her thoughts, trying to convince her that Aunt Wilma had purposely ignored her request. But her aunt had looked mortified, and if she wasn't mistaken, Beth had glimpsed tears before the older woman dashed from the room. She shouldn't have spoken that way to the only mother she'd ever known.

Who could she trust anymore? She'd always lived with the knowledge she must not have been wanted by her family, and she'd turned to Wilma Roberts for her comfort and security. Now she struggled to push aside the feelings of betrayal.

"Put your trust in Me. I won't fail you."

Beth jerked upright and listened. She slipped from her bed and limped to the door, yanking it open and stepping into the hall. Empty. Who had spoken? Had she heard a voice, or was it her imagination?

The skin on her neck prickled. She'd heard the voice before but hadn't known what He was trying to tell her. Could it be as simple as choosing to trust when it felt like so much in her life was out of kilter? She didn't see how, but a gentle peace wafted over her heart.

Men had failed her in the past. It seemed her father must have deserted her; Uncle George had died a couple of years after she arrived to live with him and Aunt Wilma. Even the man who'd promised to love her had walked away.

"Put your trust in Me." Somehow Beth knew God had spoken those words. Hopefully, being willing would count for something, because the most she could do was try.

Chapter Ten

Sleep had eluded Jeffery for two nights now, ever since he'd carried Beth to her room. What had possessed him to hold her so close? Jeffery tossed back the covers and climbed out of bed in spite of the fact the sun hadn't yet risen. He gave a wry smile. He couldn't exactly have held her at arm's length while transporting her to the house. But he should have listened when she'd insisted she could walk, and deposited her back on her feet.

His chivalrous upbringing had won out. How many times had his father insisted he play the part of a gentleman, even as a young chap? He'd once pulled a girl's hair in grammar school and been reprimanded by the teacher, and Father had switched him for it when he'd heard. Jeffery shook his head. He couldn't have allowed Beth to walk home when she was in obvious pain. But guarding his heart against the surge of emotion and yearning might be wise.

He sat in his chair and mulled over the details of his life. It had been two years since he'd seen his family. On the one hand he missed them, but on the other it was a relief not to deal with the constant pressures they exerted. He was twenty-six years old, but to his parents he'd always be their child. He wasn't sure Father would ever look on him differently. To Mark Tucker, writing was a waste of time. Somehow Jeffery must convince his parents he didn't need their money and could make it on his own. Making this novel a success might be the key.

A sudden hankering for a hot cup of coffee drove him to his feet. The sun had risen, and the household would be stirring. Hopefully Mrs. Jacobs wouldn't mind him building a fire and brewing a pot.

He came to a stop in the kitchen doorway and slowly edged backward, not wanting to intrude on the two women sipping cups of tea at the table.

Frances Cooper peered over her spectacles. "No need to leave, Mr. Tucker. Come in and have a cup of tea. Or coffee, if you prefer. We brewed both."

Mrs. Roberts beckoned, a ring on her finger glinting in the early morning light that streamed through the window. "Yes. Please do. It's nice to have a little male company. We seldom see you anymore. Are you making good progress on your book?"

His feet dragged as he entered the kitchen, and he looked askance at them both. He'd experienced more than one uncomfortable scene between these women, but they appeared friendly enough this morn-ing. "Thank you. Coffee sounds good, but I hate to intrude."

Mrs. Cooper stood and plucked a mug off a shelf. "Not at all. We are quite happy to have you. Katherine should be up soon and fixing breakfast, but we wanted to let her sleep. She looked a little peaked to me. Didn't you think so, Wilma?"

Wilma's head bobbed, and a brown curl, sprinkled with gray, broke free from the knot at the base of her neck. "She certainly did. Besides, we had a lot to discuss and decided to make an early start to the day."

Jeffery halted in front of a chair, his hand poised above the back of it. "Then I really shouldn't stay."

"Nonsense, young man," Mrs. Roberts scolded in a light voice. "Take a seat and enjoy your coffee before it gets cold." She plucked a cloth off the table, wrapped it around the handle of the coffeepot, filled the mug to the brim, then pushed it toward him. "Sugar or cream?"

He eased into the chair and cradled the mug of steaming coffee between both hands, inhaling the fragrance. "Black is perfect, thank you. It smells wonderful. You ladies certainly know how to brew a fine cup."

Mrs. Roberts leaned close. "So tell us all about your novel. We're dying to hear what you've decided to include about the happenings here. Is there going to be a romance or a murder?"

Mrs. Cooper jumped in before he could take a breath. "Of course he is not going to kill off someone at our house." She shuddered. "How could you suggest such a thing?"

Wilma took a sip of her tea. "I think it's a fine idea. We could help ferret out the killer, don't you know? Mr. Tucker could sprinkle clues for us to follow." She shivered and rubbed her hands together. "It would be positively delicious!"

Mrs. Cooper set down her cup, and it clinked against the saucer. "Why, there is not a single person I would care to have die. I am horrified you would even suggest such a thing. Although I suppose …" A gleam lit her eyes, and she cocked a brow toward the stairwell.

"What?" Mrs. Roberts clasped her hands on the tabletop. "What are you thinking, Frances? Maybe an itinerant peddler or a cowboy passing through mysteriously dies? Or perhaps outlaws come to town and hold up the bank—they could even take someone hostage...." She almost bounced in her seat.

"No, no, nothing like that," Mrs. Cooper admonished. "I was thinking of the romance question. Now mind you, I do not read that type of novel, but if you insist on writing one, Mr. Tucker, I might have just the thing."

Jeffery controlled the urge to grin. Good thing he'd awakened over an hour ago and wasn't facing this barrage with a sleep-befuddled brain. "And what would that be, Mrs. Cooper?"

"Why, you and Beth! I must admit, after I got over the initial shock of seeing her in your arms, I decided it was quite romantic. The two of you would make a fine couple." She aimed a gleeful look at Mrs. Roberts. "For your book, of course."

Mrs. Roberts glanced from Mrs. Cooper to Jeffery. "I think that's a fine idea." A sly grin crept across her face. "For a book."

Beth had been cooped up in her room for too long and couldn't countenance allowing Lucy to bring her another meal. At the moment, she was grateful she'd made the effort, after overhearing the two scheming women. What were Mrs. Cooper and her aunt thinking, planting such a foolish notion in Mr. Tucker's head? Surely he'd repudiate it.

She took a quiet step into the kitchen and waited. Thankfully both of the conspirators' backs were to her, and Mr. Tucker didn't seem to notice her approach. But then he turned his head, met her gaze, and gave a slow wink. Neither of the other women seemed to observe the gesture. Was it possible she'd imagined it?

"Ladies." He leaned forward, assuring that both Aunt Wilma and Mrs. Cooper would keep their attention on him. "While that sounds like a most creative idea, I regret to say I do not have a romance planned for this novel. Not that your niece wouldn't make a perfectly charming heroine, should the need arise."

Irritation rose. She didn't care who saw her now, and she wasn't about to go back to her room. That wink proved it—the rascal was toying with her. A charming heroine, indeed. She didn't believe that for a moment. She clenched her hands and stalked into the room. "Good morning, Auntie. Mrs. Cooper." She nodded at both women and turned her face away from Mr. Tucker.

His voice held a hint of humor. "Miss Roberts. How is your knee faring this morning?"

"Much better, thank you. The swelling is down, and I'm walking with barely a limp." She took a step toward the stove. "The coffee smells delicious."

Jeffery pushed back his chair. "Here, let me get you a cup. It's quite hot from sitting on the stove." He reached for the pot. "I wouldn't want you to burn yourself."

Beth shivered. "No thank you. I changed my mind. I'm going outside." Sudden resentment swelled a knot in her throat. No sense in staying and giving him a chance to call yet more attention to her disfigurement. She needed to gather her composure. Turning, she limped out of the room and down the hall as fast as her knee would allow.

Jeffery stared from Mrs. Roberts to Mrs. Cooper. What had happened? He'd given Beth what he thought was a compliment and offered to pour her a cup of coffee. All the color had drained from her face and then she'd scurried out the door like a woman possessed. "I hope you ladies will excuse me. I think I should check on Miss Roberts. I am afraid she might not be well."

Mrs. Roberts rose with a grunt. "No, Mr. Tucker, you will not. That's my job. I daresay she won't want to see you right now. At least not until she's had a moment." She sent him an unreadable look and plodded out of the room, head wagging.

He turned to Mrs. Cooper, who sat quite still, clutching her teacup. "What did I do to upset her? Mrs. Roberts appears to know, but she did not choose to enlighten me. I fear I am at a loss."

"I have no idea, young man. I certainly did not hear or see anything offensive, but it appears I am not in Miss Roberts's confidence either." She frowned and set her cup on the saucer with a clatter. "Or, it appears, in her aunt's."

Beth stumbled over the threshold leading out the back door, tears blinding her. She hated the weakness and brushed them away, but she couldn't as easily dispel the sorrow that had assaulted her when she'd heard Jeffery's words. He'd seen the scars on her wrist, but she'd never believed he'd call attention to them in such a heartless fashion. She'd even started warming toward him since he'd carried her home, but now all she felt was bruised. All the old taunts from childhood rushed back, sending her emotions reeling.

Had she overreacted by leaving the kitchen so abruptly? They probably wouldn't have noticed if she hadn't stomped from the room. Well, not exactly stomped with this injured knee, but she'd certainly done her best to clomp and would have if it hadn't hurt so much.

Beth headed toward a low-hanging tree in the back of the house, lifting her chin as she trudged across the packed dirt that was edged with a scattering of late-summer flowers. She must not let this bother her so much. Burying herself in her work would help her heal. As soon as possible, she'd purchase another tablet. Aunt Wilma had informed her last night that she'd hunted the brush with no results. The only good thing that had happened that day was being held in Jeffery's arms.

Beth steeled herself against the memory. She'd vowed not to allow another man access to her heart, and she'd keep that promise, no matter how kind he appeared. Jeffery Tucker might be handsome, virile, and charming, but Beth wasn't taking any chances this time around. Men couldn't be trusted. She had been burned by more than fire in the past, and emotional pain could be more devastating than anything the physical world could hand out.

Chapter Eleven

Wilma slipped out the front door as quietly as a woman her size could do. She gave a wry smile. Her husband, George, had treasured her generous figure, saying it provided lots to love and he wouldn't have her any other way. He'd been one of the most kindhearted men she'd ever known, but she would have loved him for that sentiment, if for no other reason. Not everyone understood or appreciated a woman of her stature, but she'd made peace with herself years ago.

There was no sense in hating what she'd not been able to change, and knowing that both George and God loved her without condition gave her a deep-seated peace. She emitted a low chuckle. She'd be happy to shed a few pounds, but somehow it never seemed to happen.

If only Beth could see herself in the same light—loved and accepted by God, exactly the way she was, without the need to prove herself. Her niece had been so damaged as a child she'd lost all self-confidence. Wilma prayed that the peace she had found in the Lord could be transmitted to her girl.

The porch appeared empty, and she glanced down the path. Ah. Beth had rounded the bend and disappeared under the branches of a shade tree. The girl always returned to nature when hurt or angry.

How long had she stood there listening? Could she have heard their silly banter about Mr. Tucker's book? Oh dear. Beth might be miffed at her and Frances for suggesting a romance based on Mr. Tucker's carrying her home. She couldn't imagine what else it might be.

Wilma hurried down the path, thankful the sun wasn't high enough to cast its warmth on her heavy sateen gown. Changing to a lighter frock before afternoon might be wise.

She slowed when she reached the tree and peered under the boughs, wondering what she'd find. Her niece crying or sitting dejectedly on the grass?

Beth whirled as Wilma approached. "Oh. It's you. I thought *he* might have tried to follow me."

Wilma placed her hand over her rapidly beating heart. "My goodness, dear child, there's no need to raise your voice. Whatever is the matter with you? I assumed you were upset with Frances and me, but it appears your ire is directed at Mr. Tucker." She shook her head. Young people these days were so difficult to understand.

Beth dropped her arms next to her sides. "I was at first. I couldn't believe you would conspire with Mrs. Cooper about Mr. Tucker and me having a romance—even if it *was* for his book. I almost went back upstairs but decided not to give in to mortification." She gave a tight smile. "Besides, I wanted a cup of coffee."

Wilma nodded, but her thoughts were still muddled. "Then why did you leave? All Mr. Tucker did was offer to pour you a cup."

"That is *not* all, Auntie. Didn't you hear what he said?"

Wilma scrunched her brows in an effort to remember his exact words. "No. I suppose I must not have, if your reaction is any gauge. Certainly nothing worthy of such irritation."

"Nothing worthy!" Beth gritted the words. "He said, and I quote, 'I wouldn't want you to burn yourself.' It was quite clear what he was referring to."

"I have no idea what you're going on about, dear. I see nothing but consideration for your welfare in that statement."

"I can't believe you didn't see through his comment. But then again, you aren't aware that he saw a scar on my wrist not long ago."

Wilma absently rubbed her cheek. "So you believe he accidentally referred to the scar that he glimpsed?"

"Aunt Wilma! Forgive me, but are you purposely trying to misunderstand? It's quite apparent that Mr. Tucker was not-so-subtly reminding me of my infirmity. He pretends to be one thing on the surface but is quite another beneath his kind facade. Why, look at the book he's writing. He admitted it's about a group of people living in a boardinghouse." She sighed. "I suppose it shouldn't surprise us when he gets overly inquisitive or says something unpleasant."

Wilma grasped Beth's hand. "That's nonsense." She pushed up the heavy sleeve that extended well over the girl's wrist. "Tell me what you see." Her grip tightened as Beth struggled to pull free. "Stop that. You may be a grown woman, but I am still your elder, and I expect you to listen. Now, tell me."

Beth's face paled, and she turned away from the wrist her aunt held up for inspection. "I don't have to look. I've seen it every day for as long as I can remember. It matches the rest of my body."

"But what do you see?"

Beth gave a hard jerk and took a step back. "Why are you doing this?" Her voice was barely audible. "Can't you see how hard this is?"

Wilma wrapped her arms around her niece's shoulders and drew her close. "I'm sorry, dear. I'm not trying to hurt you. I'm trying to help you understand what others see—and don't see—in you."

Beth pulled back. "By reminding me of my shame? How does that help?"

A shock went through Wilma at the confusion and anger brimming in Beth's eyes. "By trying to show you that people see you as a lovely young woman. By showing you that the scars you are so terrified others will see barely exist. Why, they are so pale and faded as to be indiscernible. I'm simply trying to assure you that your personality and inner beauty are what matter most, not the trappings of external beauty."

Beth winced. "I know I'm not beautiful, Aunt Wilma, but it's not kind to remind me in such a straightforward fashion."

Wilma shook her head. "That is not at all what I meant. I can't believe you think of yourself as unattractive."

"How could I not, since apparently my family tossed me away like unwanted rubbish? You say the scars have faded, but I say they have not. They are still as glaring and ugly as ever." Without another word, Beth stalked away, head held high.

Over the next couple of days Beth managed to avoid Mr. Tucker except for mealtimes, when she kept her focus on her plate and left the table as soon as courtesy allowed. She and Aunt Wilma had achieved a tentative peace, and her aunt had been careful not to revisit the subject of her physical appearance. Mrs. Cooper hadn't broached the subject of Mr. Tucker's book, and the atmosphere at the table had been friendly but subdued.

She sank into the comfortable damask-covered divan in the parlor and picked up her book, content in the knowledge that her aunt and Mrs. Cooper were out for a stroll and she had the house to herself. A knock sounded at the front door. Beth started and almost dropped her copy of *Little Women*.

A voice penetrated the peace of the nearly empty house. "I say, is anyone about?" A deep, masculine tone rang across the foyer and into the parlor. "This is a boardinghouse, is it not?"

Beth set her book aside and rose. "Hello. I'll try to help you if I can." She walked across the parlor and stepped into the foyer.

A well-dressed young man sporting a top hat, waistcoat, and a silver-tipped walking stick stood inside the door, a large valise on the floor beside him. His short-cropped black hair barely showed under the hat, and a frown marred his handsome face. "Are you the proprietor? I require a room."

"No, I'm not. Mrs. Jacobs usually takes care of new boarders, but she's out. I believe Mr. Jacobs is here. He's been doing a bit of work on the house lately."

The man stiffened. "Is something wrong with this establishment?"

Beth was barely able to keep from laughing. The man was positively stuffy. "I think he's been scraping some of the wood trim outside getting ready to paint before the weather turns cold. Not all the siding, you understand, only the trim." She stopped herself before she began to babble. "If you'd care to sit in the parlor, I'll see if I can find him."

He scooped up his valise and tucked it under his arm. "That's quite all right. I'll wait here if you don't mind." He appraised her, and a smile warmed his features. "You live here? Do you recommend it?"

"Yes, I do. To both questions." Beth hastened down the hall. The man was unusually handsome but a bit brusque, and his scrutiny had probed more deeply than she liked.

She scurried to the back door. Mr. Jacobs perched near the top rung of a ladder propped against the back of the house. After acquainting him with the prospective lodger, she tiptoed into the parlor, plucked her book off the divan, and slipped upstairs to her room.

Jeffery settled into his place at the supper table and evaluated the stranger—hair slicked into place, smooth-shaven cheeks, and clothes more fitting to a high-society dinner party than an Oregon boardinghouse. Jeffery shouldn't be one to criticize, as he rarely wore informal clothing himself, but the double-breasted topcoat, silk vest, gold pocket watch and fob, pinstriped trousers, and silk top hat were items not often seen at Mrs. Jacobs's boardinghouse. And the gloves the man drew off before taking his seat were quite another affair.

Micah Jacobs waited for the table to quiet, then offered a prayer. When he was finished, he lifted his head and nodded to the gentleman at the far end. "I would like to present Mr. Isaac Lansing, who will be staying with us for a few days."

A chorus of greetings welcomed the man, who merely nodded and reached for the plate of bread close to his water glass. Light chatter flowed from person to person as the meal progressed, but Mr. Lansing seemed unusually quiet, other than an occasional brief reply when addressed. Jeffery narrowed his eyes, unsure what to make of the man. Handsomely dressed and evidently well educated, the man could fit in upper-level society, but his firm mouth and the stern lines of his face didn't exude an air of friendliness.

Mrs. Cooper stabbed a second piece of fried chicken and plopped it onto her plate. "So, Mr. Lansing, what brings you to town?"

"Business, ma'am."

Mrs. Roberts brightened. "What kind of business, if I may ask?"

He gave her a long, steady look. "I am in town dealing with mining concerns. I have little time to socialize, and I don't expect to be here often. I keep to myself and mind my own business, and expect others to do the same."

Frances Cooper scowled and wiped her hands on a napkin. "No need to get uppity, sir. You are more than welcome to keep to yourself, but I assure you, no one was trying to intrude on your affairs."

"I do not care to discuss my private business, but I regret if I have offended you." The man ladled a generous helping of potatoes onto his plate. After taking several bites he turned to Beth with a winning smile. "You are the young lady I met in the parlor earlier today. I didn't get a chance to thank you for helping me. I am charmed to meet you, Miss …?"

"Roberts. Beth Roberts. You are quite welcome, Mr. Lansing. It was no trouble at all."

Jeffery stared at Lansing, not caring one whit for the man's wheedling tone or flirtatious manner. "How long will you be in town, Mr. Lansing? Mr. Jacobs mentioned you would be staying several days. Will you be returning to your home when you leave? I assume from your accent you're from the East."

"You assume correctly, but I haven't decided what I will do yet. Much depends on my business here in Baker City, and if I am able to find a pleasant way to pass the time when not employed." He leaned toward Beth. "Tell me; is there anything of refinement offered in this town? I don't imagine I will be working from dawn until dark every day, and I might enjoy taking in some entertainment. I wonder if you would consider accompanying me some evening."

Mrs. Roberts snorted and dropped her fork on her plate. "I thought you weren't here to socialize and wanted to keep to yourself. My niece has no interest in traipsing around town with a stranger."

He turned cool gray eyes her direction. "I'm sorry. I assume the lady is old enough to speak for herself."

A gasp sounded from Mrs. Cooper, and Katherine Jacobs touched her hand. "Shh, Mama. Let Mrs. Roberts handle this. It's not our concern."

Micah Jacobs shook his head. "It *is* my concern, as it's my table, and Katherine's as well. I am afraid your tone wasn't appreciated, sir."

Mrs. Roberts scooted back her chair and stood. "Thank you, Mr. Jacobs, but Katherine is correct. This is my affair, although I appreciate your kindness." She leveled a hard glare on the stranger. "You are mistaken, sir. Though my niece is able to speak for herself, what she does without a chaperone is most assuredly my business. Beth, have you finished eating?"

Beth's eyes flickered to Mr. Lansing, and Jeffery thought he caught a glint of … what? Surely not apology. "Yes, Aunt Wilma."

"Let us take our leave. I would like to lie down, if you'd be so kind as to accompany me to my room."

The two women walked toward the dining room entrance, and Jeffery worked to choke back his irritation. Had he truly seen regret, or had he misinterpreted her expression? Beth had found reason to race from the room the last time they'd been together, after he'd done nothing more than offer her a cup of coffee, but it seemed her aunt had to practically drag her away from a man who stooped to flirtatious ways and rude treatment.

He pushed back from the table. Beth glanced back, and for a second her gaze met his. His heart jolted as a memory of holding her in his arms surfaced. He shook his head. She wasn't his to hold. It was time he put his mind on his work, where it belonged.

Chapter Twelve

La Grande, Oregon

Isabelle Mason hung the last set of sheets on the line and wiped her damp hands on her apron. "I surely do miss my boy. He's been gone over a week…. No, I guess it's almost a fortnight, come to think of it."

Her old friend and confidante, Karen Luther, wagged her head and tsked. "Seems a shame his boss saw fit to make Steven traipse across the country to look at some dark old mines. Foolish, if you ask me. Why does the bank care what them miners are doing, anyway?" She plucked the empty basket off the ground and headed for Isabelle's cabin, which was situated among the trees.

Isabelle smiled and followed the short figure as she waddled around the corner of the chicken coop. "It's not clear across the country, Karen. Baker City is in Oregon, after all."

Karen pushed open the door with her foot and dropped the basket on the floor near the kitchen stove. "There's plenty of banks in La Grande. Why'd they decide to send him out of town?"

Isabelle waved to the table. "Have a seat. The water is hot. Don't know about you, but I've been on my feet too long today, and they ache. Arms, too."

Karen gripped Isabelle's upper arms and propelled her to a chair. "No, ma'am, you aren't waiting on me. I might not be much account, but I'm stronger than an ox and smarter, too." She grinned and reached for two mugs placed on a rough-hewn sideboard. "You done more than your share of work, and I don't aim to let you do more." She placed the mugs on the table and poured the fragrant tea out of the pot. "Where's your neighbor? I thought she was supposed to be helping while Steven is gone."

Isabelle lifted the mug to her mouth and relished the delicate scent of mint. The mountain snow runoff kept parts of the valley green. Dense plant life grew well into the late summer months, and she'd dried and put away a stock of herbs and plants for wintertime use. "Ina had to help her sick daughter. I've been getting along fine though. No need to worry."

Karen slipped into the chair across from her. "I do worry. You didn't bounce back this summer after being sick most of last winter. I don't think Steven shoulda left you alone all this time. The boy ought to hightail it on home. You want I should send him a telegram and let him know you're hurting?"

"No." The word came out sharper than she'd planned. "I'm fine. Tired, that's all, but Ina will be back tomorrow, and I'll rest. I promise. I can't call Steven home. He'd lose his job, and we need it." She winced, hating to have anyone, even her closest friend, know their circumstances. "I didn't answer your question about the bank sending him to Baker City." Hitching her chair closer, she placed her forearms on the table. "A couple of mines want to borrow money. The banks are getting skittish about loaning big amounts without making sure the mine is run proper."

"Guess that makes sense. They loan money out, then someone blows the place up ... it wouldn't be too good." Karen slapped her hand over her mouth. "That didn't come out right. Didn't mean anything bad by it, and I'm plumb sorry for talking foolish. Not like your boy will be in any danger looking at those mines. I'm right sure he won't."

A shiver ran over Isabelle's skin, raising bumps the entire length of her arms. Dear Lord, nothing better happen to her boy. She couldn't abide it. Losing one child was more than any mother should bear.

White pages shimmered at Beth as she smoothed the paper of her new sketch pad under her fingers. So much lost. She'd gone to the place on the trail and hunted through the bushes for over an hour to no avail. Either a person or an animal had found her treasure. No doubt she'd never see it again.

There was no use pining for what couldn't be. She'd duplicated the illustration for the magazine, along with the rough sketches for future ideas. Sending the first drawing off in the mail a couple of weeks ago had given her an immense sense of satisfaction, but that had quickly been overshadowed by the frustration she felt over the loss of her tablet.

Peace warred with grief when she remembered the picture she'd sketched while working on the hill. She didn't want that memory of the little girl lying by the fire staring her in the face each time she opened her pad, but neither did she care to lose the elusive fragment from her past.

What to do now? Ever since losing her tablet, her creativity had stalled. Or did it go deeper than that? She placed her pencil on the pad and stepped over to the window, pushing aside the gauzy drape.

Mandy Galloway sat in a swing suspended from the limb of a giant maple, one hand clutching the rope, and the other arm wrapped around the rope while holding her doll to her chest.

Beth smiled as sweet memories of her childhood sprang to life. Not all had been ugly or painful. Aunt Wilma had done her best to provide love and a sense of security those months after Beth arrived. She only had dim memories of Uncle George, who'd died a couple of years later, but they were filled with warmth.

No, it wasn't the past or the loss of her sketchbook that kept her frozen, but the questions she'd faced since the conversation with her aunt. She'd often thought she wanted a career more than anything in life—that marriage and children weren't important. Now she wondered if she'd lied to herself to avoid the pain of facing a future without either.

Her aunt thought her foolish for believing no man would want her, but Beth knew better. Too much of her childhood she'd been exposed to ridicule—and not only because of her scars. Other girls at the finishing school tittered behind her back, giggling over her past, thinking she couldn't hear or not caring that she did. She'd spent so much of her life afraid of girls her own age—their beauty, self-confidence, and often, their snobbery—that she'd had no idea how to fit in.

Now her own aunt reinforced her lack of belief in Beth's talents as an artist. Aunt Wilma thought it nothing more than a hobby, and one she should abandon for the sake of a family. Beth let the window curtain drop. Family *was* important, but if she ever married and had a child, what if she ended up abandoning that child, like her mother had? To be fair, her mother could have died, and perhaps her father couldn't keep her. Or there might have been a long line of babies, and by the time she'd come along, their money had run out. But even so, why leave her alone on the Oregon Trail? Her hands shook, and she gripped them together, willing them to stop, hating the flashing images.

Enough. She sat in her chair, clutching her pencil. Her publisher counted on her to get these sketches done in a reasonable time. Leaning over the paper she allowed the pencil to move with broad strokes, letting her mind go and not trying to decipher what the result might be.

An oval formed on the page, taking the shape of a strong jaw and broad forehead. She sketched lips, tipped in a smile, and hair falling forward a bit. She dropped her pencil and drew back. *Jeffery Tucker. Why …?*

His was the last face she'd expected to see and certainly not one she thought about enough to have memorized its features. On the other hand, his face had been alluringly close when he'd carried her up the path. She'd been tempted to touch his cheek with her fingertips, but she'd not allowed them to stray from her side. The man didn't belong in her thoughts.

Beth ripped the page from the tablet and held it in both hands, prepared to rend it in two.

She looked at it one last time and paused. What had she drawn in those eyes? They weren't blank or flat, but deep, penetrating, quizzical.

Seeking. Always seeking. If only he'd stop digging and leave her alone. She set the page back on the desk, then flipped open the pad and tucked it inside. It was a waste of good paper to destroy it when she might reuse the other side. Yes. That's what she'd do. And never, ever look at it again.

Jeffery flipped through the pages of the tablet he'd found, admiration stirring as he gazed at first one image of Western life, then another. He allowed the pages to fall open, and his hand rested on the desktop beside it. The pain and terror on the child's face pulsated in the room. He could almost smell the dust from the wheels of a wagon disappearing in the distance. What had happened to the little girl who lay huddled on the ground by the smoldering fire?

Who had drawn these lifelike illustrations? The artist's name didn't appear anyplace in the sketch pad, and only two pictures had any kind of designation—the initials E.C., nothing else. Wouldn't the artist want credit for work of such quality? He scratched his chin and frowned, trying to remember why the initials felt familiar.

And why would the person who owned it have dropped it in the brush? It appeared as though an animal had dragged it from another location, but thankfully it hadn't sustained any damage inside. Whoever lost this must surely be grieving.

He'd almost memorized the drawings since finding the tablet, but he shouldn't hold on to it any longer. Placing an ad for the tablet might alert the owner of his find, but he'd insist they describe some of the contents, for fear a disreputable person intent on getting something for nothing would try to claim it. Indeed, that would certainly be the best plan.

He shut the book and smoothed the damaged cover, then tucked it into a drawer of the desk. No sense in taking chances with something so valuable. Having been raised in the East, he knew quality art when he saw it, and this artist was exceptional.

Chapter Thirteen

Beth slipped out the front door clutching the letter from her publisher. She'd finally made progress after staring at her blank notepad the past couple of days. Ideas had trickled into her mind and gradually come to life on the page. But she'd not expected to hear from the magazine so soon—it didn't seem possible they'd had time to receive her first submission and reply. All she could do was pray they liked what she'd sent.

After Aunt Wilma's less-than-supportive comments about her work, Beth didn't care to chance the older woman walking into her room as she read her letter, so she headed for a grassy nook she'd found in a field not far from the edge of the Powder River. The air had a bit of a nip now that they were at the end of the second week of September. She glanced at the blue sky, thankful no clouds marred the fine fall day. It wouldn't be long until snow blanketed the ground and made this type of outing impossible.

She settled on a large stone close to the river and slipped her finger under the flap of the heavy, cream-colored envelope. Curiosity tugged. A single sheet slid out, and she unfolded it, taking in the contents in a matter of seconds. What an odd request for an illustration. She gave a quick shake of her head. But it wasn't hers to question what the editor wanted. At least she had time to change direction and get it sent in before the deadline.

She stared across the river and through the widely scattered trees to the buildings in the distance. Baker City was certainly an attractive town, situated as it was between two sets of mountain ranges. It might make a good study for this newest request. She smiled and smoothed the letter in her lap. Her fingers were itching to sketch.

Beth stuffed the paper into the envelope and jumped to her feet, eager to get to her room and her tablet. She took several long strides, then halted. Aunt Wilma had asked her to stop at the mercantile and pick up a copy of the *Bedrock Democrat*. It rarely held anything of interest to Beth, but her aunt liked to keep abreast of current events. The paper mostly carried local news but occasionally had articles about happenings farther away, giving a sense of connection to the outside world.

A scant half hour later, Beth sat on the parlor sofa and opened the paper, happy she'd have time alone before Aunt Wilma made her appearance. According to Katherine, her aunt and Mrs. Cooper were both enjoying a nap after their afternoon walk.

"Hello, Miss Roberts." A man's monotone voice disrupted the peace. Isaac Lansing stood in the doorway.

Beth lifted her head, annoyed at the intrusion. Of course, the parlor was a gathering place for anyone living here, but she didn't care to share it with Mr. Lansing at the moment. She'd barely had time to scan the articles. She had managed to avoid the man since he'd arrived, other than meals, when Aunt Wilma made certain he left her alone. Annoying and pompous only began to describe Isaac Lansing.

"Good day." She rustled the paper. Maybe he'd take the hint and find someone else to bother.

"A quaint paper. I've found very little of interest in it since I arrived." He plucked his watch from his pocket, glanced at its face, then put it away. "I'm happy to find you here. It seems I have an hour or two to spare."

Beth folded the paper and laid it on her lap, scrambling to think of a suitable subject to which she could turn the conversation. "How much longer will you be with us?" She tried to muster a pleasant expression. "I would imagine your business is about concluded by now."

He perched on the edge of a nearby chair and planted his hands on his knees. "Getting closer, but I'm not in a hurry to leave. I still haven't had the pleasure of your company." He leaned forward and, in a conspiratorial whisper, said, "What do you say you step out with me and get a bite of supper? I've found a couple of restaurants that serve a respectable meal." He gave her what might pass to some observers as a charming smile.

Beth winced. Only minutes ago she'd been thankful Aunt Wilma was taking a nap. Now she'd give anything if the dear woman would appear. "That's very kind of you, but Mrs. Jacobs goes to a lot of trouble to fix our meals. I wouldn't care to be rude."

He waved a hand. "She won't care. It's that much less food she'll have to supply, and I'm sure she's not averse to saving money on her food stuffs. Besides, as I've pointed out before, you're a grown woman and don't need to cater to everyone else." He stood and held out his hand. "Your name fits you, Beth. I hope you don't mind my calling you that? Let's depart before anyone intrudes."

Jeffery hesitated on the threshold of the parlor. Should he walk away? It appeared Miss Roberts and Mr. Lansing were agreeing upon some kind of tryst. Or, at least, the pompous gentleman standing in front of the young lady had certainly suggested something of the sort, and he hadn't heard her decline. It seemed she had given him permission to use her Christian name, since she hadn't corrected the man. That settled it; he had no desire to stay and listen. He swiveled and took a step.

"Jeffery?" Beth's sweet voice rang out and brought him to an abrupt halt. "I'm sorry, I didn't see you enter. You are right on time for our walk." She rose and tucked a newspaper under her arm. "I have a previous engagement, *Mr.* Lansing. But to answer your question, the name I prefer to be addressed by is Miss Roberts. Good day." She swept from the room, leaving Mr. Lansing staring after her in disbelief.

Jeffery came out of his stupor and took two long strides, catching up with her. "I am so sorry I'm late, my dear." He extended his arm. "May I?"

Beth's lips parted, and she blinked.

Jeffery turned his head and gave a slow wink only she could see.

She slipped her hand through his and held her head high, giving him an engaging smile as he opened the front door.

Jeffery glanced back and bit the inside of his cheek to prevent a grin from appearing. Isaac Lansing stood in the middle of the parlor staring after them, his mouth agape. He couldn't be more thankful—as well as more than a bit chagrinned—that he'd misread Beth's attitude toward Lansing.

Jeffery pressed Beth's hand against his side a little tighter as they walked down the front steps to the path below. "I didn't realize we'd planned a walk, Miss Roberts, but I'm more than happy to accompany you."

They strolled half a dozen steps from the porch. A scraping noise sounded above them, and Jeffery peered up at the roof. "Hello, Mr. Jacobs. You're getting the final coat of paint on the trim, I see."

Micah Jacobs balanced on the steep roof, a bucket of green paint propped against a block of wood nailed to the shingles, a brush in his hand. "Yes. It's a good thing the warm weather has hung on so long." His voice echoed and bounced. "It's rather precarious up here, but two more dormer windows, and I'm finished."

Beth shaded her eyes and looked up. "It's a lovely color. I'm guessing Katherine is pleased."

"Not as pleased as I will be to get back to my work at the livery." He dipped his brush into the paint. "I'd best get this painting done." He waved a green-stained hand.

Beth walked farther down the trail, barely out of earshot of the house, and murmured, "I am so sorry. It was truly despicable of me to use you in that fashion. I do hope you'll forgive me, Mr. Tucker, and accept my deepest thanks for rescuing me from an uncomfortable situation. I'm in your debt."

This time he allowed a grin to spill out. "There's nothing to forgive. I was more than happy to step in and whisk you away from that annoying gentleman. As for being in my debt ..."

"Yes?" Her brows arched, and a tiny smile appeared.

"You called me Jeffery in front of Mr. Lansing, so it might be difficult to go back to Mr. Tucker. Is it so abhorrent to address me by my Christian name?"

The smile faded, and she withdrew her hand from his elbow. "No, it is not abhorrent at all."

He folded his arms. "But?"

She drew in a deep breath and blew it out with a loud sigh. "My, you are inquisitive, aren't you, Mr. Tucker?"

Jeffery wanted to chuckle at her comical expression, but he schooled his features into neutral lines. "Jeff-er-y. It's not terribly hard to pronounce." Gaining this young woman's trust and friendship might be harder than he'd expected. He flashed a careful smile. "And is being inquisitive a bad thing?"

"You rescued me from a rather thorny circumstance, so I don't want to offend your sensibilities, but, well ..." She withdrew the folded newspaper from under her arm and tapped it against the palm of her hand. "Sometimes you do ask a mite too many questions for my peace of mind."

He quirked a brow, intrigued by her phrasing. So he'd disturbed her peace of mind, had he? Something to think about when he had more leisure. Probably not the best idea to pursue the subject now, if her frown were any indication of her feelings. "I apologize if I have caused you distress. I'll do my best not to plague you with an overabundance of questions from this time forward. But ..."

Now it was her turn to smile. "Yes, Mr. Tucker?"

"Yes, Jeffery. Yes, Jeffery." He waved his hand in a circle. "There, now you try."

She rolled her eyes but didn't reply.

He grinned. "You are aware I am a writer, and as such, we see questions and possibilities in almost everything we come in contact with. Not to mention, my background in the news industry causes me to look for a story in everything around me. It is difficult *not* to ask questions, if you see what I mean. Besides, I admit to a decided interest in getting to know you, and I can think of no better way to accomplish that than asking questions. But we have strayed from the issue at hand."

A light laugh escaped her mouth. "I'm afraid we have gone down another rabbit trail, Mr. Tucker, so you will need to remind me."

He tipped his head at a slight angle.

Rosy color tinted her cheeks. "Ah, yes. The matter of the names." She arched her brows and her eyes twinkled. "How clumsy of me to forget. All right. After all we've gone through these past minutes, it does seem we're co-conspirators of a sort."

"Wonderful." A deep pleasure warmed Jeffery's heart. He wasn't sure why he worked so hard to gain this woman's trust. Maybe because the task had been such a challenge. Whatever the case, it felt right now that it was settled. He extended his arm once more. "Would you care to take that walk you promised me earlier?"

A mischievous sparkle lit her eyes, and she opened her mouth to speak, then slowly closed it, giving a small shake of her head.

"What's wrong? Have I done something?"

"Mr. Lansing is coming. I suppose we should have continued our walk and not lingered so close to the house."

Jeffery turned. Isaac Lansing stood at the top of the stairs and glanced around, then lifted his hand and waved. The man was fully decked out in a suit of clothing that appeared to have come straight from one of the East Coast's finest tailors. Jeffery groaned. "Do we have to wait?"

Lansing's feet hit the walkway, and he started toward them. Good manners forbade running away at this point, although Jeffery was sorely tempted.

A shout split the air. Micah Jacobs stood on the roof, holding the paint can and waving his other arm to keep his balance on the steep pitch. He landed on his backside and dug in his boot heels to stop from sliding. He came to a halt feet from the edge of the roof, but the can of paint catapulted from his grip. It bounced once on the eave of the house and flipped into the air, curving in a wide arc. As though frozen in time, the can hung suspended for a moment, then spun in a circle and landed upside down, directly on Isaac Lansing's hat.

Beth stared at the comical sight and stifled a giggle. It was quickly apparent Mr. Lansing had suffered no damage, other than to his clothing and pride. The paint can rested upside down, leaving only the hat brim in evidence. Rivers of green ran over the brim and cascaded onto the man's nose—and every other spot that protruded to any degree. In fact, the bright color ran over his shoulders and dripped onto his shoes.

Micah scrambled for the ladder leaning against the side of the house, and Jeffery darted over to hold it as he clambered down. "You all right, Mr. Lansing?" Micah's words reached the man before he did.

Lansing stood and simply blinked.

Beth's body shook as she worked to keep her mirth at bay. If it had been anyone else at all but stuffy, pompous Isaac Lansing …

well, she couldn't help it. The man had been a thorn in her side, and she found this deliciously funny.

Micah took a kerchief from his pocket and handed it to the man, then carefully removed the can from his hat, and then the hat from his head. Dribbles of paint continued to fall from his hair, and a large green drop landed on Lansing's chin. Micah turned his head but not before Beth detected laughter dancing in his eyes.

Beth could stand it no longer. Even though she clapped her hand over her mouth, her giggle managed to break free.

Jeffery swung around and shot her a startled look.

Beth lifted the newspaper to cover her face. "I'm sorry. But it's just …" She giggled again. "Too funny."

Micah and Jeffery stared at her, then back at Isaac Lansing, whose frantic mopping with the once-clean kerchief had done wonders in turning his entire face green but little to correct the mess. All of a sudden Micah erupted in loud guffaws, his shouts of laughter ringing across the clearing.

The front door banged open, and steps thudded down the stairs. Beth looked up through the tears blurring her vision. Katherine, followed by Aunt Wilma and Mrs. Cooper, came to a stop with comical expressions of disbelief. Aunt Wilma was the first to break out of her trance. She plucked a damp cloth from Katherine's hands and trooped over to the sputtering Lansing. "Hold still. You're making things worse. Let me help get that cleaned off."

He jumped back and waved her away. "Don't touch me, any of you." He swung toward Micah and glared with as much ferocity as a green man could attain. "You did that on purpose." Then he pointed at Jeffery and Beth. "While you watched and did nothing to stop it." He shook his fist at Micah. "I'll be moving out as soon as I wash, change, and gather my things, but don't think I'll be paying for the past week. This suit cost more than two weeks' lodging at this miserable edifice."

Micah stiffened, and his face sobered. "It was an accident, and I apologize for laughing. I assumed once you got over the shock you might see the humor, but I see we've offended you. Let me help you around to the watering trough, where you can clean up."

Lansing jerked his arm away. "I don't need any help." He stalked off, paint staining the grass with every step.

Katherine touched her husband's arm. "What happened, dear? How in the world did Mr. Lansing get covered in the house paint?"

Mrs. Cooper and Aunt Wilma stood with mouths agape as Micah shared the events that led up to the accident. Aunt Wilma's lips twitched. "Can't say I'm sorry to see him go." The humor faded from her face. "But I hope he won't cause you folks trouble. He was a pompous individual while living here, but no telling what he'll be now."

Chapter Fourteen

Beth stared after the paint-bedecked man as he traipsed around the corner of the house toward the watering trough, her aunt's words ringing in her ears. "I shouldn't have laughed. I know what it's like to be laughed at by others. It's painful and ... unforgivable."

Jeffery crossed his arms over his chest. "Rubbish. I agree it might be painful if the man were injured *or* if Mr. Jacobs tossed the can off the roof on purpose. On the contrary, nothing was hurt but the man's pride—and his clothing, of course. It's a shame it happened, but it was an accident. Mr. Jacobs *did* sincerely express his regret, and Lansing tossed the apology off like a bucket of slop."

Micah rubbed his hands on the rag Katherine offered. "And if his duds cost more than a week's room and board, we'll stand the extra. I should have been more careful and not allowed that to happen. I'm to blame if anyone is, not you, Miss Roberts." He shot Katherine an entreating look.

She placed an arm around Beth and squeezed. "That's right. I'm sorry Mr. Lansing's clothing was ruined, but he might have adopted a better attitude and accepted Micah's apology." A slight smirk revealed itself. "Besides, it *was* funny. If he'd been on the other side of things instead of under that paint can, he'd have felt the same way."

Aunt Wilma placed her hands on her hips and surveyed the edge of the roof. "Well, whatever happens, you've got a mighty pretty splash of color on your shingles and another on the eaves, Mr. Jacobs." She grinned and waved a hand. "And I imagine it's going to stay there as I can't see you scrubbing it off anytime soon."

Katherine shuddered. "I certainly hope not. The dormer trim looks finished. I trust you don't plan on going up there again, Micah. It's too dangerous." She beckoned toward the house. "We'd best get inside and see if we can calm Mr. Lansing down before he leaves—if he decides that's truly what he wants to do."

Mrs. Cooper followed close on their heels, muttering something about wanting to help.

Beth looked at her aunt. "Do you think we should go in too?"

"Probably not, dear. At least, not until Katherine and Mr. Jacobs have a chance to talk some sense into that man. If that's possible, which I doubt." She grimaced. "He's rather odious, and I hope he does move, although I meant it when I said he might cause trouble for the Jacobses. Do you know what he was after when he came outside, and why he halted under the roof?" She peered from Jeffery to Beth.

Jeffery stepped forward. "I believe he was annoyed with me, Mrs. Roberts, and may have followed me outside."

Surprise left Beth floundering for a moment, then she caught her breath. "That's very kind of you, Jeffery, but he was angry with me." She addressed her aunt. "He's been looking for an opportunity to catch me alone—he said as much when he found me in the parlor. He seemed to think I'd be delighted to accompany him to town, regardless of what you might think, and, well ..." She shot Jeffery a thankful look. "Mr. Tucker—Jeffery—was kind enough to rescue me. In fact, I rather put him in a position—"

Jeffery held up his hand. "Enough of taking responsibility, Beth. You did nothing wrong. To be quite forthright, the man is a cad."

Aunt Wilma's mouth tightened. "I see. I'd say you did yourself *and* my niece proud, Mr. Tucker. Thank you. We are in your debt." She turned to Beth and her face relaxed into a soft smile. "Aren't we, dear?"

Beth hesitated, not entirely sure what her aunt might mean, but she decided to take the declaration at face value. "Yes." She touched Jeffery's sleeve. "Would you be terribly upset if we didn't take a walk? I think I'd like to go to my room for a bit, if that's acceptable?"

Jeffery bowed. "A trifle disappointed, but not annoyed. Another time, if you'd be so kind?"

"Certainly." Beth held her hand out to her aunt and drew her forward. "Come along. You can walk me to my room in case Mr. Lansing is still about." She tossed a smile at Jeffery. "Thank you again for being such a kind champion today."

She moved up the path and around to the back door, in the event Mr. Lansing might choose that minute to depart the front.

Aunt Wilma leaned closer and hissed in her ear. "What in the world are you thinking, girl? Jeffery Tucker is as fine a man as they come, and it's obvious he's interested in you and desires your companionship. I can't believe you dismissed his offer of a walk in such an out-of-hand manner. He'll think you don't care for him or his company."

Beth drew to a halt and stared at her aunt. "And I can't imagine where you'd get the notion he's interested. He was simply being polite. I allowed Mr. Lansing to believe Jeffery and I had a prior commitment so he wouldn't continue to plague me with his attentions."

"Humph. If you think that, you aren't as bright as I believe you to be—or you're choosing to shut your eyes to the facts. Either way, dear girl, you need to wake up."

Beth clamped her lips shut, unwilling to argue. She loved her aunt dearly, but sometimes her persistent attitude in voicing opinions could get a bit exasperating.

They walked to her room without speaking. Beth gave her aunt a quick hug. "Thank you. I'm going to sit and read. I think I've had quite enough excitement for one day."

"I suppose if I can't convince you otherwise, I shall do the same. This day has been rather trying." Aunt Wilma strolled down the hall to her room.

Beth shut the door and leaned against it, remembering Jeffery's disappointment when she'd dismissed his suggestion of a walk. Had she been unkind? Or missed an opportunity that her aunt recognized and she didn't? That was foolish. Jeffery was simply being considerate after the unpleasant time with Mr. Lansing. She'd never seen any real evidence that Jeffery was interested in her as a woman—maybe as a subject for his book, but not personally. Besides, after Brent had disappeared, she didn't care to trust a man quite so easily again.

She settled into her chair and spread the paper on her lap. Flipping to where she'd left off in the ad section, she absorbed the colorfully worded missives that lured patrons into various businesses to sample their wares. Not that she needed many of the frivolous items, but it was fun to look. Maybe she should take a couple of hours and browse the shops. A new hat or shoes might be in order.

She ran her finger down the column and started to turn the page when a notice arrested her attention. Leaning forward, she read it again. Someone had found a tablet.

Chapter Fifteen

Wilma glanced up from the paper she was reading in the parlor. She'd tucked herself into a corner hoping no one would bother her. Was someone tiptoeing toward the front door? Wilma craned her neck forward, making sure not to rustle her newspaper.

Beth was dressed in one of her best gowns, a matching hat crowned with an ostrich feather, and a pair of white gloves. Strange, Beth rarely dressed in such fine attire even for church. Wilma opened her mouth to call out to the girl but snapped it shut. Why was her niece acting in such a mysterious manner?

The only thing out of place was her hair, which was pinned at the side of her head with curls cascading down her back. Beth should have fastened it at the nape of her neck or piled it high, not let it hang loose like some schoolgirl. Wilma shook her head. Those scars again. The one on Beth's neck was barely visible anymore, but she'd never convinced her of that.

Wilma waited for close to an hour, and when Beth didn't return, she could stand it no longer. Time to get to the bottom of this nonsense. If the girl were shopping, she would have invited her, or at least not been secretive—or so well dressed. That good-for-nothing

Brent Wentworth must have come to town, and Beth had an assignation with the scoundrel.

Fear drove her to hasten her own toilette. She paid scant attention to her hair or clothing but grabbed her parasol on the chance it might rain—or to use as a prod to the man's backside, if the need arose.

Had they planned this since that mysterious letter had arrived that Beth had been hiding? Had her darling girl deceived her all this time? She prayed it wasn't so.

Jeffery sat at a table in the café and drummed his fingers against the table. The person coming to claim the tablet was late. He'd gotten a reply to his ad via the mail two days ago identifying the tablet, and the owner requested they meet at this restaurant. Strange the letter wasn't signed, just initialed E.R. Why all the secrecy? He'd assumed the individual would be proud of his work and not ashamed to sign his name.

Three different parties had since entered and scanned the room. He'd been certain each had been coming to see him, but then each had spotted his party and joined another table. Jeffery pulled out his watch one last time. If the owner of the tablet didn't appear in the next ten minutes, he'd head home. This was a foolish waste of time. He'd even sat close to this window as requested.

The letter didn't give any clue of what the owner would wear or how to spot him when he arrived. It was all too mysterious in his way of thinking. He picked up the letter and studied it one more time, making sure he was frequenting the proper restaurant.

A trim figure in a dark blue gown, wearing gloves and holding a folded newspaper, stepped into view and swept her glance around the room, coming to rest on him. Beth Roberts's rosy cheeks paled. Her hand went to her throat, and she appeared frozen on the spot. Jeffery couldn't imagine why seeing him there should cause such obvious distress. He set the letter facedown on top of the tablet and stood. If the gentleman who owned the tablet didn't plan to make an appearance, he might as well offer a chair to Beth. He stepped forward and inclined his head toward the table. "Would you care to join me?"

Beth wanted to dash from the room. She'd requested this restaurant since, to her knowledge, no one at the boardinghouse frequented it. Why Jeffery should be here she couldn't imagine, but it appeared there was no avoiding him. She hesitated a moment, surveying the other patrons, but no one appeared to be waiting for her. And Jeffery was sitting at the table near the window she'd requested. Oh dear. Maybe the person who'd run the ad had given up and left when he couldn't secure the table. She moved forward and stopped beside the chair he held. "Thank you. Were you waiting for someone? I don't want to intrude."

"Not at all. It appears the gentleman isn't going to keep our appointment, and I'd much prefer to spend the time with you, regardless." Jeffery seated her, then settled into the chair across from her and smiled. "What brings you to town? Shopping with your aunt?" He peered toward the entrance. "Will she be joining you?"

Beth's heart jumped to her throat. He'd been expecting someone, and the table he'd chosen was situated under the window. It couldn't be. "No. I came alone."

"You don't appear well," he said swiftly. "Should I call someone?"

Her gaze rested on the corner of a tablet partially covered by a sheet of paper. "I'm fine." She reached out and almost touched it, then drew her hand away. "What do you have there?"

Jeffery shrugged and placed his hand on the letter, moving it aside. "Something I found, but it appears the owner doesn't care to claim it. It must not be too important."

"Of course it is!" Beth's words were sharper than she'd planned.

Jeffery's brows rose.

"I'm sorry. Maybe I *should* go home."

Jeffery placed his hand on the tablet and started to rise. "I'll walk you. Or better yet, I'll hire a buggy."

"No. Please don't."

He sank down, keeping his eyes steadily on her. "What's wrong, Beth? Tell me, please."

She sagged back in her chair, her mouth dry. "It's mine."

"I beg your pardon?" He leaned forward.

She forced the words out, stronger this time. "The tablet is mine." She motioned toward it. "I answered your advertisement." Holding up the paper she'd been clutching, she added, "I even brought along a copy. You have been waiting for *me*."

Chapter Sixteen

All Jeffery could do was stare. Beth knew about his post in the newspaper and that he had the tablet. He tried to gather his thoughts. "I may have misunderstood. I assumed I was waiting for a gentleman. You say it's yours?"

She gave a short nod. "Yes."

He fingered the pages. "But your initials aren't E.C., as shown on the drawings. For that matter, the person who sent the response signed their letter E.R."

"Elizabeth Roberts." She touched the necklace at her throat.

"And the initials on the drawing? Are you claiming the pad for someone? A friend perhaps?" A recollection niggled, and he worked to unearth the nugget he knew must be buried. A memory crystallized. "Corwin. The check you dropped was made out to someone named Corwin. That wouldn't by chance …?"

Her lips tightened, and she nodded. "Yes."

"So you're picking it up for her? E. Corwin?"

"Yes. No." Beth looked at the tablet again, then gripped her hands together on top of the table. "I think I'd better explain."

"That would be most appreciated. I confess you have me a bit confused."

"*I* am Elizabeth Corwin." Beth didn't miss the flicker of disbelief that crossed his face. "Actually, that's my pen name. You understand that, being an author. When I started submitting my illustrations, I decided not to use my real name …" She hesitated a moment, then plunged on. "For personal reasons."

"I see." He flipped open the sketch pad to the first page, then turned another, and another. "So all of these are your work?"

"Yes." Beth couldn't believe her good fortune in recovering her precious tablet, nor could she dismiss her unease at disclosing her private dealings. What would Jeffery think? He hadn't said anything about her work, but it was apparent he'd reviewed her sketches.

"How many have you sold?" He lifted his hand before she could answer. "I apologize—that is none of my business, and you are certainly under no obligation to reply. I *will* tell you that these …"—he tapped his finger against the tablet—"are quite good. Extraordinary, in fact."

A brief exhilaration swam through her, then she stiffened. "Are you saying that to be polite?"

"Not at all. I don't give compliments that aren't deserved. At least not to this extent." He lifted the pad and peered at a drawing, then set the tablet down and closed it. "You're quite talented. Why, if I may be so bold to ask, do you hide that fact?"

How to answer without lying or saying too much? Beth worried the dilemma around for a moment. Jeffery had been nothing but kind. She couldn't repay him with a half-truth, but she didn't know or trust him well enough to open her heart. "I hope you won't be angry with me, but it's not something I care to discuss. At least not at the present."

"I completely understand." He beckoned to the waiter. "It's not the most private setting. Let's order coffee, or tea if you prefer, and a bite to eat, then we can leave and find someplace where you can explain to your heart's content."

Beth struggled to maintain her composure. He'd misunderstood.

"There you are, Miss Roberts." The tap-tap of a walking stick accompanied a male voice close to Beth's right. Isaac Lansing stopped next to the table. "I'd like to speak with you, if you please."

Jeffery started to rise, and Lansing held up his hand. "Please. I'd like a moment with Miss Roberts. We're in a public place, and I mean no harm."

After what had happened to the man, Beth didn't see how she could deny his request. She'd felt horrid for laughing at his misadventure and hadn't been able to adequately apologize. Possibly he'd had a change of heart about his own behavior since the unfortunate incident. "Certainly, Mr. Lansing." She turned to Jeffery. "I'll only be a moment. Do you mind?"

Jeffery eyed Isaac Lansing. "As long as you keep in mind, Lansing, that Miss Roberts is a lady and treat her as such."

Beth smiled her appreciation and took a step away from the table. "How may I help you?"

Without warning the man's genial countenance changed, and his voice became a harsh whisper. "You played me for a fool, flirting with me, then laughing when that clumsy man dumped the paint can on my head." He grasped Beth's wrist. "No woman can do that to me and get away with it."

Wilma walked as fast as her legs would allow, wishing the boardinghouse weren't situated on the edge of town. What if she was too late, and the rascal convinced Beth to run away with him? Surely he wouldn't be so bold, and she couldn't imagine her niece leaving without her belongings or saying good-bye. She placed her hand over her pounding heart and gasped for breath. *Please, God, keep her safe from that unscrupulous man.*

Wilma peered in the window of each establishment she passed. Where could that niece of hers have gone? She paused in front of the Arlington Hotel and shuddered. Surely not. Beth had better sense than to go near a man's room. Or, at least, she prayed she did. She glanced in the front door, hesitated, then stepped inside, peering around the expansive lobby. A double doorway off to the right stood open. Voices and the clinking of plates and silverware drifted out. Of course. She relaxed a little. This would be a likely place for a rendezvous.

Wilma marched into the room, pausing just long enough to sweep the room with her eyes. Satisfaction filled her. Beth stood beside a table, and a neatly dressed man stood close beside her, gripping her arm. Was the beast even now trying to drag her into his lair? He certainly wore the same type of clothing Wentworth had sported. Beth pulled back, and a soft cry left her lips.

Wilma's heart leaped into her throat as the man moved closer. Her darling girl was trying to get away. Wilma charged across the intervening yards. Out of the corner of her eye she saw another man jump up from a table. Had the rascal brought along riffraff in hopes of dragging Beth off, should she not go willingly?

A cry of rage broke from Wilma's lips, and she lifted her parasol, bringing the thick ivory handle down on the man's head. He released his grip on Beth's wrist and started to turn. Someone who was not Brent Wentworth looked at her briefly before he fell to the floor in a heap. Wilma panted, her parasol raised and ready to strike again.

Beth sprang forward and grabbed the weapon, removing it from Wilma's hand. "Auntie, I'm all right. But did you need to strike Mr. Lansing quite so hard?"

Beth stared at the man slumped on the floor, then lifted unbelieving eyes to her aunt. Jeffery stood beside the older woman and carefully lowered her shaking body into a chair. He appeared in no hurry to assist the fallen Mr. Lansing. Had she heard Jeffery whisper something in her aunt's ear that sounded suspiciously like, "Good job, ma'am"?

Of all the strange things that could be added to an already-distressful day. Beth shook her head in disbelief. Every head in the busy room had swiveled their way. Voices buzzed, and Beth wanted to sink through the floor. What could her aunt have been thinking? Mr. Lansing had been rude and inappropriate, but had he really deserved such an attack?

Lansing slowly sat up.

Jeffery bent over him and said in a low voice, "Get out of here before I call the sheriff."

Beth knelt beside her aunt and stroked her hand. Why hadn't she spoken? Beth wrapped her arm around the older woman's shoulders. It was so unlike Aunt Wilma to say nothing and allow someone else to take charge. Was she having heart palpitations after her hasty action?

Lansing floundered to his knees, rubbing a spot on his head. He glared at Jeffery, then rested a baleful expression on Aunt Wilma. "Before *you* call the sheriff? Ha. That's what I plan to do as soon as my head stops spinning." He pointed a shaking finger at the seated woman. "She attempted to kill me. I'll have her arrested and thrown in jail. Where's her club? Or was it the butt of a rifle?" He grabbed the edge of the table and hoisted himself to his feet. "Who's in charge here? I demand you hold her while I procure the law."

A short, wiry man hovered nearby, his face contorted. "Please, sir. I am the manager of the restaurant. Surely there's been a simple misunderstanding. The lady appears quite calm now. Why don't I call a doctor to see to your head? May I bring you some coffee or water?"

Lansing waved the manager away. "What I want is the sheriff." Extracting a handkerchief, he pressed it against his forehead. "She split my head open." He held out the cloth, showing a patch of blood. "Bring me some brandy."

Jeffery nodded at the manager. "Thank you for your kind offer, but no. He doesn't require anything. He'll be leaving soon."

"I will do no such thing." Lansing whirled on Jeffery, then grimaced. He pointed his finger at Wilma. "She's a menace to society. I'm sure I must have damage to my brain."

Jeffery snorted a laugh. "That and much more, if you ask me."

Wilma's back stiffened. "Help me up, Beth. I won't continue to sit here and be insulted by that—that—that uncouth individual."

Beth placed her hand under her aunt's arm and assisted her, unsure what to do next. Isaac Lansing blamed her for the incident at the boardinghouse, and more than that, he believed she'd intentionally flirted, then shunned his attentions.

Wilma stepped close to the man, raising a shaking fist. "I saw you accost my niece. If I had my way, you'd still be on the floor, not standing here issuing threats."

He held up his hands. "Put your weapon away, lady. I'll have you locked up for attempted murder with a lethal weapon if you take another step."

She stopped, then pointed at Jeffery. "Show him my lethal weapon, Mr. Tucker."

Jeffery gently removed the parasol from Beth's grasp and unfurled it. Snickers erupted around the room.

Lansing rapped his fist on the table. "I don't believe it. You've hidden the club you struck me with. I did nothing to your niece."

"No, sir, I have no weapon on my person." She drew herself up, her back ramrod straight. "Young man, you have suffered nothing but a minuscule scrape. Every person in this room saw you manhandle my niece. I heard her cry out and saw her pull away. If I were a man, I'd horsewhip you and drive you from town. It's the least you deserve."

Heads nodded, and a murmur arose.

"That's right, I saw him." A man at a nearby table spoke up.

She addressed a group of miners. "What do you say, gentlemen? Shall we escort the man out of town?"

Beth gripped her aunt's arm and drew her back. "That won't be necessary. I'm not injured." Laughter mingled with panic in her throat at the eager expressions on some of the men's faces. "Truly. Everything is over now."

Jeffery handed the parasol to Wilma, then moved so close Lansing was forced to step back. "You will apologize to the lady for touching her without her consent." He balled his fists. "Or next time you'll have me to deal with, and *I* won't be using a parasol."

The man stuttered a couple of incoherent words, his face contorting in fear.

Jeffery crossed his arms over his chest and scowled. "Not good enough."

Lansing drew in a deep breath. "I apologize for my rude behavior, Miss Roberts. It will not happen again." He walked stiffly toward the door, stopping only to scoop up his hat.

Jeffery touched Beth's arm. "Are you all right?"

She nodded, uncertain what to say.

Jeffery eyed the door, then drew the two women back to the table. "I didn't realize there was a problem until you cried out. I'm sorry I didn't react more quickly. I should have been the one to lay that scoundrel out on the floor."

Beth's heart swelled. "Thank you, Jeffery." She tried to smile, but the smile felt limp. "I think Aunt Wilma and I should get home."

"Let me call a buggy."

Wilma shook her head. "It's a lovely day, and I am in no hurry to get there. We will walk."

"Then I'll walk with you and make sure you arrive safely."

"No, young man, you will not. I need some time with my niece, and you need to keep an eye on Mr. Lansing. In fact, it might not be a bad idea if you let the sheriff know what happened."

Beth touched her aunt's arm. "Are you sure? I think Jeffery is right, and we should hire a buggy. I imagine you're quite worn-out with all the excitement."

"Fiddlesticks. I am *not* in my dotage. It will do us both good to walk." She held out her hand to Jeffery. "I will take my parasol, thank you." A smile crept to the corners of her mouth. "I think I have proven I'm capable of caring for myself. We appreciate your help, Mr. Tucker, and your offer to accompany us home. We will see you later at supper."

Jeffery nodded. "Beth. Take care of yourself."

Beth felt his gaze on her as she and Aunt Wilma exited the room. She was thankful Jeffery planned to check on Lansing and talk to the sheriff, but his company would have been nice on the way home. She and her aunt trod the street in silence until Beth could stand it no longer. "What brought you to town in the first place, Auntie, and why did you strike Mr. Lansing? Were you truly afraid for my safety?"

The older woman snapped open the parasol, keeping the edge between herself and Beth. "Humph. Well, now. That's difficult to say."

Beth gripped Wilma's arm and drew her to a stop at the edge of town. "Please explain what's going on."

A wagon rolled by and sprayed water as it passed through a puddle, barely missing their skirts. Beth tugged her aunt deeper into a grassy field and led her toward a fallen log. "Why don't you sit and tell me about it?"

"No, dear. You are wearing your good dress and are liable to get pitch on the fabric."

"I have a newspaper." Beth unfolded it and spread some sheets on the log. "I insist you sit, Auntie. I must know what's bothering you."

Wilma gave a resigned sigh and lowered herself onto the seat Beth had prepared. "All right. I suppose there's no avoiding it. To be blunt, I thought Mr. Lansing was Brent Wentworth come to take you away."

Beth felt as though someone had thrown ice water in her face and left her gasping for breath. She willed her voice to remain calm, then sat beside her aunt. "I must say I'm shocked. I can't imagine what would make you think that."

"I saw you sneak out of the house."

"Sneak?" Beth thought back over her actions earlier in the day. She couldn't deny she'd hoped no one would notice her leave as her errand had left her quaking, but sneaking seemed a bit strong.

"Maybe not, but you certainly did tiptoe and slip quietly out the door. And your clothing—" She appraised Beth from head to foot with a frown.

A tad bit of irritation rose. Her aunt was taking this too far. Beth tipped back her head, struggling to gain control of her emotions as she noted the clouds skittering along in the brisk breeze. A swallow soared overhead and lit on the branch of a tree swathed in green and yellow. She brought her gaze back to her aunt. "What's wrong with what I'm wearing? It's decent and modest."

"Certainly it is. In fact, you are quite stunning. I assumed you must be meeting someone you hoped to impress. You've socialized with very few people since we arrived. With the amount of time you spend in your room working, and no eligible men having called, that left one conclusion."

"Brent." Beth breathed his name and tried to force back the memories. Tender scenes in the garden behind her home, his declaration of unending love … and one not so lovely—his disappearance without saying a word. "You assumed he followed us out here?"

"I'm afraid so." Wilma clasped her hands in her lap.

Beth's heart contracted. Her aunt was too silent. "You surely didn't think I'd run away with him?" The truth hit her. "You don't trust me." She stood in one fluid motion.

"I am so sorry, dear one. I do trust you, although I must admit to a certain amount of concern where that man is involved. It is Wentworth I don't have faith in."

"But why? You've never given me any details, except he wasn't good for me. He walked away without a word. After he'd told me he loved me." Beth stared at her aunt for several long heartbeats. "Did you chase him off?"

Wilma shook her head, her eyes moist. "I can't discuss that. Someday, but not now."

"That is *not* fair." Beth clenched her hands. "I cared for him, more than any man I've ever met."

"You didn't know the real man, Beth. You'll find someone else who is so much better than that rascal."

"You keep calling him that, but you won't give me a good reason for it." She took a couple of steps, then turned. "We're very close to the house, and I'd like a few minutes alone. Will you be all right walking the rest of the way?"

Wilma nodded and got to her feet.

Beth waited until her aunt was a short distance ahead, then gathered the newspaper. Remorse swept her. She shouldn't let Aunt Wilma go too far without her. Truly, she couldn't fault her aunt for her concern. Truth be told, if Brent had arrived in town and sent word he wanted to meet her, she wasn't sure what she would do.

A memory of Jeffery flashed … standing over Isaac Lansing and telling him to leave or the man would answer to him. Then another of Jeffery's kind offer to accompany them home and his obvious concern for her well-being. If only they hadn't been interrupted. They'd enjoyed a nice visit after they'd realized their appointment was with each other. It was the first time she'd told anyone else the truth about her pen name as Elizabeth Corwin, and it felt good to trust him—almost as though there was hope they might become more than friends.

Beth released a soft groan. Her tablet. In all the excitement at the restaurant she'd left it on the table. She sank back onto the log and put her face in her hands. So much to think about. Brent. Jeffery. Aunt Wilma's suspicion and reluctance to tell her the truth. Would life ever get easier? She needed to collect her tablet. Sticking with her drawing and avoiding men altogether was certainly simpler than trying to figure out her past—or her future.

Chapter Seventeen

Wilma spread the missive flat on the bureau in her room and adjusted her spectacles, thankful for the strong morning light filtering through the window. She hated keeping anything from Beth, especially after upsetting the girl yesterday with her suspicions about Brent. But this was one document she didn't care to have anyone see—at least, not yet.

Her heart pounded as she bent over and read the letter from her old friend, Dr. Caleb Marshall. Disappointment struck her. She had hoped Caleb might visit Baker City, but it appeared that wasn't the case. She huffed a sigh and scanned the letter from start to finish, taking time to absorb every word.

When she finished reading yet a third time, she folded it, slipped it into the envelope, then sank into her chair, grateful Katherine had furnished each room with a comfortable seat. Caleb confirmed what she had wondered for years. Nothing else had mattered when Beth arrived at her door as a toddler. Caring for the child took precedence over digging into the finer details of her past. She'd known the Arapaho found the girl along the Oregon Trail and brought her to Fort Laramie, and that seemed enough. No one knew which wagon train she had been lost from, and Wilma never thought to inquire how long Beth had lived with the tribe.

She leaned her head against the back of the chair and closed her eyes. Caleb had talked to an Indian scout who remembered the little blue-eyed girl from seventeen years ago—the girl who spoke with a lisp and said her name was "Bethie." The Arapaho had kept her well over five months, until her burns were mostly healed and they were ready to move camp. The chief had worried that the soldiers from the fort might discover a white child in their village and cause trouble, so they'd turned her over to the garrison commander.

One of the Arapaho confirmed Beth was found near a smoldering fire with wagon tracks headed west. It would have been strange if they'd gone east, but it was still good to know. Did she really *want* to find Beth's family? Pain gripped Wilma, and she groaned. If it were solely her decision, she'd never turn a hair to track them down. She'd prefer to keep her girl all to herself and go on as they were. If only her husband were alive to advise her. But at least Caleb had given her more information than she'd had before.

Should she tell Beth or see what more could be done on her own? Wilma opened her eyes. Late-morning sunshine streamed through the parted curtains. No need to worry the girl if nothing came of her inquiries. She wasn't even sure what to do with Caleb's information. He'd promised to keep digging and let her know if he discovered anything else. Caleb had been involved from the beginning, as he'd been instrumental in caring for Beth at the fort and making arrangements for her move to Topeka.

Too bad the scout didn't have any more information, but that would have been too much to hope for. At least they knew that most of the trains traveling the Oregon Trail in the early 1860s stopped in eastern Oregon, although now they migrated farther south and to the central part of the territory. The possibility of finding Beth's family so many years later seemed nigh unto impossible. Only the good Lord could bring it to pass, and Wilma would have to leave it in His hands. And if He decided it wasn't to be, so much the better.

A pang of guilt smote her. Beth needed to know the truth. Believing she'd been abandoned or cast off by those who should have loved her was eating the girl alive. Suddenly Wilma felt much older than her forty-nine years. She didn't even want to think what it would do to Beth if she never discovered the truth. Something had to be done, even if it meant losing her girl's loyalty to another woman. Knowing Beth was finally at peace would be worth any personal cost.

Jeffery flipped through the pages of the tablet one more time, then shut it with a decisive snap. He had no right to even look at it again now that he knew it belonged to Beth, but the drawings called to him somehow. Especially the one of the little girl curled up next to the fire, her dress in tatters and pain covering her face. Who could the child be, and why did the depiction affect him so?

With all the excitement at the café yesterday, he'd not realized the tablet still lay on the table. Satisfaction had risen when he'd discovered it, along with the awareness he'd have another excuse to broach the subject of Beth's art. Maybe when he returned the sketch pad she'd be more disposed to talk. He should have done so last night, but she had claimed a headache and taken her meal in her room. And slipping it to her at breakfast this morning might have embarrassed her.

Jeffery moved from the parlor to the kitchen, drawn by the rattling of dishes. He paused at the arched doorway and surveyed the scene. Katherine Jacobs and her mother, Mrs. Cooper, worked side by side, hands busy and words flying, but not in the way they'd done when the older woman first arrived.

"Mrs. Jacobs?" He placed his shoulder against the door frame and waited.

A genuine smile lit the younger woman's face. "Mr. Tucker. Have you come to help with the dishes?"

Mrs. Cooper's brows rose. "We haven't had a man in the kitchen for some time, sir."

Jeffery tipped back his head and laughed. "As much as I'd love the pleasure of your company, ladies, I'm afraid I must decline. I was hoping to find Miss Roberts. Have you seen her by chance?"

Mrs. Cooper's brows arched. "So you *are* looking for Miss Roberts? Hmm." She grinned. "I do like the sound of that."

Warmth rose up Jeffery's neck. "Uh, no, ma'am. I mean, I have something I need to return to her. That is—"

Mrs. Jacobs chuckled. "Now, Mama, stop teasing the man, or he'll never visit our kitchen again." She tilted her head toward Jeffery. "Miss Roberts stopped in to say she was taking a walk. I think it might be on the hillside east of here. I'm not sure when she planned to return."

Jeffery nodded. "Thank you, ma'am. Much obliged. I hope you ladies have a fine day." He headed for the hall leading to the front door.

"See what you've done, Mama. Made the poor man run off." Katherine's whisper followed him, and Mrs. Cooper's voice rose in reply.

"Ha. He's not running from us. Mark my words, there's another romance stirring in this house. Just you wait and see."

"Mama! Shh ... he'll hear you."

"Good. I'm not sure the man is smart enough to figure it out for himself, even if he does write novels. Maybe he should have written a romance after all."

Jeffery bolted for the door and yanked it open, wanting nothing more than to flee the house before the two women had him and Beth married and expecting their first child. All he wanted to do was return Beth's tablet and assure himself she had recovered from her ordeal of yesterday.

He slowed his pace and grinned. If he were completely honest, though, adding a little romance to his novel—and possibly his life—might not be such a terrible idea. But there was no sense in allowing the ladies the pleasure of knowing they had come so close to the truth.

Beth spread out a rug on the grass and sat at the base of her favorite tree. Melancholy trailed its fingers over her heart. Much too soon the branches would extend bare limbs to the sky. The world would curl into a cocoon and sleep for the winter, while the earth prepared to bring new life in the spring. Spring ... the time of year the Arapaho delivered her to Fort Laramie. The tears she had shed for her mother had dried long before, but the pain still lingered. So much had returned lately as she lay in bed piecing together the shattered bits of her life. The Arapaho people had been kind, but they did not countenance children who whimpered or complained.

She'd been four when they'd brought her to the fort, as near as anyone could tell, but the wrench of leaving her Arapaho family still pricked her heart these nearly seventeen years later. If only she could remember what came before.

She had arrived in Topeka in the company of Aunt Wilma's older brother, Arthur, days before Easter. Dr. Caleb had treated her at the fort, and suggested Uncle Art contact Aunt Wilma, knowing she and her husband had lost a young daughter to dysentery.

Beth leaned against the tree and allowed tender memories to flood her soul. Aunt Wilma's face streaming with tears as she gathered Beth into her arms, and Uncle George grinning and patting her back.

She gazed down over the valley, and a deep contentment stroked her heart for the first time in days. Last night she had dreamed again. Or had it been a dream? A quiet voice had called to her in the wee hours, as she drifted in and out of sleep. She'd leaned into the night, yearning, reaching, seeking, hoping. It only lasted minutes, or it might have been seconds, but the voice was distinct.

"Trust Me. Rest in Me."

How she wanted to rest. Trust. Let it all go and not care about the past anymore.

Was that what He wanted? Should she walk away and quit trying to discover the truth? But didn't the Bible say that His truth would set us free? Why, then, did she feel so bound? So … broken?

The troubling images of nights gone by had been replaced with a warm cocoon of tranquility, wrapping its threads around her spirit and weaving an invisible blanket of peace. The sense of God's presence was real—more so than anything she'd known before.

She'd try to continue to trust, but she couldn't quit seeking the truth about her past. Would God help her find her family if she asked? Was that what He was trying to tell her? Maybe she didn't have to pretend not to care, but where was the balance between trusting and doing it all herself? So much she didn't understand. So much she wanted to accomplish and discover. And for some reason, her aunt had been little help.

A movement at the base of the hill caught her eye. Beth sat up straighter. *Jeffery.* A shiver coursed through her. Anticipation—or fear? Not that he would ever hurt her … she knew that now. Not intentionally, anyway. But there were other ways of inflicting hurt. She should know; she'd been on the receiving end often enough.

There was no place to run, no way to hide. He lifted a hand and waved. Beth sat back on the rug and moaned. She'd come up here to think about her future as well as her past. Ever since he'd carried her home in his arms, she'd had to fight to keep Jeffery out of her mind. She'd noted a spark of interest in his appraisal, but what interested him? The oddity of a woman who drew pictures she didn't want to take credit for? Or something else?

People had told her often enough that she was a mouse, hiding in her room and nibbling at the edges of conversations and social affairs, always hovering in the shadows and only darting out when she thought no one noticed. More than likely Jeffery saw her as an object of pity, not a woman he might one day care about.

As he grew closer she steeled herself against the smile brightening his face. The last thing she wanted was his pity.

Jeffery focused on the solemn girl sitting on the rug at the base of the tree and slowed his pace. What a picture she made. Her emerald-green skirt was spread out around her. Her slender fingers were clasped in her lap and wide, lovely eyes met his. Yearning, mixed with confusion, flashed in their depths before she turned aside.

So much he didn't know about this young woman, and it made him all the more determined to plumb the depths of her personality. Her intelligence had been the first thing that drew him, along with her spunk and determination. Sparkling glints at first, but apparent to someone with a willingness to see, and the traits had only grown and blossomed.

He drew to a halt nearby and swept his hat from his head. "I followed you up here. I hope you don't mind."

She averted her eyes, then a giggle escaped. "How delightfully honest you are, Mr. Tucker."

"Jeffery." The word came out automatically. "And I see no reason to prevaricate. I can't exactly claim I was out for a walk and chose this hillside to hike." He wrinkled his nose. "I enjoy the great outdoors as much as the next man, but I'll admit climbing isn't at the top of my list. A nice buggy ride or on horseback across a meadow is more pleasant, don't you think?"

"I suppose it depends on what you want."

"Ah, that does beg the question, doesn't it?" Jeffery took a step closer. "What if I said your companionship?"

Her lips quirked to the side. "I'm not sure how I'd respond." Her gaze traveled to his side. "You brought something along. Your manuscript perhaps?"

Jeffery plucked the paper-wrapped parcel from under his arm. "No. Although I would love to share that with you sometime, if you'd ever care to listen. This concerns you."

Her movements stilled—all except her hands, which clutched her skirt until the knuckles whitened. "Oh?"

He unwrapped the tablet and held it up. "You left this on the table yesterday. I wanted to return it sooner but didn't have a chance to do so privately."

Beth drew in a quick breath. "Thank you. How kind to be so sensitive. Won't you sit down?" She tucked the folds of her skirt against her leg, leaving room on the rug.

He lowered himself onto the cleared area and handed her the sketch pad. "I hoped you might be willing to discuss your art."

She dropped her gaze to the book, her lashes hiding her thoughts. "I'm not sure what you mean. It's fairly simple. I draw."

Jeffery pointed at the tablet. "Quite the contrary. Your material is complex. It has the power to stir the imagination and touch the heart. They are not just drawings; they are works of art."

Beth slowly closed her gaping mouth. The man sounded serious. From what she could tell he had nothing to gain by paying her a compliment, but hearing those words was astonishing. "Are you serious, Mr., er … Jeffery?"

His brown eyes sparkled. "Extremely. You seem surprised. Surely you know your own level of talent? You wouldn't be selling any if you weren't good." He cocked his head. "But that's not what shocked you, is it? No, I think not. More likely that I recognized your gift."

Warmth stole up Beth's neck, and she tucked her chin. "I'm sorry. I didn't mean to imply you weren't astute. That's not the case at all."

"Hmm. That only leaves one option, then. You don't believe your work is of significant consequence and find it difficult to accept that others would see your worth. Or, at the least, they might not be willing to recognize it to the point of speaking it aloud. Why is that, I wonder?"

Beth raised her head and met his eyes. "A moment ago I said I found your honesty delightful. Now I'm not so sure."

"I beg your pardon. I didn't mean to appear rude or overly inquisitive. I hope you'll forgive me?" He braced his elbows behind him and leaned back.

"Of course, but I'd prefer not to discuss my work. I hope you don't mind." She plucked a yellow buttercup from the grass and lifted it to her nose. Something tugged at her heart, darting in and out of the shadows of her mind, barely out of reach. Buttercups. They'd drawn her for years—always her favorite flower—and she'd never understood why. She'd been delighted to find some still blossoming this late in the fall.

"Not at all." Jeffery pointed at the flower. "Do you ever sketch them?" He grimaced. "There I go again."

She laughed and closed her eyes. "No, but I should. I love them."

"I suppose you used to make wishes on them when you were young, like all the other girls?"

Her head jerked up. "What did you say?"

"My sister and her friends were always picking buttercups and pulling the petals off. Saying silly things like, 'I wish this and that,' and 'he loves me or doesn't.' I'm not sure what all, as I didn't listen closely. I assumed it might be some secret code among womenfolk. Fond childhood memories and all that." A charming smile caused a dimple to appear.

An image coalesced in her mind, but not of little girls playing together. She'd not had many happy memories of times like that. This one was of a woman, her face hazy, holding a deep yellow flower. Plucking a petal and smiling, she offered it to the little girl standing so still. Where had that memory come from? Was it real or something created from Jeffery's words? She stared at the blossom clutched in her hand and tried to relax. The crushed stem fell from her fingers onto the rug.

"Is something wrong?" Jeffery extended his hand, then drew back. "Did I say something to upset you? I'm afraid I've been doing that quite often since I arrived." He pushed to his knees. "I'll bid you good day and head back to the house. You would no doubt appreciate privacy since you came up here alone."

Beth caught the wistfulness on his face. "Please don't go. I'm fine. Really …" She shook her head. "A memory I can't quite place."

"If you're sure."

"Completely. In fact, I'd appreciate the company at the moment." She drew in a breath. "I'd like to hear about your book. Tell me about it?"

Surprise burned in his eyes. "I'd be honored, but I must ask if you're certain. I've gotten the impression it wasn't a subject you wanted to broach."

She allowed a smile to emerge. "You're right, and now it is my turn to apologize. I've not been very courteous where your work is concerned."

He waved his hand in dismissal. "We've both done enough apologizing today. I'd be happy to talk about it. Do you have a specific question?"

"You mentioned that you hoped it would be under contract someday. Have you submitted it to any publishers yet, or is it in the early stages? I'm afraid I don't know much about writing, so forgive me if my questions aren't sensible."

"No more forgiveness needed, remember?" He tossed her a cheeky grin. "Your questions are quite welcome, and I'm happy to inform you that things have changed since my remarks about my prospects. An editor accepted my manuscript."

"Wonderful!" Pleasure vibrated through Beth. Where she'd had nothing but dread, she now experienced joy that this man might actually achieve his dream. She'd seen no evidence of his prying into her affairs of late—rather, she'd glimpsed something she perceived as genuine interest, although some of his questions still came too close to areas better left alone. On the whole he'd been kind and friendly. "I'm quite happy for you. When will you be able to hold your book in your hands?"

A shadow crossed his face. "I don't honestly know."

"They haven't given you any indication? Surely that's not typical."

"No, it's not. But apparently my book won't follow the normal course of publication." He plucked a blade of grass and placed it between his teeth. "They're concerned that as an unknown author and with subject matter that isn't scandalous, readers might not purchase it. So they offered another solution they believe will increase sales."

Beth laced her hands and rested them on her skirt. "That sounds hopeful."

"It's something that's being done more often of late, but it caught me off guard. They want to publish my book as a running serial in a periodical they own, the *Women's Eastern Magazine*, and accompany it with illustrations. If it is well received, they will continue until the end, then put the book in print." His brows drew together. "As though illustrations will make a particle of difference in sales." He tossed the grass blade aside. "But I must bow to their wishes or possibly never see my book in print. I suppose it's the best I can hope for, at least for now."

Beth blinked, trying to sort out her thoughts and form some type of sensible reply. *The Women's Eastern Magazine?* Illustrations? Could it be …? She pressed her hand to her forehead. Surely not. It would be too strange and certainly unlikely.

Jeffery leaned toward her. "Beth? Are you well?"

"Nothing like that. I'm sorry …" She groaned. "Let's start over, shall we?"

He grinned. "That sounds like a fine suggestion. Tell me what you're thinking."

"You'll think it's crazy."

"Please let me be the judge of that."

"I illustrate for *The Women's Eastern Magazine*."

His mouth dropped open, and he stared.

"My thoughts exactly. Recently they asked me to do a series of four illustrations." She picked up her tablet and flipped the pages. "This is the one I sent in a couple of weeks ago."

He leaned closer and peered at the paper for long moments, not speaking.

When he sat back, she closed the pad. "I also received a letter asking me to include a picture of a boardinghouse in a small town set in the West."

Jeffery choked on a sharp breath. When he regained his composure, he tapped the cover of the tablet. "I didn't see anything like that in here."

"No. I lost this before I got the letter. I purchased a new sketch pad, completed that drawing, and sent it off. Have you …"

"Gotten any proofs to look at yet?" He shook his head. "None. They have several of my completed chapters, though, and I assumed I'd be given the opportunity to view whatever they planned before the first installment goes to press." He turned a hopeful gaze on her. "But you said they've only contracted four illustrations. If it were for my book, I'd think it would be more."

She shrugged. "Maybe they plan on viewing what I send before they decide. I can't say. And it's very possible that my work isn't tied to yours."

"I'd say that's highly unlikely. What are the odds we'd both be working for the same magazine with a boardinghouse included in the subject matter and it not be the same project?" His tone held a bitter tinge.

Beth nodded slowly. "You're not happy about it." She smoothed a wrinkle in her skirt as birds chirped overhead. Now that he knew it was possible she was the artist, their budding friendship would end. Just like every other friendship she'd had. People came close, then backed away as soon as they got wind of anything "unusual."

At least Jeffery had the grace to duck his head. "You noticed. I'm s—." He clamped his lips shut.

"You don't need to say it, regardless. It *is* your manuscript, and you have a right to how you feel. In all fairness, I suppose I wouldn't appreciate someone dabbling with my work, or telling me it wasn't good enough to stand alone either."

He cocked his brow. "You think I'm upset that *you* are the illustrator?"

She hunched one shoulder and turned her face away, staring out over the valley. "I gathered as much, yes. You needn't deny it. I do understand."

Jeffery shifted beside her and touched her chin, gently urging her to face him. "I do deny it, although not entirely." His lips quirked in a rueful smile. "I was dismayed they thought my work couldn't stand alone—angry if the truth was told." He released his hold and tenderly moved one finger to the tip of her nose. "But it has nothing to do with you. I seriously contemplated rejecting their offer and continuing my quest for a publisher, in the hope my book would be printed in its entirety from the outset. But once I thought it through, I realized the serialization was an economic decision. After all, I'm an untested author with no following, and they're taking a risk publishing me. If it were a typical dime novel, it might be different, but this is more of a literary work."

Beth's heart lurched at the swelling tumult of emotions created by his tender touch. She didn't really know this man; how could she be drawn to him? Men weren't to be trusted. Brent had spoken sweet words and declared his undying love, then disappeared. Jeffery had never indicated a personal interest beyond using their Christian names. Letting a man get close either emotionally or physically was not something she cared to attempt again.

A light breeze rustled the leaves, and Beth brushed a loose strand of hair off of her face. "I think I understand."

"No. I don't think you do, and I'm making a hash out of explaining." Jeffery scrunched his brows. "It's not you I'm upset with, or that they chose you to do my illustrations. It wouldn't have mattered if they'd assigned the most famous artist in the nation, it still would have bothered me. At first, anyway." He touched her hand. "But after seeing your incredible talent, I'm adjusting my attitude." He squeezed her fingers lightly but didn't let go. "If anyone can convey what I'm trying to say and bring attention to my words, it will be you."

Peace settled again over Beth's spirit, and for a moment, she was content to allow it to stroke her bruised heart. Sitting here with Jeffery felt so right, allowing him to hold her hand. She wanted to lean into his quiet strength.

Then reality intruded. She'd heard this type of thing before. Granted, not about her work, but she'd made friends among society people, only to have them back off when they discovered grains of truth about her past. Not that any *one* thing was so terrible to drive a normal person away, but the shadows that surrounded her—the unknown circumstances of her birth, childhood, and rescue—all these served to place a wall between her and possible happiness.

She'd learned long ago to keep herself covered, and not only in a physical sense. The scars were hard enough to explain, but trying to sort through all the questions Jeffery would ask was too much to deal with. And what of his family? From what she'd learned, he came from deep roots. She couldn't allow herself to dream of a future with someone like him.

She scooped up the buttercup that had fallen to the ground. "You are too kind. I should be getting home. Aunt Wilma is probably wondering why I've stayed away so long."

He studied her for several seconds, then stood and held out his hand, a careful expression masking his features. "Allow me."

Guilt hammered at Beth, insisting on entry. He had wanted to discuss his manuscript, but she hadn't given him a chance. The subject of her illustrations had arisen, and that brought with it the fear of discovery. She was choosing to run, like she always did. Beth placed her fingers in his, gratified that he hadn't pushed. She needed time to sort through all the emotions swirling over this newest discovery.

Never would she have believed she'd be hired to create illustrations for Jeffery's novel. She didn't even know what the book was about, apart from the obvious setting of a boardinghouse in a mining town. That had been enough to keep her from wanting to know more, and now she regretted her hasty decision. Was it too late to take a step back—maybe suggest they sit and chat awhile longer?

Jeffery released his hold. "I'll walk you to the house if you'd like, then I will retire to my room." He swept the rug from the ground and offered his arm.

Beth hesitated, stung at his aloof manner. But what should she expect? He had complimented her work, and she had as good as thrown his words back at him. She took his arm, knowing this wasn't the time to try to set things right. That had been done too many times today, and from the look on his face, another attempt would only transform that hardness to marble.

They walked down the hillside in silence. When they reached the trail, Beth stepped out ahead of him, moving along the path that bordered a meadow on one side. They neared the place where she had fallen and pitched her tablet. A shiver of awareness ran along her skin. She worked to still her rapid breathing.

Beth hazarded a glance at Jeffery, then quickly turned forward. Stoic calm covered his face with no hint of the emotions cascading through her. They'd started out so amiably, only to come to this—silence. A hush that didn't denote the peaceful stroll of two friends lost in their own thoughts. No, this was more of a brooding silence of disillusionment or, at best, disappointment. And it was her doing.

Again.

They passed the place where Jeffery had gathered her into his arms. Could his heart be pounding at the same rate as hers?

Up ahead, a boot scraped over a log and someone grunted. Surely Aunt Wilma wouldn't worry and come to check on her? Though, after the doubt she'd expressed about Beth's behavior, it was very possible.

They rounded a corner to see a finely clad, masculine figure stopped in the middle of the path, the house visible not far beyond. A delighted smile tipped his mouth, and his arms were crossed over his chest. "There you are, Beth. I thought I'd never find you. But now that I have, I will not let you get away again."

Beth stumbled and nearly fell. Jeffery's hand grasped her wrist and steadied her, setting her back to rights. All other sensations faded as she stared into the smoldering gaze of Brent Wentworth.

Chapter Eighteen

La Grande, Oregon

Isabelle Mason stood on the edge of the boardwalk in front of the stage station, praying her strength would hold up until her son arrived. Steven had been gone over two weeks with only one letter. He'd assured her of his safety and advised that his employer was taking advantage of every daylight hour while in Baker City, so he'd been unable to write more often. He hadn't said a word about the other affair, but right now that didn't matter. Nothing did but having her son back home.

People bustled by, intent on their own errands. Isabelle clung to the hitching-rail post, barely able to stand. Thank the Lord no horses were tied nearby. She cast a glance at the two chairs to the right of the open doorway. Two old-timers sat tipped back against the wall, chewing the fat as though they hadn't spoken in years. She wouldn't disturb them, although she was certain they'd willingly give up their seat for her. No, the stage would soon be here, and then she'd have to get on her feet again, in any case.

Maybe she should have listened to Karen and stayed home, letting Steven come to her. She had been certain she could walk from the cabin to the station, but it suddenly dawned on her she still faced the return trip. Urgency had driven her from the confines of her home. She'd walked the five blocks—something she'd not attempted in months. She must see Steven. Must know if he'd stumbled across any information. Why didn't the stage come? Her arms trembled as she tightened her grip, determined to stay on her feet and greet her son. She'd been ill too long and hated this terrible weakness.

A rumble in the distance, accompanied by a cloud of dust spewing into the air, signaled the stage's arrival. She lifted the watch that hung on a chain around her neck—a precious gift from her father and one of the few family treasures she still retained. Right on time. She must have arrived earlier than she'd realized.

A man stepped up beside her and doffed his hat. "Ma'am."

Isabelle didn't reply. There wasn't an extra ounce of strength left in her limbs to so much as lift her hand or nod.

He touched her shoulder. "Are you all right, ma'am? Would you like to take a seat under the porch roof?"

She swayed slightly. "No. Thank you."

His brows scrunched together. "I fear you aren't well. Please—"

The stage rounded the corner a block away, the driver pulling back on the reins of his team. The springs protested, and dust rolled as the horses trotted the remaining distance. "Whoa there, fellas. You've earned your rest. This here is the end of the road for today." He leaned over the side and spat, then waved to the man standing beside Isabelle. "Grab the hitch line and tie them up, would you, mister?"

The door swung open, and Steven stepped out, his short hair covered by a hat. A fine coat of dust layered his suit, and he appeared weary. A smile flitted briefly, then he helped two ladies alight from the stage.

Isabelle's heart soared, and strength spurted through her body. Her boy was home. No harm had befallen him as she'd feared as she'd lain sleepless all those nights.

He turned, and a wide smile broke the solemn planes of his face. "Ma. I didn't expect you to meet me." Plucking his valise off the ground, he tucked it under his arm. "Let's get you home."

She loosened her grip on the rail and extended her hand. All would be well now that Steven was home. He'd have good news at last, and her world would be back to rights again. She took a step. Her knees started to shake and she wobbled, then caught herself.

"Ma? You all right?" Concern laced Steven's tone, and he dropped his valise.

"Fine. Fine." Black spots danced before her eyes, and she wobbled again. Hands reached toward her through the dark haze, but she couldn't make out a face.

Beth gaped at the man standing before her and tried to gather her wits. Brent Wentworth in Baker City? She'd never expected to see him again. Confusion exploded inside, quickly replaced by a raw, burning anger. This man had deserted her after filling her head with tales of love and commitment. How dare he follow her here?

Jeffery stepped up beside her. "Beth? Do you know this man?"

She gave him a firm nod. "I used to. He is … *was* … a … an acqaintance of mine in Topeka." Beth didn't miss the wince that passed across Brent's face. "But that was a long time ago." She lifted her chin and drilled Brent with her gaze. "This is Mr. Tucker. Jeffery, this is Mr. Wentworth."

Jeffery didn't move or offer his hand. "Mr. Wentworth. Did Mrs. Roberts send you to find Beth?"

Brent assessed Jeffery with a calculating stare, then shot a glance at the house. "I didn't stop. She's not aware I'm in town yet." He tilted his head to Beth and smiled. "I asked around and discovered where you were staying. I remembered how much you enjoy walking in the afternoon, and I waited, hoping to accompany you." He cast a dark look at Jeffery. "I'm sorry I missed the opportunity." He took a step forward and extended his arm. "I'd like to talk with you alone, if you'd give me a minute of your time?"

Beth shook her head. "I can't believe you'd even ask me that. Not after what happened." She slipped her fingers through the crook of Jeffery's arm. "Would you be so kind as to accompany me back to the house?"

"Certainly."

"Beth, wait. Please." Brent held up his hand. "What I did was unforgivable, but I can explain. Please give me a chance. I must speak to you." He took a step closer and dropped his voice to a whisper. "It's urgent."

Jeffery could feel Beth stiffen beside him. The nerve of this man, trying to force himself on a young woman of her quality. Or on any woman, for that matter. "I say, Mr. Wentworth, you'll have to excuse

Miss Roberts. She and I are returning from a walk, and her aunt is expecting her." He drew her forward.

Wentworth followed. "Allow me a few seconds. That's all I ask. I won't bother you again if you'll give me that much."

Beth slowed and released her hold on Jeffery's arm. He halted. "Do you wish to speak to this man?"

She leveled a gaze at Wentworth, then raised her eyes to Jeffery. Indecision wavered there, and then was replaced by resolve. "Not especially, but it might be for the best. Would you do me a favor?"

Jeffery bowed. "If it is within my power."

"Go inside and let Aunt Wilma know I'll be along shortly. But ..." She shivered. "Don't tell her I'm talking to Mr. Wentworth."

"I don't understand." And, most decidedly, he did not. She had appeared quite angry at first, and now she seemed more than willing to stay. Something was wrong. He stared at Wentworth. A lazy smile tipped his mouth, and he arched a brow. Sly, that's what he was—and not to be trusted. "I'll walk over to the steps and give you privacy, but I am not comfortable leaving you with this man." He lifted his voice loud enough for Wentworth to hear.

She shook her head, her dark ringlets dancing on her shoulders. "Please, if you'd do as I asked, I'd be grateful." Beth's lips puckered.

His heart wavered at the pleading expression, but wavering wasn't an option. "I'm sorry, but your reputation is more important. I'll move out of earshot, but I plan to stay where I can see you—and him."

"All right." She whispered the words and touched his hand, then drew back. "Thank you for understanding."

But he didn't. Not at all. Something was amiss here, and he planned to make it his business to find out what.

Chapter Nineteen

La Grande, Oregon

Isabelle patted Steven's cheek as he leaned over her bed. "I'm fine, Son. I probably shouldn't have walked to the stage station, but I think it was all the standing around that tired me. Now that I've rested I'll get up and start supper. You must be hungry after your long trip."

Steven gently pressed her back against the pillow. "I insist you stay put, Ma. I'm perfectly capable of fixing my own meal. I'll go wash some of the trail dust off first and change my shirt, then rustle up supper for both of us." He cocked his head. "You look like you've lost more weight. Have you been eating? Has Ina kept an eye on you?"

She laughed and waved him away. "Yes, Ina's been here, and Karen has been clucking over me like a broody hen. Quit fretting and change your clothes. A bite to eat does sound good. There's cold sliced beef in the spring house and fresh bread and butter there as well." She pushed up on her elbow. "Before you go, would you hand me a pencil and my journal?"

He looked askance at her, then seemed to relent. "All right. Let me put another pillow behind you so you can sit up. But you stay on that bed until I get back. Promise?"

"Yes, Son. I'm not going anywhere. I'll catch up on my writing while I wait." Isabelle held out her hand, eager to work on her project. She had never shared her journals with anyone, not even Karen or Steven. Somewhere inside she knew Steven wouldn't understand. Karen might, but these were too precious, too private, to disclose.

She opened the book and a yellow flower fell out, drifting to the floor. Leaning over the bed, she carefully plucked up the dried buttercup and placed it back in its hiding place. Only one of the little treasures she kept as a reminder. Her pencil labored over the paper, and sweat formed on her brow. One more page. She had to get it all down—her emotions, desires, dreams—everything Steven's sister would want to know about someday when she presented the journals to her. Bessie would come back home; she knew it. And she planned to live until she did.

Beth waited until Jeffery moved to a discreet distance, then walked the opposite direction. The last thing she wanted was Aunt Wilma looking out a window and racing out with her parasol. Footsteps crunched on the gravel walkway announcing Brent's decision to follow.

She stayed within sight of the house and drew to a stop next to a tree. Pivoting, she crossed her arms and stared at the man she thought she'd never see again. "What do you want?"

His lips quirked to the side. "The last time we met you were a quiet little thing. I admit to finding this new Beth Roberts more attractive than the old one. Did you fall in love with the stuffed shirt who walked you home?"

She slapped him. Hard.

Brent's head jerked back, and he stroked his reddened cheek with his fingertips. He studied her through the thick, dark lashes she used to love. "My comments were uncalled for. I owe you an apology."

Beth snorted. "You owe me much more than that. Earlier you said what you did was unforgivable. I agree. You also said you would explain. Do it."

He reached out, and she took a step back.

"Don't touch me, Brent. I don't trust you, and it's doubtful I ever will again."

Brent sucked in a harsh breath. "Fine. I had that coming." He managed an ingratiating smile. "I'm sorry for teasing. You used to like it."

"That wasn't teasing; it was rude." A shiver ran down her spine. "But maybe I never saw that before now."

The smile faded. "Now, Beth, honey, don't be that way. I said I was sorry, and I meant it." He touched her hand, gently tugging her toward him. "You have no idea how much I've missed you."

Beth jerked away, and anger sent her blood pounding through her veins. "Don't do that again. You said you had something urgent to tell me." A sense of freedom soared over her spirit. Brent's touch had done little to move her. Not many months ago she would have listened to his protest with a willing heart and open mind. Maybe she was growing a backbone, along with some common sense, at last.

"Won't you come with me? I don't care to talk outside in the open. Someone might overhear."

She lifted her chin. "What do you have to say that can't be said right here?"

He stripped a branch off the tree and tapped it against his trouser-clad leg. "Let's say I'd rather not take a chance of being spied upon."

"Why?" The word came out flat and harsh, but Beth didn't care. She was tired of playing games. He'd toyed with her heart in the past, and she didn't plan to let it happen again.

"Because I have … things of a personal nature I need to share, and I don't have time right now. I waited a long time for you to get back, and I'm going to be late for an appointment in town. Please, Beth. I know I don't have the right to ask, and you have no reason to trust me. But for old time's sake, won't you come and have dinner? We can go to a quiet little restaurant, if that's what you prefer."

Beth considered his request. There'd been a time she'd have gone anywhere with this man without thinking twice about it, but that was a lifetime ago. She'd longed to see Brent again, and more than once had prayed his leaving had been a mistake, but now? Warring emotions tugged her back and forth, twisting her heart and mind into knots. What if she'd misjudged, and he had a valid reason for leaving? Tiny warning bells jingled deep in her belly. "I can't go anywhere with you now. Aunt Wilma would ask questions, and I don't care to deceive her."

He leaned against the trunk of the tree with a slight smile. "Do you ever go to town alone for any reason?"

"Certainly. I often go to the post office to pick up the mail."

"Will you be there tomorrow?"

"Possibly."

"Tell me when, and I'll meet you. Surely you can take time for a cup of tea, can't you? There can't be any harm in spending a few minutes with an old friend." He straightened. "I'll head back to my hotel as soon as you promise."

Beth slowly nodded. "I suppose I might. Lately I've enjoyed stopping in a shop or two while in town, so Aunt Wilma won't worry if I don't come directly home."

"Good. You'll be glad you decided to trust me."

Beth stepped away from his extended hand. "I said nothing about trusting you, Brent. I'm meeting you and giving you the opportunity to unburden yourself, that's all."

His smile grew more confident, and he allowed his arm to drop to his side. "You won't be sorry, my dear girl. You can count on that."

Wilma stepped away from the window and sank into the overstuffed sofa in the parlor, trying to still her shaking hands. Nothing had moved outside for at least ten minutes. Had he spirited Beth away or convinced her to leave with him? Maybe she should check. Her dear girl could be in danger.

She pulled out a handkerchief and mopped her neck. *Stop it, Wilma. You raised the girl well. You must stop it, or you'll have indigestion and be awake half the night.* Look what happened the last time she thought she'd seen Brent Wentworth—she clubbed a man over the head and could have landed in jail.

Frances hobbled into the room. "Would you care for some company?" She peered over her spectacles and moved a little closer. "Your face is quite pale. Whatever seems to be the problem?"

Wilma patted the cushion beside her on the sofa and grimaced. "I do not particularly like my own company at the moment. Please sit."

Her friend settled her small frame and sighed. "It feels wonderful to be off my feet. Now tell me what is troubling you, and do not attempt to steer me off course this time with any more folderol. I can tell when a person is in distress."

"I believe I'm seeing things. Do you think it's possible I might be losing my mind, Frances?"

The older woman snorted. "That is a bunch of poppycock. Why, you are one of the most sensible persons I know. Besides myself, of course." A smile stretched across her features, and she patted Wilma's hand. "Whatever led you to ask such an outrageous question?"

"I saw Beth talking to someone outside. I thought …" She paused, hating how suspicious she'd become.

Frances leaned forward. "What? Go on, now, finish your sentence."

Wilma glanced at the window. "I came downstairs from taking a nap and wondered if Beth was back from her walk. I looked out the window and saw her talking to a man. It was impossible to see who he was, shaded by the tree boughs, but there was something about the way he stood …" She shook her head. "I am sure I was mistaken. Again."

"Again? Whatever do you mean?"

"The distressful business with Mr. Lansing at the Arlington Hotel restaurant. I am certain I told you about that."

"Only that Mr. Lansing accosted Beth and you gave him his just deserts. The man should have been horsewhipped and ridden out of town on a rail. You let him off quite easily. But what do you mean about being mistaken?"

Wilma lowered her voice. "I struck the man for two reasons. The main one being I thought he was manhandling my niece, but I also believed he was someone else."

"Why are you whispering, Wilma? I cannot see why this is such a huge mystery. For goodness' sake, spit it out."

"There is no need to get snippy." Wilma frowned and sat back against the sofa cushion. "I thought Mr. Lansing was Beth's old beau, Brent Wentworth."

"All right. But I am not sure why you would strike the man, even if he was."

"He is vile." She clamped her lips together, trying to hold in her anger. "The man wooed Beth when we lived in Topeka, and he took me in as well. I thought he was wonderful and trusted him—beyond what I should have—and lived to rue the day."

Frances touched Wilma's arm, and her expression softened. "He hurt you?"

"Yes. I … can't tell you how, Frances. It is simply too embarrassing." She covered her face with her hands and choked, then lifted her head and met Frances's gaze. "I threatened to set the law on him if he continued pursuing Beth. I suppose I should have anyway, but I knew how much it would hurt my girl, so I let him go. But the condition to my not turning him in to the authorities was that he must not contact her again—not in person or by post. So far he has kept that promise, but now …" She shuddered. "I am not so sure."

"You think that is who Beth is talking to outside?"

Wilma hunched her shoulders. "I don't know. I keep thinking I see him everywhere. I don't know why my mind keeps conjuring him when he must still be in Topeka. I got a letter from a friend earlier this summer who assured me of that fact."

"If it sets your mind at rest, she returned with Mr. Tucker not long ago. They were standing outside talking. I am guessing it was Mr. Tucker you saw."

Wilma wilted against the couch. "Oh. My. Thank you, Frances." Her hand crept over her heart and rested there. "I can't tell you how grateful I am to know that. Beth went for a walk by herself, and I had no idea Mr. Tucker intercepted her."

"You must promise to quit worrying yourself so about that rapscallion from Kansas. If he knows you will set the law on him, I cannot imagine he is going to come out here and confront Beth. Put him out of your mind." Frances waved her hand in the air. "Besides, this is the second time Mr. Tucker has been seen walking with Beth." A broad smile spread over her face. "Or, should I say, one time walking and another carrying her home in his arms. I might hazard a guess the man is interested in your niece."

Wilma smirked. "Mr. Tucker—hmm." There might be a way to get Beth to forget that worthless man from back East. She tilted her head toward Frances. "I might have an idea, and I need your help."

Chapter Twenty

Jeffery placed his pencil on his writing desk and arched his back, every muscle protesting. How many sleepless nights could a man endure and hope to get any work done? Less than twenty-four hours had passed since he'd left Beth to talk with the man who had confronted her. He still couldn't dispel the disquiet that rose when she'd agreed to speak to Brent Wentworth.

Something about Wentworth didn't sit right. His gut told him the man couldn't be trusted—least of all with a woman like Beth. Jeffery stood and prowled his room. Should he take some type of action on her behalf? He pulled to a stop. More than anything he wanted to, but did he have that right? He sank into his chair and put his head in his hands. When had Beth become so important to him?

He uttered a short laugh. Who was he trying to fool? Beth Roberts had burrowed herself into his heart even before he'd carried her in his arms. Discovering her intelligence and unique talent as an illustrator only made her that much more alluring. But every time he attempted to gain her confidence or show an interest, a wall appeared between them. She skittered away faster than leaves driven by a fall wind. Was he so unsuitable as a companion or totally undesirable as a suitor?

Be that as it may, he had more important concerns at the moment. He'd walk into town today and ask around—maybe see if he could discover where Wentworth was staying and ascertain why the man was in town.

If anything, Beth had seemed nervous since that man arrived and somewhat withdrawn. That hadn't been the case before Wentworth appeared. In fact, quite the opposite.

Jeffery strolled through the parlor and tipped his head at Mrs. Roberts and Mrs. Cooper, who were sitting with teacups in hand. Both ladies smiled in a way that raised alarm bells. "Ladies, I hope you are having an enjoyable day."

"Quite, thank you," Frances replied graciously. "I am afraid this is becoming almost a daily ritual, having late-afternoon tea together. And where might you be off to, Mr. Tucker? Joining our Beth on another walk, perhaps?"

"No, ma'am. I wasn't aware she was out for a walk. I assumed she was in her room." Jeffery's thoughts scrambled back to the luncheon. He had thought for certain she'd indicated a plan to retire and rest, but he must be mistaken. It might be better to play along with these ladies, if they were intent on continuing their matchmaking. "I would be delighted to join her, if possible."

Mrs. Roberts's eyes gleamed. "She was resting for a while after the noon meal, but she went to the post office to check the mail a short while ago. She indicated she might stay in town to shop. I would have accompanied her, but Frances had already asked me to tea." She frowned. "I do hope that wasn't unwise, but she was quite adamant that she would be circumspect."

A knot lodged in the pit of Jeffery's stomach. "I'm sure she will, ma'am. I'm headed to town myself. Would you like me to give her a message if I happen upon her?"

Mrs. Roberts shot a sly glance at Mrs. Cooper. "How kind of you to offer. No message, but if you see her, perhaps you could accompany her home? I would feel much better if I knew a gentleman of your fine reputation was escorting her."

Mrs. Cooper nodded. "Wonderful idea, Wilma. I imagine Beth would be quite grateful to have Mr. Tucker walk her home."

So Brent Wentworth was in town, and Beth was also there, alone. All he could do was hope the young woman didn't run into the rascal while shopping. He tipped his hat as he moved swiftly toward the door. "I'll be on my way then, ladies. Good day."

He pressed his hat onto his head and hurried down the path, lengthening his stride. Clouds had gathered, the sky had blackened, and Jeffery smelled a hint of moisture in the air. The area sorely needed rain after the long, dry summer, but he hoped it would wait until he arrived back home with Beth on his arm. He crossed the bridge over the Powder River, his heels thudding against the planks.

At the edge of town, he stepped onto the boardwalk lining the main street. Wagons rolled past at a leisurely pace, kicking up small puffs of dust under their wheels. Pedestrians lined the boardwalks and streets, most of them miners in town after their shift released. A smattering of women and men dressed in business attire made up the balance, giving the town a rather congested feel.

Where to begin? There were several shops that women liked to frequent, as well as hotels, and more than one restaurant. Surely

Beth wouldn't take early supper away from home when Katherine planned such exceptional meals for her boarders, but he couldn't be certain. Since Mrs. Roberts indicated Beth had come to pick up the mail, he hurried toward Harvey's Mercantile and opened the solid wood door that led directly into the diminutive section housing the post office. Disappointment hit him hard as he scanned the lobby. He'd counted on finding Beth. Only a handful of patrons stood in line for their mail or hovered in corners poring over letters. His own conscience smote him. He hadn't answered the letter from his father as he'd intended. What must his mother think? Father was probably roaring with indignation by now.

Striding to the door, he stepped out onto the covered walk. Raindrops splatted against the dusty street. Women hastened toward doorways while the roughly clad miners ignored the slight inconvenience and went on their way. Jeffery peered at the clusters of people, praying he'd spot the dark-haired young woman he sought. Why hadn't he thought to ask her aunt what she'd chosen to wear?

He strode along the boardwalk, passing Collier's Hardware with barely a glance. His steps slowed at the doorway to Snider's General Store, and he entered, making his way to the counter where an older man wearing a pair of wire-rimmed spectacles finished a transaction with a customer, carefully placing her items into a wooden crate.

The store owner nodded at Jeffery. "Be with you in a minute, Mr. Tucker." He turned to a young boy waiting nearby. "Jimmy, take this box and cart it on over to Mrs. Williams's house. She has a little more shopping to do at the butcher shop." He pivoted back toward the woman. "Will it be all right if Jimmy leaves the box on your porch, or do you want him to put it inside the door?"

She smiled warmly at the boy. "Inside would be nice, if you don't mind. There have been a number of stray dogs running loose in town lately, and I'd hate to have one make off with my eggs."

"Good enough, then. Thank you, ma'am." He dipped his head at the lady and waved at the boy. "Off with you now, and be quick. I may have another order by the time you get back."

"Yes, sir." Jimmy's grin made the freckles dance on his cheeks. "Sure will, Mr. Snider."

The older man swung toward Jeffery. "Now, how can I help you, Mr. Tucker?"

"Has Miss Roberts been in this afternoon? Her aunt suggested I accompany her home if I happened to see her in town."

Snider rubbed his chin. "Let me see. Yes, I believe she was, although it's been a busy day. It might have been yesterday, come to think of it." He gave a quick wag of his head. "It was today, yes, sir. An hour ago, maybe. Not sure where she went though."

Jeffery wasn't sure whether to feel relieved or disappointed. "Thank you. I won't take up any more of your time." He stepped aside as a man in rough mining clothes sauntered up to the counter.

"Sorry I couldn't be more help." Snider waved and turned to his customer.

Jeffery strode to the door and yanked it open, stepping out onto the boardwalk. As he pulled it shut, another thought hit him. What if Beth resented his asking for her and didn't care to be found? She might be enjoying her time alone, as she had been while up on the hill. Still, it seemed most of his time with the young woman had been spent pursuing her to various destinations and very little time making any progress toward a relationship. Somehow that needed to change.

Beth sat in the small café that Brent had suggested and stared at the man. Had she heard him right? "Please say that slower this time."

"I love you, Beth. I always have, and I came to beg your forgiveness for leaving you the way I did." He reached across the table and touched her fingers.

She drew away, not certain what she felt at the moment, but irritation rose to the top. "I have a hard time believing that, even if I wanted to."

His brows hunched together. "What will it take to convince you?"

"You haven't explained why you left me. No word, Brent. Nothing to show why you'd gone." The old pain rose to the surface, along with the fear that she *knew* why he'd gone. Her hand moved to the scar on her arm covered by the dense material of her long sleeves. Somehow he'd found out about her past—her deformity—and pitied her. Or worse yet, was embarrassed to be seen with her. The uncertainty had haunted her waking and sleeping hours since he'd left. But why find her now and declare his love?

He averted his gaze. "I should have told you long ago, but I was so ashamed."

She started at his words. "Why? What happened?"

He lifted his chin. "My mother was dying and sent a telegram asking me to come."

Dismay surged through Beth's heart, and she sat back in her chair. "You should have come to me. I would have wanted to help. I don't understand why you left without explaining, even if time was short."

He turned his face away. "Because she was …"—his voice dropped to a dull whisper—"not a woman a lady like you should spend time with."

Beth's hand crept to her throat, and she gripped the locket resting there. "What are you saying?"

"I don't know any other way to explain than to be blunt. Will you forgive me for being so, Beth?"

She nodded.

"She was a woman of the night. I found her wasting away from a sickness. I couldn't tell you, couldn't allow you to discover what kind of background I had come from. I feared you would despise me. I thought it better to disappear, rather than allow my past to tarnish you."

"Despise you? For something you had no control over? You think me so shallow as that?" Sorrow planted its seeds deep in her spirit. If only Brent realized what she'd hidden for so long, he wouldn't have worried. How well she understood the dread of being discovered—of people shunning you when they did. She couldn't judge Brent for his fear; it would make her a hypocrite. No, she could only forgive.

"Not shallow, but human. Most people can't forgive a past like mine, or a mother dying from such a rough life."

"But I am *not* most people. I thought you knew me better—trusted me more than that."

He bowed his head again. "I'm sorry." The words broke on a husky note. "That's why I came west, to beg your forgiveness. You may never agree to take me back, but I hoped you might allow me the gift of friendship. I want you to know I still love you, but I don't expect it to be returned."

Confusion turned to uncertainty. He still loved her. If only he'd told her the truth before he'd disappeared and left her wounded and bleeding. The news should make her heart race, but surprisingly, it didn't. Yes, there was a small flutter of excitement, but she couldn't claim it was love. Why did he come back now, when she was finding purpose in her life and making new friends?

He reached as though to touch her again, then pulled back. "Have you nothing to say? Am I to assume you want me to leave and never bother you again?"

Beth picked up her teacup and took a sip. "No, I'm not asking you to leave." That much she knew for certain.

His eyes lighted with … something. "So there's hope for me? For us?"

She held up her hand. "Please don't rush me."

He sat back and emitted a soft groan. "I'm sorry. I've done it again, haven't I?"

"You've done nothing at the moment, but I need time, Brent. This is all so unexpected. I can barely wrap my mind around what you've told me. After believing you had abandoned me …" A shiver ran through her body.

"I know. I'll make it up to you, if you'll only give me a chance."

Beth shook her head. "You broke my trust."

"Can you at least consider a friendship?"

She bit her lip. "That might be possible, but I'll not promise more."

"Thank you. But I hope you'll give me another chance to restore your belief in me."

The longing in his voice tugged at Beth's emotions. Her heart had gone out to him over his past, but she had no desire to travel this same path again.

Brent gripped her hand across the small table.

A boot scudded close to their table, and she tugged her hand away, then froze. Jeffery was looking at them from a few feet away, a grim frown marring his handsome face.

Jeffery stood his ground, moving his gaze from Beth to Wentworth. He should have left the café as soon as he'd seen her sitting at the table with that man. What had made him cross the room? A misguided desire to rescue her, like she was some princess needing to be saved? Foolishness. All of it. His trip to town, his eagerness to find Beth, and now this—walking in where he obviously wasn't wanted or needed. He turned away, shoving his hands deep in the pockets of his trousers.

Chair legs scraped the floor. "Jeffery. Wait. Please?" Beth hurried to his side, her fingers intertwined at her waist. "I didn't see you come in."

He let his gaze wash over her. "No. I imagine you didn't."

She winced, and color flooded her cheeks.

Could she be truly embarrassed that she'd been holding Wentworth's hand in public, or was it that she'd gotten caught? More than likely the latter. It wasn't his affair—the two of them were barely friends, if that. He certainly didn't have any claim on Beth, even if his heart desired otherwise.

Beth drew back a step. "Were you looking for me?"

Jeffery kept his eyes riveted on her, refusing to look at Wentworth. One glimpse had been enough to see the barely concealed anger simmering under the surface of the man's placid facade. Wentworth was jealous, and he might well have the right to be, all things considered. Who was this man, and why had Beth wanted to keep her meeting yesterday a secret from her aunt? Apparently Mrs. Roberts didn't know Beth was seeing Wentworth in town, or she wouldn't have sent him off with instructions to find and bring her home. Jeffery's shoulders stiffened. Or maybe that was exactly why she'd done so. "Yes. As a matter of fact, I was."

"Is anything wrong at home?" She gripped his arm. "Is Aunt Wilma all right?"

"She's fine." His words were clipped, but he didn't care. "She knew I was walking to town and asked me to keep an eye out for you. She thought you might appreciate an escort home." He shot a look at the table. "I see she was mistaken, and you *are* being cared for. I assume Mr. Wentworth will walk you home?"

Beth's lips compressed. "I, um …"

Wentworth pushed back his chair with what appeared to be a forced smile and rose from the table. "We were saying good-bye. I'm afraid I have another appointment. You can walk her home, Mr., er …?" He extended his hand.

"Tucker." Jeffery ignored the slight and addressed Beth. "Do you wish me to escort you? I don't want to impose."

She looked at her companion. "I wasn't aware you had an appointment, Brent."

"I was going to tell you, but I didn't have a chance." He stared at Jeffery. "I can cancel it if you're not happy about letting this man walk you home."

"Not at all, I was simply surprised. Why don't you come to the house tomorrow for lunch?"

Wentworth's lips tightened, and he jerked his head to the side. "Could you give me another moment before you leave, Beth?"

Jeffery opened his mouth to object but snapped it shut. This wasn't his affair. He was simply the messenger. He'd done his duty. Now all he could do was wait and see what transpired.

Beth wanted to sink through the floor, but she wasn't sure why. She and Jeffery were friends, nothing more—and at one time she'd thought Brent had been the love of her life. Yet now relief swept through her that she'd made no promises or guarantees to her old beau. She couldn't believe Brent had grasped her hand; the action had taken her by surprise.

After a glance at Jeffery, she moved to where Brent impatiently waited. "What is it?"

He took her elbow and drew her to a nearby corner. "I don't want Tucker to overhear."

She lifted her chin. "Jeffery can be trusted. You were happy he could walk me home. It's not like *you* offered." What business had brought him to town besides her? Had he been completely honest about his reasons for coming?

He gave her arm a gentle squeeze. "You're right. I'm sorry. I didn't realize until Mr. Tucker came how late it is. If it's so important to you, I'll run down the street and tell the person I'm meeting that I need to reschedule." He brushed a lock of hair off her forehead. "Will that make you happy?" The words held a slight edge.

She narrowed her eyes and took a step back. "I'm perfectly happy to walk home alone or with Jeffery. I wouldn't want to inconvenience you."

"I … I didn't mean that at all." He rubbed his chin. "My appointment can wait."

Beth regarded him for several long moments. No hint of deception hovered across his features. "Please, take care of your business. I need to get home so Aunt Wilma doesn't worry. In fact, I'm sure she'll want to know you had a good reason for leaving Topeka."

"About that, Beth." He softened his tone. "What do you think about not saying anything to your aunt for now?"

She stiffened. "Why?"

His mouth curved in a boyish smile. "I'd like to spend a little time together getting reacquainted before we let the world in—you know, just the two of us for now."

"I will not lie to Aunt Wilma."

"Of course not. I'd never ask you to do that." His grin widened. "I suppose I'm just being selfish. I wanted you all to myself for a while. But if it's important to you, we can tell your aunt."

Beth touched his arm as he started to move away. "I'm still not sure it's right to keep your presence from her, but I understand how you feel. I won't lie if she asks, but I suppose I don't have to volunteer any information right now."

"As you wish."

Beth pulled away, but he gripped her hand and gave a courtly bow. What must Jeffery be thinking? She hadn't invited that action, and although Brent hadn't kissed her hand, it made her uncomfortable.

Then, suddenly, she realized Brent's touch hadn't brought a rush of desire. Had everything they'd once shared disappeared when he'd deserted her? Somehow she doubted they could work through the obstacles that separated them and find their way back again.

Brent placed his fingers under her chin and lifted it. "I'm so grateful to have you back in my life that I'll do whatever you say. Thank you for agreeing to see me. I look forward to tomorrow."

Unease dug its talons into her stomach. "Not tomorrow. I don't usually come to the post office every day, and I have no reason to shop this soon again."

His lips drooped. "The next day, then? Please, Beth. We have so much to catch up on."

The unease deepened. "I'll think about it. I'm thankful you explained what happened."

"I hope you'll forgive me. I wasn't trying to pressure you."

She searched his face. "All right. Day after tomorrow, but only for a short visit."

"Thank you." He shot a look toward Jeffery that she couldn't quite fathom. Surely he didn't see Jeffery as a rival. No, that was silly. There had never been anything more than a casual friendship between them. Regret blew a soft breeze over her heart. Was that all she truly wanted? Could she be making a mistake giving Brent even a chance at friendship?

She bid Brent good day and turned toward the man who'd waited so patiently. A sweet contentment bathed her as she slipped her hand into Jeffery's extended arm.

Jeffery gave her a stiff nod. "I'm sorry your friend wasn't able to escort you, Miss Roberts."

Beth blinked. "Miss Roberts?"

"We should probably hurry home." Jeffery lifted his chin, his eyes cool. "The street is busy, so please be careful as we cross and don't let go of my arm." He stepped off the boardwalk and waited as a wagon passed, then moved forward. "I imagine your aunt is wondering what's keeping you."

Chapter Twenty-One

Late that night Beth woke from a dream, panting and writhing in phantom pain. Her arms and legs burned as though drenched in fire. She threw off the blankets and sat up, trying to calm her breathing. It was only a dream—not real—even if it had almost consumed her. Reaching for a match, she lit a candle on the small dresser next to her bedside, then poured water from a pitcher and downed it. The dream was still too close, pressing in on her mind.

She shuddered as the images flashed yet again. The hot coals had pushed into her tender flesh with searing agony. Her arms and legs had flailed, and a wail tore from her throat, then transformed to moans and sobs. Why didn't Mama or Papa come? It felt like days that she'd lain there. Had it been? Or only hours before dusky brown hands lifted her carefully from the ash and cradled her in gentle arms. Cool water dripped over her burning skin, and she was submersed up to her neck in the icy cold water of a stream. Terror filled her anew. First fire, then water. If she didn't burn to death, she would drown. She kicked and screamed, but the hands persisted in holding her down.

She must have passed out, for in the next image she was lying on a bed of soft furs. A woman knelt beside her, crooning words she couldn't understand, but her sweet tone had calmed her. The little girl in the dream had been almost naked, with angry red welts and oozing sores dotting her limbs, neck, and the tender skin of her belly. She moaned and waved her arms in the air, trying to make the pain stop.

The woman took her hands and held them tight while another woman edged closer. She dipped her fingers into a rough-hewn bowl and smoothed something on the angry welts and sores. At first Beth screamed, pulling away, but the woman persisted, all the while crooning soft singsong words. Blackness approached and threatened to suck her under. Beth had emitted such a shuddering cry that she awakened herself from the dream.

She had never remembered this much detail before and almost wished she hadn't tonight. Why now? Something must have triggered it. Willing her hands to quit shaking, she lay down but didn't draw the blankets over her body. If those nightmares reoccurred, she wanted to bolt from the bed as quickly as possible.

"Oh, Father God, it's been too long since I've talked to You, but I know You've tried to get my attention lately. Please make these nightmares go away. Help me sleep without darkness sinking me into another place of torment." She lifted her arm and placed the back of her hand across her eyes. If only it were so easy to block out the images that assaulted her.

"I thought I wanted to remember—to know the truth—but now I'm not sure." She whispered the words, hoping the sound of her voice would keep more memories at bay. Tears slipped down her cheeks, and she swiped them away impatiently. "I don't understand, God. Why did my family desert me or allow the Arapaho to take me? Why can't I figure out what You want me to do?"

Beth waited, hoping and praying that quiet voice she had heard in the past would speak to her spirit again, but nothing came. Had even God abandoned her? The tears welled in earnest now, and she didn't try to stem their tide. She hated being weak, hated crying, but the pain inside wouldn't be denied. First her family, then Brent, now God. Would Aunt Wilma be next? A picture of Jeffery flashed through her mind, and she pushed it away. He wasn't hers to claim.

Then why did a fresh wave of pain accompany the thought?

She needed to sleep and stop wallowing in self-pity. She was a grown woman with a promising career and an aunt who loved her. That should be enough. Besides, Brent had returned with a logical explanation of why he'd left and asked for another chance. Her heart should be rejoicing at the opportunity. It was what she'd longed for, for so many months.

But Jeffery's expression haunted her memory. What had he been thinking when he'd walked into that room and spotted her with Brent? He'd swiftly schooled his features into a calm mask, making her wonder if she'd imagined the initial flash of disappointment.

Drawing in a deep breath, she willed herself to relax. This wasn't the time to sort through the conflicting emotions where Jeffery and Brent were concerned.

There was so much she'd never fully remembered before. The Arapaho warrior who had found her had always been a shadowy, dark figure plucking her out of the ashes. Memories of the Arapaho family who'd cared for her continued to emerge, but she'd managed to block the pain that accompanied that time. The child she'd drawn who had fallen into the fire was her. Beth had known that but hadn't wanted to face it. She had worked years to forget.

She wanted her mother. A rush of memories almost suffocated her. Tender hands had smoothed her hair, and a sweet tone lulled her to sleep. A laughing voice played games, whispering things into her ear that made her giggle. Mama had loved her at one time, so why had she left her behind? Papa—he was more of a hazy figure, a man who worked all the time and didn't give many hugs. Had he been the reason her family abandoned her? Beth strove to remember. There was someone else—someone on the outer edge of her memory. She couldn't quite pull the image back to where she could see it.

Another thought struck her with an almost physical blow. From the little she remembered, her mother had cared, and it was hard to believe she would abandon her child. Perhaps they had all died. If sickness took them while traveling west, it was possible no one on the train wanted to keep her. Deep inside she had known that might be the case but hadn't wanted to face it. If she *had* been abandoned, at least there was the chance someone in her family might experience regret and still want to find her, all these years later. If they were dead, no hope remained.

Beth drove herself deeper into her pillow, determined to forget and go back to sleep. Too many years had passed. Somehow she must move on and make a new life, accepting the fact she would never have the answers she longed for. She clamped her teeth together. She'd cried enough tears in the past and wouldn't do so again. Aunt Wilma loved her, and that had to suffice.

As she drifted into the haze of near sleep, a soft voice somewhere in the distance spoke. *"Trust Me; walk in My path, and I'll show you the way."* That voice again. The same one she'd heard weeks ago. It must be God; Beth knew that with a certainty now, although she had no idea why He deigned to speak to her. She had resisted Him over the years, but He persisted. Gently. Sweetly. Pulling her into the warm circle of His embrace. Trying to persuade her to accept … something. She had yet to understand what.

She rolled onto her side, and the fingers of peace cradled her. Maybe God had heard her in spite of everything.

Wilma raised her head from her reading and listened to the voices in the nearby foyer. Katherine Jacobs's words were distinct, but the low rumble of a man's response was unintelligible. Something in the timbre sent a pleasurable tremor through Wilma's body.

Frances swept into the parlor, clutching her skirt off the floor and walking with a faster step than Wilma had seen in days. "There is a very handsome man in the parlor asking for you. I did not catch his name, but I heard him inquire after Mrs. Roberts." She cocked her head to the side. "Are you keeping a secret from us, Wilma?"

"I beg your pardon?" Wilma felt like a hen holding an attacking predator at bay. What was Frances going on about this time? "I am not hiding anything, Frances, and I do not appreciate you accusing me of doing so. Now what is this foolishness about a man asking for me?"

"It is not foolishness. My goodness, you certainly are in a dither this morning. If you are not careful, you will give yourself heart palpitations."

"Humph." Wilma scowled. No one but Frances could get her feathers ruffled to this degree.

Katherine stepped into the room, her eyes alight. "Mrs. Roberts. I wasn't sure if you were in or not. There's a gentleman caller waiting for you in the foyer."

Frances smirked. "What did I tell you, Wilma?"

Wilma rose to her feet, uncertainty increasing her heart rate. "Is he young? Black hair and dark eyes? Dressed like a gambler or some other no-account scoundrel?"

A man's laughter echoed from the doorway of the room. "No. He's old, has white hair and blue eyes, and dresses like a modestly retired doctor."

Pure joy spun through Wilma. "Caleb!" She stood frozen to the floor in disbelief. "What are you doing here?"

"Is that the only greeting you have for an old friend?" He opened his arms wide and moved toward her.

Wilma didn't hesitate. She didn't give a fig that Frances and Katherine both looked on. She flew into his arms and sighed as he enveloped her in a warm hug. How long had it been since she'd seen this man? At least a year, but she couldn't remember exactly. She drew back and inspected him. The same twinkle, the same bushy brows and tousled hair, but silver instead of the darker gray edges she remembered. Yet it suited him. As did the mustache he sported above his smiling mouth. "You look wonderful."

"As do you." He gave her one last gentle squeeze, then drew back, surveying the two gaping women nearby. "Now why don't you introduce me to these lovely ladies?"

Wilma felt color rise to her cheeks as she took in Frances's knowing look. She'd never hear the end of the way she'd greeted Caleb. "Certainly. Dr. Caleb Marshall, please meet my landlady, Katherine

Jacobs, and her mother, Frances Cooper. Frances is a friend and one I value highly." She stifled a smile. Maybe the compliment would soften the inquisition she was certain to receive once they were alone. "Caleb is an old friend of the family. He and my husband practiced medicine together for several years."

He took Frances's hand in his and bowed over it, giving her a warm smile, then repeated the gesture with Katherine. "I am delighted to meet you both." He turned to Katherine. "Might you have a small room tucked away under the eaves that you're willing to rent for a week or two?"

Wilma beamed. "You're staying? How lovely. Please, Caleb, tell us what brought you to the Oregon Territory? In your last letter you said—"

He held up his hand, and his expression sobered. "Let's talk about that later, shall we?"

Frances's brows rose.

"Of course, Caleb." Wilma sensed her friend honing in on every word the doctor spoke like a prairie hawk hot on the trail of a mouse. She shot Frances an imploring look, praying she wouldn't ask questions. How thoughtless to ask Caleb for details in front of the others. It must concern Beth. She couldn't imagine him coming all this way for enjoyment. And certainly he wouldn't have come only to see her.... Her heart beat a little faster at the possibility. Still, he'd been her husband's business partner and a dear friend, nothing more.

Katherine gestured toward the stairs. "I do have a room, Dr. Marshall. I assume you must be tired after your long trip. Would you care to go up straightaway and freshen up or rest? Do you have bags that need to be brought in?"

He nodded. "They're at the stage station. I asked the agent to hold everything until I could notify him where to deliver it. I wasn't certain I'd find Wilma here, or that you'd have room for another boarder. Actually, I would love to take a walk and stretch my legs after days of sitting." He held out his arm to Wilma. "Would you care to accompany me?"

"Very much. Let me get my wrap from my room and tell Beth I'm leaving." Wilma hurried toward the stairs. If only she could have whisked Caleb away from Frances's prying questions.

She stopped at her room to gather her wrap, then tapped on Beth's door and poked her head inside. Her niece sat hunched over her desk, pencil in hand. "Beth, dear, an old friend has arrived, and I'm going out for a walk. I may be gone for an hour or two."

Beth turned to face her. "Is it someone I know?"

Wilma hesitated, torn between telling her the full truth and setting her to worrying about why he'd come. "He's a business associate of your uncle's." She nodded at the desk. "It looks like you're busy with your work."

"Yes, but I might take a walk as well. I've been sitting too long and dearly need to stretch." She laid down her pencil and rubbed her neck.

"Oh." Wilma started at the words. She couldn't invite Beth along when she wasn't sure what brought Caleb to Baker City. "Where were you thinking of going? The recent rain has made it too wet to sit on your hillside."

"No, I was thinking of going to town and visiting a shop or two." Beth didn't quite meet Wilma's eyes. "I'm not sure yet."

"I see." Wilma didn't care for the hesitation in Beth's reply, but she was in no position to pursue it, since she didn't want to reveal all of her motives either. "Have a good time, then, and I'll see you at supper." She backed out of the room. Somehow she must get Caleb away from the house before Beth caught up with them. Almost racing down the hall, she caught herself and slowed. No need to give Frances something more to question later.

She walked sedately into the room and smiled. "I'm ready if you are, Caleb."

Frances cocked an eyebrow. "I am disappointed. I was visiting with Dr. Marshall."

Wilma's heart lurched. She slipped her hand through Caleb's arm. "We'll have plenty of time to chat when we return. We should go while we still have good light." She didn't want to pull the man's arm off, but urgency forced her out the door and down the steps so fast she almost tripped.

"What's the hurry, Wilma?" Caleb panted beside her as she struck off along the path leading toward the hillside Beth enjoyed. "I wanted a walk, not a race."

She slowed as they rounded the corner. "I'm sorry. I suppose I'm anxious to hear what brought you to town." Squeezing his arm, she mustered her best smile. "And, I have to admit, getting you away from Frances Cooper was high on my list as well."

Jeffery fingered the envelope stuffed in his pocket and scowled. He'd been traipsing up and down the streets of this town for the last half hour. With all that had been going on at the house lately, he hadn't thought about picking up his mail for days. He sidestepped a woman carrying a baby and tipped his hat. "I beg your pardon, ma'am." Better keep his mind on where he was going before he knocked someone over.

He wanted to head straight to the house to find Beth. Having a friend in town hadn't been important when he first arrived, but lately the need pressed in on him with more force. His attempts to know Beth better seemed thwarted at every turn. Right when he'd hoped they might find common ground in their work, Brent Wentworth appeared. What was the man to her, anyway? An old friend or a beau perhaps? He prayed the man was visiting and would disappear as abruptly as he'd come.

The fragrance of chocolate made his mouth water, and he backed up, pausing outside the open door of a candy shop. It had been months since he'd tasted chocolate. He jingled the coins in his trouser pocket and grinned. Maybe he'd buy a few and see if Beth cared for a piece. Most women seemed to love the dark-colored candy and considered it a rare treat. He sauntered into the store, stopping before a glass case.

"May I help you, sir?" An attractive young woman with blond hair piled on top of her head gave him a bright smile.

"Uh, yes, thank you." He pointed at a stack of round-topped chocolate. "What are those?"

"Chocolate with coconut centers. My favorite." She giggled and picked up a set of tongs. "Would you care to try one?"

Jeffery's mouth watered, but he shook his head. "No. But I'll take a dozen, if you please."

She gave a coy smile. "Buying them for yourself, or someone special?"

Annoyance made his words sharper than he'd planned. "Both. I'm in a bit of a hurry."

After wrapping the candy in brown paper, she tied it with a string and slid it across the counter. "That will be three bits, please."

He pulled out some coins and laid them on the counter. "Thank you and good day." As much as he was tempted to unwrap the package and try a piece, he'd sacrifice.

Hurrying down the boardwalk, he dodged pedestrians, anxious to return to the house. Surely Beth wasn't interested in Wentworth to any degree. More than likely the man was an old friend passing through the area wanting to renew his acquaintance. He could have misconstrued the man's actions—after all, Wentworth hadn't offered to walk Beth home and had delegated the pleasant task to him.

The door to a small restaurant opened, and he slid to a halt to keep from bumping into the exiting man, who clearly had his mind on the woman beside him rather than where he was going.

Jeffery started to apologize, then glanced at the woman. "B-Beth?" His heart plummeted to his toes, and he tightened his grip on the package of chocolates.

She drew to a halt and swiveled toward him, her smile slowly fading. "Jeffery. I didn't know you were in town."

Wentworth tucked her hand under his elbow. "Come along, my dear. We've had too little time together, and I don't care to share you." He nodded at Jeffery. "Tucker, isn't it? Have a good day." He swung around and drew Beth with him.

Jeffery glared at the couple as they moved away, suddenly wanting nothing more than to toss the chocolates as far as he could. Better yet, he'd give them to the Jacobs children. He lifted his chin and pivoted the opposite direction, his long strides pounding the board-walk hard enough to drive the spikes deeper into the wood. If only the brisk action would drown out the throbbing of his heart.

Beth started to protest, but the words died on her lips. Amazement, disappointment, and anger had flashed across Jeffery's face in the brief time they'd stood there. Annoyance swelled inside at the high-handed treatment Brent had dished out, and she yanked him to a halt. "That will be quite enough."

He raised a quizzical eyebrow. "What will?"

"I will not be whisked away like some kind of prize when a friend speaks to me. That was rude and unkind. I can't imagine what Jeffery must think."

"Jeffery, is it?" Jealousy seemed to tinge Brent's words for an instant before he cleared his throat.

Had she only imagined the jealous tone?

He patted her fingers still slipped through the crook of his arm. "I *am* sorry, Beth. I didn't intend to be rude, and I had no idea he was a particular friend. I meant it when I said I hated to share the little bit of time we have together. Please forgive me."

She glanced over her shoulder, hoping it might not be too late to hail Jeffery and convey her regret, but he had disappeared in the press of people lining the street. Frustration assailed her. Somehow she must let Jeffery know the snub wasn't her idea.

Her irritation at Brent waned but didn't quite dissolve. "You're forgiven, but he *is* a friend. I hate hurting anyone."

"I understand, and I'll not do something like that again." He drew her closer. "Let's walk awhile, shall we? It's lovely out with no wind or rain at the moment."

Beth nodded and ambled in time with his step, her thoughts drifting. During their time over tea, Brent had been a consummate gentleman. She couldn't understand why her aunt disapproved of him when they lived in Topeka.

Guilt still pricked for not letting Aunt Wilma know of his arrival in Baker City, but she needed to decide how she felt about Brent before she brought her aunt into the picture. The old dear would surely try to convince her to quit seeing him, and Beth wasn't prepared to do that as yet.

If only Aunt Wilma had confided why she disliked Brent, she might better be able to sort through her conflicting emotions. Over the past months she'd gone from hurt and despair to anger and longing. Then recently she'd actually started to forget and move on. Her growing attraction to Jeffery had done that for her, she was sure of it. But after today she doubted their friendship would still be intact.

Brent. What did she really feel about the man walking by her side? Today he'd come close to professing his love again, but she'd silenced him with a sharp shake of her head. It was too soon, and she didn't want to be pushed into a corner. She'd finally forgiven him and set aside what she'd perceived as his abandonment, but there was no reason to rush.

"Penny for your thoughts?" Brent's words drew her from her reverie, and his smile pulled her into his world.

"Kind of wandering, I suppose."

"Anything you'd care to share?" His lazy smile was beguiling.

"Thinking about our time together in Topeka." She almost bit her tongue after the words left her mouth. She hadn't planned on opening that door so soon.

"Beth." They'd reached a quiet section of town, and he paused, drawing both of her gloved hands into his. "Before we go any farther, I …" He closed his eyes briefly, sadness settling over his features.

Concern raced through her. "Go on. What's troubling you?"

"I'm not sure I should say anything." He shook his head. "It's nothing. Forgive me. Let's keep walking." He turned to go.

She gripped his fingers as they started to slide from hers. "Wait. I want to know. Tell me?"

He sucked in a breath and released it in a sigh. "You're sure? I don't want to impose or have you think less of me."

"Very sure. And I certainly won't think less of you for wanting to share what's bothering you. Please go on."

He tucked her hand under his elbow, drawing her forward. Beth allowed him to seat her on a low-backed bench tucked under the eaves of the covered boardwalk. An occasional wagon rumbled past, and footsteps thudded farther up the walkway, but Beth kept her attention on Brent. He appeared troubled, almost fearful. She couldn't imagine what could turn him from talking about their relationship when she'd inadvertently given him the opening.

He swiveled to face her but didn't touch her again. "I'm not sure how to say this."

"It's all right. I'll listen to whatever it is without judging."

"Thank you. You remember me explaining about my mother?"

Pain shot through Beth at the reminder. "Yes. You mentioned she passed away."

He averted his face. "She left a lot of debts, and the creditors are coming after me. I don't know what to do." He met her eyes. "I want to have a future together, Beth, but I can't drag you into a life of worry or poverty. It wouldn't be fair."

Her stomach clenched at the anxiety coloring his voice. All this time she had been judging him, feeling hurt and betrayed, thinking he'd abandoned her, and Brent was suffering too. "I'm so sorry. I wish I could help." Sudden disquiet swept over her. Aunt Wilma hadn't trusted him and hinted at money problems. Had she known about the debt he owed and feared a life of poverty for Beth if they married? Or had he come to Wilma and asked for help and she had turned him away? Neither alternative seemed quite fair nor like her generous, free-handed aunt.

He reached for her hand. "Thank you, but there's nothing you can do. I simply wanted you to know where things stand."

"I have a little money," she admitted. "I don't know if it would be enough, but …"

Brent hesitated, then gently squeezed her fingers. "I don't think I could accept your money. I'll have to figure this out on my own."

"But Brent …"

"Let's change the subject, shall we, dear? Move on to something more pleasant? Or maybe we should finish that walk we started. I don't want to waste another minute in your company thinking about distressful subjects such as debt and bills." He mustered a bright smile. "I'm sure it will work out. I should not have burdened you with my problems."

Beth allowed him to draw her to her feet, but all the while her thoughts swirled. Brent was in trouble, and she had misjudged him.

Aunt Wilma wouldn't lend a hand, even though Beth was certain she had the wherewithal to do so. Even if Beth no longer loved him, somehow she must find a way to help.

Chapter Twenty-Two

Isabelle's hands shook as she stirred the pot of stew simmering on the stove. Steven had only been home for five days, and his boss was already talking about sending him back to Baker City. Mines were booming there, and the bank wanted to make as many loans as possible before the winter snow set in.

Steven stepped up beside her and gently took the ladle from her hand. "Go sit down, Ma. I can care for this as well as you. You shouldn't have tried to fix a big meal. Stew was plenty without the biscuits and pie."

She perched on the hard chair he'd pulled close. "I'm fine. A little tired is all." Isabelle forced a smile. "How many more trips do you think Mr. Smothers will require you to take? Surely once you return from this next one, it will be the last until spring."

He twisted his mouth to the side. "I doubt it will be the last, but I know it won't continue into the spring." Steven's gaze darted away from hers and focused on the wall behind her.

Fear settled in. "What is it, Son? What *aren't* you telling me?"

"It's nothing. Or, at least, I don't think it will amount to anything to worry about."

"Steven, I do not have the energy to play guessing games. Out with it."

He dropped the ladle against the inside of the pot and sank into a nearby chair. "All right. Knowing you, you'll worry more if I don't tell you."

"Well then?"

"The bank is opening a new branch in Baker City in less than two months."

Isabelle brightened. "Why, that's good news, not bad. If they have a branch there, they won't have to keep sending you. So this might be your last trip. I'm glad. Why were you afraid to tell me that?" Foreboding smote her. "They aren't going to let you go because they have a man doing the same job over there, are they? That wouldn't be fair."

"No, my job is safe. In fact, it looks like I'll be getting a promotion." His eyes clouded, and he averted his gaze again.

The joy that had sprung up quickly withered. "You don't sound happy about it."

"I would be if they hadn't put a condition on it." He pivoted toward her. "They won't have a position for me at this bank once they open the new branch office, and they want me to transfer to Baker City. It means we have to move. I can take this one last trip and then move to Baker City … or find another job. They'll let me have a week or so off so we can find a place to live."

Isabelle stared at her son, unable to take in what he'd said. She placed her hand against her cheek. "You want me to leave my home? My friends? I've lived here for years." She tightened her fingers into a fist. "That's too much to ask. Everyone knows where I live. What if Bess comes asking?" Her voice rose to a high pitch, and her entire body shook. "What if she's trying to find me? She wouldn't know where to look."

Steven jumped from his chair and put his arm around her shoulders. "Calm down. Take deep breaths. We'll work it out. Don't worry. I'll quit my job and find something else." He almost lifted her from the chair. "You need to lie down and rest. Supper can wait."

She allowed him to half carry her to the bed and didn't protest as he placed her against the pillow. Weariness swamped her until she felt like a boat adrift, sinking beneath storm-tossed waves. "I can't let you give up your job, Steven. That's not fair to you either." A tear trickled down her cheek, but she didn't have the energy to brush it aside. "Not fair to either of us." She averted her eyes, saddened at her weakness and the agony reflected on his face. "I'm sorry. So sorry. I haven't been a good mother to you. All these years grieving for what might have been and making you stay put, caring for a sick old woman."

"You haven't made me do anything, Ma. It's an honor to care for you, and we'll find a way to make this work. Rest now and try to put everything else out of your mind."

Isabelle turned onto her side and pulled the blanket up under her chin. If only she could follow his advice and wipe her memory clean. *Rest.* She barely knew what the word meant anymore. It had been seventeen long years since she'd experienced a day of true peace, and somehow she didn't think it would happen anytime soon.

Wilma paced her room, unsure what she should do. She hadn't felt such a combination of joy and sadness in a long time—not since her husband had died. That event would have destroyed her had it not been for the incredible joy Beth had brought into her life. And now Caleb Marshall's arrival stirred a sense of delight that made her bounce out of bed each morning. They'd spent the past three days catching up on old memories and renewing their friendship, but she'd held back from discussing the real reason he'd come to town.

Her letter had brought him; she had no doubt of that. So many times since writing and begging him to help learn more about Beth's past she'd wished she'd let well enough alone. The girl had started to settle lately. She was even getting out more often—going to town and not burying herself in her room, hunched over that desk. It had to be Jeffery, although they didn't talk to one another at mealtimes or act as though they were interested. It must be a ploy. They didn't want anyone to inquire until they'd spent more time together and came to some type of agreement.

And digging up the ghosts of Beth's past might not be the best thing. If only she hadn't asked Caleb to see what he could discover. But if she hadn't, would he have come? Her heart lurched at the thought. She was glad he had arrived. She hadn't realized how bland her life had become. Regretting her decision wasn't to be tolerated. Trusting God with the outcome would be best.

It was time she faced what he'd come to tell her. Trust required action, and sitting in her room wallowing in fear was certainly the opposite of trust. God was big enough to take care of Beth, no matter the outcome. She grabbed the knob and wrenched open the door, then hurried down the stairs. Caleb sat in the parlor, his silver-crowned head bent over a newspaper. "Caleb? Would you have time for a cup of tea?"

He raised warm eyes. "With you? Absolutely."

Her heart fluttered. "I thought we might go to town, if that's all right."

For an instant his forehead creased; then he relaxed. "Certainly. I'll go to my room and fetch my coat and hat."

Caleb hastened across the room, stepping aside and nodding as Frances entered the parlor. "Mrs. Cooper, how nice to see you."

"Dr. Marshall, I was hoping to speak with you about a medical concern, if you could spare a moment?"

Caleb shot a glance at Wilma, and she briefly closed her eyes. The last thing she wanted was to hurt Frances, but why did she have to pick right now to swoop in with her questions? "I'd be glad to help, Mrs. Cooper, but might I ask if we could talk later? I have an appointment with this lovely lady." He held out his arm, and Wilma slipped her hand into the crook of his elbow.

A knowing look crossed Frances's face, and she smirked. "Of course not. I certainly would not want to stand in the way of you courting my dear friend."

Wilma's mouth gaped, and her words came out in a stutter. "Wh ... wh ... what are you talking about, Frances Cooper? How dare you insinuate ..."

Frances didn't so much as blink. "I did not insinuate anything. I am merely speaking what is obvious to anyone who is not blind and possibly some who are. There is no reason for you to get in a huff about it either. Dr. Marshall seems to be a gentleman, is well educated, and appears to care for you. It is not as though you are a young girl in the first blush of spring, Wilma. I would think you would be happy to be courted and not make a fuss just because a friend points it out."

Caleb actually chuckled. "Frances Cooper, I do believe we might end up becoming friends. I like you, although I'm sorry you've embarrassed Wilma. And yes, I care for her and have every intention of courting her if she'll allow it."

Frances gave a decisive nod. "She would be a fool to say no, and if she does, you can rest assured I will have something to say to her about it."

Wilma pulled from Caleb's grasp, her entire body shaking. "I'll thank you both not to discuss me as though I'm not here. I believe I'm too tired for that walk right now, Caleb, and since Mrs. Cooper wanted to talk to you about her health, this might be the perfect time." She marched primly out of the room, Caleb's weak protests almost drowned out by Frances's loud snort of disapproval.

Regret and guilt instantly pricked at Wilma's heart. She cared for Caleb but had never thought seriously about courting. He'd been her husband's friend and had never before hinted at a romantic relationship. The disappointment blanching his face before she turned away shouted his surprise and distress, and she hated that she'd hurt him. But why would Caleb proclaim his feelings so publicly and in front of Frances Cooper, of all people? Wilma was mortified—and she'd never hear the end of it from Frances.

Jeffery smoothed out the letter on his desk again and read it for the third time in as many days. The single page from his publisher brought both pain and rejoicing—for completely different reasons— but both of them centered on Beth. He had so wanted to share the contents with her, but every time he'd checked her old haunts in the house or outdoors she had been missing. He had an idea where she'd disappeared to for the past several days. He ground his teeth. That man must still be luring her to town.

Could she possibly be falling in love with Wentworth? The thought made his heart drop like a lump of coal in his chest. He didn't know when she'd carved such a deep crack in the wall he'd built or why. No, that wasn't being honest. He knew exactly why. She was lovely in every way that mattered. He longed to get better acquainted and chafed at the distance that had grown between them since Brent Wentworth arrived in town.

He straightened and set the letter aside. Did Mrs. Roberts know of the man's attentions toward her niece, and did she approve? If so, wouldn't she insist on acting as a chaperone? From all he'd seen of Mrs. Roberts, she appeared to care greatly about propriety. That might be cause for deeper reflection, especially if Beth continued to absent herself from the house.

And what about her work? Had she turned in all her illustrations, or had she abandoned her drawing while spending so much time with Wentworth? He plucked the letter off the wood surface again and held it up to the light, perusing the words once more. Yes, it clearly stated they'd hired E. Corwin as the illustrator, and the first installment was to release in the magazine a week from today.

His palms moistened. What would Beth—and the others—think when they saw his story in print? Would they approve of what he'd done?

Jeffery slipped the letter back into the envelope and placed it in his jacket pocket. Sitting in this room and moaning over not having Beth in his life wouldn't solve anything. Resolve straightened his spine. Beth would see him and talk to him, whether or not Wentworth liked it. She had the right to celebrate this news as much as he.

Jeffery strode to the door, his heart lifting at his decision. He made it all the way to the top of the staircase leading to the parlor when another thought struck him with greater force. He knew Beth was the illustrator, so it only stood to reason the publisher—also her employer—would have sent her the same letter. She hadn't sought him out to share her joy or excitement. His steps slowed, and he halted. She already knew, and she didn't care. There was no other explanation possible.

Footfalls paused outside Beth's room, then went back the way they'd come. Aunt Wilma? How strange. If she remembered correctly, her aunt planned a trip to town with Dr. Marshall—Dr. Caleb as he'd asked to be called—and couldn't have returned yet. She had been due to leave a scant thirty minutes ago, and she wouldn't have broken her appointment.

Beth read the letter again, then dropped it on her bed. She'd considered talking to Jeffery more than once since it arrived, but he'd been distant ever since he'd bumped into her and Brent in town. Besides, he'd surely have received the same type of missive as she, and he hadn't put out an effort to discuss the subject. Aunt Wilma was her priority, not Jeffery.

She opened her door and stepped into the hall, grateful her aunt's room was close by. More than likely Jeffery was hunkered over his desk working on his next book. A pang of guilt smote her—she'd turned in three of her four illustrations, but the last one was due soon. Would Jeffery be happy with the work she had accomplished so far?

Beth tapped at the adjacent room. "Auntie? Are you in there?"

"I'm resting for a while, dear." The quavering voice barely penetrated the door.

"Is something wrong? I thought you were going to tea with Dr. Caleb. May I come in?"

"No. I'm fine. You go along, and I'll join you later." The words were subdued.

Beth wanted to swing the door wide and see what was wrong, but she hesitated, hating to impose. Her aunt had been busy since the doctor arrived, so it was possible fatigue had set in. "All right. I'll check on you in an hour or so."

She moved away. Brent wanted to meet again today, but Beth hadn't felt it wise. Aunt Wilma had been so wrapped up in renewing her relationship with her old friend that she'd not noticed Beth's absences. But something else held her back. Brent had mentioned his debts again. If nothing else than because she once cared for him, she wanted to help, but this last mention bothered her. She craved time apart to think things through. Maybe a brisk walk out to her hill might be in order.

With a purposeful stride she headed down the hall and rounded the corner toward the stairs.

Jeffery came to an abrupt halt and gripped her shoulders. "Pardon me. One more step and I'm afraid I'd have toppled us both."

Beth's skin tingled under the fabric where his hands lay, and she drew away. "Jeffery. I didn't hear you come down."

He twisted his mouth in a wry grin. "That's because I stopped not long ago and stood there considering whether I should knock on your door and ask you to join me, but I went back to my room. I reached the conclusion that going to the parlor might be a better choice. I started out with that in mind when you rounded the corner."

Beth's spirits rose. "You wanted me to join you? Is anything the matter?"

"Not at all. We haven't spoken in some time as you've seemed … occupied lately." His intent gaze didn't leave hers.

Beth felt a flush steal up her cheeks, but she didn't look away. "I'm sorry, Jeffery. For everything."

He held up his hand. "It's all right. I have no right to interfere in your business or your life."

Beth glanced around the hall, hoping no one else was nearby, then nodded toward the stairway. "Should we go down to the parlor? Aunt Wilma is resting in her room, and I'd hate to have our voices disturb her."

"Certainly." Jeffery waited for her to precede him.

Beth stopped on the landing at the bottom and turned toward him. "You misunderstood. I was mortified by the way Brent treated you when we met in town. I informed him that you are my friend, and I didn't appreciate his behavior."

Jeffery lifted a brow. "Truly? I must say I'm a bit mystified by that assessment."

"In what way?" Beth peeked into the kitchen as they passed, but no one was about. Relief flooded her at the hush over the house. Katherine and Mrs. Cooper must have gone to town or to one of their quilting meetings.

Jeffery showed her to a chair in the parlor, then seated himself nearby. "We've spoken little since our time on the hillside. I had hoped we might grow to be friends—if not ..." He halted briefly, then continued. "I cannot say we've had ample opportunity to get acquainted to the degree that anything ... could develop." He sat back and crossed his ankle over his knee. "Would you?"

Beth felt as though she'd stepped from a warm bath into a cold lake. It wasn't that Jeffery was putting all the blame on her for their lack of friendship ... that wasn't the case at all. No, it was her own heart convicting her of pulling away from something she thought she'd wanted. How could she be so conflicted? Jeffery was a kind man, talented, intelligent, and handsome. But Brent—well, Brent had stolen her heart in the past, and now that she understood his situation she wanted to help if she could. But it wouldn't be kind to mention his circumstances to anyone else. "I suppose not. I *am* sorry, Jeffery. It's my fault."

His eyes widened, and he laughed.

Indignation threatened to choke her, and she gathered her skirts and stood. "If you will excuse me."

He rose and grasped her hands. "No, Beth, I was not laughing at you. Please. Sit back down and let me explain."

Uncertainty froze her, then she perched stiffly on the edge of her chair. "What is there to explain? You made it quite clear what you think."

Jeffery settled into his chair. "I laughed, not at you, but because this is what inevitably happens between us."

She wrinkled her nose, still not clear what he implied. "What happens?"

"We spend half the time we are together going in circles and apologizing. Now here we are once more. And, I must say, it's my turn." The twinkle in his eyes dimmed, and he leaned forward. "I hurt you and I didn't mean to. It was uncharitable to laugh and uncouth of me to lay any blame at your feet. I truly do beg your pardon."

Beth's lips twitched, and she giggled. He stared at her. She giggled again and covered her lips with her fingertips, but a full-throated laugh burst forth.

Jeffery watched the young woman with ever-growing admiration. Not only had she taken a step back from her chagrin, she'd turned the tables on him and laughed. Most women he'd known would have stomped off and pouted for the next twenty-four hours, but not Beth Roberts. She was truly a woman to be admired.

He coughed, buying himself time to regain his composure. "So I would venture a guess that we are in agreement. No more begging forgiveness. At least not today."

She grinned. "Not today. But earlier you said you had something to tell me. Was that it, or is there more?"

He placed his hands on his knees and leaned forward, wiping all vestiges of humor from his face. "By chance, did you get a letter this past week? From our publisher?" Now Jeffery could barely keep the silly grin from taking over his face.

Her expression stilled. "Yes. I wanted to speak to you about it, but you seemed so—distant, somehow. I assumed you didn't care to discuss it."

"I understand. I hated to trouble you as well. But that is behind us now. Did they tell you the first issue releases next week?"

Beth started. "No. Only that my work was being used in a new series of stories by Jeffery Tucker and would be releasing soon." Her cheeks dimpled in a sweet smile. ""I'll admit I felt a flash of pride that I know you."

Surprise coursed through Jeffery, and he sat back. She was proud of what he'd done? He had assumed she barely tolerated his writing. At least, she'd made it clear initially that she'd felt that way. He couldn't remember the last time someone declared they were proud of him. "Truly?" He cleared his throat. "I must say, I appreciate your confidence in me, when you haven't read the story yet. I hope it won't give you reason to regret your statement or having your name associated with my work."

Her face sobered for an instant, then softened. "Ah, but my name isn't connected to your story, remember? Only that of Elizabeth Corwin. And I'm certain I'll be more than happy with what you've written. I assume they'll send me a copy as well. Maybe we could read it together?" Her eyes lit with merry anticipation.

Jeffery nodded, his heart swelling with joy. "I would love that. Thank you." He bit his tongue to keep the rest of his thoughts to himself. If he hoped to win Beth's heart, he had to do something about Brent Wentworth.

Chapter Twenty-Three

Wilma wanted to throw something at the wall, but nothing suitable presented itself. A pillow would bring no satisfaction at all, and destroying a perfectly useful book or piece of bric-a-brac wouldn't improve her mood. She almost wished she'd allowed Beth to enter an hour ago, but she'd needed time to sort through her thoughts. Now that they were sorted, she was angrier at herself than Caleb. Confused by his response, certainly, but she had no right to be upset by his proclamation. Although she still wished he'd not stated his feelings in front of Frances.

A knock sounded at her door, and she sat upright, swinging her feet to the floor. Beth. Should she tell her what happened with Caleb or continue pretending she wanted to rest? "A moment, please." She smoothed her hair and straightened her clothing. "Come in."

"It's Caleb." His voice echoed through the thick wooden door. "I don't want to impose, but I think we should talk."

Wilma's heart pounded like a horse pulling a fire wagon to a blazing structure. Caleb. Why hadn't she thought what she'd say to him the next time they spoke? She'd spent the last hour moaning over her rude behavior and Frances's reaction. She couldn't invite Caleb into her room, and she wasn't certain she'd know what to say if she met him downstairs. "Umm, I was resting." That sounded ridiculous even to her own ears, so she walked to the door and drew it open.

Caleb took a step back. "I'm sorry I distressed you. I wanted you to know that I plan to take a room at the hotel tonight and leave town tomorrow." He turned and strode away from the door.

Wilma's stomach sickened. "Wait, Caleb. Please." She grabbed her cloak and wrenched the door wide, almost bounding into the hall.

He swung around. "What is it, Wilma?"

She halted beside him and rested her fingers on his arm. "I am the one who should apologize for treating you in such a disrespectful manner when you paid me the honor of declaring your interest. My behavior was unforgivable."

Caleb laid a gentle hand over hers. "You weren't disrespectful. I took you by surprise, and I spoke out of turn in front of a virtual stranger."

Wilma gave a weak laugh. "Frances is a friend, although at times she does act more like a fencing partner. While I would have preferred she not be privy to your declaration, there's no lasting harm done. Would you still care to walk to town and have tea together?"

A cautious smile warmed his face. "What do you say we tell Mrs. Jacobs we won't be here for supper? Would that be acceptable?" His eyes darkened. "That is, if you care to be in my presence that long?"

"I'd love to." She withdrew her hand from his. "But Caleb— about what you said downstairs …"

He shook his head. "Wait. You don't have to say anything. Let's set it aside for now, shall we? We'll go have a bite to eat and visit about other things."

"I'd like to explain, if you don't mind?" Wilma managed. "And I'd prefer to do so here, with no one around, rather than in a crowded restaurant or down in the parlor."

"All right."

"You did surprise me. I had no idea you felt that way."

He started to reply, but she held up her hand. "Please. I need to finish. I care for you, Caleb, but I'm not certain if it's only friendship or something more. I don't even know if I want to be courted. It seems so strange at my advanced age to think about courting."

He snorted. "You are not a bit old. You're almost a decade my junior and still a young woman. Quite a lovely one, if I may be so bold."

She felt warmth creep into her cheeks. "I'm close to fifty, and I'm not foolish enough to believe your sweet flattery, but I thank you for your kindness. All I'm asking is that we remain friends."

Caleb's brows drew together. "Friends?"

"For now. I can't make any promises, but …" She plunged ahead, wondering if she'd regret her words. "I think it's possible I might be interested in courting sometime in the future, if you're willing to wait and give me a chance to get used to the idea."

His expression softened, and he grasped her hands. "I could kiss you right now, Wilma Roberts, but I won't. I'm not going to push you, even though it's what I long to do. I'll give you as much time as you need." A grin tugged at his lips. "Keep in mind we're neither one of us getting any younger."

Something delicious fluttered in her heart. "I certainly will." Wilma tucked her hand into the crook of his arm and sighed. So this is what had brought Caleb to the West, not news about Beth.

Maybe she could wait a little longer to ask if he'd discovered anything else. They'd waited all these years, so another day or two surely wouldn't make a difference. Tonight belonged to her and Caleb, and she intended to enjoy every minute of it.

Beth had lingered long enough. The past few days of meeting Brent she'd swung from anger to cautious acceptance to a willingness to help, if not to rebuild a friendship. After today she was bordering on anger again. She snatched her reticule off the chair beside her and rose.

A waitress bustled over, carrying a coffeepot. "Would you care for a refill, miss? I'm sorry to take so long getting back to you. Are you ready to order?"

"No, thank you. The person who planned to join me was detained, so I'll pay for my coffee." She smiled, hoping to soften her departure, and made her way to the cashier. After pressing a nickel into his hand, she hurried out the door.

Beth shivered and rubbed her hands over her arms, suddenly conscious of her scars. This was exactly what had happened in Topeka. She'd made an appointment to meet Brent, and he hadn't appeared. No word, no letter waiting at home, no hint of what might have happened. Fear had almost driven her to despair until she'd gone to her aunt. That lady had promised her Brent was well and intact but had left town suddenly and wouldn't be returning.

Beth had always assumed that somehow Brent had gotten wind of her past, but Aunt Wilma assured her that wasn't the case. But she would never explain *why* he had left, only pressed her lips together and made it clear she had no use for the man, and Beth was better off without him.

Now she thought she understood why, although she'd never seen her aunt as a snob. Somehow Aunt Wilma had discovered Brent's mother's past and didn't want Beth soiled by her reputation. Was it possible Aunt Wilma had learned of Brent's arrival in Baker City and told him to leave? She paused outside a bakery, and her stomach grumbled at the delicious smells wafting out the open door.

How unfair of her aunt if that were the case. Determination pressed Beth forward. It was time to seek out Aunt Wilma. She had waited long enough to hear the truth.

Beth stepped off the boardwalk and wove between the wagons parked in front of the mercantile. She stopped to check for traffic and lifted the hem of her skirt, stepping over the spots of mud left by last night's rain shower.

"Miss Roberts." A man's voice that sounded vaguely familiar swung her around. Isaac Lansing peered at her from under his bowler hat. Clearly not the same hat the bucket of paint had landed on, as this one appeared quite unscathed.

Beth drew back, not caring for his frown. "Yes?"

"Meeting you has saved the sheriff a trip to the Jacobses' boardinghouse. I assume you still live there?" He cocked his head toward the silent law officer standing nearby.

The sheriff reached into his vest. "I'm terribly sorry to do this, Miss Roberts." He extended an envelope. "You'll need to see that Micah Jacobs reads it, as well as your aunt. Is that clear, miss?"

Beth stood stupefied. "I have no idea *what* you are talking about. What does Mr. Lansing have to do with you or Mr. Jacobs or my aunt?"

"I can't tell you more, Miss Roberts." The sheriff jerked his chin toward Lansing. "I am required to serve you the papers this gent's attorney drew up."

Lansing smirked and stuffed his hands in the pockets of his tailored jacket. "What it means, Miss Roberts, is that you all are being sued. Have a good day." He stepped back onto the boardwalk, his retreating footfalls beating a tattoo that matched the pounding of Beth's heart.

Jeffery couldn't sit still. The hours since he and Beth had talked yesterday had dragged, and he'd been haunting the parlor hoping to catch a glimpse of her again. He'd assumed she'd be around this afternoon after their friendly parting, but Mrs. Roberts and Dr. Marshall had returned minutes ago with no sign of Beth. Could she still be seeing Wentworth? The thought sickened him.

Footfalls pattered up the outside steps, and the front door flew open. Beth launched herself over the threshold, panting and clutching an envelope. "Aunt Wilma? Katherine? Is anyone here?" She slammed the door shut but didn't appear to notice.

Jeffery stepped into the foyer and touched her arm. "Is anything wrong?" He moved to her side. "Do you need to sit down?"

"Nothing. Everything." Her eyes closed for a second. "I need to see Katherine or Mr. Jacobs. Are they home?"

A skirt rustled behind them, and Katherine appeared in the doorway. "What's all the fuss about?" She laid her hand on her stomach. "Are you all right, Beth?"

Mrs. Cooper appeared behind her with Mrs. Roberts and Caleb right on her heels. Mrs. Cooper stared at the envelope. "Did you receive bad news, my dear? You are quite pale. Wilma, I do believe your niece could use a cup of that tea we were sharing in the kitchen."

Mrs. Roberts nodded at Mrs. Cooper. "I'll be right back. Take care of her, Frances."

"Of course." She ushered Beth to the sofa and settled her into it.

Jeffery followed, wishing he had thought of the tea or even leading her to a chair. The three women who'd descended on the parlor seemed to have things well in hand. "Maybe we should leave you ladies to deal with this. I'm not sure I'm needed." He eyed Dr. Marshall.

Caleb shook his head. "I was thinking the same."

Beth's chin rose. "No. Please don't go. You need to hear this too." She patted a place on the sofa. "Sit down, all of you." She turned to Katherine. "Is Mr. Jacobs at home?"

"No, he's at work, and then he's going to pick up the children from school, but that won't be for another couple of hours." Katherine smiled at Mrs. Roberts, who set a cup of tea on the table near Beth's elbow. "Take a sip of tea, gather your thoughts, and as soon as you're able, tell us what happened."

Beth drew in a shaky breath. "Thank you." She held up the envelope. "This is addressed to all of us. Well, excepting Mr. Tucker, I suppose."

Jeffery had no desire to sit. He wanted to rip open the envelope and discover what had distressed Beth so. But it wasn't his place. She said it didn't concern him directly, but she wanted him to stay. He wished he'd had the nerve to take the seat beside her.

Mrs. Roberts edged onto the sofa beside her niece. "What's this all about?"

"I bumped into Mr. Lansing in town."

Jeffery stiffened. "Lansing? Did he accost you again?"

"No," Beth managed, "but he gave me this. Or rather, he had the sheriff hand it to me, as he was planning on coming out here to serve it, he said. I don't understand, but it sounded ominous."

"Have you opened it?"

"No. He said I should give it to Mr. Jacobs, so I hesitated to read it." She held out the missive to Katherine. "He's suing us."

Mrs. Cooper erupted. "The nerve of that low-down, calculating, miserly snake of a man. Suing us? Whatever for?"

Katherine held up her hand. "Give me a moment, and we'll see." Her face had paled but her voice was calm. She perused the document, then raised troubled eyes. "Micah needs to see this, as I'm certainly no lawyer, but it doesn't sound good."

Jeffery stepped close to her side and held out his hand. He hadn't planned to share this information, but it seemed the right time to do so. "My father is a retired judge, who comes from a family of statesmen. Maybe I could help?"

Her brows rose, but she gave him the paper without comment.

Jeffery took it to a lamp and took his time, digesting each word. Finally, he raised his head. "Mrs. Jacobs, in short he's suing your business, but naming you and Mr. Jacobs, for damages to his person

and mental faculties after the ... ah ... incident with the paint can.
Mrs. Roberts, he's suing you for harassment and assault with intent
to do bodily damage. Beth is named along with you, although it
doesn't specify why. Possibly because you were there when it happened, although I'd be more apt to believe it was because Beth
rejected his advances."

Mrs. Roberts waved her hand in the air. "You were there also,
Mr. Tucker, and you aren't named."

"No, ma'am, I'm not. I don't think he could come up with a
reasonable charge against me, or I'm sure he would have. Your and
Beth's names are simply linked together, but I'm guessing any judge
worth his salt will dismiss the allegation against Beth."

Mrs. Roberts slumped into the sofa. "I could be ruined." She
turned to Katherine. "I'm so sorry. I shouldn't be thinking of myself
right now. This is my fault. If I hadn't struck the man, your home
and business wouldn't be at risk."

Katherine gave a stiff shake of her head. "Nonsense. It all started
when Micah accidentally toppled that paint can, but we compen-
sated him by not charging a full week's board, which he accepted. We
even asked if he'd care to stay longer, and he declined."

Beth slipped her fingers over her aunt's. "I laughed at his misfor-
tune. I was as much to blame as you, Auntie."

Mrs. Cooper snorted. "Hogwash. Everyone who was there laughed.
The man made a comical sight with that bucket upside down on his hat
and green paint dripping off his chin. He had every right to be upset,
but it is ridiculous to cause such a fuss. And Wilma should have beaten
him within an inch of his life for laying hands on you in that restaurant.
She merely did her duty as your guardian and protector."

Jeffery tucked the letter into the envelope. "I agree. No judge would fault Mrs. Roberts for her actions. I believe she should be commended." He stepped away from the window and extended the missive to Katherine. "You will want to show this to Mr. Jacobs when he arrives. If there is anything I can do to help …"

A heavy foreboding settled over the room. This was the first time in years that Jeffery could recall wishing his father lived nearby. But the thought only lasted for a moment. He didn't want his parents meddling any more than they'd already done, trying to make him return home and take up his father's practice or live on the family's wealth. He needed to handle this himself and show Beth he was more than a drifting writer with only a few prospects.

Not for the first time Beth wished she could have time alone with Jeffery. His calm demeanor and caring attitude soothed her nerves. Why had she ever thought him intrusive or obnoxious? Her thoughts flitted to Brent. Would *he* take the time to speak reassuring words to the others or simply whisk her off to some secluded place where they could be alone? But Brent had been caring since he returned, even if he hadn't evidenced any desire to meet the other boarders in her home. She could only assume that was a result of Aunt Wilma's animosity toward him. "What do we do now? Should we try to find an attorney?"

Jeffery perched on the edge of an overstuffed chair. "I have no idea if there is a law firm in town. It's possible Mr. Lansing has secured the only one, although not probable." He grimaced.

"Where there's a need, there are typically more." He swiveled toward Katherine. "You have lived here for years, Mrs. Jacobs. What is your recommendation?"

Katherine didn't reply, and Beth glanced at her, wondering at the lengthy silence. The pink in her cheeks had faded. Beth got swiftly to her feet and hurried to her landlady's side. "Are you all right?"

She placed her hand over her belly. "I feel a little sick to my stomach."

Frances grunted. "I am not a bit surprised. This business is enough to sicken anyone." She peered at her daughter. "But it is not at all like you, Katherine, to wither under pressure, no matter how troubling. You need to lie down." Frances cut off her daughter's protest. "I know you are a grown woman, and the mistress of this house, but *I* am still your mother, and I know what is best." She rose and took Katherine's hand. "Come along. We cannot take any chances with you in such a delicate condition."

Aunt Wilma emitted a sharp cry, and Beth gasped. Could Mrs. Cooper be implying …?

Her aunt rushed to Katherine's other side and placed a protective arm around her waist. "I had no idea. Why didn't you tell us? You should not be doing as much work as you do, or waiting on any of us." She cast an anxious look at Frances. "You haven't said a word."

Frances lifted her chin. "It was not my place to speak about such things."

Katherine gave a strangled laugh. "*I* haven't said a word to anyone except Micah. Not even to Mama or the girls. Mother, how did you know?"

Frances smirked. "I am not an imbecile, Daughter, nor am I blind. I will admit I did not know for certain until now, although I had my suspicions for a while. If you will remember, I gave birth to two children myself." She eyed Jeffery with amusement. "I beg your pardon if we are causing you embarrassment, Mr. Tucker, but it will be apparent soon enough that my daughter is with child. I see no reason to beat around the bush."

Jeffery tipped his head, but Beth was certain she saw a smile creep onto his face. "I have two younger siblings, ma'am, and a mother who has a fondness for being frank as well. Pray do not concern yourself with injuring my sensibilities."

Beth stepped forward, all thought of the impending trouble from Isaac Lansing suspended. "I can set the table or help prepare the meal if you'd like."

Katherine shook her head. "Lucy and Amanda can take care of the table, thank you." Then she smiled. "I suppose I could allow you to help this one time with supper preparation, if you truly don't mind. The bread is already baked, as well as a cake set aside. Lucy can get jars of applesauce from the pantry when she gets home, and I have vegetables to go in the stockpot for soup."

Beth nodded. "I'll get started right away while Aunt Wilma and Mrs. Cooper get you settled."

Jeffery moved to her side. "And I will assist if you'll advise me what to do. I might not be the best cook, but I can fetch and carry. That is, if you'll permit me the honor of helping?"

Pleasure warmed Beth's heart. "That would be lovely, thank you." She wanted to hold on to this happiness and forget the worries the letter from Mr. Lansing had stirred. Then a cool breeze blew over her spirit, dispelling the warmth. If only this additional trouble hadn't happened right when things seemed to be improving.

She headed for the kitchen with Jeffery on her heels. No sense in worrying about what she couldn't change. The Bible mentioned there being enough trouble in the current day without worrying about tomorrow, and she needed to take that to heart. She'd had more than enough anxiety over things she couldn't control in her life. Surely it wasn't a sin to enjoy some time with Jeffery and allow the business with Lansing and even the problems with Brent to be forgotten—at least for now.

Chapter Twenty-Four

Jeffery watched Beth's graceful form move ahead of him toward the kitchen and had to rein in his thoughts. Shame coursed through him. This woman wasn't his fiancée or even someone he was courting. He had no right to imagine their relationship, which had yet to evolve into anything deeper, was more than casual friendship.

He averted his gaze and tried to concentrate on the document he'd read. Surely Lansing would know the Jacobses weren't wealthy people, and he didn't stand to gain much by pursuing his suit. It was spite, pure and simple. He'd met men of a similar nature. They hated to be thwarted, ridiculed, or held in low esteem—and it had been apparent from the first that Isaac Lansing had the highest regard for his own person, whether warranted or not.

They arrived in the kitchen and Beth halted, hands on her trim hips. She tipped her head to the side, resembling a princess surveying her kingdom. "I'm always surprised by how perfectly Katherine maintains this room. I don't know how she keeps up with all the work, even with Lucy's and Mrs. Cooper's help."

Jeffery moved over to the cupboard where a stockpot rested. "I'm quite certain you will do an admirable job in your own home someday." He gave her a warm smile.

She busied herself at the washbasin. "I imagine I'll live with Aunt Wilma until I'm old and gray." Her light laughter tinkled musically across the kitchen. Happiness filled every corner of the room.

"I'm guessing some fortunate man might have other ideas," he quipped back.

Her laughter stilled. "Somehow I doubt that, but it's kind of you to say so. The vegetables are laid out and clean; they simply need chopping. Are you handy with a knife?"

He smirked. "Yes, I believe I can handle that task." He moved up beside her and peered into the basin. "Do you want me to cut them in the basin or into the pot?"

"The pot, I think." Beth scrunched up her nose. "I guess I should have asked more questions, but I don't think it will hurt to toss them all in at once. Katherine has the stock ready to go. I'll scrub the potatoes while you slice the carrots and onions." She giggled. "I hate chopping onions; they make me cry."

They worked side by side in silence for several minutes until Jeffery could stand it no longer. Just being near her stirred his senses. She stood so close that a loose strand of her hair persisted in finding its way onto his shoulder as she bent over the sink. Everything about her intrigued him. It amazed him that she could still laugh with all the troubles piling around her. Where did that kind of peace come from?

He rocked back on his heels and set the knife down on the counter. "How do you do it?"

She raised a startled gaze to his. "What? Clean potatoes?"

He choked on a laugh. "No. I mean, how can you still smile and joke when you and your aunt are being named in the lawsuit?

I've seen you upset before, but you never appear to let things go very deep."

"You're wrong, Jeffery. If only you knew …" Thoughtfulness smoothed her face. "I've worked hard lately to trust the Lord and not carry everything myself. You're a Christian, aren't you? I've seen you in Sunday services several times since we arrived."

He shrugged. "As much as the next man. My family was faithful in their church attendance while I was at home, and I was baptized at an early age. I accepted Jesus when I was a child, so yes, I'd say I'm a Christian. I'm not certain what God has to do with the lawsuit or anything else that's going on though." He let the chopped carrots fall from his hands into the pot. "All done but the potatoes."

"Thank you." She handed him a clean spud and resumed her work. "I'm discovering that God wants to be involved in everything we do."

Jeffery snorted. "I'm sorry, but I cannot see God being concerned with the mundane details of our lives. I suppose it would be appropriate to ask for His intervention on behalf of everyone named in the suit, but anything much smaller than that, I can't agree."

"But why?" Beth turned wide eyes on him. "If He created us, why would He then abandon us to our own devices and problems?"

"I assume He has enough on His hands running the universe and wouldn't care to be involved in the petty things of earth."

Beth poured a pot of water over the remainder of the peeled potatoes in the basin. She reached for a towel and wiped her hands, then picked up another knife.

Jeffery wondered at her silence. Had he offended her with his views? He hadn't realized she took her Christianity so seriously. His parents had always given money to their church and been faithful in attendance, but he'd never heard them advocate ideas like this. "Did I say something wrong?"

"No. I guess you're simply making me think about my own beliefs. Aunt Wilma raised me in church as well, and I've often questioned why God lets so many bad things happen to good people. But I don't think it's because He's busy elsewhere. I was taught that He loves us and cares about every detail of our lives, although I'll admit I've wondered at times how that could be true." She worried her lip.

Jeffery studied her, intrigued but concerned at her evident distress. "What's bothering you, Beth?" He spoke the words quietly. Tumbling the last bits of potato into the pot, he laid his knife on the countertop. "I think we're done, and the teakettle is on, as well as coffee. Let's sit for a bit, shall we?"

She nodded, plucking two cups off a shelf and placing them on the table.

Jeffery poured coffee for himself and tea for Beth, then took a seat opposite her. "Would you care to talk about it?"

"Maybe I should." She wrapped her hands tightly around the cup, then lifted it to her lips. "I'm terrified to, but somehow I want to trust you." She murmured the words. "I need to trust you. There have been so many times in my life I …" Tea sloshed over the side as she set the cup on the table.

As soon as the words slipped out, Beth wanted to take them back. What had she been thinking? Maybe she should try to lighten the mood and change the subject. She'd never talked about her past to anyone but Aunt Wilma. Not even Brent.

Jeffery touched her hand. "You can, Beth. I will never betray your trust in any way. Tell me only what you want to, and I swear to you, I'll listen and try to help."

Beth's heart jumped at the warmth of his touch. She longed to intertwine her fingers with his and never let go. How much to tell him, and where to begin? She shuddered at the thought of him knowing about her physical scars, but was there a way to tell him the rest without that? Surely she could. "It's about my past."

He didn't speak, but the pressure of his hand urged her forward.

She plunged ahead. "Aunt Wilma isn't really my aunt."

"I see." He smiled. "So it's a courtesy title, then. She's your guardian."

"Yes. No. I guess I need to start over, as I've already given you the wrong idea." She withdrew her hand, hating to do so, but knowing propriety demanded it. What if someone walked in and saw them? Besides, it was too hard to concentrate on what she was saying when he was touching her, and she'd already started badly.

"I beg your pardon?" Jeffery leaned forward, giving Beth his full attention although his gaze drifted to her fingers entwined on top of the table.

"Aunt Wilma is my guardian, but she never adopted me. I'm an orphan." She blurted out the words, unsure how else to present them.

He gave a slow nod. "That's not unusual, although I'm very sorry it happened. Is that what's been bothering you?"

"Not entirely. It's possible my parents abandoned me when I was young. The doctor who examined me believed I might have been four or nearing four years old when the Arapaho brought me to Fort Laramie."

Jeffery leaned forward in his chair. "The Arapaho. How surprising. Why did they have you?"

"We're not exactly sure, but I've gotten inklings lately. I've had some dreams, and bits of old memories are returning. At first we wondered if they'd kidnapped me, but now I don't think so."

"What kind of memories?"

"I have a vague recollection of a wagon train. I was sitting by a fire, crying …" She wasn't sure she wanted him to know the rest. Why had she ever broached this subject? She sat up straight. "I was injured, and I remember a dark shape looming over me. He picked me up and placed me on some kind of litter pulled behind a horse. That's all I remember about that day. I woke sometime later in a teepee with a woman putting salve on my wounds."

"How were you hurt?"

She paused, unsure how much to tell him. "I may have fallen on some hot coals. I'm not certain."

Jeffery shifted in his chair. "Do you think the Arapaho might have snatched you from your camp while your parents were scouting? Maybe you *were* kidnapped, not abandoned."

"I've wondered that, as well. But the Arapaho weren't on the warpath when I was young, and there was no record of a wagon train being attacked by them. Do you remember seeing a drawing in my tablet of a little girl sitting on the ground crying?"

"Yes. It was quite striking."

"It came to me while I was sitting on the hillside one day. I remembered dust disappearing in the distance, running, crying, falling, then terrible pain. I didn't put it all together at the time. I simply drew what I saw. But lately, I've had dreams …"

"And what of your parents? Surely they wouldn't have left you alone with an injury. Do you have any recollection of them at all?"

"Do you recall when we were sitting on the hillside talking, and I picked a buttercup?"

He nodded.

"That brought back a memory of my mother holding the same flower and plucking off the petals, playing a wishing game with me. I think she loved me when I was little. There are other hazy ones, of a woman holding me and rocking, but I'm not certain if they're of my mother or the Arapaho woman who cared for me."

"So they were kind to you?"

"Very. I even picked up some words. From what Aunt Wilma discovered, I may have lived with them up to five months. They brought me to Fort Laramie in the spring, and the last wagon train went through before the snow closed the passes the winter before, probably no later than early September."

"So you might have been lost from a wagon train." Jeffery sat forward, his glance intent. "Do you remember anything about traveling?"

"No." She fingered the necklace that never left her throat, then lifted the locket so he could see it. "This is the only clue I have to my past." Carefully, Beth pried open the two halves and leaned forward so he could see the miniature portraits.

He stared at it for a minute. "She looks like an older version of you. Of course you have no idea who she or the man might be."

"None. The pictures haunt me and give me hope, both at the same time. Aunt Wilma replaced the chain years ago. The one I was wearing as a child was delicate. For years she made me put the locket away, fearful I'd lose it, but when I turned thirteen I insisted on wearing it. I've not taken it off since."

"I understand." His face was grave. "Not knowing what happened must be difficult. It's possible you could have fallen out of a wagon, you know. Or they might have died on the trail. I can't imagine your parents abandoned you."

"I've thought of that, but don't you think someone would have come looking? Surely they'd have missed me before much time went by. How far could a small child walk in a day? And wouldn't I have run after the wagons?" She shook her head. "There's no telling how long I was out there before the Arapaho found me. That's one of the reasons I believe I was abandoned."

Jeffery gave her a shrewd look. "One reason? Is there another?"

"I'm sorry, it's not something I care to talk about right now."

"I didn't mean to be overly inquisitive." A smile tipped the corners of his mouth. "And don't worry, I would never mention it to anyone or use this in my book."

Surprise surged through Beth. She'd completely forgotten about his novel. She searched his eyes. "Thank you. Truth be told, I hadn't worried you would. Not this time, anyway."

"Hmm, not this time?" Jeffery grinned and winked.

Color rose in Beth's cheeks.

He pushed back his chair, then walked to her side of the table and held out his hand. She accepted it and Jeffery drew her to her feet, retaining his grip. "I'm sorry, Beth. Sorry I ever worried you." His tone softened, and he stepped closer. "I am so glad you felt you could trust me with the pain of your past. I am deeply honored."

Beth barely dared to breathe. The air in the room felt too warm, and she wanted to tug at the collar of her gown. When had Jeffery grown so handsome and—her mind searched for the right word—*charming*? Brent's image rose to her mind, but she pushed it away. She didn't want to be reminded of anything right now except the man who stood so close. "I've never told anyone about my past before. Not even …"

He stiffened. "The man you've been meeting in town? Wentworth?"

She nodded, her heart lodged somewhere in her throat. How could she have forgotten they'd met?

Jeffery dropped her hand. "Are you in love with him, Beth?" His tone held a rough edge.

She bit her lip, unsure of her reply. So much still confused her about Brent, although *love* was too strong a word. He was part of her past, and she had yet to decide where to relegate those memories.

He gave a short nod. "Somehow I hoped …" He turned his head. "Never mind. It is of no consequence."

Beth touched his arm. "Jeffery?" How could she convey the confusion warring inside?

"You do not owe me anything. We're only friends, remember?" A wry smile tugged at his lips, and he touched her cheek with a gentle finger. "Only friends." He took a step back. "I must be going. I have a lot of work to do on my second novel." He cast a look around and frowned. "Did you need any more help with supper?"

"No. The girls will be in to set the table, and all else is ready. Thank you. For listening—for … everything." She paused. "Jeffery?"

"Yes?"

"Maybe I could help you sometime on your story? By listening, I mean. That is, if you'd ever care to share it with me?" There was so much more she longed to say, but the words wouldn't move past the lump in her throat.

He hesitated, then said slowly, "Sometime. I'll see you at supper, Beth."

A deep sense of loss descended upon her as he walked from the kitchen. Only friends he'd said, but from the yearning she'd glimpsed in his eyes, she believed he might have hinted at more. Was that what she wanted? She stepped to the stove and stirred the simmering pot. Why did life have to be so difficult?

Resolve stiffened her spine. Brent hadn't met her for their last appointment, and she still didn't know why. She needed to find him and decide once and for all where her heart stood and what Aunt Wilma was hiding. Strange. She'd never really considered opening her heart and telling Brent her life story. Or maybe it had crossed her mind, but something inside warned her that the risk would be too great.

Wilma scrubbed the last breakfast pot the following morning and gave a sigh of satisfaction. "It feels good to be back in a kitchen again."

Caleb placed the pot in the cupboard. "Mrs. Jacobs tells me she'll be seeing her own physician later today, but the past two days the morning sickness has lightened by dinnertime."

"I'm thankful she allowed all of us to pitch in and help." Wilma smiled at Caleb. "Although I do believe Frances was quite put out that she was given the cooking instead of the cleaning."

Caleb quirked a brow. "But Mrs. Jacobs said her mother was a good cook. I can't imagine why she'd rather scrub pots and pans."

Wilma laughed outright. "She was hoping to keep an eye on the two of us, that's why. She's kept silent for now, but mark my words, she's biding her time."

Caleb tossed the towel on the rack by the sink. "For what?"

"To meddle in my business. It's killing her not knowing what's going on. I can't believe she hasn't tried to pry the information by force." Wilma tsked. "That woman will be the death of me yet." She stopped in front of the window. "What a lovely fall. I'm not sure how much longer it will last, as winter can set in quite suddenly, but this last week of September has been perfect."

He stepped up beside her. "I can't imagine the winters being any more bitter than in Kansas."

"I'm not certain, having yet to experience one, but I've heard the snow gets very deep in the mountain passes."

"How about here in town? Do they frequently get cut off from the outside world?"

"I believe it happens, but the snow can come and go quickly as well. I suppose we'll have to wait and see. Hopefully we won't find out until after Thanksgiving."

Caleb turned to face her. "Why are you still here, Wilma?"

"There are no rentals to be found in town, and I don't have the money right now to build, even if I wanted to. The boarding-house has come to feel like home, so we've not felt any urgency to move."

"That's not what I meant, my dear." He took her hand in his. "Why didn't you return to Topeka? I know you came here hoping to discover more about Beth's family, but from what I understand, you haven't been successful. Do you ever plan to go home?"

Her heart lurched, and she tried to still the trembling that seized her. *Home*. She had longed for it at first, but now …? Wilma shook her head. "I don't think so, Caleb. I wrote to my solicitor and asked him to sell the house."

"What? Why?" His grip tightened. "Is something wrong? You aren't ill, are you?"

She patted his hand. "Of course not. Would you care to take a walk and get out of this house while the weather is still fine? If you don't mind, I don't care to discuss it here."

Caleb cast a glance toward the parlor. "Certainly. I was going to suggest the same. Let me go to my room first and retrieve something."

Wilma plucked her shawl from the back of a dining room chair and swung it around her shoulders. Curiosity and dread pricked her. What could Caleb be retrieving? Surely he wasn't going to propose after she'd made it clear she wasn't certain she was ready to be courted. She smirked. How foolish to even consider such a thing. More than likely it was an article that related to the medical field. George used to love discussing new medical finds.

Hurrying footsteps clattered down the stairs and Wilma smiled. Caleb was fifty-seven, eight years her senior, but you'd never know it. She still hadn't figured out why he'd retired and headed west.

He slowed at the kitchen doorway. "My lady." He swept her a courtly bow and extended his arm. "May I have the honor of escorting you?"

She giggled, then slid her hand through the crook of his elbow. "With pleasure, kind sir."

"Is your shawl warm enough, or do you need a cloak?"

"It will be fine, thank you. The sun is shining, and there's no wind today." Wilma kept a firm grip as they walked out the door and down the stairs, thankful no one followed. Frances must be upstairs taking her midmorning rest, and Beth had headed to town shortly after breakfast. She frowned. The girl had been traipsing to town more than normal lately. It might not hurt to ask about that. However, nothing more seemed to be developing with Mr. Tucker. Frances had been keeping her ears open as well and had reported no romance blossoming. What a disappointment. Even though Mr. Tucker wasn't a wealthy man, he was steady and decent, and his prospects were good now that he'd acquired a contract for his book. He might even become a famous author someday.

Caleb placed his hand over hers and squeezed. "What are you smiling about, Wilma? You look quite happy with your own thoughts."

"I suppose I was wandering. How rude of me."

"Not at all. If it's not something you care to talk about …"

"It wasn't important. Simply thinking how nice it would be if Beth and Mr. Tucker were to start courting."

"Tucker?" Caleb arched his brows. "I didn't realize. So Beth is interested in the man?"

"Frances and I thought so, but now I'm not sure." She tipped her head to the side. "It doesn't matter." They passed the spot in the yard where Mr. Lansing had encountered the bucket of paint, and Wilma winced, remembering the lawsuit. Hopefully whatever Caleb brought from his room wasn't bad news.

"I asked about selling the house in Topeka. I'm curious … what made you decide to do that?"

How much to tell him? Caleb was a dear friend, and he desired even more. Trust wasn't an issue as much as her own stubborn pride. Somehow she hated admitting she'd made poor choices, but deep inside Wilma knew that telling the full truth would be the better option. "Several things. Partly, I thought Beth needed a change. There was a man in Topeka of whom I didn't approve, paying court to my niece. I believe he left town at my urging, but I didn't care to take unnecessary chances. Also, I determined she needed a change."

Caleb pressed her fingers. "She needed one, or you did?"

She drew to a stop on the path and peered at him. "What do you mean?"

"When you left, I wondered if you decided to cut all your ties to home. You didn't say good-bye, and if mutual friends hadn't informed me, I wouldn't have known where you'd gone. I was pleasantly shocked when I received your letter, as I didn't know if I'd hear from you again."

"I am so sorry." She tried to still the trembling of her fingers. "All I could think of was protecting Beth and trying to find answers about her past. I didn't realize I had hurt you. Please forgive me for my callous behavior."

"No forgiveness necessary, Wilma. I'm grateful you weren't running away from me."

"Never." As soon as the word left her lips, she knew it was true. It wasn't the time or the place to let him know, but her heart was stirring toward this kind man.

"Good." He drew her forward along the path, tucking her hand closer under his arm.

"May I ask what you brought from your room? Does it have anything to do with what drew you west?"

He nodded and slowed his pace as they crossed the wood bridge over the Powder River. "Let's stop here for a moment." They paused, and Caleb leaned against the railing. He pulled an envelope from his breast pocket. "I received this in the mail yesterday. I've been sending out inquiries to people I thought might know more of Beth's history."

"What, Caleb? What did you find?" She placed her hand over her pounding heart. "Do you know who her parents are, is that it?"

He shook his head. "I'm sorry, no. I didn't mean to get your hopes up."

She slumped, not sure if she was relieved or disappointed. "What, then?"

Caleb withdrew a paper and unfolded it carefully, exposing a dried yellow buttercup.

Wilma touched it with a tentative finger, not wanting to destroy the fragile specimen. "Beth loves these." She looked up. "I don't understand what it means."

"I have a friend who works as a scout for the military. He married an Arapaho woman and works out of Fort Laramie."

A jolt went through Wilma. "That's where the Arapaho brought Beth."

He nodded. "I know. Carter wrote and sent this. He questioned his wife about the little white girl who came to her tribe many years ago, and Dancing Water remembered her."

Wilma gripped her hands together. "Go on."

"His wife was twelve years old when Beth was brought to their camp. Apparently, Dancing Water's mother was the woman chosen to care for her. She said the child had burns on many parts of her body and cried all night when she arrived. But the little girl was clutching something in her fist and wouldn't let go."

Wilma looked at the dried flower resting on the paper Caleb had partially folded. "This?"

"Yes. When Beth finally fell asleep, Dancing Water took it, thinking it was powerful medicine and kept the child from dying. She pressed and dried the blossom and guarded it carefully. When Beth was taken to the fort she wanted to send it, but the brave who returned her refused. Dancing Water kept it all these years in memory of the child she came to think of as her baby sister."

"Did she say how they found Beth or anything about her family?" Wilma gazed down into the water flowing below the bridge. The years had sped by almost as quickly as this river moved through its channel, but sometimes it seemed like yesterday that the frightened young girl had arrived on her doorstep.

"Dancing Water told her husband that Beth was found beside an abandoned campfire. From the signs, she'd apparently been running, tripped, and fell over the rocks surrounding the coals and into the sizzling fire. It appeared the wagons had been gone for some time. The hunting party followed her back trail. They saw where she'd played in a field earlier in the day and picked the buttercups. She was so badly burned they didn't want to take the time to find her people. Their camp was close, so they loaded her on a travois and took her to their medicine woman, Dancing Water's mother."

"Then she wasn't stolen." Tears filled Wilma's eyes. "I'd almost hoped she had been—at least that way Beth wouldn't have to continue believing her family abandoned her."

Caleb touched her hair. "I know, and I'm sorry."

"There's nothing more? No other clues to her people?"

"I'm afraid not. The braves took Beth to the fort about five or six months after finding her, when she was well enough to travel. Dancing Water said both girls cried when they parted. Has Beth mentioned remembering her time there?"

Wilma thought for a moment. "She told me not long ago that memories are returning. I'll ask if she recalls Dancing Water."

He tucked her hand back into his arm. "Would you prefer to walk to town or stroll back toward the house?"

"I don't think I'm in the mood for town, but I'd love to continue walking for a little longer, if you don't mind."

"Certainly. But about your house? I understand you wanting to come out here to help Beth, but why sell? I assumed someday you'd move back to Topeka."

A hawk swooped overhead, its shrill cry rending the air. Wilma raised her head and watched its flight, wondering what it would be like to experience that kind of freedom. "When we left, I had every intention of returning, but things have changed. Beth and I are both making a new life here. It's a nice change living simpler and not being pushed into the center of the social whirlwind. And while George left me comfortably well off, I made some poor choices last year that affected my finances." She hesitated, unsure if she should continue.

Caleb nodded. "So selling the house is partly financial? That makes sense. I assumed since George bought it when you married you'd not want to leave."

"It wasn't an easy decision, but it was time to let go. I loved George deeply, but the years have softened the loss." She met his gaze. "I'm ready to move on." She held her breath, wondering if he'd grasp what she hoped to convey.

He stopped and gently gripped her shoulders. "Are you saying what I think, Wilma Roberts?"

She tipped her head to one side and smiled. "I'm not sure. What is it you think?"

"That you'll consider my suit? You'll allow me to court you?" His hands tightened, but she could feel his fingers tremble.

"I will." Wilma nodded, her heart bubbling with joy and gratitude that God had sent such a kind man into her life. "And I'm proud that you'd ask, Caleb Marshall."

"Then I hope this will help you make up your mind in the days to come." He lowered his head and his lips brushed hers, gently and tentatively.

Wilma's lips tingled, and her body felt as though she might burst into flames. When Caleb lifted his head, she drew in her breath. "My goodness gracious!" She stared up at him, taking in the expression of happiness that slowly changed to one of near panic. Poor man—he must have thought she didn't care for the experience. Raising her chin, she smiled. "I do believe I might need one more to help me make up my mind."

Chapter Twenty-Five

Jeffery paced from the parlor to the base of the stairway and back. Beth had stood him up. He glanced at his pocket watch. Ten o'clock—fifteen minutes late. From what he knew of her, this wasn't typical. Maybe he should go upstairs and knock on her door. He placed his foot on the first tread and paused. What if she was ill? He hadn't seen Beth since breakfast, but she'd appeared quite well.

He'd worked hard to allay the stiffness between them created by his mention of Brent Wentworth a number of days ago. It had seemed foolish to dwell on such a trivial incident, and his heart kept tugging him in Beth's direction. They *had* made this arrangement yesterday, but he hadn't forgotten and assumed Beth wouldn't either. He ought to find Mrs. Roberts and ask her advice.

The front door opened and closed softly, and Jeffery spun around. Beth stood in the foyer, her cheeks pink and hair tousled. "Jeffery, I'm so sorry. Am I terribly late?"

His heart somersaulted. She looked positively adorable in her burgundy gown and matching hat. "Certainly not enough to worry over. I didn't realize you had gone out. I hope coming back didn't inconvenience you."

A shy smile blossomed as she drew off her hat. "I should have asked you to come with me, but I was hoping to surprise you." She held up a slender package with a flourish. "I rushed to the post office this morning …"

Jeffery caught his breath. "Is it …?"

She giggled and waved it in the air. "Yes! It's from *our* publisher. It has to be the issue with your story and my illustrations, don't you think?"

Wonder pulsed through him. "But you have yet to open it. You brought it all the way from town and didn't find out for sure?"

Beth swept into the parlor, her skirt billowing around her. "Of course not, silly. I would wager your copy is at the post office as well. I would have wanted you to wait. It's only fair, since we both contributed."

What an amazing woman. He didn't believe he knew anyone who would possess that kind of self-control. Jeffery waited as she sat on the sofa and arranged her skirts to the side, leaving him room to sit. "I would like to think I'd have done so, but I am not so sure I'd have been so considerate. Thank you." He perched on the edge of the sofa and stared at the brown-paper parcel clutched in her slender fingers.

Beth plopped it down on his knees. "It's your story, and it's only right you open it."

"What?" He stared at her, not certain he'd heard correctly. "You waited long enough." He placed it back in her hands and leaned over the parcel. He inhaled the scent of jasmine, and his heart turned over. Her hair brushed his cheek, sending a ripple of desire through his body. Right now he'd give anything to take this woman in his arms and kiss her. "Please go ahead. Besides, I'm guessing the illustrations you drew are what will make my story shine."

Beth searched his face, then nodded. "All right." Slowly she peeled back the wrapper and revealed the front cover of *The Women's Eastern Magazine*. She gasped.

Jeffery leaned closer. "What is it? What's wrong?"

Beth held out the magazine with shaking hands. "My picture." She stared at the illustration of the boardinghouse set in a grove of trees.

His brows hunched together. "What?"

"This." She held it up. "It's mine." Never had she dreamed they'd use her picture on the cover of this prestigious magazine. "And both of our names are at the bottom."

Jeffery took it and gazed at the drawing. Long seconds ticked by. Finally, he raised his head, and deep admiration shone from his eyes. "Amazing. Your work will sell out this issue."

Beth exhaled in relief. "You really think so?"

"Yes." He placed the periodical back on her lap. "Let's see if there's more."

Realization tempered the joy dancing inside. "I'm so sorry. I was caught up in the excitement of seeing the cover and forgot to look for your story. If it weren't for your book, my art wouldn't have been so prominently displayed."

"Not true. Your work will stand the test of time, whether it is attached to a book or on its own. Never doubt that, Beth."

Warmth stole into her cheeks, and she ducked her head.

He placed a finger under her chin, tipping it up. "I am very serious. You are a talented woman."

The touch of his hand sent shivers running through her body. Was it right to feel this way? She hadn't seen Brent the past couple of days and had come away from their last meeting more confused than ever. He'd sworn he'd been ill the day she'd waited at the restaurant and hadn't been able to send word. She didn't know what to think, and now Jeffery's touch and nearness created a response she'd never thought she'd feel again.

"What's wrong, Beth?" He released her chin. "You look so sad. Can I help?"

Beth started and pulled back. Those were the exact words she had said to Brent. He had denied anything was wrong, but the comments about his finances belied his adamant words. Why did she have to compare everything Jeffery did to Brent?

"Nothing," she managed. "I'm sorry. I guess I felt bad that we haven't looked at your story yet."

It wasn't a lie, but Jeffery frowned. An ache filled her chest, but there was no turning back time. Moving forward was best. The last thing she cared to do was let him know she'd been thinking of Brent, even if the comparison *had* leaned in Jeffery's favor. "Let's take a look, shall we?"

Beth thumbed through the pages until a bold heading caught her eye: "Frontier Friendships."

"Jeffery." She breathed the word and ran her fingertips over the paper. "Look." Awe filled her at the sight of his words in print. Having her illustration on the front was a thrill, but seeing the opening lines of Jeffery's work was something more. *Honored* and *privileged* were the two words that came to mind—especially having her art woven together with his story. It really was true that things happened in real life that almost seemed too far-fetched to put in a story. Who would believe that two people would end up living in the same house and be hired by the same magazine located two thousand miles away? And, on top of that, to put the two together, each to complement the other? It was almost unbelievable.

Jeffery hadn't moved since she'd placed the double-page spreads in his hands. He looked up, wonder shining from his dark eyes. "They put it in the center." He flipped to the next page. "Five pages in all. Amazing. The first three chapters are here, along with two of your drawings."

She squinted and looked closer. "Two? I sent them four."

He swiveled the magazine so she could see it better. "They repeated the one of the house from the cover and this one of the valley, town, and mountains in the distance. You did a wonderful representation of Baker City. Anyone living here would recognize it."

Her heart sank. Why hadn't she thought of that? "Do you think readers will assume I live here?"

He frowned. "Not necessarily. Would it bother you if they did?"

Beth shrugged. "I suppose it wouldn't be terrible, but I've tried to stay anonymous. That's why I use a pen name."

"I still don't quite understand that. Aren't you proud of what you do? You're so talented. I'd think you'd want everyone to know what you are capable of."

She pulled away and settled against the sofa. Since meeting Jeffery, her confidence had risen, but she'd never told him her full story. He didn't know about the ugly scars she still carried. She rubbed her forearm, feeling the raised flesh through the fabric, and ducked her head. "It's … complicated, Jeffery."

A gentle touch on her hair turned her around. Jeffery smiled. "Why don't you believe in yourself, Beth? What are you so afraid of?" He took the hand that covered the hideous spot on her arm. "Won't you let me help?"

The silence stretched out, and Beth forgot to breathe.

Jeffery leaned closer, his gaze capturing her own. "I care about you, Beth."

She closed her eyes and felt his lips brush hers, ever so gently. She swayed toward him, suddenly longing to be held in his arms. His care ignited a smoldering fire that all of her months of caring for Brent had never stirred.

The front door banged open, and Aunt Wilma strode into the foyer. "Hello, anyone home?"

Warmth rushed into Beth's face. "I'm sorry—so sorry." She stood with effort. "I'm not what you think. Forgive me." She felt as though hounds nipped at her skirt, snapping with sharp fangs at her tender flesh. Almost running, she dashed up the stairs and into her room, leaving Jeffery to deal with the rash of questions her aunt was certain to have.

"But I thought you didn't have to go back to Baker City until the new bank is finished?" Isabelle hated the way her body shook and tried to steady her voice. She wasn't ready for Steven to leave yet. Her strength ebbed and flowed like the tides she'd read about in a book but had never been privileged to see. Only one of the *many* regrets of her life.

Steven kissed her forehead, then straightened with a weary sigh. "I know, but we need a place to live if we're going to move there. The bank doesn't provide housing, and the town is growing faster than the buildings can be erected. We may have to stay in a hotel until we find something better."

"Then why go now? Can't we load the wagon and arrive before your job starts, and find something then?" She settled deeper into her rocker and tucked the lap robe around her waist. It seemed she was always cold nowadays, as they were well into fall with winter fast approaching in this high mountain valley.

Her son eased onto the only other chair in the living area of the cramped cabin. "I don't want to put you through that, Ma. And it wouldn't make sense to take all our belongings if we don't know where we'll live when we arrive. I need to do this. I'm sorry."

Isabelle nodded. "I suppose you're right. How long do you reckon you'll be gone this time?"

"They want me to look over the progress at the bank, so I'll be tied up two or three days with that, plus travel. No more than a week, at worst."

"All right. Karen and Ina promised to stop in and keep me company. I wish I could go with you and see what it's like. Get prepared, if you know what I mean?"

"I do, but you're not strong enough. The move will be hard. We'll camp on the trail one night if the travel wears you out." He sighed. "Maybe I shouldn't take this job. La Grande is growing too. I'm sure I can find something better here if I try."

"No." Isabelle said the word with more force than she'd planned, but if she hadn't done so, she'd have grabbed on to his offer and not let go. She didn't want to leave her home, even though it wasn't large or fancy. Her friends were here, and leaving the farm a few years ago when her second husband died had almost done her in. The grief of his loss, leaving the land they both loved and couldn't afford to hold on to, along with her ongoing illness, had almost put her into an early grave. "I won't have you give up your opportunity for me. There's no telling how many more months or years I have on this earth, and it's not going to be wasted holding you back from your chosen career."

"Don't talk that way, Ma. You're going to get well, and you aren't holding me back. We'll keep this cabin, and if you're not happy in Baker City, we'll return. I won't stay any longer than I have to, and we'll talk it over again next week." He pushed to his feet. "I love you and want what's best for you too."

"Thank you, Son. I'm so blessed God didn't take you when your father died."

"I wish I could remember him better." Steven straightened. "Most of my memories are with Papa Garvey instead of Father."

"He would have been proud of you, as am I." She waved her hand toward the door. "Now, get along with you so you don't miss the stage, and I'll see you when you come back."

Chapter Twenty-Six

Beth had to make a decision; she could wait no longer. After her talk with Jeffery, she'd left a note at the hotel desk telling Brent that she'd meet him this morning. She'd thought she'd loved Brent for so long that she wasn't sure what to do with the growing affection for Jeffery. The memory of Jeffery's tender kiss created an ache that extended clear to the tips of her toes.

They had more in common than she'd realized when they'd first met. She had thought him a stuffy, self-absorbed man with his head always in a book but had come to recognize a tender, humorous side. But that kiss put expectations and desires on the table that she didn't care to face at the moment.

She gazed across the restaurant at the doorway, wondering if Brent would come. A number of things he'd said and done didn't add up, and over the past few days her misgivings had grown. She was tired of sneaking around and keeping things from her aunt, and the thought that Jeffery might stumble on her and Brent again convulsed her stomach.

Brent wove his way through the tables and stopped beside her. He doffed his hat, then slipped into his chair. "You look lovely. I'm sorry I'm late. I hope you haven't been waiting too long?"

"Not at all. Only five minutes or so."

"Good." He picked up a menu card and scanned it. "What would you like?"

She lifted a brow. "I'm not terribly hungry, and I know you need to save your money to pay your mother's debts."

A smile emerged. "Nonsense. If we can't enjoy money occasionally, what good is it?"

"You seem in an exceptional mood today. Has something happened?"

He placed the card on the table. "I have a wonderful business opportunity that could get me out of debt and put me in very good shape financially."

A waitress stopped by their table. "What can I get for you folks?"

Beth touched the rim of the cup sitting on a saucer. "Tea, please."

Brent nodded. "I'll have black coffee and a slice of your rhubarb pie. How about you, Beth? Something sweet to go with your tea?"

"No, but thank you just the same."

The waitress returned and set the coffee and pie in front of Brent, then filled Beth's cup with tea.

As the woman walked away, Beth took a sip of her tea. "Tell me about this new business venture."

"It's a chance to invest in a new mine. I stand to make a large sum of money. In fact, it would give me the start I've needed and enable me to take care of you."

"I beg your pardon?"

"I wasn't going to do this yet, Beth, but I can't help myself." He gripped her hand across the table. "I love you and want to marry you.

I want to care for you the rest of our lives." He hesitated and dipped his head. "There's one small problem."

She withdrew her hand and sat back, tucking it in her lap. Apprehension jolted her at Brent's declaration. "And what problem would that be?"

He mustered a smile. "Is something wrong?"

Everything stilled inside her.

"Wait."

For what? She wasn't sure, but she remained quiet, trying to listen for that familiar inner voice.

"Beth?" Urgency filled his voice.

Glasses clinked at a nearby table, reminding her they weren't alone. "I'm sorry," she murmured. "I would like to understand what you are saying. It didn't quite sound like a proposal, somehow. Not if there's a problem attached."

His mouth drew down in a frown. "Of course it's a proposal. I said I love you. Don't you believe me?"

In the past Beth would have nodded and given her heartfelt assurance, but not today. There was a distinct hesitation inside and that continuing sense she needed to wait. "Why don't you tell me what's troubling you first?"

Brent leaned back with a sigh. "I'm sorry. I suppose I understand your caution, since I hinted at a problem. I should have left that until later and simply asked you to marry me."

She gave a short nod. "Now go ahead and explain."

"This investment is a once-in-a-lifetime prospect, and the owner is pressing me to put the money down fast, or he'll move on to the next investor."

"How fast does he expect it?"

"In two weeks." His gaze dropped.

"I see."

"Beth?" His lips thinned. "Never mind. It doesn't matter."

Beth narrowed her eyes. Discouragement and shame covered Brent's face. Was it possible she'd misjudged him? "Please go ahead."

"Are you sure? I don't want anything to come between us."

She furrowed her brow. "Why do you say that?"

"I don't want to lose you. No amount of money is worth that to me."

A chair scraped across the wood floor at the nearby table, and a man rose, helping a woman to her feet. Beth focused back on the matter at hand. "I don't understand."

He sat back and stroked his chin. "I don't have enough money. I poured everything into my mother's debts. It's only a matter of time until I am back on my feet. If this offer had come six months from now, it wouldn't be a problem. As it is …" He shrugged and spread his hands.

"You don't have enough." Beth nodded, understanding dawning. He hoped she could help. Or maybe her aunt. "Were you expecting me to ask Aunt Wilma for a loan?"

He winced. "Never. But I thought … never mind."

"What? Brent, be honest with me. Quit talking in circles."

"Fine." He drummed his fingers on the table. "You're twenty years old. I assume you'll come into money when you turn twenty-one. I hoped you might borrow against that and loan me the money. It wouldn't take long for me to pay you back." Brent paused. "And, of course, if we marry soon, it wouldn't matter."

"I see." A chill descended over her, and she shivered.

"Wait."

There was that internal caution again. She wasn't any closer to understanding than she had been the first time she'd heard it, but heeding it would be wise. "You said you have two weeks?"

"Yes. I need to give the man an answer."

"I will pray about it." Beth reached for her reticule and slipped the loop over her wrist. "It's getting late. I should be going."

His face fell. "Pray about it? Why?"

Surprise encompassed her. Why had she never realized they hadn't discussed God or Brent's relationship with Him? She'd assumed he was a Christian, as he'd attended a church in Topeka. But the more she saw of life, the more she realized church attendance meant little. Brent had never talked about faith in God. "It will help me decide the right path to take. Don't you ever pray?"

Annoyance darkened his countenance. "I've never seen it do much good or why it matters. When you marry me, I'd think you'd want me to succeed."

Beth lifted her chin. "I beg your pardon, but it matters very much to me. And I didn't say I would marry you."

Contrition softened his features, and he reached for her hand again, but she yanked it away. "I spoke without thinking. Take all the time you need. I understand if you want to pray about it." His eyes searched hers. "But you can trust me. I love you, and I'd never do anything to harm you."

"I didn't say you would. I'm not sure why you'd speak so, Brent." The root of suspicion expanded.

His attention darted around the room. "No reason at all. I suppose I'm nervous, wanting you to say yes to my proposal. You understand, don't you?"

"Which proposal? For my hand in marriage, or for my money?" She leveled him with a steady gaze. He had no way of knowing she had no inheritance, but she did have a tidy amount put away from the sale of her illustrations, with more coming. "What if I were to tell you I have no inheritance? Would you still want to marry me?"

His face paled. "I told you the money doesn't matter."

Beth plucked her shawl off the back of her chair. "I'll meet you here tomorrow at the same time. Good day, Brent." She didn't look back as she walked from the room.

One thing loomed in her mind—his request for money. Brent's lips had tightened when she'd asked if he'd still love her if she were poor. Jeffery wouldn't care if she were a beggar on the street. Then why did she keep pulling away whenever he tried to draw near? It was too much to sort out, and at the moment she wanted to get to the bottom of what Brent was after and why.

God would lead her in the right direction. Relief swept through her that she hadn't allowed Brent to pressure her into anything. Maybe she was growing up, at last.

Wilma pushed her chair away from the breakfast table. "Thank you for the wonderful meal, Katherine. I'm so glad you're feeling better, but be sure you let me know if there's anything more Beth and I can do to help."

Beth nodded. "I'd be happy to do whatever you need."

Katherine braced one hand against the door lintel and tugged on Lucy's braid. "I've got a good helper who promised to do the dishes this morning since it's Saturday and there's no school. Thanks for offering, but we'll get along fine."

Mandy snuggled against her mother's other side. "I'll help too, Ma. I want you to rest so the baby doesn't get too tired."

Lucy tweaked the little girl's nose. "Silly. The baby is what's making Ma tired, not the other way around."

Mandy scrunched her nose. "Nuh-uh. Babies can't make a big person tired; they're just little people."

Katherine rolled her eyes and sighed. "Come on, girls. If you start bickering, I'll leave all the work to you and go climb into bed."

Frances put her arm around her granddaughter. "Come, Amanda. You and I will heat water on the stove while Lucy clears the table." She turned toward Wilma. "Would you care to have tea later this morning and visit? It feels like a long time since we chatted."

Wilma glanced at Beth disappearing from the room and frowned. The girl had been slipping out of the house more frequently lately, and the last two times Jeffery had been home, so she couldn't be meeting him. Her niece hadn't been forthcoming, and now that she thought about it, she'd seemed somewhat evasive. Something felt off, and she needed to ferret out the trouble.

She stepped closer to Frances and lowered her voice. "I'd love tea, but I have a bit of sleuthing to do first."

Frances's eyes gleamed. "Can I be of assistance?"

Wilma's gaze traveled the length of her friend's gown to her feet. "I wish you could, but I'm afraid it involves walking to town."

"My feet and ankles have been quite strong lately, and I would not mind taking a walk, if you care to include me."

Wilma gave a grim smile and nodded. "I'll help Lucy clear the table while you get the water going. Between the two of us we can have the kitchen put back to rights in no time."

Jeffery stepped in front of Beth as she stopped at the bottom of the staircase. "I think we need to talk, Beth. About what happened the other day in the parlor."

She stepped around him. "I'm sorry, I don't have time now. I'm headed to town."

He touched her arm, and she stilled. "Please. I want to apologize for my behavior."

Beth raised her eyes, then swung quickly away. "There's no reason. Let it go, Jeffery."

"But I acted like a cad and took advantage of you. I must have frightened you, and I'm afraid I ruined our friendship. You've barely spoken to me since."

"No. You didn't frighten me at all." Her hand went to her throat, and she clutched the locket that always hung there. "I ... I don't care to discuss it now, if you don't mind."

"Later, perhaps?"

"Perhaps. Now, forgive me, but I have an appointment and must go." Beth moved away, then turned. "I'd hate to lose your friendship, Jeffery, truly I would." Color rose in her cheeks. "And, to be honest, you didn't offend or upset me at all. In fact ..." She shook her head. "It doesn't matter. But there are things I haven't told you...."

Relief surged through him. The kiss hadn't made her angry. Maybe there was hope after all. Then he remembered those last words. *There are things I haven't told you.* He tensed. "Is it that Wentworth man you've been meeting in town?"

She blinked two or three times. "I beg your pardon?"

Jeffery gripped her arm. "You were with him a week or so ago. I've seen you with him before. Is he your beau, or something more serious? I don't trust him, and I think you need to stay away from him."

Beth gave a gentle tug, and her eyes saddened. "I must go, Jeffery. I'm sorry." She spun away, the click of her heels fading as she hurried down the hall.

Chapter Twenty-Seven

Beth wasn't sure if she could make it all the way to town without breaking down. Had she done the right thing, leaving the house and not responding to Jeffery? She couldn't respond to him, or what had happened in the parlor, until she settled things once and for all with Brent.

She'd been confident in the trust that seemed to be growing between herself and Jeffery, as well as their mutual love for literature and art. But he didn't have the right to demand answers about Brent. It wasn't like Jeffery had openly declared his intentions, even if he had kissed her. Then why was it so hard to put Jeffery out of her mind?

It didn't matter; it would be over soon. She wouldn't give Brent money, no matter how much he declared his devotion. She pulled her linen shawl closer around her as a wagon rolled past. Beth glanced at the sky. Blue, almost to the horizon, but clouds that looked like mounds of white confectioner's candy peeked above the mountains.

She loved the slower pace of Baker City and enjoyed her friends at the boardinghouse. Beth had never wanted to put down roots or make deep friendships in this town—until now. Was it because of Jeffery or her new success with her art?

Dodging around pedestrians and horses, Beth lifted the hem of her burgundy gown and stepped onto the boardwalk, making her way to the restaurant.

She peeked through the door and spied the table where she and Brent usually sat. Empty. He was late ... again. It didn't matter; he'd probably be along shortly. A waitress motioned her toward the table, and she breathed a short prayer. *Protect me from any mistakes, Lord. Help me to follow Your perfect will.*

Wilma clutched Frances's arm as they hurried down the main business street of Baker City, intent on keeping her friend from stumbling, should her ankles start giving her trouble. Bringing her along might not have been the best idea, but she couldn't deny she appreciated the company, even if they'd barely drawn a breath to speak to one another.

Without warning, Frances reared back on her heels, and Wilma slowed to a stop. "What's wrong with you? Are your feet hurting?"

Frances glared. "I am not taking one more step until you explain yourself, Wilma Roberts. What kind of shenanigans are you up to?" She stared pointedly at the parasol Wilma clutched in her other hand. "Are you intending on lighting into Mr. Lansing again because he brought suit against the house? Micah plans to consult the local judge as soon as he can, and I don't think you'll help his cause if you rush in, causing trouble."

Wilma planted her hands on her hips. "Me, causing trouble for Micah? That's the furthest thing from my mind. Where in the world did you conjure that idea?"

"It is not too far-fetched, considering the haste with which you are dragging me through town. Why, you have been perusing the inside of every establishment, including the saloons, and you are clutching that parasol like a sword. What else should I think, pray tell?" She plopped down on a bench outside the mercantile and pointed. "Sit. Talk. I am not moving until you explain why we are here."

Wilma grunted and slumped onto the hard surface. "We are wasting precious time."

"No. *You* are wasting it by arguing with *me*. Go on." Frances leaned back and crossed her arms.

There seemed no help for it. Frances appeared entrenched. "Fine. As you wish. I am hunting for Brent Wentworth."

Frances sat upright. "The man you told me Beth thought herself in love with?" She gaped. "What makes you think he might be in town? As I recall, you believed Mr. Lansing was Mr. Wentworth before you mashed him over the head and incapacitated him."

Wilma waved her fingers in the air. "That is neither here nor there. I was only guessing he might be in town at that time. Now I know." She tried to keep the smug triumph out of her voice but didn't quite succeed.

"Oh? And what makes you think that?"

"I saw him."

"When? Where? Are you certain it was him?"

"Yes. I was in town yesterday as he strolled the boardwalk. Thankfully he didn't see me. I tried to follow, but he was too far ahead. I lost him, or I would most assuredly have accosted him on the street and demanded to know what he is doing in town."

"It *is* a free country. I would assume Mr. Wentworth has the right to walk these streets the same as any other."

"No, he does not. I told that trickster to never come near Beth again, or I would turn him over to the law."

Frances cocked her head to the side. "And if he is not aware your niece is in town? You could be misjudging the man."

Wilma snorted. "Highly unlikely. But that is what you and I are doing. Checking up to be sure. I lost Wentworth in this section of town." She gestured across the street. "If I were a wagering woman, I'd say he's spending his time in one of those saloons."

"Drinking?"

"And worse. He liked to frequent gambling halls in Topeka. After he left town, I did some digging and found out quite a bit of unpleasantness. Why, I could tell you stories—" She gasped. "Oh my. There he is, across the street."

Frances craned her head. "Where? Point him out, Wilma. There are too many men crowding the walkway."

Wilma jumped to her feet and grasped Frances's wrist, hauling her off the bench. "Hurry, we need to duck inside. I cannot allow him to see me." She tugged her protesting friend into the mercantile and slipped to the front window, peering outside.

A clerk stepped up beside them. "May I help you ladies?"

Wilma remained frozen where she stood, and Frances shook her head. "No. Go away and help someone else. We are not in need of your assistance, or we would ask for it." She motioned with a flip of her fingers. "Shoo."

Wilma peered back in time to see the clerk cast them a dark look and depart.

Frances scowled. "That man follows me around the store, nagging whenever I come here. He is quite the pest." She moved closer to Wilma and whispered loudly, "What do you see?"

Wilma broke into a wide smile. "He is heading down the street. Come on. Let's follow. I do not intend to lose sight of him this time, and when I catch him, he is going to get an earful, let me tell you."

Beth smiled as Brent entered the restaurant and made his way toward her. "Hello."

He tugged at his collar. "Sorry I'm late. I was meeting with the miners who want me to invest." He seemed to pull himself together and mustered a smile. "You look lovely today. Is that a new hat?"

She touched the brim of the burgundy felt. "No, I've had it since …" She hated to bring up the subject of Topeka. "For two years."

He nodded absently. "How nice."

Beth tried to catch his eye. "You seem upset."

His brows drew together in a fierce frown. "I am. Someone on the street bumped into me and picked my pocket." He patted the breast of his jacket. "I was going to stop at the bank to deposit my cash, then swing by the telegraph office to send a wire letting my mother's creditors know I could make the final payment. Now the money is gone." He put his head in his hands. "I don't know what I'm going to do."

"How horrible! You must go to the sheriff at once." She started to rise.

"No." Brent's head lifted. "Please sit down, Beth."

"But why not? You were robbed." She eased herself back onto her chair.

"I didn't see what the person looked like; the streets were too crowded. What would I tell the sheriff? Someone jostled me, and I was careless enough to let them slip their hand into my pocket?" He rolled his head back and forth, then shrugged. "I don't know which direction they took, as I discovered the loss when I reached this building." Brent covered her hand with his. "But if I can make that investment, none of this will matter. I'll make back everything I lost and more. We can live like royalty for the rest of our lives. I simply need a small nest egg to give us a start. Tell me you'll marry me."

Beth tugged her hand away. She opened her mouth, then stopped at the sound of footsteps pausing beside Brent's chair. She turned her head.

Aunt Wilma drew herself to her full height. "She will do no such thing, you scoundrel. No niece of mine will ever carry your worthless last name if I have anything to say about it."

Beth stared at the two women. "Aunt Wilma! Mrs. Cooper. What are you doing here?"

Brent's face paled. He sat unmoving, not turning his head to look at the woman who towered above him.

"I have come to save you from the biggest mistake of your life." She jerked a thumb at Brent. "This … this …" She sputtered. "Words fail me. I am not a cursing woman, but nothing else would possibly do this *person* justice. He is trying to hoodwink you. I should have told you the truth months ago."

Beth shook her head. "You don't understand."

Brent winced, then managed a smile. "Hello, Mrs. Roberts. Beth is trying to explain that I was robbed on the way here."

Wilma emitted a cackling laugh, and several patrons in the restaurant turned toward her. "Robbed, were you? On the way here? Well now, that's a mighty convenient story, since Frances and I followed you from the saloon, and no one touched you."

Warmth stole into Beth's face. "Brent was in a business meeting at the bank. I'm not sure what you're implying, and I do believe I am able to take care of my own affairs."

"Is that what he told you? More like a meeting with his gambling buddies, and he lost all of his money in a poker game. He is nothing but a two-bit gambler who preys on innocent women. Why do you think he left Topeka so suddenly without telling you good-bye?"

Beth stared at her aunt. "Brent's mother came down ill.... She wanted to see him before she died. He … he was too embarrassed to tell me, because of his mother's …" A memory returned. God's voice whispering, *"Wait."* She'd wondered at the time, but her uneasiness had intensified the past couple of times they'd met. Had it all been a lie from the time he came to town?

Beth stared at Brent, but he slumped deeper into his seat. "What's going on, Brent?"

Wilma grunted her disgust. "There is no honest reply." She stepped closer to him. "He knows that I understand everything about his conniving schemes. When he left Topeka, I had him investigated. His mother passed almost ten years ago in the Cincinnati fire. Her name was listed as one of the many lost."

Beth stiffened. "What are you saying, Aunt Wilma?"

"That I believed him to be a fine, upstanding man when I first met him as well. In fact"—she blasted him with a harsh glare—"I went so far as to fall for an investment scheme he proposed where he promised a large return in only a few months. I trusted him."

Brent cleared his throat. "You can't believe that, Beth. It's all a lie."

Beth focused on the ashen face of the man she'd once thought she loved, anger forming like a fireball in her stomach. She turned to her aunt, her voice choked. "Why did you keep it from me?"

Mrs. Cooper moved up beside Wilma and placed her hand on her friend's arm. "Tell her the full truth, Wilma. Your pride no longer matters. I think you owe her that, don't you?"

Wilma slowly nodded. "Yes," she whispered the word, then raised her voice a notch. "That I do." She nodded at Brent, then scanned the room. "I don't care to cause a scene, but you deserve the truth, and I won't keep it from you any longer."

She placed her hands on the table and leaned toward Beth. "I started having second thoughts and talked to a banker. He had never heard of Brent Wentworth, but several of his patrons mentioned someone offering the same claim to riches. I went back to this, this …" She gestured toward Brent. "I demanded my money back, but he had spent every penny. I informed him I was turning him over to the sheriff, but he reminded me that your name would be linked with his, and my good name would be dragged in the mud as well." She gave a harsh laugh. "And believe me when I say there was no consideration for either of our feelings or reputation. No, it was purely self-preservation that prompted his request to let him go, nothing more."

Brent drew himself up. "My good woman, you exaggerate."

Beth glared at him. "So you let him walk away? You did noth-ing?" She couldn't believe her aunt's words. Anger at Brent's betrayal bubbled, but bewilderment stirred the pot of her emotions into a kettle of confusion.

"Yes, I regret to say I did, and this is what I get as a result." Wilma drew herself up. "But I warned him that he was to leave town and never contact you again. I assured him that I would press charges for everything he stole from me and reveal him as the blackguard he is. I did not expect to see him again, although I admit I had twinges of doubt. I am guessing he believed you would be coming into an inheritance soon and was trying to cozy up to you again." She cocked her head at Beth.

Beth met her aunt's gaze without flinching. "He asked me to marry him and needed money for a new investment. I planned to turn down his marriage proposal, as I realized I don't love him, but I toyed with the idea of helping him." She rose to her feet and faced Brent. "How dare you lie to me? I can't believe I was so naive as to believe you."

Wilma stepped aside as Beth pressed close to the table.

Brent crafted a weak smile. "Darling, I am *so* sorry. I would have told you the truth, but I thought you'd hate me. Believe me when I tell you my love for you was never false. I'll marry you today and never ask for a dime. I swear."

Beth swung as hard as she could, her open palm making contact with his cheek. The sound echoed through the room, and a buzz arose from the remaining patrons.

Brent placed his hand over his reddening cheek. His lips twisted. "Truth be told, I never wanted you anyway. You and your aunt are nothing to me." He pushed back his chair and stood. "I would have overlooked your background for a price, but I should be thanking my stars I didn't marry someone taken by Indians. If word had gotten out, I'd have been a laughingstock in the East."

It was all Beth could do not to cringe, but she lifted her chin instead. "Get out of my sight. You are despicable."

"Not so fast, Beth." Wilma beckoned toward the door. "Sheriff, I'm glad you have arrived."

A middle-aged man strode across the room, weaving between the empty tables. Beth turned to her aunt. "But you said you followed Brent from the saloon." Her glance flew from her aunt to the sheriff.

Wilma smirked. "A boy standing outside this establishment hoping to earn a coin fetched him for me." She nodded at a towheaded boy hovering near the doorway. "Come here, son."

He trotted across the room. "You already paid me, lady. You don't owe me nothin'."

She dug into her skirt pocket and pulled out a two-bit piece. "You earned this as well."

He stared at it for a long moment. "Golly! I ain't ever had two of these of my very own. Thank you, ma'am. Ma will be tickled." He dashed for the door and disappeared.

Wilma nodded to the sheriff. "This is Brent Wentworth. I believe he is wanted in several states. I shall come by later to inquire about filing charges."

"Yes, ma'am." He grasped Brent's arm and pulled him to his feet. "Let's go. I've got a tolerably comfortable cot waiting in my jail." His boots echoed against the wood floor as he drew Brent toward the door.

Wilma slumped into a chair. "I hope you will forgive me, Beth, for not telling you. I never thought we'd see him again."

Beth bent over and wrapped her arms around her aunt. "I forgive you, Auntie. But after today, it's going to be hard to trust another man again."

Chapter Twenty-Eight

Jeffery hadn't touched his book in days. Gloom had surrounded him since Beth had turned her back on him and walked out. She had been cordial at meals, but distant, and already he missed her companionship. He glanced across the dining table at her and frowned. She was avoiding his gaze again. What had happened to change her attitude toward him? Was it possible Beth wasn't being forthright with him about her feelings? He'd hoped she might understand his desire to court her, and he would have said so if she had given him the chance.

A knock sounded at the front door. Jeffery scooted his chair from the dinner table, suddenly eager to get away. "I'll get the door if you'd like me to, Mrs. Jacobs."

Micah stood. "Thank you, Mr. Tucker, but I'm expecting a visit from an attorney. He has put me off several times, and I'm hoping that might be him." He disappeared down the hall, and the muted sound of male voices drifted from the foyer.

Swift footsteps made their way back to the dining room, and Micah stepped into view, a wide smile creasing his face. "I suppose I should have taken you up on your offer, Mr. Tucker. The caller is here to see you."

Jeffery stood, looking from Mr. Jacobs to the front of the house, wishing he could see through walls.

Mrs. Cooper waved toward the doorway. "Do not stand there with your mouth agape, young man. You have a visitor. Go greet him, and if it is someone you care to visit with, I will bring you coffee in the parlor."

He gave a brief bow. "Thank you, ma'am. You are correct. I should not keep the gentleman waiting." He turned to Mr. Jacobs. "Did he happen to give his name?"

Micah hesitated. "He did, but he asked that I send you in without saying. Forgive me, but I think it's better if I follow his wishes. I seated him in the parlor."

Jeffery shot a look at Beth. Was it possible someone from the magazine had arrived in town? Something between dread and excitement danced along Jeffery's spine, and he hurried out of the room.

A man with his back turned stared out the window. His erect form and perfectly tailored clothing sent splinters of awareness through Jeffery. He cleared his throat, almost hating to have the man turn. No matter that he hadn't seen that stance in two years, he would know it anywhere. Jeffery's boot echoed on the hardwood floor, and the man swung around.

"Hello, Jeffery." Mark Tucker didn't extend his hand or move toward him. He simply stood there, hands locked behind his back, an unfathomable look cloaking his expression.

Jeffery's entire being stilled as he attempted to process the emotions that assaulted him. "Father." So much he wanted to say, but only that one word escaped. He longed to rush across the intervening space and pump his father's hand but another part of him wanted nothing more than to dash the other direction.

He took a step forward and halted as another thought pushed to the fore. Why was he here? Mark Tucker did nothing by halves and certainly not without careful consideration. It was a long journey from their family home in Ohio to Baker City, Oregon, and not one the older man would have taken without a specific reason. And Jeffery was certain he knew exactly what that purpose might be.

He tucked his hands deep into his pockets. As much as he wanted to greet his father with warmth, he wouldn't allow it to show. Not yet, at any rate. "What brings you so far west, sir? I'm guessing it's not pleasure." Jeffery carefully schooled his features.

His father tapped his toe against the floor. "That's all you've got to say?"

Jeffery lifted his chin. "Are you staying at a hotel?"

"Not any longer than I must." He brushed a thin film of dust from his sleeve. "I'll be returning as soon as I've gotten what I came for."

"And what might that be?"

He drilled Jeffery with a hard stare and strode forward. "You."

Wilma clucked to herself as she headed through the parlor to answer the firm knock at the front door. It seemed the entire household was falling apart. It had all started when that good-for-nothing Isaac Lansing sent his letter of intent-to-sue. Then Jeffery's father had arrived, and Jeffery had been scarce as hens' teeth. Beth appeared to do everything in her power to avoid the poor boy. Why, the air was drawn as tight as a bowstring when those three were in the same room. If it weren't for Caleb's presence, she'd pack her bags and return to Kansas, now that she knew Brent Wentworth was safely behind bars and not apt to bother Beth again.

On the other hand, if she did that, Jeffery would be left alone with his difficult father. Wilma hated the thought. She liked the young man and had hoped Beth's affections might swing his way. The knock repeated, a little louder this time. Wilma hurried across the foyer. "Give me a moment; I'm coming."

Breathing hard, she swung open the door and stepped aside, waving the person inside. "No need to knock." She surveyed the young man, possibly a few years older than Beth, as he gave a slight bow, then stepped past her. His day-suit and top hat were clean and serviceable, but she was happy to note they weren't reminiscent of either Wentworth or Isaac Lansing.

He offered a hesitant smile. "I beg your pardon, madam. I wasn't certain if I should enter or announce my presence first. I hope I didn't disturb your rest this fine morning."

"Fiddlesticks, the sun has been up for well over an hour. Were you looking for a room, or visiting someone?" She smothered a grin that tried to escape. The plain-spoken question almost sounded like Frances. Had she been around the woman so long she'd begun to imitate her behavior? "Forgive me, I did not mean to be rude." Wilma spread her hands and smiled. "How can I help you?"

"My mother and I will be moving to town in November. I'm hoping there might be two rooms available."

Wilma peered into his deep-blue eyes, trying to gauge the type of man he might be. If he *was* another Isaac Lansing, she'd send him packing without so much as a howdy-do.

He returned her gaze without flinching, and Wilma slowly relaxed. Nothing but honesty shone from his face, and those eyes—they seemed vaguely familiar.

He twisted the hat in his hands. "I'm sorry if I've come at a bad time."

"I'm sure it's fine. Why don't you wait here a moment? Mrs. Jacobs is finishing breakfast preparations. I'll fetch her."

Wilma entered the kitchen. Beth cracked an egg into the bowl on the counter and set the shell on the growing pile to her left. She looked up. "Getting hungry, Auntie?"

Wilma halted and glanced from Beth to Katherine. "I didn't realize you were helping this morning."

Beth nodded. "Katherine's been tired recently, so I decided she needed an extra pair of hands." She gestured in the direction of the dining room where Lucy and Zachary were setting the table. "Not that she doesn't already have two wonderful helpers."

Katherine brushed the back of her hand across her forehead, moving an errant curl. "I told her she isn't expected to lend a hand with the cooking, but she insisted."

Wilma looked around the room, then directed her attention toward the stairway. "It feels like we're family, and with you in a family way, it's not going to hurt either of us to help. Is Frances not well this morning?"

Katherine lifted a brow. "I'm not certain, but I didn't want to bother her in case her gout has flared up. Besides, Beth appeared quite early, so there was really no need."

"You seemed in a hurry to get here, Auntie," Beth added. "Is everything all right?"

"Oh my." Wilma pressed the palms of her hands against her cheeks. "I nigh forgot. You have a visitor, Katherine. Or I should say a prospective boarder. I told him I'd fetch you right away."

Katherine heaved a sigh and put down the spoon she'd used to stir the oatmeal. "We don't have another room available. I hate turning anyone away, but Mr. Tucker's father took the last one."

Beth placed the last platter of food on the table and surveyed the area critically. Everything looked perfect. She wasn't certain why it mattered so much, but she wanted Jeffery's father to approve of the home where his son had chosen to live.

Discovering Brent's deception and betrayal had been difficult, but she was starting to see she couldn't live in a world of anger. She'd spent far too many years dabbling around the edges of hurtful emotions already, and her friendship with Jeffery had helped put her feet on a more solid foundation.

But could she trust him? Really trust him? So many fears had shaped her life since her earliest memories, but Beth was determined to rise above them, with God's help. The words breathed into her spirit. She knew God could be trusted, but a tinge of sadness seeped through her heart thinking about her possible future.

Lately, in spite of what happened with Brent, she'd come to realize she wanted a relationship with Jeffery, if God allowed. But she'd made such unwise choices in the past. She touched her fingers to her lips. The gentle kiss Jeffery placed there didn't feel like a poor choice.

She couldn't forget the warmth of his lips on hers and his tender solicitude. But Brent had been the same way when they'd met—charming, caring, and ever attentive—and look what he had done. All to gain access to her aunt's money.

Beth shivered at the realization of how close she'd come to committing herself to him while in Kansas. Loathing nearly choked her. She should have seen through his declaration of love.

She adjusted a chair, hesitant to call everyone to breakfast with her mind still in a whirl. Could a man like Jeffery be seriously interested in courting her?

Footfalls sounded behind her, and she swung around. How much time had passed since Katherine left the room?

Aunt Wilma stopped beside her and patted her arm. "It looks very nice, but I think we'll need another place setting."

"Oh?" Beth looked the length of the already full table. She could squeeze another plate at the far end.

"Katherine asked the young man who arrived to stay to breakfast. She felt terrible she couldn't offer him and his mother rooms."

"Is his mother with him?" Beth glanced toward the parlor.

"I don't believe so. He said they're moving here, and he's come to find lodging. Seems like a nice young man. He reminds me of someone, but I can't quite recall who it might be."

"Did you get his name?" Beth's heart beat faster. Surely one of the young men she knew from home hadn't arrived. None of them had paid her much mind when they'd lived in Kansas, and she couldn't think of a single one she'd care to see. "You don't think it's one of Brent's friends, do you?"

Aunt Wilma started. "Certainly not. Whatever made you say such a thing?"

Relief weakened Beth's muscles, and she shrugged. "I suppose I'm still a little anxious."

Wilma planted her hands on her hips. "If one of his friends shows up, it won't matter. The scoundrel is in jail, and that's where he'll stay, if I have anything to say about it."

"I can't believe I trusted him." She shook her head.

Wilma drew Beth into the circle of her arms. "I am so sorry you had to endure that. But you can't let it cloud your perception. Why, Jeffery Tucker is a fine man, as is Caleb."

Beth broke free of her embrace. "What are you up to, Auntie? What does Jeffery have to do with this?"

"Nothing at all," her aunt replied swiftly. "I don't care to have you think every man is cut from the same cloth as Wentworth. Jeffery is simply an example of an honest man."

Katherine stepped into the room followed by a well-built man a full head taller than Beth. "I'd like to introduce Mr. Steven Harding. Mr. Harding, this is Beth Roberts and her aunt, Mrs. Roberts."

Mr. Harding inclined his head. "I'm pleased to meet you both." He studied Beth. "Something about you …" He appeared thoughtful. "Is Beth a family name? Short for Elizabeth, and after your aunt, no doubt?" He smiled warmly at Aunt Wilma.

Beth tilted her head. "Yes. I mean, no." The words almost stuck in her throat. She'd nearly told him her pen name was Elizabeth.

"My aunt's name is Wilma, and mine is Beth. I'm not certain it's a family name." She bit her lip, aware she'd said too much.

He smiled. "No matter. Are you from this area originally?"

Aunt Wilma stepped forward and placed her hand on Beth's arm. "We're from Kansas. What brings you to Baker City?"

"Business. My bank is putting in a new branch office in town, and I'll be transferred from La Grande next month. I'm hoping to find a place for my mother and myself."

Aunt Wilma nodded. "I saw the new brick building; it's quite fancy for a bank. Will you be managing it, Mr. Harding?"

"I'm afraid not, but I am one of the officers. I will be handling the loans to miners, ranchers, and such."

"I see."

Masculine voices mingled with a childish one neared the room, and Beth turned, her heart skipping a beat. Jeffery and his father entered, accompanied by Mandy. She clung to the older man's hand, chattering so fast Beth could barely make out a word. Mr. Tucker gazed down at her, apparently intent on catching every syllable, his face drawn in concentration.

Jeffery approached Mr. Harding and extended his hand, shooting a glance toward Beth. "Hello, I'm Jeffery Tucker, and this is my father, Mark Tucker. Will you be lodging here?"

Steven Harding shook his head, his fine blue eyes clouding. "Pleased to meet you both. I regret Mrs. Jacobs doesn't have room and doesn't believe that will change before we move."

Mark Tucker straightened and looked from his son to the stranger, a slight smile curving his thin lips. "Oh, but I'm sure there will be, Mr. Harding. Two in fact."

Beth sucked in a breath. "Whatever do you mean, Mr. Tucker?"

"I understand it could snow in the mountain passes any time, and I don't care to be stranded here. Jeffery and I will be returning home soon."

Chapter Twenty-Nine

Jeffery couldn't get Beth's face out of his mind. Apparently, his father's declaration had shocked her. It had been hours since those words were uttered, and her image was as clear as though it happened moments ago. Dismay, chased by—what? Resentment? Alarm? He couldn't be sure. She'd walked out of the room right after the announcement. When she returned, she had avoided looking at him the rest of the meal.

He glared into the mirror above his bureau and jerked at his tight collar, hating the thought of not seeing Beth this evening. Somehow he must let her know he hadn't agreed to go home with his father. He gritted his teeth. The record would get set straight with his parent at dinner tonight, that he could promise. That was the only reason he'd agreed to dine with him at the Arlington Hotel. He didn't know when he'd have the opportunity to speak with Beth alone, but speak to her he would. Did she care if he went home? Hope pulsed through Jeffery's veins until he recalled the resentment that had shone in her eyes.

Time to turn his attention elsewhere before he choked. He loosened his grip on his collar, picked up his jacket, and shook it. The man who'd arrived at breakfast … what was his name? Steven

Harding. He seemed a pleasant enough sort, and Beth didn't appear at all interested in pursuing his acquaintance. Dark hair, a firm jaw, and an erect bearing, all things that seemed to attract women, but Beth had barely spoken to Harding throughout the meal. Jeffery grimaced. Of course, she hadn't deigned to speak to *him* either.

Enough, Tucker. Jeffery shut the door behind him and headed toward the parlor. Laughter and the buzz of voices drew him forward. It had been so long since he'd heard his father laugh.

Frances Cooper looked up as he entered. "Young man, you have a delightful father. I hope you are aware of how blessed you are."

Jeffery halted, and his gaze went to Beth, sitting on the far end of the sofa, before swinging to the older woman. "Good evening, Mrs. Cooper. I hope you're feeling better tonight." He was not getting drawn into a discussion about the merits of his father's personality. "Mrs. Roberts, Beth, you both look lovely, as always."

Beth met his gaze. "Thank you, Jeffery. Your father was telling us he's taking you to supper." Her voice sounded breathless, and a tiny smile emerged.

"Would you care to join us?" The words left his mouth before he could stop them.

His father leveled him with an unpleasant glare, but Jeffery squared his shoulders. "I would love for the two of you to get better acquainted."

In for a penny, in for a pound, he thought. And the truth was, he would like his father to see how much he cared for Beth. No longer was it only the need to learn the stories of the townspeople that kept him from returning home. It was this woman he'd come to care for the past few months. Maybe if his father got better acquainted with Beth, he'd understand.

Frances exchanged a knowing look with Wilma.

His father inclined his head, the smile on his lips not quite reaching his eyes. "I'd be most pleased to have you accompany us, Miss Roberts."

Beth looked from one to the other. Finally, her tense stance relaxed. "Thank you. That would be very nice. As long as I'm not interfering."

Jeffery stepped over beside her. "Not in the least. We haven't had a chance to talk in days, and I would love your company." He prayed the warm look he gave her would convey more than his desire for her companionship at this one meal.

Jeffery pulled out Beth's chair and seated her, hoping his father would recognize his desire to stay in Baker City. Not that he'd leave regardless, but he hated the idea of more hurt occurring within their family. If only Father could come to terms with the idea that not everyone wanted to sail through life on someone else's money or follow in their footsteps.

Beth leaned toward his father with a smile and replied to something he'd asked. Jeffery's heart stirred. He wanted to court her, but more than that, he longed to earn her trust. Yet something seemed to prevent her from opening up to him that he didn't understand. A certain reticence in her behavior and a withdrawal when he got too close. He'd searched his memory for anything he'd said that might have created a rift, but he couldn't come up with a single thing.

Other than the conversation in the kitchen concerning his relationship with God.

Jeffery leaned back in his chair. Could that be the problem? Beth had shared her confusion over certain aspects of religion, but she'd stated she had a true friendship with God. That wasn't something he'd attempted to develop and lately he'd wondered if he'd missed out on an important facet of life. From what Beth had said, that was highly likely. He'd have to study on it some more, and in the meantime, he'd take a closer look at his Bible and perhaps strike up a conversation with God.

Beth placed the napkin back in her lap and smiled at Jeffery. "Thank you for inviting me. It was a wonderful meal." The atmosphere had been comfortable since they arrived at the restaurant, but it was apparent now that Mr. Tucker was chafing to talk to his son alone.

Jeffery glanced at his father, then back at her. "I'm glad you agreed to accompany us."

Mark Tucker shifted in his chair. "I'm sorry I haven't been a better host." He tapped his fingers on the table. "I've had a lot on my mind, but our time together this evening has been most enjoyable. I'm truly happy you came, Miss Roberts."

"Thank you. But I wish you'd call me Beth."

He smiled and nodded. "All right then, I will. You mentioned that you and your aunt are from back East?"

She nodded. "Yes, from Topeka, Kansas."

"Have you lived there all your life?"

She hesitated. "Most of it, sir." Her mind scrambled, trying to find a way to open a new topic before this one got out of hand. "How about you? Were you raised in Cincinnati?"

He propped his forearms on the table. "I was. The Tucker family has lived in Ohio for two generations—three counting our children—but my grandfather emigrated from Virginia. Our ancestors arrived in this country about fifty years after the *Mayflower* landed. We have a heritage that Jeffery can be proud of passing along to his children someday." He straightened and trained his gaze intently on her. "What of your family?"

Beth swung her eyes to Jeffery, uncertain how to reply.

Jeffery pushed back his chair and rose, holding out his hand to Beth. "It's getting late. Were you ready to return home?"

She gave him a smile that she hoped conveyed the relief rippling through her. "I am a little tired, although I've had a delightful time." Transferring her attention to Mr. Tucker, she attempted to soften the abrupt departure. "I imagine you'd appreciate some time alone with your son before the evening ends."

He dipped his head and got to his feet. "I've enjoyed getting to know you, Beth, but you are correct. I don't feel I've had enough opportunity to talk with Jeffery since I arrived."

Jeffery took her cape from the back of her chair and settled it around her. Beth briefly closed her eyes, savoring the touch of his hands.

Stepping back, Jeffery turned to his father. "We'll be glad for the buggy with the chill in the air." He offered his arm to Beth and guided her outside.

Mark Tucker untied the horse while Jeffery walked Beth to the buggy and extended his hand. "Allow me?"

Beth placed her gloved fingers into his and stepped up. The toe of her slipper caught in the hem of her wide gown, and her other hand grasped at the air as she attempted to find the handle.

Strong hands encircled her waist and steadied her. Jeffery stood close behind her but didn't loosen his hold. Beth could feel the pound of his heart as he drew her against his chest and waited. "All right now?"

She nodded, trying to quiet her breathing. "I think so." Moving her head a little, her cheek touched his, and a jolt ran through her. Her hands shook as she reached for the buggy's handhold again. "I'm glad you were there."

"So am I." Slowly he released his grip from her waist. "If you're sure." He waited for her to get settled in the backseat, then swung up beside his father.

Beth was thankful for the darkness that shielded her rosy cheeks. If only Jeffery had chosen to occupy the seat beside her. It was only a half-mile to the house, but if the state of her emotions were any indication, the journey would have been quite fulfilling.

The next morning Beth leaned her head against the overstuffed chair in the parlor, reliving the evening before.

She knew exactly why she'd gone—Jeffery had asked her. The longing in his expression had been so intense she couldn't say no, even with his father glowering his disapproval. And when Jeffery had stepped to her side and looked down at her, she had almost melted at his nearness. Beth relaxed, remembering the strong touch of his hands as he'd kept her from falling.

"Beth?"

She sat upright and blinked. Jeffery leaned against the door frame of the parlor. Had thinking about him made him materialize? "Hello. Is your father with you?"

"No, he's working on some correspondence. Writing to Mother, I assume."

Beth smiled up at him. "I had a wonderful time last night, and I'm so glad you asked me to come." She hesitated before plunging into what had been on her mind since awakening that morning. "I hope you don't object to my asking, but are you going home with your father? He made it quite clear last night that he expects you to."

Jeffery indicated the sofa across from her chair. "Do you mind if I join you?"

"Please do."

He frowned. "I'm afraid I will continue to be a disappointment to my parents."

"I'm sure you aren't a disappointment, Jeffery."

He offered a rueful grin. "Oh, but I am. I have been so for several years, and when I refuse to accompany him home, it will only intensify." Leaning forward, he held her eyes. "I do not care to leave Baker City."

Beth's breath caught, and her heart tripped before settling into a faster rate. "I know you are working on your second book, and I'm so sorry we've not had a chance to discuss it." She bent her head.

Jeffery scooted forward to the edge of the sofa cushion, his knees only inches from hers. "That is not why I'm choosing to stay, Beth. I hope you know that."

"I'm not sure ..." She shivered at his nearness, and she didn't know whether to move back in her chair or inch closer toward him. Her heart pulled her toward him, but she settled for staying exactly where she was.

"I think you are." A smile hovered around the corners of his mouth. "We haven't discussed that I kissed you. I must admit, I am not sorry at all. In fact, if I had it to do over again ..." Jeffery took her hand in his. "Surely you know by now that I care for you. We haven't had a lot of time to get properly acquainted, and I'll confess I took unfair liberties when I kissed you, but I couldn't help myself." He squeezed her hand. "If I stay here in Baker City, would you allow me to court you?"

"*If* you stay?" Visions of Brent's desertion so many months ago loomed, and she drew back in the chair, her hand slipping free of his. Almost immediately she longed to grasp it again.

"I'm sorry. I did not mean to imply I might leave," he explained. "I plan to stay, regardless of your decision. I know that you've been hurt by Wentworth. I'm not sure what he promised you, but I understand he lied to you and cheated your aunt. I am not that kind of man." His tender gaze held hers. "Won't you give me a chance?"

Beth hesitated. If she said yes, and Jeffery later discovered her terrible scars, would he flee in revulsion and horror? The only reason Brent returned was the hope of gaining access to her aunt's money. He'd said as much himself. And he had scorned her womanhood and cast aspersions on her past.

Jeffery *wasn't* that type of man. If she said no and walked away, would she ever be certain she'd made the right decision?

She drew in a quick breath. "All right. I'll trust you, but let's move slowly, all right?"

He nodded, his eyes shining with hope. "I'm praying you'll learn to believe in me before too long."

October 15, 1880, La Grande, Oregon
The creak of the wooden door signaled Steven's arrival, and Isabelle eased up from her chair. She held the magazine carefully extended before her, unwilling to crumple the pages she'd been staring at for what seemed like hours.

Steven shrugged out of his coat and hat and hung them on a peg behind the door. "It's getting mighty cold. I wouldn't be surprised if we get snow early this year. Maybe we need to think of moving sooner." He turned and studied her. "Is something wrong?"

A strangled cry broke from Isabelle's throat. "Look." She thrust the magazine into his hands, open to the page that continued to haunt her.

He glanced down, then raised his eyes. "It's a story about a boardinghouse. What is it you want me to see?"

"The illustration." She pointed a shaking hand to the picture near the top of the page.

"It's very nice, but I don't understand …"

"Look at the name of the person who drew it, Steven." Isabelle held her breath, almost afraid to breathe in case the name should disappear. Had she imagined the connection? Was it possible the past had finally caught up to her?

He stared at the illustration but only saw the initials E.C., so he flipped to the front of the magazine and purused the scant information about the story and the illustrator. "Elizabeth Corwin." He stepped over to the window and placed the page squarely in the dim light filtering through the heavy clouds. "I'm still not sure what you're upset about."

Isabelle moved to his side and peered over his arm. "Surely you remember that name."

"Yes, I know Corwin was your maiden name, but we don't know any family members called Elizabeth Corwin. Do you think it might be a relative we haven't met?"

She plucked the magazine from his hands. "Could it … do you think it possible, Steven?" Her shaking hands could barely hold the magazine as hope and fear collided, leaving her weak.

He jerked as if hit with a branding iron. "Now, Ma, don't get your hopes up. How many times have you thought you'd found her, only to be disappointed? If Bess is alive, why would she use Grandmother's name?" He shook his head. "It seems highly unlikely this person is Bess. It's possible she's a distant relative … or not related at all." Steven gently took the magazine and flipped to the first page. "It says here it's published in Pittsburgh, Pennsylvania. Do you know of any family back East?"

Isabelle struggled to keep the tears from spilling onto her cheeks. She couldn't be disappointed again. All day she'd been staring at this story and imagining her little girl all grown up and drawing these pictures. Bess had liked to draw when she was a wee thing, always scribbling on any scrap of paper or making pictures in the dirt. "Do you think we could contact the publisher or talk to the man who wrote the story? He might know who she is or where she lives."

Steven shrugged. "I don't know if the magazine would give a stranger that kind of information." He flipped the pages until he located the story again. "It says the author is Jeffery Tucker, but no address or other information is given."

She sank into her rocker and pushed with her toes, the creak of the old wood a comfort to her ears.

Her son suddenly stilled. "I met this man." He lifted his head. "On my last trip to Baker City." Steven jabbed at the page. "And it says right here he's working out West writing the story but originally comes from Cincinnati. And the picture of this valley and town could easily be Baker City."

Isabelle slumped against the wooden spindles and started to sob. "You've got to go back." She grabbed his sleeve. "Please, Son. And you must take me with you."

Chapter Thirty

October 18, 1880

Jeffery fiddled with his spoon and glanced around the restaurant, wondering if the man would put in an appearance. Why had Steven Harding sent word asking to meet him away from the boarding-house? What could he possibly want? He pulled out his pocket watch and glanced at the face. Ten after four. A glimpse out the window showed the October sky was already growing dim with heavy clouds, and the sun sank over the mountains toward the western horizon.

Hard to believe it was already the eighteenth of October, and his father had yet to depart. If he didn't leave soon, he could be trapped by an early snowfall, if what he heard from the old-timers was true. Most years, winter didn't set in until the middle of November, although the Wallowa Mountains could get a coat well before then. He'd noticed a dusting of white on the Elkhorn Mountains while walking to town today and brought a heavy neck scarf to tuck into his woolen coat.

He pushed back his chair. It appeared Harding wasn't going to appear. Just as well—dusk would arrive in a little over an hour.

"I beg your pardon, Mr. Tucker, for keeping you waiting." Steven Harding strode the last several paces to the table and held out his hand. "I had to stop by the bank, and they kept me longer than I expected."

Jeffery rose and took the man's hand, appreciating the firm grip. "I'm glad I waited, then. Would you care for something to drink? It's quiet this time of day."

Steven seated himself and nodded. "A strong cup of black coffee sounds perfect." He twisted around and caught the server's eye.

She hurried over, coffeepot in hand, and filled his cup. "Anything for you to eat, sir?"

"This is fine for now, thank you." Steven took a sip and closed his eyes.

Jeffery chuckled. "Your first time to sit today, I take it. You can always tell a tired man by the way he appreciates his coffee."

"It has indeed been a long day." Steven took another drink and set his cup down, cradling it with his hands. "I'm sure you're wondering why I asked to meet."

"I am." Jeffery saw no need to waste time. The man was tired, and he had no desire to linger after dark.

"All right then. I'll lay it out for you. I didn't care to bother Mrs. Jacobs, and I didn't spend much time with anyone else for the short amount of time I was at your boardinghouse." He drummed his fingers on the table, then his body tensed. "I'll get right to the point. I want you to tell me everything you know about a Miss Elizabeth Corwin."

Jeffery sat back and stared. "I beg your pardon?" Anger caused his muscles to tighten. Was this another good-for-nothing like Brent Wentworth, out to discover a young woman he could take advantage of? He hadn't gotten that impression on their first meeting, but this type of question was highly unusual. He suddenly jerked up short. Harding had asked about Elizabeth Corwin, not Beth Roberts—he apparently didn't know they were one and the same—and Jeffery had no intention of disclosing that fact. "Why do you ask?"

Steven shrugged. "I saw your name in a magazine alongside hers."

Jeffery nodded and relaxed his clenched jaw. "She's the illustrator for my book that's running in *The Women's Eastern Magazine*. But, to be blunt, I don't care for your question."

Steven held up his hand. "I'm sorry. I went about that wrong. Let me back up and start over."

Jeffery crossed his arms over his chest. "That would be wise."

"My mother begged me to return to Baker City, and she wanted to come along, but I wouldn't allow it. Her health is poor, and the trip is too long. It will be hard enough moving her here in a couple of weeks, and I'm wondering now if that's even possible, the way the weather is looking."

"What does your mother have to do with Miss Corwin?"

The tension seemed to ooze out of Steven, and he slumped in his chair. "She thinks it is possible Miss Corwin might be my sister."

Jeffery stiffened, his mind abuzz. Slowly he reexamined the man sitting across from him. Similar eyes, hair a shade darker, and a warm smile that somehow resembled Beth's. He had known Harding looked familiar the first time they'd met him, but had no idea—

He jerked his thoughts to a halt. Having a family resemblance meant little. There were swindlers on every corner these days. Just look at Brent Wentworth. "What makes your mother believe that?"

He narrowed his eyes as another thought occurred. "And why would you not know your own sister?"

Steven placed his forearms on the table. "Both good questions, but not ones I care to explain fully at the moment. I will tell you that we've been separated for a number of years, but beyond that I'd prefer not to say."

Jeffery straightened his frame. "Then I'm afraid I am not at liberty to give you more information."

Steven drew in his breath and expelled it with a soft grunt. "All right. My sister disappeared when she was very young, and Corwin is a family name. I would rather not go into a lot of detail now, if you please. Can you at least tell me if you know her?"

"I might." Jeffery's mind shot forward, trying to work through the scant information. "Although I don't see why you can't tell me more."

"I'm sorry, but I don't know you, Tucker. I didn't come here to tell you my family history, but to inquire if you have a way for me to get in touch with Miss Corwin. Is that too much to ask?"

"Why don't you tell me a little about your mother first?"

"Fair enough." Steven settled against his chair and took a drink of his coffee. "She was widowed a number of years ago and lives in La Grande. Her health is poor, and she's been holding on, hoping to find Bess again."

Jeffery started. "Bess? Your sister's name?"

"Yes."

"I see." Jeffery drummed his fingers on the tabletop. "I can't personally introduce you to Miss Corwin, but I'd be willing to see that a letter gets to her, if you'd care to give me one before you return to La Grande."

Steven's face fell. "I was hoping she might live here, and I could meet her."

Jeffery shook his head. "A letter will have to do." Uncertainty twisted his gut, but he held firm. He needed to investigate this man and his mother before he allowed this to go any further. Beth had been deeply hurt once already. The last thing she needed right now was two people posing as long-lost relatives hoping to latch onto money they might envision as a result of her prominent placement on the magazine cover. Harding didn't seem like that sort, but according to Mrs. Roberts, Wentworth had fooled her at first meeting as well.

Steven placed his cup on the table. "Shall I bring it by your boardinghouse tomorrow before I leave town?"

"No." Jeffery gave a decisive shake of his head. "I'll come by the bank if that's convenient."

"Fine. I leave on the morning stage. Meet me at half-past eight."

Beth peered at the watch pinned to the front of her dress. Nine thirty. She'd been up for three hours already and had gotten some much-needed work done on a new illustration before she'd attended breakfast. After the meal, Jeffery had agreed to meet her in the parlor at nine o'clock, and she'd already waited for thirty minutes. She gathered her skirts. Maybe trusting Jeffery was a bad idea.

A light patter of footsteps sounded along the hall and Mandy entered, tugging Mark Tucker's hand. Beth hid a smile. She hadn't envisioned Jeffery's father as someone to spend time with a young child, but since he'd arrived, Katherine's young daughter had been very much in evidence, and he didn't seem the least perturbed.

Mandy slowed to a halt and grinned, her wide smile showing a space where her front teeth used to be. "Mr. Tucker is going to read me a book." She tipped her head to the side. "Do you want to listen?"

The man in question ruffled Mandy's hair. "We don't want to disturb you, Miss Roberts. Maybe we should wait for another time, or we can take the book to the dining room if you'd prefer."

"Certainly not. You are more than welcome to stay. I was waiting for …" She clamped down on her lip, wondering how much to say.

Mr. Tucker gave a sage nod. "My son. Earlier he mentioned running to town. He told me he was meeting someone and hoped it wouldn't take too long. Is he late?"

"I'm afraid so." Beth relaxed against the sofa cushions. So Jeffery had told his father where he was going. Maybe he did have a good reason for the delay. "I'll wait a little longer, if the two of you don't mind my listening in. What are you reading?"

Mandy ran over to a bookshelf and pointed. "*Alice's Adventures in Wonderland*." She stood on her tiptoes but couldn't quite reach the volume.

Mr. Tucker stopped beside her. "Allow me, Amanda." He plucked the book from its place and handed it to her with a flourish.

She giggled and hugged it to her chest. "I love this book. Come on, Mr. Tucker."

He obediently followed her to the sofa, and Mandy curled up beside him as he spread the volume across his lap.

Beth watched the scene unfold. *How fascinating.* From the little Jeffery had said about this man, she'd expected him to be cross, but other than pressing Jeffery to return home, he'd appeared quite pleasant. She leaned her head back, allowing the words to flow over her and enjoying the smooth cadence of the voice that reminded her so much of his son's.

"Father?" Jeffery's voice interrupted her reverie, and she sat up. He stood in the doorway, his expression curious as he looked from the duo to Beth and back again. "I'm sorry to interrupt." His gaze swung her way. "I hope you'll forgive me for being tardy." A shadow seemed to darken his eyes. "It was unavoidable."

Beth straightened her sleeves, making certain her wrists were covered. "The time has flown. I've enjoyed listening to your father."

Mark Tucker closed the book. "Amanda, do you mind if we finish this another time? I think Miss Roberts and Mr. Jeffery had an appointment, and we don't want to interfere."

Jeffery nodded gratefully. "Thank you, sir. That is, if you really don't mind."

"Not at all. Amanda and I will go to the kitchen and see if Mrs. Jacobs can spare a cup of tea." He rose and held out his hand. "Would you care for some tea, Miss Galloway?"

Mandy giggled and slipped her hand in his. "Yes, sir. I love tea parties."

Mr. Tucker set the book back on the shelf and directed his attention to Jeffery. "I hope you can find time for me a little later. I'd like to talk to you concerning an idea that might be of benefit to Mr. and Mrs. Jacobs." He turned and nodded to Beth. "Miss Roberts, you're welcome to sit in on our reading anytime."

"Thank you." Beth smiled as they left the room. "Your father can be quite charming."

He sank into a chair. "I had no idea. I remember him reading to my sisters when they were young, but ..." He ran his hand over his hair and glanced at the doorway. "It's been a while since I was home, and this doesn't fit the picture I've had of him."

Beth settled against the soft cushions, wondering at the confusion so evident on Jeffery's face. What she'd give to have a parent who cared enough to go halfway across the continent to see her and attempt to persuade her to return home. A pang of apprehension hit her. Mr. Tucker was a decent man, and it seemed Jeffery's eyes were getting opened more every day. "And what picture did you have of your father?"

"A man intent on getting his own way, whatever the cost." His forehead wrinkled. "He was so adamant about me going back to Ohio when he first arrived, but lately ..." He shook his head. "I don't know, but something is different. In fact, I believe it started when you accompanied us to supper the other night."

Beth smiled. "I can't imagine that could be true. He didn't speak to me much, and I got the impression he was upset I'd come along."

"I wondered at the time, but now I'm not so sure. Did he reveal anything before I came in about why he wants to speak to me? He mentioned Mr. and Mrs. Jacobs."

"Not at all. Do you think he's considering extending his time here?" Beth's heartbeat quickened. If Mr. Tucker decided to remain in town for a time, he might come to like it and quit urging Jeffery to go with him. She repositioned herself on the sofa and tucked a pillow under her elbow. "Were you able to take care of your business in town?"

Jeffery's face smoothed, but she thought she caught a glimpse of … something.

Jeffery flicked at a piece of lint on his trousers. "Yes, I suppose so. There was someone I needed to see before he left town." The letter Steven Harding had given him at the stage station lodged like a boulder over his heart, pressing in and making small rivulets of sweat run down his back. He had promised to give it to her, but the matter of whether it would hurt or help her weighed on his mind.

Beth leaned forward. "Jeffery."

"Hmm?" His glance darted to hers, then edged away. "Sorry. I guess I'm a bit distracted."

"What's wrong? Is it anything I said?"

His attention centered squarely on her. "No. Of course not. I've been trying to sort through a knotty problem." Was this the right time? What if Harding was a fake, and she were hurt again? He didn't want to be a part of that happening. If only he had time to investigate the man before he handed over the letter. But would she forgive him if he kept it a secret, and it turned out Harding was telling the truth?

"Is there a way I might help? Are you concerned about your story?" She laced her fingers together in her lap.

Jeffery brought his thoughts back to the woman sitting across from him. The letter could wait. He'd distressed her and needed to make it right. "It *has* been on my mind lately. Now that I've finished the first book, I'm trying to work out all the details for the second."

The lines in her face smoothed out. "Ah, I see. I haven't had a chance to tell you, but I read the first three chapters."

Delight drove out the last lingering vestiges of worry. "What did you think? Please be completely frank, and don't try to spare my feelings."

Her face sobered, and Jeffery experienced a moment of dread. Had he misjudged Beth's initial reaction? He straightened his shoulders.

"I think"—she cocked her head and a smile peeked out—"that your book will be a bestseller one day. As much as I determined not to like it when you acquainted the household with the idea, I must admit I was captivated. The characters drew me in immediately. Of course, I don't have a strong sense of the story line yet, but enough to know I shall enjoy it immensely, as I'm sure anyone shall who reads it."

He released the breath he held. "How very kind. Thank you."

She shook her head. "I am not being kind. My words were honest, as you asked. So you see, you don't need to be troubled."

A lump formed in Jeffery's throat, and he swallowed. He couldn't deceive her, couldn't allow her to think the book was his only concern. Lately he'd been trying to pray, working to develop a personal relationship with God. Somehow he didn't think keeping the letter a secret would further that relationship. "Thank you, but that wasn't what has me distracted." He stared at his hands laced between his knees, then lifted his eyes. "I'm not sure how to tell you what's bothering me, other than to come right out and say it. I pray it will bring you peace and not added distress."

Every thought in Beth's mind halted as she absorbed Jeffery's words. Had he received word from their editor about her work not being satisfactory? But if that were the case, he wouldn't think it could bring her peace. She tried to shake the disjointed thoughts. "Has something happened with your story? Are they unhappy with my illustrations?" She focused on his face, determined to catch even the slightest hesitation.

"No, no. Nothing like that at all." He plunged ahead. "It happens to be a bit more personal."

Curiosity swarmed Beth's thoughts like a hive of bees getting ready for winter. "I can't imagine ..." She peered at Jeffery's firmly clamped jaw. "Please. Tell me."

Jeffery scooted his chair closer to the sofa. "The reason I was late ..." He licked his lips as though trying to find the courage to continue. "The man I met in town claims he might be your brother."

Chapter Thirty-One

Wilma stopped on the path to the house and placed a kiss on Caleb's cheek. "You are a wonderful man. I do hope you know that."

He slipped his arm around her. "I may forget that on a regular basis and need to be reminded, especially if that reminder comes with an accompanying kiss."

She settled her head against his shoulder and sighed. Why had she assumed for so many years that love would never find her again? Caleb hadn't asked her to marry him in so many words, but he'd been hinting so strongly she knew it was coming. "Thank you for all you've done to try to help me find Beth's family—or, at least, to discover what might have happened to her so many years ago. It means a lot to have your support and understanding."

Caleb drew her onto the boardinghouse porch. "As much as I'm enjoying this time together, we probably should go in. I don't want to tarnish your reputation, should anyone happen to look out the window." He tucked a wayward curl behind her ear. "If you were to allow me to make an announcement …"

Wilma's heart galloped at an alarming rate. "Announcement?"

"This isn't the way I planned on asking, but I'm not sure I can stand it much longer." He gathered both her hands into his and placed a gentle kiss on her knuckles. "Wilma Roberts, I love you and want to marry you. Would you consider taking on an old man like me this late in my life?"

Wilma stood silent for what felt like minutes. Then happiness radiated through every part of her being. "I'd be proud and honored, Caleb Marshall. In fact, I can't think of anything that would make me happier."

He placed a tender kiss on her lips. "I promise you won't be sorry."

She wiggled an eyebrow playfully. "I don't intend to be. What do you say we get inside where it's a little warmer and share with Beth, and then the rest of the family? That is, unless you want to keep it a secret for now?"

His face transformed into one huge smile, and he pushed open the door. "No more secrets. I could shout it from the rooftop, you've made me so happy."

Wilma sailed into the foyer and tugged Caleb toward the parlor. They stopped at the doorway as Mark Tucker came up the hall from the dining room.

He tipped his head. "Good afternoon."

Caleb stuck out his hand and gripped Mr. Tucker's. "A fine one, indeed." He pumped the other man's hand.

Wilma peered into the parlor. "Jeffery. Beth. I'm so glad to see you both. Is Frances or Katherine about?"

Beth raised her head, her face pale and tight. "I don't know, Auntie." She scooted to the edge of the sofa. "Would you like me to go look?"

Wilma stared at Jeffery, then back at Beth. "We've come at a bad time, haven't we?" How foolish. Why hadn't she bothered to look into the room before speaking? It was quite apparent the two young people were having a serious conversation. She turned to the two gentlemen standing behind her. "Let's go to the kitchen and see if Katherine and Frances are there."

Beth pushed to her feet. "It's all right. Mr. Tucker needs to speak to Jeffery, and I'm going to my room. I hope you'll all excuse me." She brushed past Wilma with barely a nod.

Wilma's stomach twisted in a knot. She hadn't seen that lost look on her girl's face for many years. Not since the day seventeen years ago when Beth had arrived at her door.

Beth had kept the letter Jeffery had given her tucked in the folds of her skirt as she made her way out of the parlor. She lay on her bed, though she didn't remember climbing a single stair.

If only Aunt Wilma and the others hadn't come in when they did. Beth had so many more questions to ask Jeffery, but she didn't care to make this situation public—especially since the letter Jeffery had handed her was addressed to Miss Elizabeth Corwin.

Her hands shook so hard she wasn't certain she could open the envelope. Jeffery told her Steven Harding had given it to him before he boarded the stage heading back to La Grande. The young man who'd asked for rooms for himself and his mother.

His mother.

Was it even remotely possible the woman could also be *her* mother? Why hadn't he spoken to her personally, rather than using Jeffery as a go-between?

Beth groaned and rolled her head against the pillow. Her pen name. But why did he think Elizabeth Corwin might be his sister?

She propped her hand on her elbow and stared at the envelope with the flowing script across the face. The only way to get the answers to those questions was to gather her courage and see what this contained.

And would it contain the truth? Jeffery had expressed concern and reminded her of Brent's scheme to gain access to her finances. What if it *was* a hoax?

She swung her feet over the edge of the bed. *Please God, don't let Aunt Wilma come up to check on me.* Beth wanted to fall on her knees and cry out to her heavenly Father, begging Him to make this be true. But another part of her wasn't so sure. Would the cords of her life begin to weave together with the reading of this letter, or would they unravel worse than before?

Beth slid her fingertip under the glued flap and raised the edge until she exposed the creamy stationery inside. She stared at it, drawn to the paper like a child to a candy counter.

Gathering her courage, she pinched the exposed portion of paper, tugged it out, and lay it facedown on her skirt.

How childish. It was only a letter from a stranger and might have no meaning at all. Resolutely Beth flipped over the missive. She closed her eyes, then took a deep breath and opened them, staring down at the beautifully scripted words.

Dear Miss Corwin,
I'm not certain how to present this. At best, you might find it ridiculous, or at worst, it will come as a shock. My name is Steven Harding, and my mother's name is Isabelle Mason, as she married again after my father's death. I would like to inquire—

Forgive me, I find it hard to know how to proceed. I've rewritten this letter five times now and am on my last sheet. My mother and I have been searching for a missing family member for a number of years. She saw your drawings in The Women's Eastern Magazine and noted your name. I realize it will sound fanciful and presumptive, but my sister's name was Elizabeth. We called her Bess. My mother's maiden name was Corwin, and when she saw your name, it gave her hope that you might know something about her daughter.

Mother felt you might be she, but after careful reflection, I am more of the opinion this is a mistake. But I must keep my word and inquire, as Mother has numerous spells of weakness, and I fear another disappointment could cause grave consequences. Is it possible you might be related to our family? My father was Charles Harding, and my maternal grandmother was Mary Ann Elizabeth Corwin. We traveled by wagon train to Oregon seventeen years ago.

I am hesitant to go into much detail by post, as my mother has suffered deep guilt over the loss of her child, and it is something she should explain. I am feeling most foolish writing this, as my sister's name was Harding, not Corwin. But if you can convey any information concerning a young woman named Bess, I would be forever in your debt. You can reach me by post, and we'll await your reply with humble gratitude.

Yours most sincerely,
Steven Harding

Beth fell against the pillow, clutching the letter. *Seventeen years ago. Headed to Oregon. His father was dead.* The thoughts flew through her mind faster than she could process them. Why hadn't he explained how his mother had "lost" her child? What did that mean, anyway?

Hope tried to surface but was quickly replaced with a deep sense of dread. Was it possible a child could be accidentally lost for so many years, or was the woman having pangs of supposed "remorse" after seeing the illustrations in a national magazine?

Beth rubbed her hands over her face, not sure what to think. Jeffery had admitted he'd found Steven Harding to be a decent sort, but they'd only spent a short amount of time together, and anyone could put on airs if the need required. She'd certainly learned that from personal experience.

She could conceive of no reasonable explanation as to how they could have lost a three-and-a-half-year-old child. And even if they had, why hadn't the parents come looking? Plucking the letter up, she scanned it again, searching for the sentence that struck her so hard.

My mother has suffered deep guilt over the loss of her child, and it is something she should explain.

Why would the woman be suffering guilt if she hadn't done something inherently bad? Beth's fingers relaxed, and the letter fluttered to the floor while her thoughts continued to race. And why care now, so many years later, unless she had something to gain?

Beth had waited seventeen years for the truth, and right now she wasn't positive she could handle it. Too often truth only brought pain and deeper loneliness.

Maybe she would pray about it and talk to Jeffery, then give it a few days, or weeks, and see how she felt.

Footsteps sounded on the stairs and grew louder as they progressed up the hall. Beth bolted from the bed and swept the letter off the floor. She stuffed it into the envelope and hurried to her desk. This was not something she cared to discuss with her aunt. Not now, and possibly not ever. The last thing Beth wanted to do was to hurt the woman who had poured so much love into her life.

Jeffery paced the floor of the parlor across from his father, situated on the sofa. He had wanted to dash up the stairs after Beth, hold and comfort her, and assure her everything would be all right. Hope had blazed in her eyes when he'd given her the letter from Steven Harding, but within minutes it had withered, replaced by anxiety. Had he done the wrong thing in conveying the message? Why hadn't he thought it through longer, rather than rushing home and delivering the envelope? He should have known how it would affect her.

"Son, why don't you sit down so we can talk?" his father requested. "I would guess your trouble has to do with a certain young woman who appears to be in distress. But I have something I want to discuss with you as well." He waved toward the chair flanking the sofa. "Sit."

The habit of boyhood years made Jeffery halt, but he took his time doing his father's bidding. His guard slipped into place. He had little doubt that the subject up for discussion was returning home at the earliest possible convenience. It didn't matter—he had no intention of going anywhere. Not with Beth upset and her future at stake.

He leaned back in his chair and crossed his arms over his chest. "I'm afraid I don't have a lot of time. You're correct. Beth is upset. I appreciate you noticing, but I doubt there's anything you can do to help."

Mark Tucker gave a slow nod. "Perhaps so; we'll have to see. But, first, the item I want to discuss."

"Yes, about that."

His father quirked a brow. "Tell me a little more about Miss Roberts and her aunt."

Jeffery's heart stilled, and he eyed the parlor door. "Anyone could walk in, you know."

His father nodded. "Quite so. But I do have a reason for asking, and I'd appreciate an answer."

Jeffery restrained a snort. It was amazing how kind his parent could be one moment and how haughty the next. "Then I suggest we retire to my room, if you don't mind."

"Lead the way."

They traveled upstairs in silence. Jeffery pulled the door shut and motioned toward the overstuffed chair, then took his own seat at the straight-backed chair next to his desk. "What did you want to know?"

"From what Beth said, I gather they traveled here from Topeka, but I didn't catch what brought them so far west. Do they have family here?"

Jeffery winced. A couple of days ago he could have honestly answered in the negative, but now that he knew about Steven ... yet what did he really know? No proof had been offered by Harding or his mother, and Beth had not confirmed their suspicion as correct.

"I can't say, sir. From what I understood when they arrived, Mrs. Roberts made the decision to travel for personal reasons."

"Do they plan on relocating here or returning to Kansas?"

"I'm not certain, but I haven't heard either of them discuss leaving."

"It's curious they would be content to remain in a boardinghouse and haven't found a home of their own."

Jeffery laced his fingers around his knee. "May I ask where all of this is leading?"

His father hesitated, then gave a short nod. "I suppose that's a fair question. I am trying to determine if you will ever be willing to move back to civilization where you belong."

Jeffery could not tolerate another round of pressure about returning home. "Father, I'm sorry. Let me make it clear for the last time. I am not going to Cincinnati with you. I want to visit, but I have no immediate plans to live there again."

"I understand that, and I imagine I have enough sense to decipher the reason. But that is not what I have on my mind at the moment."

"What do the Roberts ladies have to do with it?"

"Everything, from my perspective, as it appears you are in love with the young woman."

Jeffery could only stare. He finally shook his head. "I beg your pardon?"

"Come now, Son. You never have been good at hiding your emotions—at least not from your mother or me. If she were here, I'm confident she'd make the same observation. The only thing I'm not positive of is whether the young lady returns your affection. At times I would swear she does and then at other times I am not so certain."

Jeffery dropped his gaze to the floor. "That is an interesting observation, sir."

"Enough dithering. I find it difficult to believe you can't—or won't—own up to your feelings for Miss Roberts. She seems an intelligent person who is well spoken and decent. Are you ashamed?"

Jeffery sat upright, fighting to contain his astonishment and temper. "Absolutely not! I simply do not see a reason to discuss my business."

His father rubbed his hands over his knees. "Not even with your father?"

Jeffery couldn't be certain if he'd imagined the slight trembling in the older man's hands. "I'm sorry, sir."

He shook his head. "I am saddened our relationship has grown so strained these past years that you can't trust me. What have I done to earn that, Jeffery?" He ran his hand over his hair, disrupting it from its normally orderly state. "I am most sincere in asking and quite tired of the constant strain between us."

Could his father truly want to know? How many times had he tried to talk with him in past years, only to have him turn a deaf ear? He couldn't imagine things would change now, and he hated to chance baring his soul, only to be ridiculed.

"Please, Son. I did not travel all the way from Cincinnati to continue fighting. In fact, in spite of my demands when I first arrived, I find my eyes are opening to certain facts. I promise to listen this time."

Jeffery took a deep breath, wondering where to begin. "I appreciate all you and Mother have done for me. Please understand that. You were more than generous, and I know I've been a disappointment by not studying law. All I've ever wanted is to write." He rubbed his hands on his trousers. "I do *not* want to sit through one social occasion after another, trying to impress the right people, nor do I care to live off your money."

His father started to interrupt, but Jeffery raised his hand. "Wait. Hear me out. I know you and Mother desire the best for me and feel I'm wasting my life. But I love what I'm doing. My first book was contracted and three chapters were printed in *The Women's Eastern Magazine* with more to come. It's not huge, but it *is* a start, and one that I am proud of—because I accomplished it alone. They did not offer the contract because my father is Mark Tucker or because I travel in the correct social circles or because I may inherit money someday. They offered it because they saw merit in my work. That is all I have ever hoped for or wanted." He dropped his voice. "I wish you and Mother could understand that and be proud of me as well."

Mark Tucker sat as though frozen in ice, his gaze never wavering. "We are more proud of you than you can imagine. I had no idea ..." He blinked. "Writing means so much to you, then?"

Jeffery nodded. "It does. A year ago I would have said more than anything, but now I'm beginning to see there are other things more valuable. But it still holds a very important place in my life."

"I see. I wish we had understood—had listened before—so you wouldn't have felt the need to leave home. You could have pursued your dream there just as well."

Jeffery gave a sharp shake of his head. "No, sir, I couldn't. It was essential I strike off on my own. I needed another perspective. I had seen so little of real life. It was important that I experience disappointments and work for what I wanted, for it to have meaning.

Besides, if life always comes easily, there would be very little passion to pour into one's work."

"I meant it when I said your mother and I are proud of you. We were angry at first that you chose to leave, but the longer you were gone and the more determined you were to find your own way, the more we began to understand what a strong man you'd become." He gave a dry laugh. "Not that I was willing to accept that for a long time, but your mother has a way of being … persuasive." He raised his brows.

Jeffery chuckled. "I remember."

"She told me to come out here and ask if you would return home, but if you insisted on staying I was to accept your decision and assure you of our love. I'm afraid I didn't handle it the way she would have liked when I arrived. I was so certain that all I'd have to do was crook my finger and beckon." He hung his head. "I owe you an apology, and I will have to give your mother one as well."

Shock rippled through Jeffery. "Thank you. I appreciate that more than you know. But, sir?"

His father's head came up. "Yes?"

Jeffery offered a smile. "I won't tell her if you don't."

His father exhaled, then laughed. "I would be most appreciative. Your mother can be quite formidable when she's angry." He placed his hands on his knees. "Now. You mentioned there are other things in your life you're coming to realize are important. I assume that includes Miss Roberts?"

Jeffery gave a brief nod. "It does, but it goes deeper than that. Not long ago she challenged me to reexamine my relationship with God."

His father rubbed his hand over his chin and frowned. "Why? Haven't you attended church since you arrived?"

"That's basically what I said to Beth. She informed me there is more to faith than church, and I need to dig deeper. That God wants me to know Him more intimately."

"Interesting concept. What exactly have you done with it?"

Jeffery smiled. "For starters, I'm reading the Bible that sat in my trunk for the past year. It's amazing what I'm learning—that God actually has a plan for my life. And I'm talking to Him more." He shrugged. "I'm not certain where it will lead, but I know I've had more internal peace than ever before."

His father tipped his head. "Hmm. I like the sound of that. Now, back to Beth. There is something troubling that young woman, but I haven't been able to put my finger on it. I like her, Jeffery. Truly like her. And should you ever decide to marry Beth and bring her back to Cincinnati—" He laughed. "There I go again. But all the same, she would be an asset to the family should that happy event transpire."

"Thank you, sir. That's good to know."

"On another subject, I have decided to deal with the man who is tormenting Mr. and Mrs. Jacobs—Isaac Lansing, I believe." His lips tightened to a stern line. "The Jacobs are a delightful family. I have taken a fancy to all of them, but particularly their little girl, Amanda. If Lansing has his way, she could lose her home, and I cannot countenance such an action."

Jeffery knew that look well. He'd seen it more times than he could remember, when his father came home fired up over a case he was determined to win. And rarely did he lose. "What do you propose?"

"I am still quite well known in legal circles, and I believe my name will carry weight even out here in this uncivilized country. I propose to speak to Mr. Lansing's attorney and acquaint him with some facts."

"Such as?"

"That I am prepared to take the case myself and stay as long as needed to see it through to completion—and I plan to win."

A new degree of respect settled in Jeffery's heart. This was a side of his father he hadn't seen for years. Could the trip out West have softened him somehow—possibly helped him glimpse life from a different perspective? Jeffery leaned an elbow on the arm of the chair. "I wouldn't expect anything less from you, Father—than to win, that is. But I must say I am elated you are offering to help. I know it will be a burden off Mrs. Roberts and Beth as well."

Jeffery hesitated, not wanting to break the fragile thread of newly woven trust. "There may be something more you could do. But you must keep it a secret as I don't want to get Beth's hopes up for nothing."

Chapter Thirty-Two

October 23, 1880, La Grande, Oregon

Isabelle could only stare at her son. Steven had been home from Baker City for two days, and his explanation still didn't satisfy her. "Tell me again why this Mr. Tucker wouldn't give you more information about Elizabeth Corwin and why you came home instead of staying to press him further."

Steven pulled the hard chair close to her rocker. "I'm not sure what you want to hear, Ma. I've told you at least four times now that I didn't feel we should give our private information to a stranger."

"I know what you said." Isabelle relaxed her pursed lips. "But I had such high hopes you could get her address or that she might be living out West." She blinked, trying to quell her tears. "I suppose it was too much to expect you might speak to her and find out if she's actually our Bess."

Steven patted her hand. "I'm sorry it wasn't better news. But at least Mr. Tucker promised to send her my letter."

"Yes." She swiped at the lone tear making its way down her cheek. "As saddened as I am, part of me wonders if it might be better this way."

"What do you mean?" Steven tilted his head.

"I've been stewing over this since you left, trying my best to push the thoughts aside, but the worry keeps returning." She heaved a sigh and tried to straighten her weary shoulders. "I realized something. If Elizabeth Corwin is our Bess, then I reckon she's living a fine life with a good family and won't care about poor relations. Why, she's a talented illustrator, more than likely raised in a big city. I couldn't stand it if she looked on me with shame."

"You can't mean that," Steven said, startled. "We aren't poor. I have a decent job, and I'll be making more money. In time we can get a better house."

Isabelle mustered a smile. "I mean no disrespect, Son. You've made a good name for yourself, there's no denying that." She waved a hand around the cabin. "But look around you. We live in a simple home. We have good neighbors, but before you got your job, people would have said we were no-account farmers barely scratching a living. I had trouble paying the bills after your stepfather died, and if it weren't for you, we'd probably be in the poorhouse by now." She shook her head. "If she writes back, and it is our Bess, we'll need to talk it over before we let her come visit. I don't think I could endure it if she looked down her nose on us."

Steven jumped to his feet. "If she does, then she's not fit to be called by your name. But I don't believe it will come to that. At least, I pray it won't. Somehow we have to trust that God wouldn't bring her back into our lives only to lose her again." He stepped over to the pegs by the door and swung his coat off the hook. "I'd better head to the bank."

"You go on, Son. I'll see you when you return." Isabelle watched him walk out the door, her heart heavy. She'd been trusting God for seventeen years, but not once in all that time had it occurred to her that her little girl might have grown up and found a life of her own—or that she and Steven wouldn't fit into that life.

Isabelle trudged to the shelf next to her bed and carefully lifted one of the worn books she'd written in for so many years. Should she continue? Would a young woman who'd been long separated from her family care about the ramblings of an old, sick woman, even if she was her mother? She turned the journal over in her hands, then laid it back on the perch near her pillow, too heartsick and fearful to write another word as yet another fear niggled its way into her mind. What if all this time Bess thought they didn't want her because they hadn't found her yet? What if she hated her family and didn't care to see them at all?

The front door slammed, and Beth rose from her chair. Jeffery and his father were somewhere about, but the rest of the household were gone and not expected anytime soon. She hurried toward the foyer.

Isaac Lansing stood inside, his hat shoved firmly on his head, and his coat buttoned up to his neck. He raised a gloved hand and shook an envelope. "How dare he send this!" The cords of his neck stood out.

Beth halted a good distance away from the red-faced man. "I don't know who you are talking about, but please do not shout."

"Mark Tucker, that's who." He waved the envelope again. "I demand to speak to him!"

"What seems to be the difficulty?" Jeffery moved from the hall to the foyer and positioned himself in front of Beth, his father close on his heels. "Mr. Lansing, you have no business raising your voice at Miss Roberts, regardless of your problem."

Mark Tucker cleared his throat. "I believe you mentioned my name?"

Lansing strode forward, stopping inches from Mr. Tucker, his chest heaving. "My attorney gave me this letter. He's dropping my suit. How dare you interfere in my business!"

Mr. Tucker stood his ground without flinching. "I simply filed a reply with the court, then had a talk with the judge. Your attorney was wise enough to understand he wouldn't win based on outrageous charges."

Lansing snarled, planted his hands on Mark Tucker's chest, and pushed. The older man staggered backward and landed hard on the floor. Lansing glowered down. "If you know what's good for you, you'll stay out of affairs that don't concern you."

Jeffery sprang forward and swung his arm, his fist connecting with Lansing's chin. The man's head jerked back, and he crashed against the wall. Jeffery grabbed him by the front of his coat. "And if you know what's good for you, you'll leave and never come back. We'll call the sheriff and bring our own suit if you so much as speak to anyone in this house again." He opened the door and shoved him onto the porch. "Be thankful I'm not having you hauled off to jail right now." He slammed the door behind Lansing and turned to his father.

Beth gazed at Jeffery, her heart thudding. Then she bent to Mark Tucker's side. "Are you all right, sir? Is anything broken?"

"I'm fine." He placed his hand on the floor and pushed to his feet. "I hope that's not the case for that upstart, however." After brushing off his jacket, he extended his hand to Jeffery. "Good work, Son. I have never been more proud to be called your father."

Wilma stood in the foyer trying not to wring her hands. Things had been going so well. Mr. Tucker's actions had ended the lawsuit within two days, and the entire household had breathed a sigh of relief. Now this. It seemed they couldn't go more than a few days without one problem or another cropping up.

If only Beth would appear before Jeffery and his father left for the stage, then the decision to keep silent would be taken out of her hands. Why did Caleb have to choose this afternoon to ask Beth to go to town with him so they could spend time together?

She clutched Jeffery's arm. "I still say you need to speak to Beth about this. Can't you wait till the early stage tomorrow instead of going now?"

Jeffery patted her hand. "I'm thankful business has picked up so much the stage company has two runs per day now. It's almost November, and we can't afford to wait another minute. According to the driver, we can be in La Grande by tomorrow night. We'll stay one day, two at the most."

Wilma wanted to throw back her head and wail. Where was Frances when she needed her? *She* could talk Jeffery out of this nonsense. Maybe she should run up to Frances's room and rouse her from her nap. She half turned and stopped, heaving a sigh. That wasn't fair to her friend. "But what shall I tell Beth?"

Jeffery shot a glance at his father, and the older man gave a slight nod. "That Father and I needed to take a little trip on business, and we'll be back soon."

"I don't understand why you won't tell her yourself."

A troubled look passed over Jeffery's face. "We've talked about this, Mrs. Roberts. I need to meet Steven Harding's mother and see if she's telling the truth. If I tell Beth where I'm going, or even that I am leaving, she'll ask why. I cannot and will not lie to her, so it's best if I simply slip away. It won't be dishonest for you to tell her my father and I are on a business trip."

Mark Tucker nodded. "Quite so. I wanted to meet a business associate who settled in La Grande while I was out West and haven't had a chance to do so. This is the perfect opportunity."

Jeffery looked deep into Wilma's eyes. "I do not want Beth hurt even more. She told me she decided not to answer the letter, but I know the decision has been hard on her."

Wilma nodded. "On me as well. Beth confided in me a few days ago." She gripped her hands together, trying to still their shaking. "I don't know what to think about all of this. I am terrified I'll lose her, Jeffery. What if this woman is her mother and sweeps in here and takes her away? Have you thought of that?" She peered up at him, noting the concern knitting his brows. "You can't hide it from me, young man; I know you care. You wouldn't be doing this if you didn't."

He gave a slow nod. "I do."

"Have you told Beth?"

"Yes. But that's as far as I've taken things. After hearing Harding's questions and handing his letter over to Beth, I've reflected on some of the same things as you. I can't tell you what will happen if this is her family. I can only tell you I feel it is the right thing to do. Beth has suffered too many years wondering what happened and who her people are."

Wilma winced. "I know. But I've been there for her since she was four. I can't lose her, and I'm not even sure I want to share her with someone else. Have you considered that this woman believes Beth is a well-known illustrator? What if she only wants her back because of that? Beth could get hurt even more." She glowered. "I think you and Mr. Tucker should remain here. After all, if Beth decided not to answer that letter, who are we to interfere?" She wanted to say who was *he* to interfere, but good manners forbade her from being so crass.

Mark Tucker pulled out a pocket watch. "I am sorry to interrupt, but we must be going if we plan to make the stage. Mrs. Roberts, my son's mind is made up. We would ask that you keep your own counsel on our behalf. You can simply tell Beth that Jeffery is accompanying me on business."

Wilma bit her lip to keep it from trembling, then drew in a soft breath. "All right. I will do as you ask. But it's going to be difficult to keep the truth from Beth, so please don't delay any longer than necessary."

Beth stepped through the front door in the company of Caleb Marshall and drew off her gloves. "It's getting quite cold, and the clouds are building. I'm glad I wore my heavy cloak."

Caleb nodded. "I shouldn't have kept you in town so long. I didn't realize the temperature would drop so quickly."

"Yes, it's getting dark so much earlier. But it was still wonderful to get out of the house. And I loved spending time with you over lunch. I'm very happy for you and Aunt Wilma."

He patted her arm. "I appreciate that, my dear. Your aunt has been a bit distressed, not knowing if you were being kind about our plans to marry, or if you were truly happy."

Beth pushed away the whisper of sadness that tried to wrap its tendrils around her heart. "Truly. She deserves to be happy again after all these years." A memory surfaced, and she giggled. "I still can't get over the triumph on Mrs. Cooper's face when you made your announcement. It was like she took personal credit for what had happened."

Wilma swept into the foyer. "She did."

Beth turned. "Oh dear, I didn't know anyone was around. I hope no one else heard me."

A smile blossomed on Wilma's face. "If you mean Frances, there's no need to worry. She convinced Katherine to lie down and take a nap while the girls and Zachary are at school, then she did the same."

"Oh, good. I wouldn't want to hurt her feelings. But how do you know she took credit?"

Wilma hunched a shoulder. "She told me. The woman is nothing if not forthright."

Caleb laughed and placed his hand on Wilma's back. "I must agree. But from what I've seen, she's been a good friend."

Wilma nodded. "Yes. And it's amazing, considering how our relationship started. You remember, don't you, Beth?"

"I certainly do. I wondered for a while if this house was big enough for the two of you." She hung her cloak on the coatrack beside the door. "Is Katherine not feeling well again?"

"Simply tired, from what I could tell. I told her you and I would start supper. I hope you don't mind."

"Not at all. I'll go upstairs and change."

An hour later, Wilma directed Zachary and Lucy as they set the table, and Mandy scurried from the kitchen to the table with a plate of sliced bread. Beth put the final touches on the meal, feeling a deep satisfaction at the work she and Aunt Wilma had done.

Katherine stepped through the door and sniffed. "Oh, it smells wonderful in here. The cornbread is making my mouth water." She lifted the lid on a steaming pot and dipped in a spoon, raising it to her lips. "The beans and ham are perfect."

Frances hobbled into the room and nearly toppled into a chair near the stove. "My old bones don't stay warm the way they used to." She rubbed her hands up her arms. "Mark my words, winter is coming soon."

Beth smiled. "You can't be much older than Aunt Wilma. But I don't mind winter, although I haven't spent one in Oregon, so I'm not sure what to expect."

Frances peered at Beth. "Dear girl, I'm a good ten years your aunt's senior. As for Oregon winters, they can be quite fickle. We could have snow tomorrow and have it all gone three days later with the sun shining down like it was fall. Or it could snow and we wouldn't see the ground again until spring. You never know from one year to the next."

Wilma shot her a strange glance.

Beth wrinkled her brow. "Auntie? Is something wrong?"

"No, child. I'm pondering what Frances said, that's all."

"Well, it's time to call everyone to supper." Beth beckoned to Zachary. "Would you run upstairs and ask Mr. Tucker and Jeffery to come down?"

Wilma's eyes darted to Katherine.

"What is it, Aunt Wilma?" Beth stepped forward and touched her aunt's arm, not caring for the pained expression on the older woman's face.

"I'm afraid Jeffery and his father are gone."

Chapter Thirty-Three

Jeffery held the stage door open for his father, thankful the conveyance had finally rolled to a stop on the main street of La Grande. His legs and back felt as though they'd taken a pounding from a prizefighter.

He stood on the boardwalk and peered through the semidarkness of the early evening. A lantern hung on a post next to the hitching rail, and another illuminated the door leading into the stage station. He loved the bustle of Baker City, but his writer's soul also craved isolation and calm—the hush of this small town poured a gentle peace over his mind.

He grabbed the valise his father handed out. "How are you feeling, sir?"

"Well enough, I suppose, considering the driver managed to hit every rut and ridge along the road. I must say the train is more comfortable."

Jeffery nodded. "I hear a line is planned in the next couple of years." He caught the bag the driver heaved over the side before it landed in the dirt. "Looks like that's it. We'd best find a hotel. It's too late to look up Harding and his mother tonight."

"That sounds good to me, but I'd like a hot meal before bed."

"Of course." Jeffery beckoned to the driver who had walked up to the lead horse. "Excuse me, can you recommend a hotel?"

The man nodded toward a brightly lit building across the street. "That one over yonder is clean and don't have bedbugs, from what I hear. How-some-ever, they don't have an eatery. You'll have to get your grub at Ella's Place a block up the street."

"All right, thank you kindly." It only took a matter of minutes to make their way to the front desk of the plain, sparsely appointed establishment and secure two rooms. Jeffery would have been happy with one room and two beds, but his father insisted on paying the bill and acquiring one for each of them. He couldn't deny his gratitude at the thought of sinking into peaceful oblivion.

They moved away from the long wooden desk, their footsteps softened by the worn carpet lining the foyer floor. Candlelight and two lanterns lit the area, and heavy velvet drapes hung parted at the large front window. A lone wagon rolled past, the clop of the horses' hooves muted by the rain that had fallen earlier in the day.

Jeffery's stomach reminded him quite forcefully of the lack of nourishment over the past hours. He placed his hand over it and grimaced.

Mark Tucker sighed. "Your stomach sounds like mine feels. Empty. I'm *almost* tempted to forego a meal and fall into bed. I'd forgotten how much a trip by coach could take out of a man my age."

Jeffery grinned. "Then I must be getting up there along with you, because I'm not in a lot better shape. You want to go lie down for a while or go eat right now?"

"I think I'll put my bag in my room and head on over, then retire early. I assume you want to get an early start tomorrow?"

"Yes. We can meet for breakfast at half-past seven if that suits you, then I'll see if I can get directions to Harding's place."

"I still wonder if it might have been better to wire ahead and let them know we're coming."

Jeffery nodded. "Possibly, but it seemed like the right decision at the time. I guess I was concerned they might say it wasn't convenient for us to come, and I didn't care to be dissuaded."

The next hour passed quickly as the men left their bags in the room and partook of a simple but filling meal. Then Jeffery crawled into his bed and blew out the lamp on the bedside table with a sigh of relief. At least nothing had gone wrong in the first part of this journey. His thoughts drifted to Beth as his eyes closed.

Had it been a mistake not to confide in her about his trip and explain his reason for leaving? What if she didn't appreciate his efforts to uncover the truth about Steven Harding's inquiry and his mother's claim? Surely Mrs. Roberts could calm any concerns that might arise, and it wasn't like he'd be gone long enough for Beth to miss him. A deep-seated desire rose to the surface—as much as he didn't want to cause Beth distress, he prayed she *would* long for his return. If he could deliver good news, that should go a long way toward securing her forgiveness for stepping into her business.

Longing swept over him as he remembered the light touch of her lips that day in the parlor. Jeffery could only hope Beth had finally put aside all of her feelings for Wentworth. She had cautiously agreed to a courtship, but he wanted a serious one with nothing standing in the way.

Another memory stirred, and he embraced it wholeheartedly— Beth's suggestion of pursuing a relationship with God. "Thank You,

Father, for making Yourself real to me." He whispered the words, amazed anew at the peace that blanketed his spirit.

Beth stepped to the parlor window for what must surely be the tenth time and peered outside. Nothing stirred. The trees had shed their autumn finery by this last week of October and raised mostly stark branches to the overcast sky. Jeffery and his father had been gone for four days with no word. He hadn't left her a note or a message with her aunt or with Katherine. She turned to her aunt and planted her hands on her hips. "Tell me again what Jeffery said?"

Wilma glanced down at her skirt and smoothed out imaginary wrinkles. "I've told you so many times, I'd think you'd have memorized it by now."

Beth stuffed down her irritation. There was no point in getting upset with her aunt. It wasn't her fault Jeffery had left without saying good-bye. She willed her voice to be calm. "I know, but I'd like to hear it one more time." Sinking onto the end of the sofa she stared across the cozy room at her aunt.

"All right." Wilma nodded and met her gaze. "He said they were going on a business trip to La Grande. His father had someone to see and apparently there was a rush to make the stage before it left. You were gone with Caleb so he left word with me."

Beth couldn't quite put her finger on it, but something was missing in the explanation. "But he didn't leave me a letter. You're sure he said they'd only be gone a couple of days?"

"No. It takes two days to travel, and he thought they'd only need to be there one day. So I assume five days in all."

Beth gave a short nod. "So if all goes well, they should return on tomorrow's stage." She touched the locket at her throat, longing for the sense of peace it usually brought.

"I would assume that's the case."

Beth's head snapped up. "What aren't you saying, Auntie? Is there something you aren't telling me?"

Wilma harrumphed. "Stop plaguing me, girl. I've had as much of this as I can stand. I'm sure he'll be home tomorrow night, and all will be well. You're fretting too much. You need to find something worthwhile to keep occupied." She grunted as she got to her feet. "I'm getting stiff. I'm going to find Caleb and take a walk, if I can tolerate the cold."

Beth clamped her lips shut to keep a sharp retort from slipping out. There was not one thing she could think of that would get her mind off Jeffery's leaving. She'd tried working on her illustrations to no avail. All she wanted to do was pace and stare out the nearest window. It might be foolish, but she couldn't quell the sense of dread that had consumed her for the past two days.

When Aunt Wilma first told her Jeffery was gone it came as a shock, but knowing Mr. Tucker, she assumed he'd pressured his son to accompany him and not given him adequate warning. Now she had to wonder. As the days progressed, her aunt seemed more reticent and tense, as though she were hiding information. Was it possible Jeffery hadn't waited to talk to her or left her a note because he regretted his hasty offer to court her? Maybe this was his way of putting distance between them, so he'd have time to think and reconsider his decision.

She pulled an embroidered pillow onto her lap and hugged it against her chest. Jeffery wouldn't do that; he was honest and genuine in all of his dealings. Fear pricked at the edges of her mind. She'd thought that about Brent at one time as well. Had she put too much trust in Jeffery?

There had been so many disappointments and losses in her life, and she couldn't stand the thought of Jeffery being another. She laid her cheek against the pillow. It wouldn't kill her if Jeffery changed his mind, but it would be one more horrid blow. Tears pricked, and she blinked, unwilling to allow them to fall. It might not kill her, but if the pain piercing her right now was any indication, it might come close.

Chapter Thirty-Four

Wilma wasn't certain she could stand it much longer. Beth had been like a caged bear pacing the house and barely contained her worry since they'd awakened to over two feet of snow three days ago. Jeffery hadn't returned, and no stages were running. She'd promised Jeffery not to mention his intention to visit Steven Harding and his mother, but she hated the anxiety filling her girl's eyes. She plunked her empty teacup on the saucer. What would it change if Beth knew? She blew out a breath of frustration and snatched the newspaper from a nearby table in the parlor, shaking it open.

Frances harrumphed. "Can you not sit still for five minutes, Wilma? Something is plaguing you, so why don't you spit it out and be done with it? Are you fretting because Caleb and Beth went to town and did not take you along?"

"Not at all, although I'll admit it would be nice to get out of this house. But I don't care to push my way through snowdrifts two feet deep and can't imagine why Caleb would want to attempt it."

Her friend smirked. "Because he is a man. Men are contrary creatures and do not always follow reason. Besides, Beth went as well, and you said nothing about wondering why *she* would go." She drummed her fingers against the arm of the sofa. "From what

Micah said, the drifts are melting, and the road to town is open. I understand it was worse to the west, and Baker City got off easy in comparison."

Wilma groaned. "That is *not* what I wanted to hear."

"Jeffery and Mr. Tucker are grown men. You worry too much. I would imagine they stayed put in La Grande like sensible people and will be along soon."

"I suppose, but I can't seem to convince Beth of that possibility." Wilma placed the paper facedown on the table. "That's why she went to town, you know. To see if there's any word at the stage station."

"Ah, I thought that might be the case. She has been drifting around like a lost waif the past few days." Frances leaned forward. "Do you think the girl has finally realized she cares for Jeffery?"

Wilma couldn't answer past the lump in her throat.

"And high time, if you ask me. It has been as obvious as the day is long that he is smitten with her, and I thought she would never wake up in time."

"In time? For what?"

"To keep from losing him, of course. An intelligent man like that is not going to sit around and wait forever, you know. Why, not long after he arrived, his father told me there is a young woman at home they had hoped might be a suitable match for their son. I do believe that might be one reason he came, in hopes of persuading Jeffery to return and marry."

Wilma bristled. How like Frances, to stir a pot that didn't need stirring. "I don't care how many women are waiting in Cincinnati hoping to find a husband. Jeffery is interested in my niece, and that's that."

A sly smile edged Frances's mouth. "Ah-ha. I am certainly happy to see you willing to assert yourself at last. However, we should not borrow trouble where the two young people are concerned. These things seem to have a way of working themselves out." She smirked. "Although a little nudge in the right direction never hurts."

"I'm not sure what good that will do, with Jeffery and Mr. Tucker off who-knows-where with no idea when they might come home." Wilma gripped her hands together to keep from wringing them.

Frances narrowed her eyes. "What else is bothering you?"

Wilma opened her mouth, all hesitation at sharing her secret gone. She must tell someone, and Frances was as good a choice as any. Besides, she had made it clear where her heart was in the matter and would certainly understand.

Just then the front door banged open, and the rush of footsteps sounded on the hardwood floor. Beth burst into the room with Caleb on her heels. Snow fell from their garments and drifted to the floor, but Beth didn't seem to notice. "Aunt Wilma, Mrs. Cooper." She placed her hand over her heart and drew in a long breath. "I'm afraid something terrible has happened to Jeffery and Mr. Tucker."

Wilma bolted upright, her nerves all aquiver. "What in the world?" She shot to her feet and stopped in front of her niece, grasping her arms. "Calm down." Drawing her forward, she pressed her onto the sofa. "Caleb, why don't you sit as well, and help sort this out? Tell us from the beginning, and take your time."

Katherine came into the room, wiping her hands on a dish towel. "I heard the commotion. Is everything all right?"

Wilma shook her head. "We're not sure yet. Why don't you join us, and Beth will fill us in."

Beth took a sip of the tepid tea her aunt offered and worked to calm her racing heart. Dread had given her feet wings on the way home, and poor Dr. Caleb had barely been able to keep up. She'd prayed all the way, not even feeling the bite of the wind. Surely God wouldn't let anything dreadful happen to Jeffery when she'd finally discovered how much she cared?

Her aunt reached over and patted her hand. "Better now, dear? Can you tell us what happened?"

She set the cup down. "Thank you, yes." She turned to Caleb. "Please remind me if I forget something important?"

He nodded and settled himself on the other side of Wilma. "I'd be happy to."

Each person in the room exuded caring support, and Beth's fear waned. As much as these people cared, God loved her even more. She had to choose to trust Him in this, come what may. "We stopped by the stage station to see when another coach might be coming or going to La Grande. A man had ridden in a couple of hours earlier, and made it by horseback, but said it might be days before a wagon or coach could get through." She stopped and strove to quell the trembling in her limbs. Sucking in a breath, she tried again, then shook her head.

Caleb raised his brows, and at her nod, he continued. "He brought word that there was a death along the trail. Two, actually."

He looked from one face to the next. "Two men attempted to ride from La Grande to Baker City the night the storm hit. They must have gotten lost in the blowing snow and wandered in circles. They were found frozen stiff a ways off the road, and their horses were gone."

Wilma gasped, and Katherine choked back a cry.

Frances shook her head. "Nothing says it is Jeffery and Mr. Tucker."

Caleb gave a short nod. "I agree. That's what I've been trying to tell Beth."

"Have they brought their …. I mean … are they here, in town?" Wilma croaked out the words.

"No." Caleb glanced at Beth. "We asked. Apparently they were found closer to La Grande and were taken there."

Frances clucked her tongue. "So sad. No one has identified them yet?"

"The man didn't know. All he heard was it was a young man and an older one. At this point we have to pray it wasn't Jeffery and Mr. Tucker and hope for the best."

Chapter Thirty-Five

Three days had never dragged by so slowly in Beth's entire life. Much of her time was spent here in the parlor, but staring out the window didn't change a thing. She'd thought it hard when Brent left her back in Kansas, but nothing compared to this present agony. No word had come from La Grande as to the identity of the two bodies. More riders arrived in town, but the stagecoach still wasn't running. Any day, the stage company promised. The wait left Beth sick to her stomach and unable to sleep.

Lucy swept into the parlor, looking more like a young lady each day with her long blond curls piled on her head. Zachary trailed along behind, carrying a board game.

Mandy perked up and wriggled in Beth's grasp. "Can I play too?"

Lucy wrinkled her brow. "How about I play something else with you later? This is a word game for big people, and you're not old enough."

Mandy slid off Beth's lap and planted her hands on her waist. "I am *too* old enough. I go to school, and I can spell lots of words."

Katherine entered carrying a tray of tea, coffee, and cookies. "I thought you all might enjoy a snack since it's still a while until supper. I'm thankful for the rain that's washing away the snow, but it's still too cold and wet to spend any time outdoors." She heaved a sigh. "I'll be glad for spring for more than one reason."

Micah took the tray from her grasp. "And you shouldn't be carrying anything heavy. Doctor's orders."

Katherine smiled. "It was not heavy, Micah." She directed her attention to Frances. "Mama, would you care to pour the tea for whoever wants a cup?"

Frances straightened and smiled. "Certainly." She waited until her son-in-law set the tray close to hand. "Wilma? Coffee or tea?"

"Tea, thank you."

Frances eyed her friend. "You have been awfully quiet all afternoon."

Wilma hunched her shoulder. "I suppose I'm tired."

Beth shook herself from her reverie. How had she missed noticing her aunt's pallor? Guilt pricked at her conscience. Because she'd had her mind on her own troubles instead of caring what anyone close to her might be going through. "Aren't you sleeping, Auntie?"

Wilma dropped her gaze to her lap. "Not too well."

"Is something amiss more than worry over Jeffery and Mr. Tucker?" Beth wasn't sure where the question came from, but she suddenly knew the answer. Aunt Wilma *knew* something and had been keeping it from her. The puffy eyes and reluctance to meet her gaze, not to mention her unusual silence, spoke volumes.

Wilma opened her mouth, then shook her head. "Nothing I can discuss, thank you." The words were so low Beth barely heard.

Beth hurried across the room, kneeling beside her aunt's chair. "Whatever is the trouble? Is something wrong with Dr. Caleb?"

Wilma waved her hand. "No, no. He's fine. Taking mail to the post office since they expect the coach to go out soon."

"Then what?" The air in the room seemed to still, and no one spoke.

The front door banged open. "They're back! Everybody!" Dr. Caleb's excited shout rang through the house. He rushed into the open doorway and waved his arms. "Jeffery and Mr. Tucker. They made it through with a wagon, and they'll be here any moment." He turned to Katherine. "Mrs. Jacobs, would there be somewhere that an invalid could rest for an hour or two after they arrive?"

Beth had pushed to her feet, her heart pounding almost out of her chest. "Invalid? Who's hurt? Is Jeffery all right?" She plucked her skirt up and raced for the front door. "I'm going to meet them. How far are they from the house?" Grabbing her heavy cloak from a peg behind the door, she struggled to wrap it around her shoulders.

The doctor placed his hand on her arm and shook his head. "Wait, child. Let them come here. There's no sense in you trudging through the slop out there. As far as I could tell, Jeffery is fine. He's driving the wagon."

Relief shot through Beth, but another thought hammered at her mind. "His father then?"

"I don't think so. They'll be here in a matter of minutes. Please trust me and wait here."

Beth's hands shook so hard she could barely hang the cloak back on the peg. Jeffery was alive.

Jeffery reined the buggy to a stop and stared at the house. Would Beth welcome him? Eleven days with no word. If only the telegraph line hadn't gone down in the storm, and if only there hadn't *been* a storm. None of that mattered now. He'd left without explaining his actions, and his skin crawled at the knowledge of the hurt he might have caused. She'd agreed to give him a chance when he asked permission to court her, then he'd disappeared without an adequate explanation.

He had gone over the details in his mind a thousand times since leaving Baker City, and every time he arrived at the same conclusion. Beth's happiness and her desire to know her history were most important. But he hated the thought that the long delay might have heaped pain on the woman he loved.

He smiled at the older woman reclining in the backseat of the buggy. "I won't be long. I need to give Beth some warning before we take you in. Are you sure you're warm enough?"

Isabelle Mason nodded. "You made a fine bed for me, Mr. Tucker, and there's enough blankets covering me to warm an entire village. Take your time. I don't want to scare her." Her lips quivered, although she attempted a brave smile. "I hope we aren't making a big mistake coming here unannounced like this."

Steven Harding tucked a woolen blanket closer around her neck. "Shh. We've been over that ground a dozen times already. Jeffery knows Beth well. I'm still finding it a struggle to think of her as anything but Bess, but I'll get used to it." He cocked his head. "You go on in now. You, too, Mr. Tucker. We'll be fine out here until you say it's time to come in. And if she decides she doesn't want to see us, we'll understand and move on."

Jeffery wrapped the reins around the brake and climbed down from the buggy. He glanced at his father, who still sat on his horse. "You're coming in, aren't you?"

Mark Tucker shook his head. "Not yet, son. I'll wait with these folks for a couple of minutes. I think you need a little time with your girl alone before we all barge in and start answering questions."

Warmth shot through him. He'd never realized before his father could be so perceptive. "Thank you, although I have no idea if she's my girl or if she's even still speaking to me." He tugged at the top button of his coat. "I guess I'd better go find out."

His foot hit the last step of the porch when the front door swung open and a blur of deep green burst out. With skirts swirling around her and arms outstretched, Beth flew across the porch and into his arms.

Stunned, Jeffery could only hold her. Muffled sobs rose, and she trembled in his embrace. "Shh, Beth, it's all right. You're shivering. We need to get inside where it's warm." Keeping her tight against his side, he pushed open the door and drew her into the foyer. He lifted her chin and ran his thumb down her cheek, stroking the tear-wet skin. "I am so sorry. I didn't mean to worry you. Truly, I thought I was doing the right thing. I had no idea I would be gone so long."

She inhaled a long, shuddering breath and lifted a gaze filled with lingering despair. "I thought you were dead."

The idea that he'd hurt and worried her nearly paralyzed him. "We were delayed by the storm and stuck in La Grande for a number of days, but we were never in danger." He brushed a lock of hair off her forehead and pressed his lips where it had lain. "Why would you think that?"

She closed her eyes for a moment. When they opened again, Beth met his gaze without flinching. "Someone rode into town and said two men were found frozen along the trail to Baker City. They weren't identified, but one was younger and the other older. They were found three days after the snow hit, and when you didn't return …" She took a step back. "Why didn't you talk to me before you left, Jeffery? I've been sick with worry."

"I'm sorry." He stroked another curl off her face. "I'll explain it all soon, I promise. But right now there's someone in the wagon who needs to come in out of the cold."

Her hand went to her throat. "Your father. Oh dear, I forgot. Dr. Caleb said someone was ill and needed to lie down, but he didn't think it was Mr. Tucker." She turned and reached for the doorknob.

Jeffery stepped around her. "It's not Father. I need to tell you something first." He'd rehearsed this so many times, but the words had melted like the rain-chased snow. "I wish I had more time to explain, but I guess I'll just have to say it. I went to La Grande to investigate Steven Harding's claim that he and his mother might be your family. The woman in the buggy is your mother, Beth. She's terrified you won't want to see her. Will you allow her to explain what happened so many years ago?"

Beth's legs shook so hard she could barely stand. Her mother was in the wagon outside? And Steven was truly her brother? How could Jeffery possibly know that, and why was he keeping them outside? Her thoughts darted around, barely making sense. She wrapped her arms around herself, hoping to still the tremors. He said he'd gone to investigate the claims in Steven Harding's letter, but she'd never anticipated the man or his mother would arrive on her doorstep.

Steven had written the letter and tried to find her before Jeffery left, and he'd hinted at the guilt his mother carried. They had made their way here, braving the cold. She wrapped her arms more tightly around herself, a shiver coursing through her. "Yes, I want to see her."

But what if they didn't like her? Would it change her relationship with Aunt Wilma? And could she believe what they told her?

Reason took over her racing thoughts, and she worked to relax her tense muscles. "I'll admit I'm frightened. I have no idea what to expect."

Jeffery placed a gentle finger under her chin and raised her face. "*I* know what to expect, and I can assure you it is nothing to be afraid of. They are good people, Beth, with a story you need to hear." He stepped to the door, then turned back. "I imagine you'll want your aunt to listen as well, but you might ask Mrs. Jacobs if you can have the parlor to yourself for the next hour or so."

Beth's heart pounded, and she stretched out her hand. "Will you stay as well?"

His gaze grew warmer still. "If you want me to."

She nodded, then slipped out of the foyer toward the parlor.

A few minutes later, voices sounded in the entry. Aunt Wilma slid closer to Beth on the parlor sofa and captured her hand. "Are you all right?"

Beth swallowed hard. "I think so. Did you know he was doing this?"

Wilma's gaze didn't waver. "I did, and I'm sorry I couldn't tell you. Jeffery wanted to protect you and didn't want to get your hopes up if it turned out to be nothing."

Beth nodded. She couldn't blame her aunt for her silence and should have realized Jeffery wouldn't do anything to hurt her. All those days wasted in foolish worry and nights without sleep. Why was it so difficult to trust God when hard times came? Somehow she sensed His hand had been directing her for months. The memories that had surfaced, along with the knowledge of His growing presence, should have reassured her, and would have if she'd taken the time to pray and think it through this past week instead of assuming the worst.

Jeffery walked through the open portal behind a frail woman with wide blue eyes, her shoulders encased protectively by her son's arms.

Mr. Tucker stopped in the doorway and nodded toward the kitchen. "I think I'll get a cup of hot coffee while you folks talk."

Beth's throat closed over the emotion that swelled at his tender expression. "Thank you." She couldn't manage another word. She could only grip her aunt's hand.

Jeffery glanced at them both. "Before we go any further, I think we should introduce Beth's aunt Wilma." He tipped his head her direction. "This is Mrs. Wilma Roberts, the woman who took Beth in and raised her, and this is Steven's mother, Isabelle Mason."

Aunt Wilma squeezed Beth's hand and nodded to Steven and his mother. "It's good to meet you both. I understood there was someone who needed to lie down. Are you sure this is a good time to talk, Mrs. Mason?"

The woman dipped her head. "Please, call me Isabelle. And I cannot rest until this is done." Her gaze was riveted on Beth.

Steven helped his mother into a chair across from Beth, then took one close by. Jeffery settled into a chair. Silence blanketed the room with an expectant hush, like everyone waited for angels to pronounce a momentous event. Steven touched his mother's hands, which were gripped in her lap. "Would you like me to start, Ma?"

She drew her shawl closer around her neck with quaking fingers. "I want to tell her. It was my fault, not yours."

Chapter Thirty-Six

Isabelle's mind was completely blank. All she could do was stare at Bess. It *was* Bess. There was no doubt in her mind. She would recognize that face even if it were mixed with a thousand others. A wave of remorse hit her, and she reeled against her chair. So many lost years. So many missing memories. Isabelle slumped deeper into the chair, praying the words would come.

Their glance met, and the girl paled and stiffened. Did Bess hate her for not being a part of her life? She couldn't blame her. How many times had she lain awake in bed hating herself for not working harder to find her baby girl? All the years of torment and imagining the worst—but Bess was alive!

Someone moved beside her chair, and she looked up. Jeffery, the thoughtful young man who'd come to La Grande, stood holding a cup on a saucer. He placed it on a table near her elbow, then walked back to his seat. The fragrance of mint enticed her, and she picked up the cup and sipped. No one else moved. Her girl sat beside the woman who had raised her, whose head was bowed over their clutched hands.

Why hadn't she thought of what this might do to the person who had taken Bess in? Would her presence cause damage to Bess's life rather than the joy Isabelle had always longed for? She pushed those worries away. It was too late for questions or concerns.

They were all waiting.

For her.

She set the cup on the saucer. "I have so much I want to say to you, Bess."

The girl winced and gave a slight shake of her head. "My name is Beth."

Isabelle started. "I'm sorry. I forgot that's what you've been called all these years. I will try to remember. Do you want to ask questions, or would you prefer I simply tell the story of when you were lost?"

Beth tipped her head in one fluid motion. "I'd rather hear what you have to say first. I might have questions, but I won't interrupt unless I don't understand, if that's all right?"

"Yes, that's fine." Isabelle slipped her icy hands into the folds of her shawl. "You were three years old when we started for Oregon, and Steven was eight."

Beth leaned forward. "I'm sorry, but who exactly is we? You and Steven?"

"No, there were four of us. Steven, you, me, and your father."

"So my father isn't still alive?"

Isabelle's face twisted as pain knifed her heart anew. "I'll get to that, but no, he's not."

Beth sank against the sofa cushions, her expression drawn. "I'm sorry. I won't ask anything else."

Isabelle shook her head. "Don't be. We left in the early spring and by late summer had arrived in Wyoming." She tried to form the next sentence, and she shivered. "That's when it happened." She stifled a groan.

Steven patted her shoulder. "Take your time, Mother."

She smiled at him weakly. "Thank you, Son. It's hard talking about what came next. There is no way to soften it. Cholera hit the wagon train, and a number of people died."

Her gaze strayed to Beth, and her heart shook. "Your father was one of the first we lost. We stayed in one place for several weeks, praying the sickness would pass, but more continued to sicken. Finally, the wagon master made the decision to move on, even though our forces were depleted. He worried we'd be trapped by winter snows before reaching our destination. Steven had helped me watch you while I cared for your father, but by the time we moved on, both he and I were ill."

Isabelle twisted her hands in her lap. Would Beth understand and be able to forgive what happened next? She had blamed herself for so many years she couldn't imagine anyone else doing less. "I grew so sick I couldn't care for you, and we feared you'd get the disease as well. Another family took you in, promising to care for you like their own. Unbeknownst to me, the mother took ill and died not many days later. Her husband asked someone else to take you, but they were overwhelmed. It was decided that three families would share your care, along with two other children whose parents had died."

Mrs. Roberts interrupted. "Shared their care? Why wouldn't each child be in the care of one family?"

"Because there were too many deaths, and not many were left intact. Those who didn't die were sick or caring for others. Everyone did the best they were able, but"—her voice choked—"it wasn't enough."

Beth barely dared to breathe. This woman was sharing so much—almost too much to take in. She'd found her mother and brother, and lost her father all within a matter of minutes. Why had it never occurred to her that a plague might have hit her family? Of course, that still didn't explain what happened or why she wasn't found, but so much was starting to make sense. "So I never took sick?"

The woman who claimed to be her mother shook her head. "That was the only thing that gave me hope. I was told later, when I recovered, that you'd never shown any sign of the disease. But I always worried that you might have done so, and no one realized it." She shuddered and rubbed her hands up and down her arms. "I had so many horrible nightmares of you lost and sick in the wilderness, with no one to care for you. We never knew what happened or if you were alive."

Beth nodded. "I understand, but how did I get separated from the wagons? Why was I alone?"

Isabelle hunkered deeper into her chair, her face drawn. "My fever broke, and I wanted you back, but they said no. I needed to wait another week or so, to be certain you wouldn't fall ill. They assured me you were being cared for, and there was nothing to worry about." Her voice rose. "I should have insisted! It was my fault for not demanding you stay in our wagon."

Steven laid his hand over hers. "Ma, quit blaming yourself. I was still ill, and it wouldn't have been safe."

She drew in a shaky breath. "I know, but it doesn't change what happened." Chewing on her bottom lip, she stared at Beth for several seconds. "You were apparently playing in the woods with some of the other children. The wagons were ready to move, and the wagon master was determined to put in a long day of travel to try to make up for lost time. The children scattered to their wagons, but no one realized you hadn't come." She closed her eyes as though reliving the memory, then slowly focused back on Beth. "Each of the three families assumed you were with one of the others. In the rush of departure, no one checked to be sure all the children were accounted for."

Isabelle shook her head. "There had been so many losses, so much sickness, and still many who were weak and ill. It wasn't their fault. All of them had their own children to care for, and you were my responsibility, not theirs. I was to blame. I should have gotten out of bed and made sure you were where you belonged. I have never forgiven myself, and I doubt I ever will." She bowed her head and placed her hands over her face, her body shaking as her sobs filled the room.

Beth sat as though clamped by chains to her seat. The cries of the broken woman sitting across from her slashed her heart to a depth she hadn't known possible. The pain was palpable and fresh, as though the event had happened yesterday. As hard as it had been not knowing where she belonged or why she was alone, Beth couldn't begin to imagine the agony this woman had gone through at the loss of her child. "Then what happened?" She whispered the words. "Did anyone search for me?"

Steven straightened and drew in a breath. "No one realized for three days that you were missing. I was starting to recover, but I remember it well. Mother asked for you on the third day. She said it had been long enough, and she wouldn't be separated any longer. Finally one of the women relented and went to the family she assumed was caring for you. They didn't have you and assured the woman that another family was responsible. Each of the three placed the blame on the others, and no one could remember the last time they'd seen you."

Isabelle pulled a handkerchief from her pocket and wiped her cheeks. "I spoke to the children you were with. They remembered you sitting in a field picking buttercups. Each of them believed you had come when they were called, but none of them knew for sure if you had. I demanded the train go back to find you, but by that time winter was close. The wagon master had to make a decision. The time we'd lose turning around, searching, then retracing our steps could be the difference of arriving safely in Oregon before the snow hit, or perishing."

Beth stared in horror. "So they just … left me?" She wanted to rail at someone—to demand answers and find someone to blame, but one look at the anguished woman closed her lips.

Isabelle raised a trembling hand. "No. They sent a man back on horseback to search. He returned five days later. He'd discovered your tracks coming out of the meadow but lost them again. As he widened the circle, he stumbled across the prints of several unshod ponies. At the time, the Arapaho weren't attacking settlers, but they weren't above taking captives. He spent a full day scouting, but you were nowhere to be found." She swiped the handkerchief across her cheeks, catching the rolling tears. "He couldn't go after a party of braves on his own, and by the time he would have come back to the wagons and mustered a rescue, the tracks would have faded. We had already passed Fort Laramie, and there was no way to get word to them. Believe me, I tried."

Steven nodded. "She did. The wagon master had to stop Ma from taking a horse and riding out on her own. In her weakened condition, she would have died before she reached the fort, and he didn't want another death, or to leave me orphaned."

Aunt Wilma shifted position beside Beth. "So you've been looking all these years? And it wasn't until you saw Beth's drawings in the magazine that you had any idea she was alive?"

"That's right." Isabelle smoothed the handkerchief on her lap. "Can you tell us why you chose to use Elizabeth Corwin?"

Beth scrunched her brows and thought for a moment, her hand almost automatically going to her locket. "I'm not sure. I thought it possible my given name might be Elizabeth. I can't say where Corwin came from. It kept haunting me for some reason that I couldn't understand. It didn't *feel* like my last name, but it was familiar somehow."

The woman gave her first tentative smile. "It was my name before I married. You were named after your grandmother, Mary Ann Elizabeth Corwin. That's why the story and pictures in that magazine struck me so hard, and I convinced Steven to come talk to Mr. Tucker. I couldn't believe it when I saw that name. All I could think was, God must have put it there to lead me to you." She squinted at Beth. "I saw you touch something at your throat. Is that a locket?"

"Yes." Beth fingered her one treasure from her previous life, trying to contain her amazement.

"Have you had it long?"

She hesitated, not sure why she didn't want to reveal the contents. If this woman was her mother, wouldn't she recognize it and be able to tell her what it contained? "Since before I was found on the trail by the Arapaho."

Isabelle sucked in a breath. "Mr. Tucker didn't tell us …"

Beth glanced at Jeffery, who gave a slight shake of his head. "So you don't know my story?"

"Only that you were rescued and taken to Topeka where you were raised by a kind woman."

"I see." She drew the locket from between the folds of the fabric at her neck and held it out so it could be seen. "Do you recognize this?"

"Oh my." Isabelle's hand flew to her mouth.

Steven leaned forward, his face excited. "Is that Grandmother's locket? The one you told me about?"

His mother nodded. "Yes. I put it around my little girl's neck when I got sick. She was so afraid to go with another family. I told her that Grandmother and Grandfather Corwin loved her, and she could look at their pictures anytime and know she had family close by." She turned toward Beth. "That should contain a portrait of a woman with eyes that match yours, her hair swept up on her head, and wearing a dress with a cameo pin at her throat. Opposite is a portrait of her husband wearing a hat and looking very grim and proper. He was terrified to smile, for fear of ruining the picture."

Beth felt all the blood drain from her face at the perfect descriptions. Wonder nudged confusion out of the way as realization dawned. "You really *are* my mother? And my brother? You didn't abandon me?"

A soft cry broke from her mother's lips. "Oh, my darling girl, I would have gone to the ends of the earth if I'd only known where to look. I loved you more than life itself. I don't know if you'll ever be able to forgive me for not finding you."

Beth pushed up from her seat and moved across the short space separating her from the woman she barely remembered. She stopped beside her chair and stared down, trying to take in the astonishing revelation. Her family was alive, and they loved her. Sinking onto her knees, she extended her hands. "Mother? Mama?" The tears spilled onto her cheeks, but she didn't care. "It's really you?"

Her mother drew Beth into a hungry embrace. "Yes, honey. And I promise that I will never leave you again."

Chapter Thirty-Seven

Jeffery felt as though he stood on hallowed ground. He breathed a prayer of thanksgiving, grateful beyond measure to have witnessed Beth's reunion with her family and humbled to have played a part in it. He ventured a glance at Mrs. Roberts. Her cheeks had lost their color, and her eyes brimmed with sadness. Was it possible she wouldn't be happy for Beth?

Another thought gave him pause. Mrs. Roberts was afraid of losing the young woman she thought of as her own. Beth had found her real family, and from all appearances, the cords that bound them in her childhood would be rewoven and an enduring strand formed. How would that affect his relationship with Beth? Would she be so caught up with her mother and brother that she would forget him? He got to his feet and cleared his throat. "I think I'll excuse myself now and give you folks time to sort out the rest of the details."

Beth turned to him, her hand still clutching her mother's. "Will I see you later? You aren't leaving again before we have time to talk?"

Her breathy question did much to soothe his worry. "I'm not going anywhere. But Father is planning on leaving for home tomorrow, and I want to spend a little more time with him before then."

He made it partway down the hall when the light footsteps behind him gave him pause. Beth hurried toward him, her hand outstretched. "I'm so sorry, Jeffery. I really wanted to talk to you as well. I didn't realize … didn't expect …" Her voice caught and held.

Jeffery took her hand and drew her close, his heart pounding. "I know, and it's all right. I'm so thankful you've found your family at last, Beth. I pray they will be able to help heal the broken places in your life."

She stood on tiptoe and placed a brief kiss on his cheek. "It's all because of you. I will never be able to repay you for what you've done. You'll have my gratitude and affection for the rest of my life." Whirling, she made her way quickly back to the parlor.

Gratitude and affection. Jeffery clenched his jaw. That was not what he'd been hoping for. Not at all.

Three days had gone by since her mother and brother had arrived in Baker City, and Beth still hadn't been alone with Jeffery. It almost felt as though he were avoiding her, but she couldn't understand why. She'd thought her kiss and request to spend time with him would help him see how she felt. The only thing left was to salvage what pride remained and pour all of her time and attention into her family—not only her mother and brother, but Aunt Wilma as well.

She knocked on her aunt's door. "It's Beth. I'd like to talk if you feel up to it?" Worry nipped at her. Aunt Wilma had looked peaked lately and not her usual outspoken self. Even Frances had a hard time prying more than a dozen words from her friend. She tapped again. "Auntie? Are you there?"

A quiet voice answered, but Beth didn't quite catch the words. She pushed open the door and looked inside. Her aunt stood over a carpetbag, placing items of clothing inside. "What are you doing?"

"Packing." The word was flat.

Beth's heart lurched. She covered the intervening space in two strides and placed her hand on her aunt's arm. "Why? Where are you going?"

"To a hotel until I decide what to do next. Or until Caleb and I marry."

Beth's thoughts raced from one thing to another but couldn't seem to land on anything that might have caused this sudden departure. "I don't understand. Has something happened to upset you? Is Frances being difficult again?"

"Frances is fine. I simply think it's time I move."

Beth sank onto the end of the bed, sudden awareness dawning. "Is this because my mother is here?"

Wilma frowned. "Your brother should be here, not me. You need your family together in one place. You've been apart long enough."

She stood and took the clothing out of her aunt's hands. "Look at me, Aunt Wilma." Beth waited a moment before continuing. "*You* are my family. That hasn't changed and never will. Finding my mother and brother again doesn't mean you aren't one of the most important people in my life. I love you and don't want you to leave."

Her aunt's gaze wavered, then tears flooded her eyes. "I love you, too."

"Come here." Beth gathered the older woman in her arms and held her tight. "Did you honestly think I wouldn't need you anymore? I will always need your wisdom and strength." She pulled back a half step. "You believe me, don't you?"

Wilma hiccupped and nodded. "I suppose I'm a foolish old woman who's being overly sensitive."

Beth brushed the back of her fingers down her aunt's cheeks, wiping away the tears. "Not at all. You're being perfectly normal. I wish you would have talked to me about this sooner though. I didn't realize you felt this way."

"You're certain you don't want me to leave so Mr. Harding can live here?"

"I'm certain. Now come on, let's go downstairs and have a cup of tea and a chat."

"But how about Mrs. Mason?"

"She's resting in her room."

Wilma nodded. "I wondered. It was good of Katherine to allow her to move in when Mr. Tucker headed home. Is she very ill?"

"Steven said she has frequent attacks of weakness since her illness so many years ago. I urged him to have Caleb examine her, if he's willing, to see if there's anything more that can be done."

"That's a wise idea. Have you caught up on reading the journals she gave you?"

"I'm taking it slow." Beth smiled. "It's still hard for me to take in that she filled six of them, all written to me. It's allowing me to see into her heart and thoughts. Some of my favorite entries are on my birthday and holidays, when she was reminiscing on what I might have been doing if we'd been together. I'm also happy to know my real birthday at last."

"We weren't too far off. We always celebrated on the day you arrived at the fort in March, not knowing your actual birthday was in early February."

"Yes, that will take a little getting used to, but at least I'm only a month older than we thought. I've been thinking of something else, Auntie. Since Caleb located Dancing Water and her people, I'd like to see her again. Maybe someday you and I can travel back East together and visit her. I want to thank her for all she and her people did for me." She linked her arm with her aunt's and tugged her through the open door. "Enough of the past for now. We need to celebrate the future. You will always be an important part of my life, Auntie."

Her aunt sighed and squeezed her arm against her side. "And you mine. Shall we go see if that handsome Jeffery Tucker is about anywhere? I haven't chatted with him in too long, and we have much to thank him for."

Beth slowed her pace toward the stairs. Somehow she didn't think he cared to be found, although she still didn't understand why. She tucked the remnants of her bruised heart back out of sight and put on a smile. There was no sense in alarming her aunt for no reason; she'd had more than her share of anxiety lately. "I suppose. We can see if anyone is about who wants to take tea with us and make it a party."

Chapter Thirty-Eight

Jeffery stood at the bottom of the stairs wondering if he dared go up and tap on Beth's door. He could stand the uncertainty no longer. Either she cared for him as much as he did for her, or he'd leave this town and not look back. The idea of staying in Baker City and only garnering Beth's friendship and gratitude was not something he could tolerate.

He started up and made it halfway, then paused at the sound of firm heels padding along the hall at the top of the staircase. The chatter of women followed.

Beth and her aunt swung around the corner of the hall and came toward him, faces alight with laughter. "Why, Jeffery, there you are." The older woman lifted the hem of her skirt and started down ahead of Beth. "We were hoping to find you and ask you to tea."

"You were?" He kept his grip on the railing and backed down the stairs, keeping his gaze on Beth. No frown marred the beauty of her face. "Actually, I was coming up in hopes of enticing Beth to take a buggy ride. Now that the snow is gone and the weather has moderated, it's quite a pleasant day and might be one of our last to venture out before another storm comes along." He moved aside at the bottom and allowed Mrs. Roberts to pass.

She gave him a subtle wink. "Wonderful idea. You young people get quite restless cooped up in the house. I'd like to find Frances anyway."

Beth gaped at her aunt. "I beg your pardon? You asked me to tea."

Wilma waved her hand. "Fiddlesticks. Everyone is welcome to change their mind once in their lifetime. And Mr. Tucker is correct. You might not get many more of these fine days. Why, even though it's the middle of November it feels like fall again. Go along with you and have a good time. I'm perfectly content to visit with Frances." She walked away, head held high.

Jeffery peered at Beth. Had he pushed too hard to get his own way? Surely not. Mrs. Roberts was the one who insisted that Beth accompany him. "Would you care to come with me?"

Her smile warmed his heart. "I'd love to, Jeffery. Very much. But we'll need to ask Katherine or Mr. Jacobs if we can use their buggy."

He grinned. "I hope you'll forgive me for presuming, but I was so excited about taking you for a drive that I already obtained permission and harnessed the mare." He stuffed his hands in his pockets and rocked on his heels. "I also warmed two bricks in the oven to place at your feet in case it gets cold."

"How thoughtful." Her face glowed with pleasure. "I'll get my gloves and hooded cape and meet you outside."

A few minutes later she stood on the porch as Jeffery stopped the buggy before the house. He wiped his damp palms on his trousers, then tugged on his gloves and jumped down from the seat. *Please, God, be with me today and bless my endeavor.* If only this would go as planned, he'd never beg God for another thing as long as he lived.

Beth allowed Jeffery to tuck a lap robe around her, relishing the feel of his strong hands. "Thank you, I'm quite comfortable. I'm so glad you thought of this. It's wonderful to be outside." What she really wanted to add was, "with you," but couldn't quite muster the courage. She peeked from beneath her lashes at his handsome profile as he urged the horse forward into a slow trot. "Where are we going? Or are we simply driving and enjoying the day?"

He laughed, and to Beth's ears it was absurdly satisfying. "I have a destination in mind, but you'll have to wait and see."

"All right. I'm perfectly content to sit beside you and enjoy the day." There, she'd said at least a little of what she felt and hoped he would understand the rest.

"As am I." His dimple showed at the corner of his mouth before he turned his attention back to the mare. "Is your aunt all right?"

Beth wrinkled her forehead. "Yes, why do you ask?" Was it possible Jeffery could be so perceptive?

"I noticed her eyes were rather red-rimmed when you came downstairs, although she was smiling. I hoped she hadn't been ill … or something." He glanced at her.

"We had a good talk and cleared up her concerns." Beth didn't hesitate. How wonderful to know she could confide in Jeffery. "She was worried my mother and brother would usurp her position in my heart. I assured her nothing could do that, and she'd always be my family. I've simply added to it, not replaced her."

Jeffery nodded. "Wise answer." He shook the reins as the horse slowed. "We're almost there." The buggy pulled up a rise and topped out with a view looking toward both mountain ranges, the valley spread out between. "I discovered this on our trip to La Grande and thought you might enjoy it."

Beth absorbed the quiet beauty that lay on all sides, taking in the peaks in the distance tinted with snow, and the valley dotted with cattle and horses, and the outer edges of the town within sight. The man beside her completed the image of peace and wholeness. "What a lovely picture. I'm so glad you brought me here."

He set the brake and wrapped the reins around the handle. "Maybe you could draw it sometime. That is, if you stay in this area."

She turned her attention to him. "Why wouldn't I? I see it as home now. Even more so than I did Topeka."

"I wasn't sure, now that you'd found your family, if you might move."

"Steven says his position at the bank here will be permanent, and his mother"—she felt warmth blossom in her cheeks—"*our* mother is content to stay where her children are. How about you?" Her voice faltered. "I know your father wants you to return home."

"I want to visit them in the future, but I feel the same as you."

She relaxed, gratitude sweeping aside the tiny residue of worry.

He swept his arm in a wide arc toward the valley. "This is where I want to live—assuming I don't have to live here alone the rest of my life."

Beth's pulse quickened, but she offered a demure smile. "Were you thinking of adopting a pet? A dog or cat, perhaps?"

Jeffery threw back his head and emitted a shout of laughter, the joyous sound echoing across the valley. "That might be an option someday—should I have a child who has a yearning for one." He gave her a meaningful smile.

Beth ducked her head, not caring to have him see her blush.

He lifted her chin with a gentle touch. "You mentioned earlier that you were adding to your family, not replacing it. Do you think you have any more room in your heart for another addition?"

"I guess it would depend on who that was, and what position he or she wanted to fill."

He stroked his finger down her cheek, and she leaned her face into his touch, loving the feel of his skin against hers. His voice deepened. "I was thinking of applying for the position of husband, if it happens to still be available."

She opened her lips to reply but stopped short. How could she have forgotten? He wouldn't want her when he knew. Beth drew back against the seat.

Jeffery dropped his hand to his lap. "Beth? Did I say something wrong? Is it too soon? I'm so sorry if I've rushed you."

She turned away. "That's not it at all. You did nothing wrong."

He gently drew her around to face him. "Then what? Please explain it to me, so I can make it right, whatever it is."

Sorrow swelled in her heart. "No one can make it right. It all happened so long ago, and there's no changing it."

"Beth, look at me. Please." He waited until her eyes met his. Warmth flowed into her, and she drank it in like someone too long in the cold. "If you're talking about the fact that the Arapaho had you for a number of months, or that you didn't know who you were much of your life, that doesn't matter. I wouldn't care if you still didn't know, or if you'd lived with the Indians for years instead of months. I love *you*, Beth, and your past is part of who you are. Surely you see that." He tucked a wayward curl under her hood, and the touch of his hand sent shivers up her spine.

She wanted to pull away—insist he drive her back to the house and allow her to go her way—but she didn't have the strength to break free of his touch. Longing for his love drew her, but disillusionment from so many rejections in her past pushed her away. She felt like a piece of warm taffy, tugged first one way, then the other, stretched almost to breaking. "It's not that either, Jeffery. You don't understand."

"Then make me understand. Tell me what is troubling you."

Beth grasped her sleeve and shoved it up almost to her elbow. She thrust it toward him, the rigid scar uppermost. "Look."

He wrinkled his brow as he peered at her arm, then raised a quizzical glance to hers. "What am I supposed to see other than your perfectly lovely arm?"

Was he teasing her or trying to make her feel better? "The scar." The words were more curt than she'd planned, but she needed to disguise her hurt.

"I see that. Does it have some significance?"

She slumped in her seat. He didn't understand. "That is only one of many. The bits and pieces of memory have been coming together these past weeks. I'd been playing with the other children and got tired. I must have fallen asleep in the tall grass of a meadow and maybe that's why no one saw me. By the time I woke, the wagons were gone. I don't think I actually saw them leave. That memory might have come from being used to walking behind at times and watching them roll across the prairie."

Jeffery nodded and offered an encouraging smile.

She rubbed her hands up and down her arms. "I remember running and crying. I stumbled and fell into a fire pit still full of hot coals. My arms, legs, and part of my back were burned." She shivered at the dark memory that returned stronger each time she revisited it. "I am horribly scarred, and even I have a hard time looking at some of the more deformed places." She shook her head and drew farther away. "I don't think you could see them and still love me."

Jeffery grasped her hand. She tried to pull away, but he clasped it tighter. "Is that all?"

She stared at him, not sure she understood. Was the man daft or being purposely obtuse? "All what? I told you I have many of these." She lifted her arm again, determined he appreciate her words this time. "All my life I've lived in fear of these scars. At an early age I recognized they set me apart from other children—made me less desirable as a person in their eyes. I was damaged and not someone they cared to bring into their innermost circle. I learned to live on the outside and raised the walls of my heart to keep out the pain, but I always knew. I am not like other women and never will be."

Jeffery gave her a tender smile. "And thank the good Lord for that wonderful fact."

She pulled back, stung by his words, but somehow comforted by his tone. "I'm not sure I understand."

He sobered and squeezed her hand that he'd managed to retain. "I meant that you are not like other women, or I wouldn't have fallen in love with you. You are not silly or obnoxious or flirtatious, or any of the other half-dozen things that often irritate me about young women. You are beautiful in form as well as actions, intelligent, kind, well-spoken, talented—the list goes on. I do not see what those scars have to do with my feelings for you."

More than anything Beth wanted to believe his words— longed to trust that he wouldn't change his mind when he truly saw what her dress kept hidden—but the hurt of the years went too deep. Brent's betrayal still lingered in her thoughts, even while she worked to push it away. "But you can't know that, Jeffery. What if you were to see more and be repulsed? I don't think I could stand that." She dropped her voice to a whisper. "It would destroy me."

Sympathy mixed with tender love warmed his expression. He scooted closer to her side and stroked her wrist, his fingers running over the ridge of skin on the inner surface. "Does it hurt?"

She shivered at his touch. "Not anymore. It hasn't for years."

He gently picked up her arm and leaned over, placing his lips against the scar. "Nothing about you could ever repulse me." He kissed her again, allowing his lips to linger a little longer. "I don't care if your entire body is covered with scars ten times worse than this one. A hundred times worse. It does not matter to me. *You* are what matters. The woman who resides inside and who shines out for the entire world to see. That is who I fell in love with, and who I will continue to love, regardless of the condition of your skin. That is nothing to me and never will be." He raised his face to hers and drew her close. "Do you believe me, Beth? And do you love me?"

Tremors of pure joy ran over her skin, and she leaned toward him. "Yes, I love you so much, Jeffery."

He dipped his head as though to kiss her but stopped. "But do you believe me? Do you trust me?"

Everything within her seemed to slow as she searched for the answer.

Trust.

God had asked her to trust Him in those still times of the night.

To wait.

She hadn't understood what she was waiting for at the time, but now she knew. For this moment, this man, this declaration of love. The hope for her future. And, more than that, the opportunity to open her heart and be vulnerable—to trust another person fully and completely—without reservation or fear.

God had given her this gift. There would be no more wishing on buttercups, wondering if the man of her dreams would love her, or love her not. Through God's grace and in so many ways, Jeffery had proven that he did.

And now she would make the choice that would change her life forever. "Yes, I believe you. And I trust you more than any person in the world."

He bent his head and brushed her lips with a sweet, soft kiss. "Will you do me the honor of becoming my wife?"

"I cannot think of anything that would bring me more delight. I love you, Jeffery, with all that is within me."

His face broke into a deeply satisfied smile, and he lowered his head once again.

She clung to him this time, drinking in his love like nectar from a flower. She'd waited for this man all of her life ... a man who looked beyond the scars of the past, a man who had shown a steadfast love and helped her to trust again ... and she would never let this man go.

... a little more ...

When a delightful concert comes to an end,

the orchestra might offer an encore.

When a fine meal comes to an end,

it's always nice to savor a bit of dessert.

When a great story comes to an end,

we think you may want to linger.

And so, we offer ...

AfterWords—just a little something more after you

have finished a David C Cook novel.

We invite you to stay awhile in the story.

Thanks for reading!

Turn the page for ...

- **Author's Note**
- **Great Questions for Individual Reflection and/or Group Discussion**
- **A Sneak Peek at Book Three: *Dreaming on Daisies***
- **About the Author**
- **Other Books by Miralee Ferrell**

Author's Note

Why I Wrote This Story

A question many authors are asked is, "What prompted you to write this particular book?" I had to think about it for a while to truly decipher what drove me this time. I discovered it was more than one thing—in fact, one issue came to light that I hadn't realized until recently.

Naturally I hoped to find a story line that would entertain readers, and I wanted to continue with the characters created in *Blowing on Dandelions*. But each book needs a theme. I don't ever want to write a simple romance without something that drives it. In this case, it was a young woman who'd been damaged—not only physically, but emotionally, due to the scars from her childhood.

As I thought about that, I realized many of us carry hurts and scars from words spoken or actions taken that we had little or no control over. I had a wonderful childhood with caring, supportive parents, and I grew up having a best friend, Kit, from the time I was three. At first I wasn't sure I could relate to Beth and her inner turmoil; then memories started to surface. My third-grade teacher, disgusted that I couldn't write cursive (I'd transferred from a school that taught it starting in grade two), openly ridiculed me before the class and other teachers. Her actions colored my self-perception that entire year and the next, and my eagerness to learn and belief in myself declined.

Later, as a committed Christian attending a public high school, I didn't fit in with any of the popular kids. I didn't endure the bullying that so many do now, but I was often on the outside looking in. Thankfully my personality is such that it didn't affect me to a deep degree, but nevertheless, I understand the angst so many teens endure at the hands of their peers.

Later, as an adult, I endured an unintentional wound from a friend who allowed me to believe something within my personality was unattractive enough to sever our friendship—that blow set me back emotionally to the point that, for a while, I struggled to even attend church, certain others must see the same flaws.

My hope in writing this book is to show that God is able to take even the wallflowers of this world and cause them to blossom. No matter what we've been through in our past, He is able to heal the deepest hurt. Our Lord accepts us where we are, for who we are, scars and all. He looks beyond our overweight bodies, our acne-scarred skin, and all our other "deformities" we think or know we might have, and sees what's inside—the lovely person He created us to be.

I used my daughter, Marnee, as my role model in my first historical romance—and she's another of my "treasures." Now it's my son's turn. I dedicated this book to my son, Steven, even though he's a different personality type than the character by that name. Steven is a US Marine who served in Iraq, a husband, and a brand-new father, but he's also the epitome of an excellent son. I named a character after him because *my* Steven has a similar trait—he's tenderhearted and compassionate toward his family. He was always the one who noticed if I was upset and was the quickest to apologize or show compassion. I'm so proud he's my son.

Within the confines of *Wishing on Buttercups*, there are a couple of true threads. One is the Oregon Trail, which lies within a mile of the outskirts of Baker City, Oregon. Many trains passed along that route, although by the time of my story it had dwindled to only a trickle. Baker City was on the edge of being a booming mining town and would see rapid growth over the next few years, and many historical buildings built during that time period still stand today.

When possible, I try to weave either a historical or family event into my plot, and the episode with Micah losing his grip on the paint can and it toppling onto Isaac Lansing's hat is a perfect example. When my father was a child, my grandfather accidentally lost his grip on a can of paint while working on a roof. It bounced over the eaves and landed upside down on the head (and hat) of a neighbor who caused trouble every time he showed up at the farm. My grandfather exploded in laughter, and quite understandably, the neighbor left in a huff. No lawsuit or action was brought against my grandfather, but the neighbor found fewer reasons to come around from that time forward.

I hope you've enjoyed this second book in the Love Blossoms in Oregon series and will join me again in book three, *Dreaming on Daisies*, Steven and Leah's story. The first chapter is included beginning on page 401. I hope they'll whet your appetite and keep you reading!

Miralee Ferrell

Great Questions

for Individual Reflection and/or Group Discussion

1. What was Beth's dream? What was Jeffery's dream? What is your dream?

2. When Beth receives a letter from a publisher about her illustrations, she experiences the fulfilling of a dream. When have you experienced the first-time fulfillment or renewal of a dream? How did you get to that point in your life? How did it feel when you accomplished that dream?

3. Jeffery looked to his family—especially his father—for approval. Whose approval is important to you, and why? How have you handled that longing for approval?

4. Have you, like Beth, ever felt scarred and unlovable? Afraid to love for fear of being hurt? If so, when … and why? How have those feelings influenced your life now?

5. In Chapter Three, Wilma Roberts tells Beth, "Physical marks and family connections mean nothing, my dear. God looks at the heart, not the outward appearance. Never forget that." Do you agree with that statement? Why or why not?

6. When has a person seen you—with all your scars—as worthy and lovable? Tell the story. How did that moment change your perception of yourself?

7. In Chapter Four, Jeffery approaches Beth with good intentions, but she views his efforts differently. When have you found yourself at odds with someone because you didn't understand each other's communication? What happened as a result? Looking at the situation now, what would you do differently if the situation arose again?

8. In Chapter Eleven, Wilma tries to help Beth understand what others see—and don't see—in her. What do you think others see—and don't see—in you? How can viewing yourself that way encourage you to change … for the good?

9. Isabelle feels regret and guilt for a situation in the past that wasn't within her control. How has that affected her life from that point forward? How did it affect her relationship with her surviving son?

10. Have you felt regret or guilt over a past situation? If so, how might you take a step forward today into a healthier frame of mind, instead of staying mired in the past?

11. Frances Cooper and Wilma Roberts have a unique, hard-won relationship. They don't always agree, and they often rub each other the wrong way. But they also play the role of loyal friend

and truth teller in each other's lives. What benefits do you see in their lives as a result? What person(s) or group serves as loyal friend and truth teller in your life? How has that person's or group's insight influenced you to become a better person?

12. How does Jeffery view his father? How do others view Mark Tucker? Why do we sometimes view the ones we love so differently than others do?

13. In what way(s) does Beth's insecurity about her past and family, as well as her prior relationship with Brent, cause her not to trust others? Is it easy for you to trust others? Why or why not?

14. Beth Roberts carries a heavy burden of secrets. How does trying to protect those secrets cause her problems? What secrets are you carrying that weigh you down? How might you lighten the burden of, or bring to light, those secrets so you can live in freedom both now and in the future?

15. Beth's favorite flower is the buttercup. After spending so many years "wishing on buttercups," what dreams of hers come true by the end of the book? Of your own dream(s) that you listed for the first question, how might you move from "wishing on buttercups" to actually holding that dream and drinking in its beauty and scent, as Beth did at the end of the story?

A Sneak Peek at Book Three:

Dreaming on Daisies

Miralee Ferrell

Chapter One

One mile outside Baker City, Oregon
Mid March, 1881

Leah Carlson kicked a wicker chair out of her way and stormed off the porch, angrier than she'd been in years. Well, years might be a stretch, but at least weeks. Or perhaps several days. Maybe riding to town and finding Pa would be a good idea. She glared at the ground, her mood not improved by the thick mud clinging to the bottom of her boots, and scraped the mud off on a horseshoe nailed to the bottom step. March, her least favorite month, always felt somewhere between winter and spring with none of the benefits of either.

She trooped up the steps and righted the chair. Not the chair's fault Pa had gotten drunk again and stayed all night in town. Buddy, their aging ranch hand, had seen Pa go into the saloon when he'd headed home from the mercantile last night. At first he hadn't told her in hopes that his boss would return at a decent hour, but that hadn't happened.

Leah wrapped her coat closer around her shoulders. Now most of the chores would fall on her, Millie, and Buddy, Millie's husband. With Buddy's back giving him fits, she couldn't ask him to do the heavy work, although his pride would force him to try. Why did Pa keep falling off the wagon whenever hope set in that he'd finally beat that horrible habit?

Empty promises, that's all she ever got. Promises he'd change. Promises he'd do better. Promises he'd broken ever since Ma died nine years ago. And lately it had only gotten worse. She'd gone from a child at the tender age of fourteen to a caretaker and ranch foreman almost overnight, and to this day she still felt robbed.

At least the ranch was safe as long as she worked hard to pay the bills—as long as Pa didn't try to use it as collateral for his drinking debts. But something needed to change. Maintaining this place was too much for her and Buddy alone. Pa had to stop drinking. Of course, he appeared to think everything was fine and even bragged in town about his successful cattle and horse business.

She plopped down into the righted chair. Over the years she'd done her best to cover for him, but he'd had enough "episodes" lately that she knew people were talking. All she could do was keep up appearances and find at least one more hired hand—the sooner the better. Digging up some extra cash and increasing her herd of horses by a couple dozen wouldn't hurt, either.

Dragging Pa home and shaking some sense into his noggin sounded very tantalizing. But knowing her father, he would ignore her efforts or embarrass her in public. No, accosting Pa in town wouldn't work. Somehow she had to beat him at his own game and bring him to his senses. She had no idea how, but she'd find a way, if it was the last thing she did.

The front door creaked on rusty hinges, and Millie poked her head outside. "Girl, you goin' to sit there all day starin' at nothin' or come in and get ready for that weddin' you've talked about for the past two months?"

Leah bolted upright and jumped to her feet. "Oh, my goodness. I can't believe I forgot Beth's wedding." She brushed a strand of hair out of her eyes. "How much time do I have to get decent?"

Millie gestured at her mud-caked boots and stained trousers. "Not near enough, from what I can see. Guess you could stay at home. It's not like you're close friends with either the bride or the groom."

Leah shook her head. "I promised Katherine Jacobs I'd help with the refreshments since they're entertaining a few close friends at the boardinghouse after the ceremony. Besides, Beth has attended our quilting group occasionally since Christmas, and we've become friends." She stepped past Millie and headed for the stairs leading to her room. "If Pa comes home while I'm gone, see if you can make him stick around, will you, please?"

Millie grunted. "Can't nobody make that man do nothin' he don't want to, girl. You should know that by now, especially if he's been drinkin'. But I'll try." She waved her hands as Leah paused. "Get on with you. Nothin' you can do here, anyhow. It's about time you had some fun before you're old and gray like me. Who knows? Maybe some good luck will rub off the bride and land on you." She wrinkled her nose. "There's got to be at least one man in this world who's marriage material that don't irritate you."

Leah grinned. "Of course there is, but you snatched him up years ago. I'm destined to be an old maid the rest of my life and live here with you and Buddy, so quit trying to fix me up. I'm perfectly happy the way things are."

"Humph. Likely story." Millie crossed her arms and scowled, the creases beside her mouth deepening. "We're not going to be around forever, you know."

"You are too. Neither of you have permission to leave me alone." Leah choked on the last word and fled to her room. Millie had been the closest thing to a mother she'd had for more years than she cared to remember.

Steven Harding hauled on his horse's reins, his heart galloping so fast he thought it would burst from his chest. Had his horse trampled that man lying in the road? He set the brake and wound the reins around the handle, then leaped from his buggy and ran forward.

The man seemed almost burrowed into the mud, his shoulder muscles twitching and right leg jerking. He lay flat on his back, eyes closed, with one arm flung over his forehead. A guttural groan broke from his parted lips.

Relief swept over Steven. At least the man wasn't dead. But where had he come from? The busy streets of Baker City were behind Steven, and the boardinghouse where his sister and mother lived was only a few blocks away on the outskirts of town. Had he been day-dreaming and not noticed the man crossing the road?

He leaned over and touched the fellow's arm. "Are you all right, sir?"

The fallen man mumbled before rolling to his side and pushing to a sitting position. He swiped a filthy hand across his cheek, flicking away a glob of mud and blinking his eyes. "Wha' happened?"

Steven recoiled as the stench of alcohol hit him. Was he drunk? It was only midmorning. Surely no one started their day drinking enough to be intoxicated at this hour. He pulled his thoughts back where they belonged. It wasn't his place to judge, especially after he almost ran over the fellow. "I'm not certain. I didn't see you crossing the road in time to stop. Can you get up? Nothing's broken, I hope?"

The man groped for his hat resting on a flat rock a short distance away. He slapped it against his hand, then jammed it onto his head, covering the ring of gray hair. "Don't think anything's broken. I don't recall what happened. I need to get home and do my chores."

Steven gripped his arm and hoisted him to his feet. "Let me give you a ride. Unless you have a wagon or horse nearby?"

"Don't rightly remember if I do." He gazed around with a bewildered stare and took an unsteady step. "Reckon I can walk." Taking another stride, he staggered, his boot plopping into another section of mud, sending a spray of dirty water only inches from Steven's clean trouser leg.

Steven sprang forward and caught the man with one hand before he pitched onto his face. With his other hand, Steven took out his pocket watch and gave it a hurried glance. Two hours before he had to pick up his sister, Beth, and his mother for the ceremony. "Do you live far?"

The man shook off his grip. "'Bout a mile or less. My ranch is the closest one to town. Don't need no charity from strangers, though."

"I'm headed that direction, so it's not charity. Please. It's the least I can do."

Bloodshot eyes met his. "Guess it won't hurt nothin' if you're headed that way."

Steven stayed close as the older man lumbered into the passenger side of the buggy. He'd have to scrub out the mud before taking the womenfolk to the church, but it couldn't be helped. It was possible this individual was already lying in the mud when he came along.

That would account for Steven not seeing him until he was almost on top of him. But it didn't matter. He wouldn't drive off and leave anyone needing help, whether his fault or not.

The ride to the ranch was silent, and Steven kept his gelding at a hard trot, intent on making the best time possible. He drew to a stop in front of a two-story white house sadly wanting paint and repair. Setting the brake, he leaped from the buggy and hurried to the other side, intent on keeping the man from falling as he disembarked. His gelding dropped his head and nibbled at a clump of soggy grass near the base of the hitching post. Steven came to a halt on the passenger side and lifted his hand to the man still sitting inside.

The front door of the house slammed nearby, but Steven kept his attention on the fellow climbing unsteadily to the ground.

The older man ignored Steven's extended hand. "Don't need no help, mister. I'm right as rain." He grasped the handrail next to the seat and swung his legs over. Planting his boot on the step, he edged down, but as soon as his feet hit the ground, he lurched forward, almost into Steven's arms. Steven grabbed the man's arm and held him upright.

"Pa? What in the world?" The feminine voice was accompanied by a light patter of steps on the porch. "So I see you finally decided to come home and got another one of your cohorts to bring you."

Steven loosened his hold on the man's arm and pivoted, arrested by the undercurrent of anger tingeing the words. His heart jumped. A young woman who looked just a bit younger than he was stared at the man she'd called Pa. Her emerald-green gown matched her bewitching eyes, but the glow emanating from them certainly wasn't warm or friendly. "I beg your pardon, miss, but I think you've misunderstood."

The fiery redhead stood with her hands planted on trim hips, her green eyes shooting sparks. "I doubt it. You aren't the first man to bring my father home in this"—she shot an irritated look at her parent—"condition." She nearly spat the last word. "I appreciate the ride, but I'll thank you next time not to buy him any more drinks when he's had more than enough."

Steven's heart sank, and he took a step back. The last thing he wanted was to add more sorrow to this woman's life, but he hated that she thought him responsible. But did it really matter? He wasn't apt to see her again. He tipped his head. "Sorry for the trouble, ma'am. Now that he's home and safe, I'll be on my way."

Leah gritted her teeth to keep back the words threatening to spew out as the handsome, dark-haired driver picked up the reins and clucked to his horse. This one was certainly younger and better mannered than her father's other cronies who had delivered her inebriated parent to their door in the past. Anxiety struck her as she remembered the crisp white shirt beneath the suit jacket and the stiffly starched collar. What were the chances he'd come from a saloon dressed like that? She'd probably stuck her foot in her mouth again with her impetuous accusation. Someday she must learn to think before she allowed words to blurt out.

Swiveling, she glared at her father tottering up the path toward the porch. "What do you have to say for yourself, Pa? I've been worried sick, not to mention having to do most of the chores myself. Was that man who brought you home drinking with you at the saloon?"

"Who I drink with is my own business, not yours," he tossed back. "I told that fella I didn't need his help, and I'm tellin' you too. If you already did the chores, I'm gettin' a short nap."

"Pa! We need to talk."

He squinted red-rimmed eyes at her. "Done talkin'. I'm hungry, and I'm tired. Millie can fix me a sandwich; then I'm goin' to bed for an hour or two. Nothin' to talk about, anyhow." He waved a dismissive hand. "Go on with you, and leave me alone."

Leah moved closer, barely containing her frustration. "There is a lot to discuss, Pa. Starting with your drinking. It's getting out of hand, and it needs to stop or you'll put this ranch and everything we've worked for in danger."

Pa reached for the newel post at the bottom of the short flight of steps leading to the porch, clamped his hand on top, then maneuvered himself onto the first step. "I won't tolerate no daughter of mine preachin' at me about my responsibility or my sins. And it's my ranch, so I'll do what I see fit with it. I've worked hard makin' it what it is all these years. You got no call to tell me what to do." He headed for the door. "Now leave me be whilst I get somethin' to eat. My head hurts, and I don't wanna hear anymore."

Leah looked at the chair propped against the wall, wishing she could kick it again and allow some of her aggravation to escape. Better that than allowing the tears building behind her eyes to spill over.

Charlie Pape plunked into a kitchen chair and slid the plate holding his sandwich closer, happy Millie had fixed it and left. The last thing he needed was another well-meaning female trying to tell him what to do or insisting he change.

He picked up the sandwich and took a bite, working hard to hold onto his aggravation toward his daughter. The girl had no right to tell him what to do or how to live his life. It was his business if he drank, and nobody else's. And she was dead wrong thinking she knew better than he did how to run this ranch. It had been his for years.

A thought pricked at his conscience, but he pushed it away. It was his ranch, and he intended to make sure it stayed that way.

Leah was a good girl and meant well. He couldn't fault her there. But she was too much like her mother. Always trying to fix things to swing her own way and not taking into account what he might want. Leah wasn't his child by birth, but he'd taught her all he knew and was plumb tickled that she seemed to love the ranch as much as her old pa. The girl had been raised here since Charlie married Leah's ma when Leah was only a baby. He'd always figured he and Mary would live here until their sunset days, and then Leah and whatever man she married would take over for him. Not once had he considered the unthinkable might happen, leaving him alone with only his misery to keep him company.

Steven Harding paced the parlor at the Jacobs's boardinghouse and took out his pocket watch for at least the tenth time since returning from dropping the stranger at his ranch. Ten minutes after two o'clock—only a minute since he'd last checked. He would have

wagered a guess that much more time had passed. Did his sister want
to be late to her own wedding?

Women's voices mingled not far down the hall. Moments later
Beth's adopted aunt, Mrs. Wilma Roberts—or, rather, Marshall,
since she'd recently remarried—and her friend, Mrs. Cooper, swept
into the room, arms entwined and faces aglow. They came to an
abrupt stop and stared, then both erupted in giggles.

He tugged at his tight collar and frowned. "What seems to be
the problem, ladies? I can't imagine what could be so amusing."

Mrs. Cooper's grin broadened. She shook her head, and a gray
curl slipped loose from under the brim of her dark blue hat. "A
stranger might assume you are the groom, if your distraught appearance is any indication. Are you terribly nervous about accompanying
your sister down the aisle this afternoon?"

Mrs. Marshall patted his shoulder. "Why don't you sit down,
Steven? It won't do any good wearing a path in the carpet. Beth will be
down soon, and my Caleb will be back to pick up Frances and me."

"I'm not nervous at all. I simply don't understand what's taking
so long. We still have to drive to the church. Mr. and Mrs. Jacobs
and their children left long ago, and I'm sure Jeffery has been there
for hours."

"Caleb drove my daughter and her family over early to ready the
sanctuary for the wedding. And your mother is putting the finishing
touches on Beth's hair. Your sister is going to make a beautiful bride,
and Jeffery is blessed to get her. I am quite certain she will be worth
whatever amount of time he must wait." Mrs. Cooper pointed at
a chair. "Sit. You are making me nervous, pacing like some caged
animal."

"That's exactly how I feel." He sank into the seat indicated and ran his fingers over his closely cropped hair. He glanced at Beth's aunt, a woman he'd only known for a few months but had come to respect. "How can you be so calm? You weren't even anxious when you and Caleb married at Christmas. And why aren't you upstairs helping? I'm sure Beth wants you there."

Mrs. Marshall frowned. "I don't know what you have to be so fretful over." Her face softened. "Beth asked me to stay, but she should have this time with her mother. Isabelle has missed so much of Beth's life these past years, which I was privileged to enjoy while raising her. I won't rob your mother of an instant alone with her daughter on this special day. Besides, the ceremony doesn't start for almost an hour, and the buggy will get us to the church in plenty of time."

Steven nodded but didn't reply. He was happy for his mother and sister but longed for this day to hurry to a close. Maybe once Beth was married to Jeffery Tucker, life would return to normal. Finding Beth again after a seventeen-year separation had been exhilarating, but he'd struggled to find his place in the family with the ensuing changes.

He'd been an only child since Beth was lost when he was eight years old, and while he rejoiced at their recent reunion, part of him longed for the time when Ma leaned solely on him for advice and support. Then, suddenly, he was ashamed at the direction his thoughts had taken. More than anything, he was lonely. Steven had thought his sister's return would unite their family. It hadn't happened that way. With Ma living at the boardinghouse to be near Beth, and him living in a mining shanty on the outskirts of town to be close to work, he didn't have much time with either of them. But Ma was happier than he'd ever seen her, and he couldn't begrudge her that. It was high time he moved on with his life. He'd better get used to being alone.

About the Author

Miralee and her husband, Allen, live on eleven acres in the beautiful Columbia River Gorge in southern Washington State, where they love to garden, play with their dogs, take walks, and go sailing. She is also able to combine two other passions—horseback riding and spending time with her grown children—since her married daughter lives nearby, and they often ride together on the wooded trails near their home.

Ironically, Miralee, now the author of eight books, with many more on the way, never had a burning desire to write—at least more than her own memoirs for her children. So she was shocked when God called her to start writing after she turned fifty. To Miralee, writing is a ministry that she hopes will impact hearts, and she anticipates how God will use each of her books to bless and change lives.

An avid reader, Miralee has a large collection of first edition Zane Grey books that she started collecting as a young teen. Her love for his storytelling ability inspired her desire to write fiction set in the Old West. "But I started writing historical fiction without even meaning to," Miralee says, laughing. She'd always planned on writing contemporary women's fiction, but God had other ideas. After signing her first contract for the novel *Love Finds You in Last Chance, California*, she decided to research the town and area. To her dismay, she discovered the town no longer existed and hadn't since the 1960s. Though it had been a booming town in the late 1880s, it had pretty much died out in the 1930s. So her editor suggested switching to a historical version, and Miralee agreed, although she'd never even considered that era.

It didn't take long to discover she had a natural flair for that time period, having read and watched so many Western stories while growing up. From that point on she was hooked. Her 1880s stories continue to grow in acclaim each year. Her novel *Love Finds You in Sundance, Wyoming* won the Will Rogers Medallion Award for Western Fiction, and Universal Studios requested a copy of her debut novel, *The Other Daughter*, for a potential family movie.

Aside from writing and her outdoor activities, Miralee has lived a varied life. She and her husband have been deeply involved in building two of their own homes over the years, as well as doing a full remodel on a one-hundred-year-old Craftsman-style home they owned and loved for four years. They also owned a sawmill at the time and were able to provide much of the interior wood products. Miralee has done everything from driving a forklift to stoking the huge, 120-year-old-boiler, from off-bearing lumber to running a small planer and stacking boards in the dry kiln.

Besides their horse friends, Miralee and her husband have owned cats, dogs (a six-pound, long-haired Chihuahua named Lacey was often curled up on her lap as she wrote this book), rabbits, and yes, even two cougars, Spunky and Sierra, rescued from breeders who didn't have the ability or means to care for them properly.

Miralee and Allen have lived in Alaska and the San Juan Islands for just under a year each, where she became actively involved in women's ministry. Later, she took a counseling course and earned her accreditation with the American Association of Christian Counselors, as well as being a licensed minister (not a pastor) through her denomination. She spends time each month in her office at church praying with and ministering to women, as well as occasionally speaking and filling the pulpit.

Miralee served as president of the Portland, Oregon, chapter of ACFW (American Christian Fiction Writers) for four years and now serves on the board in an advisory capacity. She belongs to a number of writers' groups and also speaks at women's groups, libraries, historical societies, and churches about her writing journey.

www.miraleeferrell.com
www.miraleesdesk.blogspot.com
miraleef@gmail.com
www.facebook.com/miraleeferrell

Books by Miralee Ferrell

Love Blossoms in Oregon Series
Blowing on Dandelions
Wishing on Buttercups

Love Finds You Series
Love Finds You in Bridal Veil, Oregon
Love Finds You in Sundance, Wyoming
Love Finds You in Last Chance, California
Love Finds You in Tombstone, Arizona

The Other Daughter
Finding Jeena

Other Contributions/Compilations
A Cup of Comfort for Cat Lovers

Faith and Family: A Devotional Pathway for Families

*When God Answers Your Prayers: Inspiring Stories of
How God Comes through in the Nick of Time*

*Faith & Finances: In God We Trust, A Journey to Financial
Dependence or the Biblical Keys to Financial Freedom*

*Fighting Fear: Winning the War at Home
When Your Soldier Leaves for Battle*